Spark of Resistance

C A Lewis

ISBN: 979-8-9863413-2-3 (Paperback)

ISBN: 979-8-9863413-3-0 (Ebook)

Cover Design by Rachel Goering

Map created with Inkarnate

Typeset created with Atticus

This one's for you, Grandma.

Love you, always.

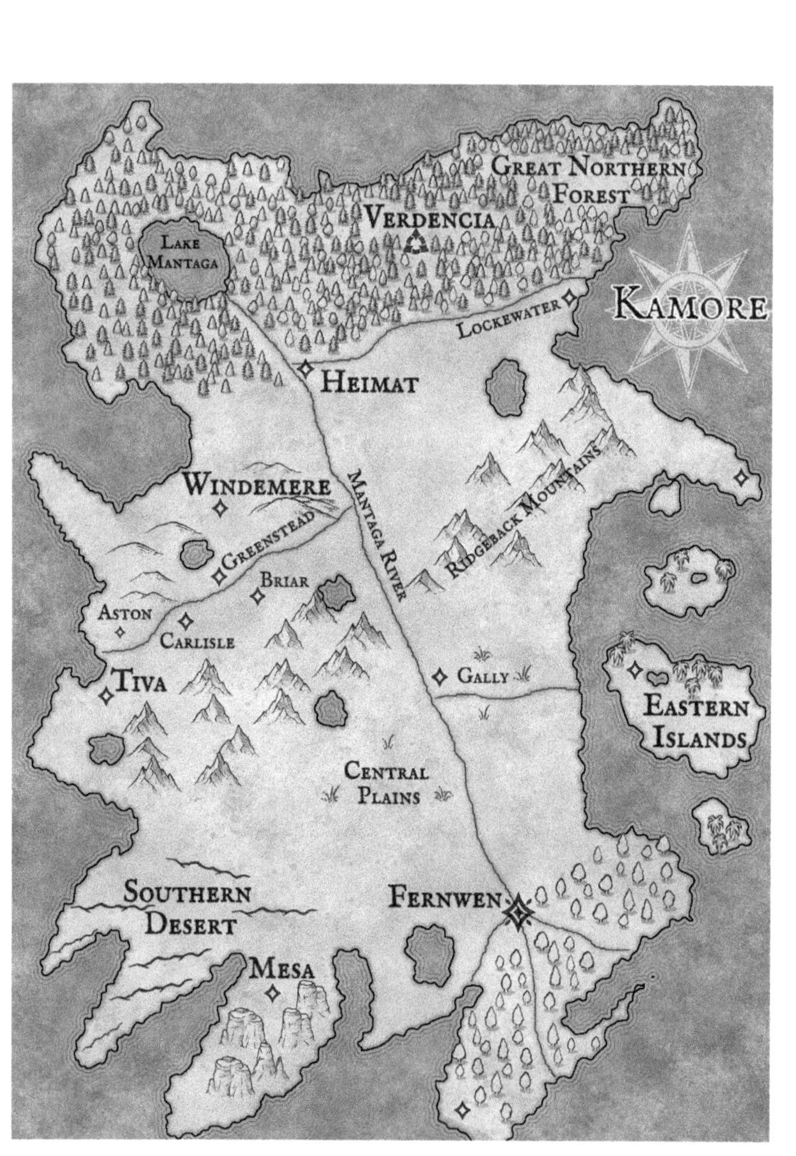

KAMORE
GREAT NORTHERN FOREST
VERDENCIA
LAKE MANTAGA
LOCKEWATER
HEIMAT
WINDEMERE
GREENSTEAD
BRIAR
ASTON
CARLISLE
TIVA
RIDGEBACK MOUNTAINS
MANTAGA RIVER
GALLY
EASTERN ISLANDS
CENTRAL PLAINS
SOUTHERN DESERT
FERNWEN
MESA

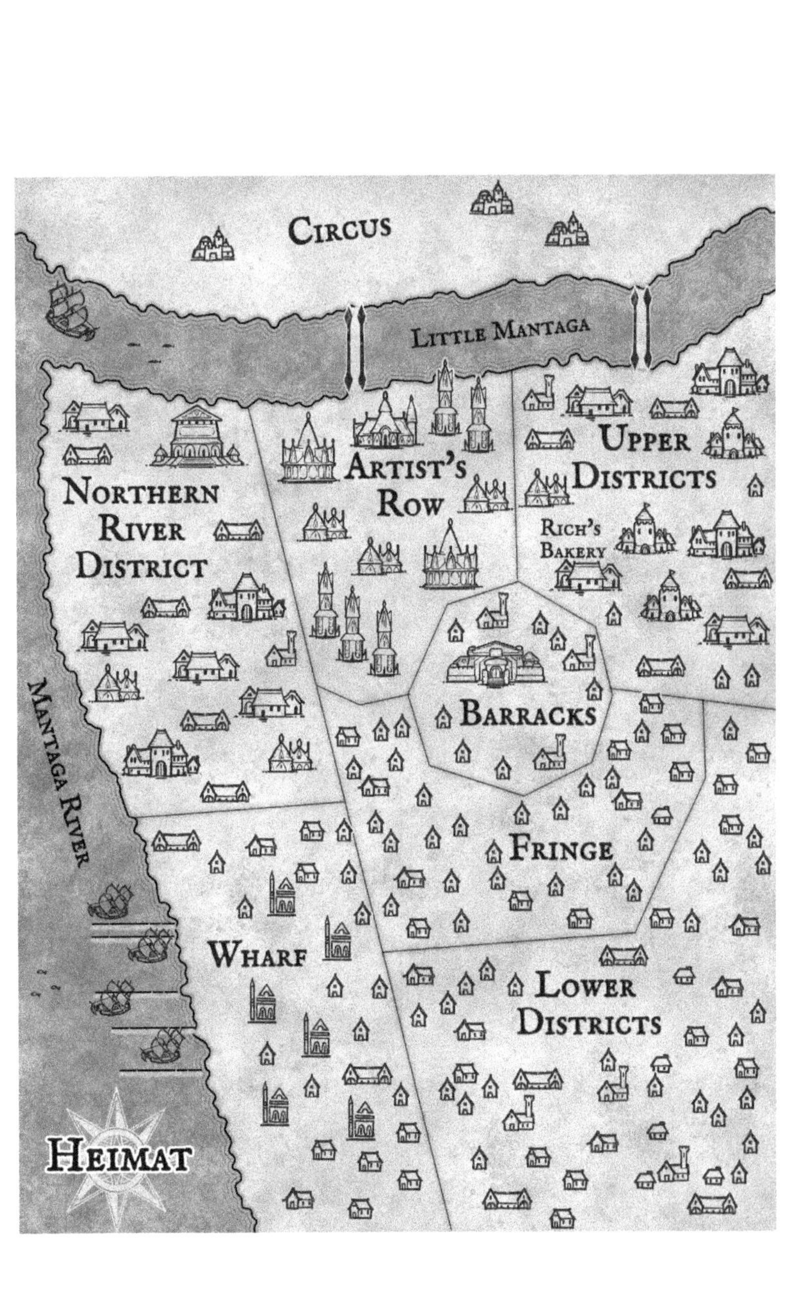

CIRCUS
LITTLE MANTAGA
NORTHERN RIVER DISTRICT
ARTIST'S ROW
UPPER DISTRICTS
RICH'S BAKERY
BARRACKS
MANTAGA RIVER
FRINGE
WHARF
LOWER DISTRICTS
HEIMAT

Chapter One

Fernwen, the capital of Kamore, was not what it once was.

The city sat just upriver from the coast, where the Mantaga broke into three distinct branches, named for the three faces of their deity; the Huntress, the Prophetess, and the Goddess herself. Before the Uprising, it was filled with merchants, artists, and academics, making it the true cultural hub of the country.

Now it felt abandoned.

Before the Uprising, Magicae comprised half the population of Kamore. Now they barely totaled a quarter of the country's population.

Losing that many people was devastating.

Fernwen was devoid of the color and richness of a thriving metropolis. The Uprising halted the city's progress, destroying the community forged between Magicae and Mortals and leaving the bitter taste of power and control in its wake.

Those that could, fled to country or island estates, putting as much distance between them and the people that followed the madwoman controlling the government. Those that couldn't leave bore the brunt of their ruined city. They lived in the slums and worked the brothels, slaughterhouses, and bars along the river. They lived in fear of the flesh markets and the prisons in the old castle keep where Myra Falkenwrath kept her residence.

Kamore was ruled by a monarchy centuries ago. The castle in Fernwen was one of the few surviving structures from the wars that followed after the monarchy failed to produce an heir. The civil war that ensued only ended when leaders from all sides proposed a democracy to unite their people and stop the bloodshed.

Andre Freeman was the last president to be elected before Myra took power. And she had no intention of letting that power go until the Magicae were brought low, once and for all.

She paced the length of the massive room in the middle of the former fortress. It was once the throne room and now the only one fitting enough to be her office. It was the safest in the castle, surrounded by stone that stood the test of time, with only one entrance that needed to be defended against. The secret exit dropped to below the castle, too far up to mount a feasible attack and covered by a latched door and heavy trunk, providing the security she demanded.

Myra wore her signature breastplate with a sword at her hip, not feeling fully dressed without her armor and weapon on her person. She strode back and forth across the stone floor, contemplating what her next move should be. The country had more moving parts than she thought possible, and the public were obsessed with being involved in matters that did not concern them.

Damn democracy. If only they could see how much better things would be if they stopped resisting. Myra shook her head. Reason never worked with the uneducated. They would never understand until she proved her ways were the only ones that mattered.

Once the Magicae were dealt with, they would see. Everyone would see.

A rap on the door broke through her reverie, halting her pacing as she strode to the massive desk in the center of her command center. It was the only piece of furniture present, making it clear who held the power. The office was all hard lines with only cold stone accents that did nothing to soften the room itself.

Much like the woman it belonged to.

"Come in." Myra's voice boomed, echoing off the stone in her chosen place of residence.

A young soldier stood in the doorway as the double doors of the entrance swung open, held by two of Myra's personal guards, her closest and only friends, in the castle. Being a dictator left few options for genuine relationships. Her personal guard was filled with the soldiers she had trained with, bunked with, and climbed the ranks with. They were the only people she truly trusted in this viper's nest of a city.

The young man walked forward with his head bowed and a scroll in his hand, doing his best to keep his legs from trembling at the presence of the legendary military general.

Myra waited a moment, studying him in disgust. They let just about anybody into the barracks these days. *I'll have to have a talk with Jakob about training the weakling out of these new recruits.* The burly woman crossed her arms, a scowl on her face, as she addressed the young soldier, "Are you going to stand there and piss yourself, or are you going to tell me something useful?"

The soldier looked up with wide eyes, thrusting the scroll forward. "This came for you, Your Excellence. It's from the North."

Myra snatched the scroll from the poor lad's hand, noting the unbroken seal on the front. She sliced through it with her finger and unrolled the weathered paper, holding it flat with two weights from her desk.

She narrowed her hazel eyes, flashing an annoyed look at the boy still standing in front of her. "Is there more, soldier?" The woman growled, leaning towards him, hands flat on her desk.

The soldier's face reddened, but he held his ground. His voice was the only thing that wavered from his position in front of the country's acting President. "Your Excellence, the bird came with two letters. One for you and the other for the bird master. Pigeons from Heimat are being transported as we speak to be used for a reply. The bird master will be awaiting your response."

Myra pursed her lips, frustration mounting that Vincenzio would dare presume she'd reply like a lovesick teenager. "Noted. Back to your post, soldier." Myra's eyes went back to the letter on her desk, a clear dismissal of the young man.

He saluted the general despite her lack of attention and left her chambers.

Myra's eyes darted across the page, only her subconscious noticing the click of the doors behind him. Her training meant she never missed a detail, despite her mind being otherwise occupied.

Her brows knitted together and her scowl deepened the more she read. Vincenzio was thorough in his explanation of the events in Heimat. He was informing as well as asking for reinforcements and permission to go after his daughter.

Myra pounded one fist on the desk before crumpling the piece of paper bearing the unfortunate news. She ripped it several times before throwing it in the fireplace behind her to join other correspondences she meant to destroy. That could wait. She needed to visit the dungeons and demand answers.

She strode through the doors, her short, dark brown hair swinging just below her ears. Not waiting to see if her guards followed, she marched to her destination, descending stone steps that led to the windowless cells in the depths of the castle.

Myra's boots sounded on the steps, only stopping to grab a torch from one of the wall sconces. The smell of dank stone, sweat, and excrement hit the guards behind her with force, but didn't faze the general herself. She swept in, not waiting for the guards to salute or greet her, and moved to the last cell on the right.

She shot an impatient glance at one guard, gesturing for her to unlock it quickly, hissing about the guard's lethargy under her breath.

Once the key turned, Myra shouldered past the other woman and pushed into the small space. Closing the door behind her, she jerked her chin, signaling for her guards to keep watch outside the cell. Nobody could overhear this next conversation.

She turned to the gaunt woman sitting on the cot opposite her. One ankle wore a chain attached to the wall, the skin beneath it rubbed raw from years of wear. The woman herself looked like a ghost. Her body was all angles; her bones poked through the surface of her body, sores covered her pale skin from being immobile for so long, and her hair was reduced to long, tangled strings protruding from her head.

Myra faced the poor excuse for a woman and snapped her fingers in front of her, trying to get the woman's attention. The shell of the once eloquent woman remained motionless. Myra gave a cry of frustration and slammed her hand into the wall behind her prisoner.

"Damn it! You pathetic excuse for a Mortal. You lied to me all those years ago and said Duncan was dead!" Myra's eyes blazed with anger as the woman still sat motionless, not moving despite the outburst.

Crack! The sound of Myra's backhand echoed throughout the prison. Captives and soldiers shuddered in tandem, imagining the general taking her frustration out.

"Well? Say something, Naomi. Or has your mind finally given up after all these years?"

Naomi Freeman, the former First Lady of Kamore, returned to her sitting position, refusing to say a word or even look at the woman who had imprisoned her for almost two decades. Instead, she leaned over and spat on the woman's boots.

Even the vicious beating that ensued couldn't take away the small smile on Naomi's face.

Chapter Two

It had been two days since they left Heimat.

Two days since his city burned.

And two days since he felt blessed solid ground beneath his feet.

What he wouldn't give to be on solid ground right now.

George held onto the gunwale with white knuckles, gritting his teeth as the ship rocked beneath him. He leaned over the side and spilled his guts into the rushing river below. The lanky thirty-three-year-old with dark brown hair used his sleeve to wipe his mouth, removing the last of the residue from his face. He stumbled against the side of the ship as it pitched violently with the current of the river.

He groaned, closing his eyes and sliding down the gunwale until his knees hit the rough planks of the deck.

Bloody ship. George cursed the vehicle that made his stomach churn and left him vulnerable to the stares and whispers around him. He prided himself on his ability to remain unseen in a crowd, but this cursed sickness brought the entire ship's focus onto him.

His only saving grace was the lack of passengers awake in the early hours before dawn. This time, only the crew members on duty witnessed his upset stomach. He needed to get a handle on his seasickness before his people woke to see their leader in such a compromising position.

His reputation depended on it.

Eyes still closed, George took a deep breath through his nose and exhaled through his mouth. He took a second and a third before standing up, still holding tight to the gunwale. His eyes opened to the predawn gloom, staring across the river to its bank. He took one more deep breath before turning around and taking halting steps on shaky legs. Making it to the mainmast, he wrapped an arm around it, gritting his teeth and holding tight as the ship pitched again.

Around him, the crew shouted orders and went about their tasks in a flurry, preparing for a shift change. They were the reason the ship made it out of Heimat and kept to the middle of the river. The crew members were constantly readjusting the sails to take advantage of the wind, using the rudder to steer through the rough waters. He appreciated the skill they demonstrated with envy. He would give anything to settle the discontent in his stomach.

Two days since they left Heimat and still no sign of pursuit from the mayor. George knew blowing the docks would hinder the military man, but he'd never dared to believe they would avoid pursuers indefinitely. They kept up their breakneck speed, not daring to stop. The crew worked in shifts, taking turns catching sleep when they could, and making sure the ship stayed its course.

If they still didn't have pursuers by day's end, it would be almost impossible for any ship to catch up with the *Vengeance*. His interactions with the ship's captain had been brief, but he knew their progress was thanks to the shrewd captain. She knew how to inspire and motivate her crew to get impressive results.

George didn't hide his curiosity as he watched the crew scramble up and down the rigging. They moved like spiders, gripping the ropes with hands and feet, constantly moving but never falling. He simply stood and watched with wide eyes, moving when someone approached his perch by the mainmast to stay out of the way.

"Georgie! How ya doing?" Reg hailed him as he walked toward his friend. George's best friend and adopted brother seemed unaffected by the two days at sea. He shook his curly dark brown hair and studied George's pale face and hunched form. "Been sick already, eh?"

George tore his gaze away from the activity of the crew and rested it on his closest friend. He cracked a wry smile. "Aye. It seems I ate too much stew last night." He ran a hand through his hair. "Just when I thought I was getting used to this bloody ship." He trailed off and shook his head, staring past his friend as the sun crested on the horizon.

Reg followed the man's stare and patted him on the back. "You'll get yer sea legs eventually, mate. Jus' bend yer knees and move with the ship, not against it." He demonstrated by crouching slightly and moving side to side with the gentle rocking of the deck beneath his feet. He motioned for the man who had welcomed him into his family to follow his lead.

George sighed. "You've told me that more times than I can count. It doesn't make it any easier, Reg."

"Pft. That's because you've failed to try it. Let go of that mast and give 'er a go." Reg goaded.

George knew it was pointless to keep fighting his stubborn mule of a friend. He unwrapped his arm from the mast and rested his hand on it, locking eyes with the man still demonstrating the rocking motion.

He took a cautious step from the mast, hand stretched out towards the comforting solidness of the wooden pole. His stance was wide as he bent his knees and felt the planks rock underneath him. He tried to sway with the ship but wasn't prepared for the motion underneath his feet. George stumbled, arms wheeling, and fell forward, hitting the deck with his elbows. He swore as he lay prostrate, cursing the ship and its inhabitants.

A peal of laughter sounded in the crisp autumn air.

George flushed and stayed in his position on the deck, contemplating whether he should disappear below deck or face his humiliation. He heard light footsteps coming towards him, causing him to scramble to his feet. He felt an arm wrap around his waist, steadying him as the deck shifted beneath him yet again.

"You gotta move your hips there, Scally." The woman leaned into him as the boat dipped, moving his hips, and leaned away as it crested, pulling him along with a gentle tug on his waist. "Like this." She did it again, gently leading George as the ship moved with the river. Her eyes sparkled as she looked up at him. She smirked as she leaned towards him one more time. "Now you."

The arm around George's waist disappeared as quickly as it had appeared. He focused on shifting his weight with the ship.

"There ya go, Scally. Still a little rough, but maybe you won't fall on your face anymore." She winked and strutted away, yelling at and cajoling her crew as she made her way topside to her usual spot on the quarterdeck.

George's neck flushed as his gaze followed the captain of their ship. All his interactions with the formidable woman seemed to end with him looking incompetent or tongue-tied. He stumbled as a sharp turn disrupted his swaying. He shuffled back to the mainmast and grabbed a hold of it.

"Bloody ship," George growled.

Reg moved closer to his friend and chuckled. "Even the Cap can't teach this old dog new tricks." He clapped his friend on the back as he shook his head in misery.

"George still seasick?" Tamara asked with a scowl as she joined the crowd at the mainmast. The silvery tattoos that covered the exposed skin of her hands and neck seemed to glow in the morning sun; her dark skin providing the perfect contrast to the incandescent lines.

"Aye. He's quite crabby, too. I think it's from the lack of sleep."

George put a hand to his temple. "Could both of you say something helpful for once? I need to be presentable before our people wake up." He looked to the horizon, the sun now fully visible.

"Get ready to kiss me, George," Tamara said with a smirk and reached into her pocket. She pulled out a vial and held it up to the light of the early sun. It glinted as the glass caught the sun's rays.

George's eyes widened, and he lunged for the vial. Tilting his head back, he uncorked it and guzzled the liquid inside. He wiped his mouth with his sleeve and pocketed the vial.

Tamara's eyes glinted. "How do you know that wasn't poison?" She raised an eyebrow.

"Was it?" he asked, straight-faced.

Tamara gave an exaggerated sigh. "Come on, George, at least humor me a little. Put some sort of worry in your tone." Her expression was amused as she goaded Heimat's leader.

"I told ya he was crabby!" Reg chimed in.

George rubbed his temples as the seasickness draught did its job. The few Herbalists on board had limited ingredients to work with, which made creating the correct mixture for combating seasickness an arduous process. George was just grateful they were finally successful in creating one.

Tamara and Reg continued on about the weather and what the kitchen was fixing for breakfast. They shared a concerned look when George groaned and moved both hands to his head.

"Ya good there, Georgie?" Reg placed a hand on his friend's shoulder. He looked at Tamara. "Tam, go grab one of the Healers." He helped his friend to a sitting position on the ground while Tamara ran down to the infirmary below deck. "Put yer head between your knees and breathe. There ya go. Tam will get this sorted out."

Some of the crew had gathered to watch the spectacle. They stood to the side or watched from the rigging above. The surrounding congregation brought the attention of their commanding officers.

"What's gotten into your crew, Adams?" The Captain asked her first mate, pointing to the crowd around the mainmast with one hand on her hip.

"One civilian is having a rough go of it. I'll sort them out." Sebastian Adams left his Captain to go talk to their crew.

Cleo Starski admired the way her first mate strode towards the mainmast to give their crew an earful. She and Adams had crewed together for the past five years. He was straight-laced, loyal to a fault, and the best navigator on this side of the Mantaga.

Everything that made him off limits only seemed to make Cleo's blood hum with more desire.

She wrenched her gaze from her first mate's retreating figure and focused on the river ahead. Their inevitable romp in the sheets could wait, the river would not. The Mantaga was a beast, several miles wide and deep enough for even the largest boats to travel fearlessly. She commanded the respect of all ships and their crews.

Cleo's calloused hands rested on the worn wood of her ship's wheel while she kept a lookout for rocks and rapids posing a threat to the ship's hull. She cut an impressive figure and didn't let her inexperience as a captain show. Cleo, Adams, and most of the crew came from merchants' ships that traveled up and down the Mantaga River, sometimes traveling along the eastern coastline. Cleo came from a wealthy family that resided in the Capital but was never satisfied with the lifestyle her parents provided.

She felt the wind on her face and couldn't keep the grin from her face. Leaving home was the best decision she could have made.

Cleo left Fernwen when she was sixteen, stowing aboard a vessel headed to Heimat, the trading hub of the North. She had been crewing and working her way up the ranks since then.

First mate was the highest position she'd climbed to until now.

She relished the challenge and knew this crew like the back of her hand. They only had to deliver these civilians and they could start their new career as an independent sailing ship. They could start transporting goods and taking a heavy cut of the profits for themselves. Cleo could almost taste the opportunity and freedom she hungered for.

Her gaze flitted to where Adams bellowed at the crew. One Healer hustled towards the mainmast, finally parting the crowd so Cleo could see who caused the ruckus. Her eyebrows pulled together when she saw George in a huddled position.

The man the civilians looked to for leadership was unassuming and moody. He clearly didn't belong on the ship, but something about the way he quietly persevered, not giving in to hiding in the infirmary, earned him a little more respect from the Captain. Her green eyes watched his two friends lift him to his feet and slowly help him follow the Healer to the steps leading belowdecks.

If only the Magicae in their group were as seasick as that one. Cleo thought with a sigh. The past two days, their civilian passengers had kept to themselves, but she knew it was only a matter of time before they became restless and exercised their Gifts in full view of the crew.

The *Vengeance* and her crew were no strangers to the Magicae, employing an Herbalist to man the infirmary was one of the best decisions she made. But that didn't erase the ingrained distrust and fear present in so many of her crew.

Cleo squeezed the bridge of her nose as she recognized what trouble it could be if any of the Magicae ignited her crew's fears. *Hopefully, it won't come to that.*

The Captain knew it was a false hope. As soon as that Crafter woke up, she would need to take action if she wanted to keep her crew in line.

She caught movement in the corner of her eye, rousing her from her musings.

Adams made his way back to the quarterdeck once he was satisfied the crew had returned to their duties.

"It was the civilian you tried teaching how to dance," he said gruffly.

"Do I catch a hint of jealousy in your tone?" Cleo raised an eyebrow with a smirk.

"Of that guy? Hell no. He can't handle more than an hour on deck the *Vengeance* of all ships. This is one of the finest I've ever served on. I can only imagine how he'd have fared on something like the *Aurora* or the *Scarlet Wench.*" Adams scrunched his face at his captain's comparison.

Cleo laughed loudly. "Prophetess, he would've died if we were on the *Wench.* What a terrible ship. Remember the way she would pitch with every change in the current?"

"Or anytime Tiny moved to the opposite side of the deck. Remember when he got drunk and thought he could dance or some shit? What an idiot."

Cleo was soon roaring at the memory of the large man. She kept one hand on the wheel as she doubled over, caught in a laughing fit. She let herself savor the moment with her friend before composing herself. Both hands went back to the wheel and her gaze caught sight of the rocks ahead.

"Looks like we've got some fun ahead of us." Cleo pursed her lips and veered the ship away from the rocks. "Tell the crew to reef the sails. We need to slow down a bit until we've passed the Teeth."

Adams gave her a salute before heading down to give the crew their orders. Reefing the sails entailed gathering and tying them off, leaving less sail to catch the wind and propel them forward. The men and women in Cleo's crew began climbing the rigging of all three masts, moving to the sail they were in charge of, and tying the intricate knots needed to hold them in place.

"Teeth ahoy, Cap!"

Cleo looked to the crow's nest, at the top of the mainmast. She saluted the woman on duty, acknowledging the warning she gave.

"I could give you a better idea of what's coming, if you wish." A voice sounded to her right.

Cleo jumped, releasing the helm of her ship for a moment. Her heart pounded in her throat as she gripped it forcefully, throwing a glare at the person at her shoulder. "Never sneak up on the captain of a ship when she's at the helm. You could end up damaging the keel or hull." She took a moment to gaze at the young man next to her.

One of the civilians stepped forward so he was in her eyesight, keeping his hands in his pockets. The muscular man wore only a pair of ragged shorts, and no shoes or shirt to speak of. "Sorry, Captain. I was only trying to help."

Cleo focused on the river before saying, "What? You got the eyes of a raptor or something?" She gritted her teeth and yelled, "Damn it, Adams! Tell them to get that main sail reefed tighter! It's come loose again." She pulled hard on the wheel in her hands, pitching the ship hard to one side, narrowly avoiding a cluster of rocks that took her by surprise.

"Yes, actually." Cleo raised her eyes in surprise, finding them captured by eyes so dark they looked black. Deep brown filled every space, leaving no white coloring, and surrounding large pupils, almost indistinguishable from his dark irises.

"Prophetess above!" Cleo focused on keeping her grip on the helm as she rode the wave of shock she felt. She shook her head. "Sorry, mate, you surprised me. Been a while since I last locked eyes with a Shifter." Her focus drifted back to the river. She banked hard, avoiding a large rock to their left. She turned back to him when she saw him in the corner of her eye. Cleo raised an eyebrow. "What are you still doing here, Scally? I thought you were going to scout for me."

"You never confirmed you wanted me to."

Cleo gave him a long look, eyes traveling up and down his form. "Oh, I always want you to make no mistake about that," she purred. She dismissed him with a wave. "Just send a cry to the crow's nest and Miriam will send me a signal."

The man took off at a run, Shifting as he did, shrinking and growing feathers. The shorts he wore landed in a heap as he took to the skies. He did one lap around the ship before climbing high into the sky.

Cleo kept her focus on the rushing river, keeping her ears perked for Miriam's warnings above. "Adams! Tell them to hand the sails! We're still moving too fast." Adams bellowed orders, making sure all the crew bundled their sails entirely, leaving their ship at the full mercy of the river.

"Starboard!" Miriam shouted above.

Cleo caught sight of the trio of rocks just under the surface seconds later. She cut to the left, being mindful there was no wind to act as a buffer. She straightened the ship out as they passed by the rocks unscathed.

"Starboard!" Miriam called again.

Cleo kept the log protruding from the shore to their right in sight as she stayed steady on the course.

She caught sight of silver wings from the corner of her eye, but kept her focus on the river ahead and the wheel in her hands. All she heard was the roar of the river as she grounded her feet and willed her arms to become an extension of the ship.

The Captain didn't hear the falcon's cry, but the woman in the crow's nest did.

"Port!" She frowned when Cleo didn't hear her. "CAPTAIN! PORT!"

Roused from her musings, Cleo over-corrected in her desperate attempt to avoid the rocks that seemed to come out of nowhere. The ship spun rapidly, too far to the right, aiming straight for the bank. Cleo gritted her teeth and readjusted her grip on the wheel, throwing all of her weight into correcting the ship's course.

Once the bow of the ship successfully faced the middle of the river, Cleo let out the breath she was holding. Her arms shook from the effort, but she had learned her lesson. She kept her ears perked for calls from the crow's nest and her eyes on the water in front of them. There was no way the Captain was going to let the Teeth take this ship or her crew from her. When Miriam called once more, Cleo was ready, directing the *Vengeance* out of harm's reach.

They continued in this way for almost an hour. Cleo's arms grew tired as she pushed and pulled the wheel beneath her fingers, fighting against the currents in the river. Her eyes strained from squinting towards the water below. Still, she only wore a look of concentration as they battled the rapids and currents of the Mantaga. She refused to let her exhaustion be the reason they didn't make it.

"We're through it, Cap!" Miriam flailed her hands. Silver wings glinted in the sun as the Shifter wove through the rigging, letting out a cry in jubilee. He banked and landed on the captain's shoulder, chattering in her ear.

She shooed the raptor away and called to Adams, "Ready the anchors! On my signal!" She guided the ship into a small inlet protected from the wind. They would anchor for the night before braving the next part of their journey. Her crew needed and deserved the rest after pulling off the feat of making it through the Teeth unscathed. Vincenzio's lackeys would have a rough go of it if they followed behind them. Cleo wasn't convinced he'd be able to find enough experienced men and women to crew a ship, even if they had one. When they left, the explosions from the docks hit the ships moored there pretty hard.

"Anchors ahoy!" she yelled at the top of her lungs, stepping to the raised wall of the quarterdeck. She let her fingers trace the rough planks as she listened to the metallic bangs of the anchors dropping. "Good job, old girl. You did splendidly," she murmured to the ship beneath her feet. Her gaze traveled to her first mate, making his rounds, clapping sailors on the back, and taking part in the celebrating they were doing. Her heart tugged, knowing she couldn't take part like she once did. She sighed; being a captain was a lonely affair.

The Shifter returned with the discarded shorts in his beak. He dropped them on the deck behind her and Shifted. She watched him with interest, anything to distract her from the self-pity she'd felt moments before.

Watching someone Shift was an exercise in disbelief. The man's feathers receded as his form grew in size, his claws extending into hooked fingers, and his beak flattening into full lips. The feathers on his face thinned into eyebrows and stubble, while the ones on his head did likewise, becoming the cropped cut he wore.

Cleo stared as the Shifter's body became human, impressed by the magic running in his veins. Once fully human, he spun and pulled on his shorts until they hung loosely on his hips. He faced the captain of their ship and raised an eyebrow.

Cleo chuckled darkly. "Nothing I haven't seen before, Scally. Although I will say that package is quite impressive," she winked.

The Shifter remained unfazed by the Captain's flirtatious tone. "Your crew is impressive, Captain. Who was the woman in the crow's nest?"

Cleo narrowed her eyes. "Trying to make me jealous already? I'll bite. Her name's Miriam, but she's off limits." Her words became hard as she stared at the Shifter.

Bane furrowed his brows. "I wanted to commend her work, not take her to bed. She spotted some rocks before I did. I won't distract your crew, Captain." He walked towards the mainmast as Miriam descended. Cleo watched the two talk and noted that he kept his word. He leaned away from her instead of into her, as one did when they were enamored by someone. She took another moment to observe before making her own rounds and praising the efforts of her crew.

She might not celebrate like she once did, but she could affirm the bonds already forged and let her appreciation show.

Screams. Fires raging. Her mother hugging her tight, whispering words of love. Running through corridors, holding tight to Helene's hand. Riding hard, feeling Helene slump behind her. Wandering the countryside, hungry, cold, and scared to death. Luc and Damien struck down by soldiers. Duncan's body laying in a heap on the ground, his limbs sticking out at unnatural angles. Nan's eyes glazed over and unfocused, with an arrow sticking out of her chest while her body lay prostrate.

And blood. Bright red and sticky, everywhere.

A strangled noise broke out, full of anguish. Rae put her hands to her ears, only to realize the sound came from deep within. She pulled her arms across her middle, trying to hold herself together as the pain and fear wracked through her.

She felt a tug on her shoulder that became a consistent shaking. Garbled words sounded as if she were underwater, but she fled deeper within herself. The pain was too much; the darkness was safer.

Rae retreated to the inviting blackness, allowing herself to remember a whisper of deep, warm maroon and a man's figure astride a black stallion. She imagined a hand reaching down and pulling her up behind him, the faint scent of leather and horseflesh wafting toward her. She sighed as she leaned into the solid warmth in front of her.

Rae slipped into unconsciousness while the ship pitched and fumbled through the Teeth. She was in a bed bolted to the floor of the infirmary. All the patients in the small cabin were lashed to their beds to keep them from moving as the ship rocked with the raging river.

There was one resident Healer aboard the ship, considered part of the crew, along with two civilian Herbalists from Heimat. One civilian was a Healer while the other was a Grower. The Grower was trying to coax the few plants on board to grow and release the seeds they needed. The two Healers made rounds in the infirmary and worked diligently to create needed tonics for their patients and the supply cabinet.

Rae and George were joined by two other civilians battling seasickness and one crew member nursing bruised ribs after losing his footing on the rigging. The five beds barely fit in the small cabin, leaving only inches between each.

Rae finally stirred in the early evening on the day they passed through the Teeth. The resident Healer bustled toward her and brought a glass of water to her lips after helping her sit up. Rae drank greedily and nodded her thanks. She winced and brought a hand to her temple as the Healer checked her pulse for signs of a fever.

"What hurts?" she asked, turning Rae's hands over.

Rae cleared her throat. "My head is throbbing. Everything else just aches." She motioned to muscles stiff from disuse.

The Healer reached into her apron and pulled forth a tonic. She added it to Rae's water and helped her take another drink. Rae gulped down half of what was offered and sank back into her pillows.

"Thank you," she croaked. The Healer nodded as she moved to the bed across from her, where the sailor moaned, clutching at his ribs.

"Welcome to the land of the living, Freeman." A voice sounded from the bed next to hers.

Rae looked to find a pale George grimacing at her, and she rolled her eyes. "You're welcome," she replied.

"For what? Getting on this cursed boat? Not happening."

"Asshole. I saved your life. The least you could do is say thank you."

"I think I would be better off dead at this point."

"Finally, something we can agree on." The pair glared at each other, neither willing to back down. Tension filled the air between them. George broke eye contact first, fists clenching the blanket on his bed.

Rae turned her back to him, ending the conversation. Her mind drifted back to a certain dark rogue as the tonic worked through her system, a whisper of power returning to her core.

Chapter Three

The Circus was on the run. In the wake of everything that happened in Heimat, Duncan pressed them hard, putting as much distance as they could between themselves and the city they once took refuge in. It was the end of their second day in the forest, yet traces of smoke still wafted through the trees, floating upward as the caravan moved swiftly through the night.

Tyee pulled another child onto Koko, settling the young girl in front of him as two more sat behind him. He'd seen the girl stumbling, fighting to stay awake and keep up with the only family she'd ever known and acted on instinct. He felt her slump against his arm as sleep overtook her. The horseman hissed his frustration, urging his stallion to move to the front.

"Duncan!" Tyee shouted as he approached the Ringmaster. "We need to stop for the night. Our people can't keep up."

"We have to keep moving, Tyee."

"Duncan! Look at me." Purple eyes met his. He gestured to the three kids he carried. "We need to stop. We're going to lose them."

Duncan narrowed his eyes. "They should be in the wagons."

"The wagons are full, Duncan. They won't make it. We need to stop and make camp. We've gone far enough," Tyee pleaded.

Duncan looked behind them and saw haggard, dirty faces lit by the torches they carried. He looked back at Tyee, seeing the sleeping children pressed against him. Duncan sighed and hung his head, a lost look in his eyes.

Tyee shifted his position in the saddle and readjusted the girl in front of him.

Her head lolled to the side, but she didn't wake. Duncan lifted his head and stood up in his stirrups, addressing the entire caravan.

"My friends!" He cupped his chin as his voice rode the wind, carrying to everyone in the caravan. "Take heart! A little further is all I ask. Once we reach the next clearing, we'll stop for the night." His gaze met Tyee's, and they shared a nod. Duncan sent Jess and Kaiser to scout for a place to rest. Conrad and Nymeria joined them in feline form.

Duncan kept riding but slowed his pace. The people in the caravan kept moving, heartened by the promise of rest. They were weary from the frantic pace and the fear that was their constant companion. They kept their ears strained for any sounds of pursuit.

The unknown was worse than anything they could imagine.

Duncan led a handful of riders in the front, followed by the wagons and individuals on foot, with another squadron of riders in the back. A few riders like Tyee were interspersed throughout in case something was to attack from the sides. Every individual carried a weapon, whether it be a sword, a dagger, a bow, a large stick, or even a kitchen knife.

A sound came barreling through the forest, and Nymeria, the lioness Shifter, appeared. She Shifted quickly, grabbing the blanket from the back of Duncan's saddle and wrapping it around her.

"Duncan, we got company. There's a clearing up ahead. Get the wagons there and we can form a barricade around them."

"How many?"

Nymeria frowned before cocking her head to listen. "Two dozen Shifters." Her eyes narrowed as she concentrated. Tyee felt ice drench his insides.

Duncan waited for her to say more.

Nymeria's eyes widened, and she thrust the blanket back at the Ringmaster. "Hurry!" she yelled, not looking back while she shifted back into her powerful lioness form.

"Get to the clearing!" Duncan projected his voice and took off at a gallop. The caravan followed, spurred by an urgent sense of panic, clutching their weapons close.

"Put all the wagons in the middle, elderly and the young too. Everyone else, make sure you have a weapon and fan out around the perimeter. Hurry now." Duncan waited by the entrance of the clearing, directing his people with a torch in hand.

"Duncan, what's going on? Everyone is panicking, but no one knows why. Explain," demanded Chiara, pulling her horse alongside his.

Duncan looked into her concerned eyes, "We're not alone. We need to protect as many as we can." He turned to the next batch of incoming Circus members.

"Wagons, elderly, and children in the middle, everybody else needs to be ready to defend them." They nodded and kept moving into the clearing.

"Who hunts us?" Chiara asked, unwilling to leave without knowing more.

"The Shifters of the Forest." Duncan looked to the forest as something came crashing towards them. His eyes betrayed his concern, but his tone was like steel as he said, "Go, Chiara. Protect the children."

Chiara's eyes widened but did as she was bid, taking charge as soon as she reached the circle of wagons.

"Hurry! Elderly and children to the wagons!" Duncan shouted to the last trickle of riders and those traveling by foot.

He was too late.

The sounds of bodies breaking the treeline resonated throughout the clearing. Predators of all species burst from the trees, snarling, growling, and snapping at the caravan. Duncan watched with a grimace as wolves, big cats, foxes, a wolverine, coyotes, and many more beelined for the wagons gathered in the clearing.

A wall of fire flared up and around the wooden vehicles. Zalia held out her hands, keeping the predators at bay but separating Duncan, Tyee, and a handful of their people from the group.

Tyee kept his eyes on the Shifters prowling around the wagons, looking for an opening in the flames. He drew his throwing knives from Koko's saddle, tensing for the moment they realized their prey was closer than they thought.

Duncan held an arm out and signaled for them to slowly make their way to the trees. If they could reach the treeline, maybe they could go unnoticed. Tyee silently urged their people to hurry, trusting Koko to remain quiet as he moved to the trees. One cook tripped, landing with a thud.

Almost in tandem, the enemy Shifters turned as one.

Duncan dropped from his saddle, preparing to use his Craft should it come to that.

"Tyee, take the kids and run." He pushed his mare towards Tyee as the horseman's stomach dropped, watching the animals stalk toward them.

"Never." Tyee grabbed the mare's bridle and pulled her alongside Koko. He transferred the children in his care to the smaller horse's back.

"Go, Tyee."

"Don't be stupid, Duncan. I don't run." Finishing his task, Tyee handed the mare's reins to the cook who had fallen. On instinct, the man led the mare and her charges to the back of their group, anticipating the need for protection.

Duncan groaned, clenching his fists tight enough to draw blood.

"Everyone get behind me," Duncan said through clenched teeth. He stepped forward, not bothering to see if Tyee and the others followed his command. His eyes narrowed as the Shifters advanced.

Tyee moved to Duncan's left. The wind Crafter shifted to the right begrudgingly. Tyee knew there would be hell to pay after they got through this but now was not the time. He gave Koko his head, knowing the stallion would be a bigger asset if he could maneuver on his own. His hands clenched his throwing knives, his mind racing as he focused on the Shifter leading the charge and wearing the coat of a wolf.

The wolf pulled its lips into a sneer and gave a low growl.

Tyee's heart pounded. He didn't want to kill the Shifter, not after living with so many. Doubt clouded his thoughts as he wondered how Duncan knew they were Shifters and not simply animals. He tried to shake the thoughts from his head.

The evidence was in front of him: wolves mixed with big cats, badgers, coyotes, and foxes; these animals would not form packs naturally. He licked his chapped lips and forced the tremor from his hands. His eyes hardened. He didn't want to kill, but that didn't mean he was a stranger to defending his own.

Tyee was a survivor first and foremost.

If these Shifters couldn't see reason, he would make them. He spared a quick glance at the Crafter next to him.

Big mistake.

The wolf saw Tyee's break in concentration and lunged.

Tyee heard the wolf jump towards him and tensed for the impact that never came. A tremendous gust blew through the small group outside the safety of the wagons.

The wolf was thrown into the dirt meters away from their people, but the impact caused the other predators to remember themselves. They pressed forward, driving towards the two men and the people they protected. Tyee readied his first knife.

Before he could let the blade loose, a low roar came from behind them. An enormous body crashed through the underbrush before anyone could react.

Two giants leaped from the forest, over the heads of the members of the Circus, and squared off with the Shifters in front of them. The roar came again before Tyee realized Conrad, the tiger Shifter, and Nymeria had joined the fight.

The tiger and lioness puffed out their coats and bared their teeth. The predators cocked their heads, recognizing the two as their own. Several looked to where the wolf still laid in the dirt. He finally stirred and lumbered to his feet, taking care not to put much weight on his back right leg. His yellow eyes stared straight at the two felines in front.

He raised his chin and let loose a haunting cry, howling to the sky.

The Shifters tensed, trying to decide whether to continue with their attack or listen to the wolf's cry. Some relaxed and melted back into the shadows they came from. The predators surrounding the wagons came closer before doing the same. More and more left the clearing as the wolf continued his cry until only one other Shifter remained.

The large mountain lion padded towards the wolf and rubbed against him. They shared a look before the feline bobbed her head and turned back to Conrad and Nymeria.

The mountain lion started Shifting, but stopped once she stood on two legs. Fur still covered her body and claws dripped from hands still resembling paws. Fangs glinted when she gave a wicked grin.

She spoke in guttural tones from a throat thick with disuse. "Who are you?" She narrowed her eyes at Conrad and Nymeria as they Shifted. Unlike the mountain lion, they Shifted entirely into their human forms, taking the blankets Tyee offered from his saddle.

He watched Duncan step forward to speak with the powerful woman, but the Ringmaster stopped when she bared her fangs and glared.

"Not you, Crafter," she spat. "My words are for them." She nodded toward Conrad and Nymeria. Her gaze moved to them as she said, "We are the Shifters of the Northern Forest, protecting its secrets and creating a safe place for our people. I will ask again, why do you travel with these Furless?"

Nymeria put a hand on Conrad's arm and took a small step forward. "These people are our family and dear friends. We travel to find sanctuary within the Great Forest, as you have found."

The Shifter devolved into grating noises. Tyee frowned when he realized the Shifter was laughing in its half form. He looked to the wagons, relieved to see them devoid of any enemies. A wall of fire still burned but was shrinking. Tyee swallowed and refocused on the strange Magicae in front of them. They needed to get her on their side before the fire Crafters used all their energy.

Nymeria tensed as the Shifter kept laughing. "Care to share the joke?"

The wolf leaped between his leader and the lioness Shifter when Nymeria took another step toward the pair. He emitted a warning growl from deep in his throat despite the limp in his back limb.

"Calm yourself, love." The Shifter placed a hand on the wolf's head, quieting his protests. She furrowed her brows and addressed the lioness. "Forgive my outburst, but this is comical, no? You mean for us to believe two as powerful as you degrade yourselves and travel with so many Furless?"

Nymeria's mouth was set in a grim line. "My son is what you consider Furless. You're no better than the Mortals we ran from." Nymeria bared her teeth.

The Shifter studied Nymeria before moving her gaze to Conrad. "Come now, the time for games is done. Speak true or we will have to take action." She showed her fangs.

Conrad's expression turned sour. He glanced at Tyee, eyes falling to the knife in his hand. He locked eyes and motioned to the knife with his gaze. Tyee's grip tightened, and he blinked once, indicating he understood. Conrad tossed the cloth aside and Shifted. He took care to stop the process halfway, entering a half-form like the two Shifters they faced.

He looked at their adversaries and bared his own teeth.

The mountain lion Shifter hissed her approval. "You look much better in this form. It's your first time, no? Feel the power."

Conrad's sneer turned into a low growl. Nymeria put a hand on his arm, reminding him of what was at stake. He narrowed his eyes but quieted and turned to the mountain lion.

"Think what you want, but I am the same, no matter my form. The lioness speaks true. These people are our family and we travel together because of our shared purpose. We mean to liberate all of Kamore from the tyranny she remains under. Disrespecting them will not get you very far," he spat.

The mountain lion Shifter gave Conrad a long look, noting his squared shoulders and set jaw. She frowned. "You truly travel with Furless by choice?"

Her gaze moved to Duncan and Tyee, trying to comprehend what made the Shifters so devoted to them. Her eyes widened as she took in their smells. "Mortals? You have Mortals in your party? Fools." She looked at the wolf in alarm and Shifted into her animal form. They took off into the forest after their pack.

Conrad growled in rage, Shifting back into his tiger form, and bounded after the pair.

"Conrad! Imbecile." Nymeria took off after him, Shifting as she went.

Tyee watched the pair go, eyebrows furrowed in concern. *I should go after them.* He thought before catching sight of the wagons still surrounded by fire. His heart panged uncomfortably as he gazed at the dancing flames.

The orange glow reminded him of a certain golden girl and the guilt and fear he felt for her. He shook his head to clear his thoughts.

Brooding wouldn't serve anybody.

He urged Koko towards the wagons, not bothering to see if Duncan or the others followed him.

"Zalia!" he bellowed as they approached. He dismounted and yelled, "They're gone! Let down your walls."

When the wall of fire descended, Tyee hurdled over the last of the flames, leaving Koko to keep a lookout. His eyes widened when he saw Zalia on the ground and the two green fire Crafters panting.

"Where's the other fire Crafter?" Tyee's eyebrows furrowed.

The two Crafters shared a look. "He didn't make it. He left the caravan days ago, and no one knows why."

"What happened?"

"Zalia used our energy for as long as possible, but we think it overwhelmed her. She's been knocked out for a while now," replied the young woman.

"So you two kept the wall up?" Tyee looked between them as the woman hung her head, but the man met his stare.

"We had to, so we did," he stated matter-of-factly.

"You should be proud of yourselves. You protected our people." He knelt next to the unconscious Crafter. "Let's get her to Abuela for a fire tonic." The two scrambled to help him as Duncan and the others reached the wagons.

Duncan took the scene in quietly, moving between the wagons and giving encouragement to his people. He took a moment to stare in the direction Conrad and Nymeria had disappeared.

So, the long road begins.

With that thought, Duncan prepared his people to sleep through the night, posting sentinels to keep watch for the things that prowled in the night.

Chapter Four

The sun beat down on Rae's face for the first time in what felt like weeks. She lifted her chin to catch as much of the early morning light as she could. Breathing deeply, she took in the smells of the river, the fishy smell of water mixed with that of leaves falling from the trees on its banks. An icy wind bit against her exposed skin, but she couldn't help the smile tugging her lips upward.

The cold was worth getting out of the infirmary below deck.

She pulled her cloak tighter around her but took off the gloves one of the crew had given her. She turned her hands palm-side up and reached within. Flames ignited in each palm, making Rae's grin bigger. She went through her Crafting positions, twin flames in her hands. She lost herself to the movements, focusing on her breathing. After a few minutes, she stood up, remembering the wood beneath her feet. She closed her palms, trapping the heat inside, and returned to a crouch, one arm in front of her and the other above her head, ready to strike.

Within her core, she tugged one wind from the complex braid giving order to the storm. She went through more positions, winding the wind around her hands, concentrating on adding more and more each time she went through the positions.

Rae took a misstep and fell to one knee.

The wind went flying out of control, filling the sails and pushing them towards the bank.

A cry sounded and crew members scrambled up the masts, reefing the sails against the sudden wind.

Rae gritted her teeth and called the wind back, surprised by how stubborn it could be. She jumped when a hand fell on her shoulder. She looked up into Zeke's silver eyes and pursed lips. He kept his hand on her shoulder but closed his eyes while he delved within.

Rae bit her lip as Zeke concentrated. A tense awkwardness still hung in the air between them, despite Rae's attempts to dispel it. She watched as Zeke pulled her unruly wind towards him. It resisted at first, but then gave in as the pull of the hurricane in Zeke's core became undeniable. He seemed to pass it through his hands a couple of times before opening his eyes and moving to face Rae head-on

He looked into her eyes and cocked one eyebrow. She swallowed the relief that rushed through her at seeing that familiar expression on his face.

Later. She insisted, pushing the hope of reconciliation aside.

Determination filled her eyes as she released her lip and nodded, holding out her hands. He passed the wind to her and watched her bend the will of the gale.

"That's it. Remember, you can bring it around your waist too. Sometimes that keeps it occupied longer than just using your hands."

"What do I do when I want to release it without causing damage?" Rae asked, moving the wind to whip around her trunk.

"Release it slowly, keep ahold of it, and run it through your hands as if it's a rope. Use your hand to cut it, if you will, limiting how much wind leaves at a time."

Rae took a deep breath, grasping one end and forcing it to drift through her hands as Zeke instructed. The wind balked but acquiesced after realizing its ticket to freedom. She kept one hand by her waist and the other pointed towards the trees to the north, careful to aim away from the sails. After a while, she closed the fingers of the hand she held aloft, letting go of the wind that had already passed through her hand.

She clenched her jaw as the wind around her trunk reeled with the loss of itself. It bucked, trying to follow its brethren. Rae used the hand near her waist to hold on, coaxing it through her other hand. Eventually, the wind settled and jumped towards the promise of freedom.

She repeated this two more times until the wind was gone. Breathing hard, the Crafter moved to the side of the ship and placed both hands on the hull. Zeke joined her but stayed silent. Rae felt the tension return without the distraction of the wind acting as a buffer. Their easy banter and ribbing hadn't been the same since that night in Heimat.

Rae studied the wind Crafter's profile. His silver locks had grown into a mess of short, wild curls, and his body hunched forward as he leaned on his elbows against the gunwale. The lines of his jaw were sharper, but his face was red from the wind, a ruddy hue coloring his normally pale skin.

She looped her arm through his, craving the closeness they once had. "I'm sorry, Z. Please, talk to me. I hate this," she whispered.

Zeke met her gaze with silver eyes full of emotion. "I know you are, Rae. But betrayal doesn't run its course overnight." Noting the anguish in her eyes, he softened his features and flashed her a smirk that didn't reach his eyes. "You're going to have to do better than that." He pulled away from his trapeze partner and walked to the bow of the ship.

Rae's stomach dropped, noticing the way Zeke used her name, but she couldn't help the hope blooming in her chest. Determination filled her eyes as she called after him, "Challenge accepted."

Zeke sent her a look over his shoulder, a little more light in his eyes. "We'll see about that."

I can fix this. Even if it's the last thing I do. Rae vowed to herself and the friend she loved like family. Zeke had a history of being betrayed by the ones he loved the most. Pushing her Craft into his veins without warning during her moment of desperation was the worst thing she could've done. Rae didn't blame him for holding a grudge and was grateful he seemed to be open to reconciliation, even if he still needed a little space.

Rae let herself rest from wrangling the wind and kept her gaze on Zeke as he joined Bane at the bow. The pair began stretching and conditioning their muscles as Rae brainstormed ways to combat the rift between her and her trapeze partner.

Rae threw her hands up and pushed off from the side of the ship. Brainstorming was getting her nowhere, the right idea refused to spark and left her emotions to their own devices. She knew she couldn't waste this perfect opportunity to practice the Crafts still unfamiliar to her.

Taking a deep breath, she focused on releasing the tension in her shoulders and back.

Then she concentrated on the riverbank and set her feet shoulder-width apart. She bent her knees and released the gunwale, flipping her hands so they rested palm-side up. Rae had only called on her earth Craft once before and it resulted in her passing out. She needed to practice in shorter bouts to build endurance.

Earth Crafting was the most consuming of the Crafts. It took more endurance to force the earth to bend to a Crafter's will than the three other elements. One had to be steadfast and unmovable in order to master such a Craft.

Rae kept her knees bent as she reached within and called forth the might of one spire from her core. Three of the Crafts were kept in check by the plaiting she had done, weaving the winds, flames, and currents into tapestries that kept them from overwhelming her. Her earth Craft was the difficult one, requiring her to coax it into spires of rock that formed a tight circle.

She bit her lip as she tried to figure out how to pull a small amount of power without causing everything to collapse.

She closed her eyes and focused on one pillar of rock. She willed it to enter her veins, feeling her blood become sluggish as particles of soil concentrated within it. Once the spire disappeared from her core, Rae opened her eyes and focused on a spot of grass along the riverbank. She closed her hands into fists and watched as the grass rumbled before bursting, soil gushing to the surface.

She widened her eyes in surprise and slowly relaxed her hands, watching the geyser of earth reduce to just a trickle. She held on as the last of the earth left her veins, sweat dripping from her brow. Taking a shuddering breath, she gripped the gunwale once again. She focused on the feeling of the wood beneath her fingers, willing herself to remain conscious.

"Not another one." Rae heard a voice to her left. She gripped harder, unable to turn her head in fear of passing out and being sent back to the infirmary.

"Well? Best to get it over with, lass. Your stomach will feel better once you do." Gloved hands gathered and held her hair before she felt pressure against her back, moving her head over the side of the hull.

Rae saw spots and struggled against the hands holding her firm.

"Whoa there, lass. Easy now, I'll let you go."

When the pressure released, Rae straightened, feeling a little better and less likely to pass out. She turned to get a look at the person trying to help her.

Rae met dancing emerald eyes and sun-kissed skin. She noticed the woman's dramatic trench coat covered in haphazard patches that hung loosely on her shoulders. Gold glinted on her right earlobe and a maroon bandanna covered her dark hair.

The woman raised an eyebrow in challenge, waiting for an explanation.

Rae narrowed her eyes and placed a hand on her temple. "It's my head, not my stomach. And I'm not your lass."

"Oho! You got a bark on ya, but do you have a bite to match?" The woman unsheathed her cutlass and balanced it on one finger. She focused on the blade for a moment before flashing Rae a feral grin.

Rae gave her a quizzical look but still drew two daggers. Movement at the edge of her vision caused her head to turn. Some of the crew inched closer to watch.

"Two blades against one? Guess you're more lily-livered than I thought." She gave a fake pout to the gathered crew. Many sneered at the fire Crafter.

Rae struggled to comprehend what was happening and dropped her guard slightly. *Am I supposed to fight this woman? Who the hell is she, anyway?* She thought, trying to see where Zeke and Bane had gone. Again, she only found sneers from the surrounding crowd.

Cleo strutted back and forth, cajoling the crowd and hurling insults at her chosen adversary. Inside, she was cringing, sending prayers for forgiveness to the Prophetess. She knew this was the first time the Crafter had ventured out of the infirmary and that the woman was still recovering from her ordeal in Heimat.

But Fate favored the bold.

Cleo had observed from her place at the helm as Rae went through the motions of commanding her Crafts. There was no denying the woman was powerful, or the ignorance she took for granted, not expecting she needed to hide on a ship from Heimat.

Such a farce. Cleo thought with disgust. Her crew should be held to higher standards. *I can't make changes until Lockewater. We just need to make it that far.*

But promises for the future wouldn't change the present. As Captain, Cleo was expected to maintain order on the ship. Her crew's fears and distrust for the Magicae on board would be abated if she proved they were still no match for their Captain's hand-to-hand combat skills.

Taking on their strongest fighter would settle the matter before it became an issue. And the only way to ensure a win was to take her on now when Cleo had the element of surprise on her side.

She kept a close eye on the Crafter as she brandished her cutlass for their audience's delight, waiting for the perfect opening.

Cleo noticed Rae's daggers dropping and smirked. The time was now.

Rae instinctively threw her arms up when Cleo attacked, but her arms trembled as her daggers caught Cleo's blade.

Cleo didn't slow down. Too soon, the blade was gone, leaving the Crafter to scramble for footing on the slippery deck. She kept her eyes on Cleo as they circled each other.

Cleo sported a wicked grin as she prowled along the deck. "We fight til first blood, lass. Any problem with that?" She raised one eyebrow.

Cleo knew it was dangerous to goad a Magicae as powerful as Rae, but she needed to appear confident and unbothered. She felt her heart pounding but didn't let it show as the Crafter took a deep breath to center herself. Rae spread her feet out, one slightly in front of the other, and nodded, steel in her golden eyes, daggers at the ready. With her jaw set, the Crafter watched Cleo's every move.

The Captain's grin faltered slightly, but she hid it and pressed her lips into a thin line. She was impressed by the Circus performer, whether she wanted to admit it or not. She'd expected Rae to be less eager after spending so many days in the infirmary. No matter, Cleo could only hope she was clever enough to take the upper hand.

"As the Prophetess is our witness, we fight for first blood. May the better fighter win!" Cleo announced to the waiting crowd. The crew's cries drew an even larger audience, hungry for a reprieve from the monotony of life on board. She looked to the Crafter and said lowly, "Just don't destroy my ship. No fire, golden eyes, savvy?"

Rae bit her lip but nodded. Cleo felt relief flood her eyes before she hardened them once more. The request was a strategic one. She knew the Crafter would be off balance, not being able to use the Craft she knew by heart.

Cleo was no stranger to doing her research. She wasn't the youngest captain in the North by chance, after all.

The two women crouched, studying each other, muscles coiled for an attack. They circled once again, narrowing their focus to the fight ahead.

Cleo attacked first, swinging at Rae just outside her dagger's reach. Rae moved quickly, leaning away from the curved blade, and swinging a leg out, trying to take her opponent by surprise. Cleo jumped nimbly over the clumsy move but went spinning into the crowd as Rae thrust her daggers forward, punching the wind towards the woman.

Cleo twisted in the air, missing the mainmast by a hair, and tucked her legs, rolling into a somersault as she hit the deck. She used her momentum to thrust herself into a standing position. Cleo heard movement behind her and immediately whirled around, cutlass sweeping in front of her as she crouched low.

Rae halted her attack when Cleo stood up, leaning back just in time to avoid the bite of her blade.

Cleo gave a frustrated grunt as her sword met the empty air. Rae danced away, but the Captain pressed forward, trying to fluster the other woman into making a mistake. Sweat beaded on Rae's brow as Cleo kept coming, swinging and thrusting her cutlass as if it was an extension of her arm. Cleo gave one more powerful downward strike, forcing Rae to use both daggers to stop her. With a flick of her wrist, Cleo dislodged one of the Crafter's weapons and sent it clattering across the deck.

The two women jumped away from each other, both breathing hard.

Cleo flashed a triumphant grin to the crowd and passed her cutlass between her hands, while Rae tried to catch her breath. The time she spent in the infirmary was showing. Both took a ready stance and watched the other's moves. Cleo, once again, made the first move. She feinted right before arcing her short sword and descending on the acrobat's unprotected left side. Rae wasn't fast enough to stop the seasoned sailor, so she tried contorting her body away from Cleo's blade.

She could barely avoid the curved weapon, but the sudden change in her weight distribution caused Rae to stumble.

Cleo saw her chance and tackled her opponent, putting one boot on the arm that held Rae's last dagger. With one knee on the ground, Cleo loomed over her. Rae tried to use the wind to get the older woman off of her, but Cleo chuckled and brought the cutlass to Rae's throat.

Rae squirmed, fear punching a hole in her gut as her life flashed before her eyes.

"Damn it, Cleo! Make the cut and be done with it!" A voice sounded above the crowd, earning boos from most of the crew.

Cleo's eyes glittered when she smirked at the Crafter. She said lowly, "Don't worry, lass, I'm a woman of my word." She dipped the cutlass to Rae's cheek and drew a thin line across the woman's flushed skin. A line of blood followed the tip of the sword. Cleo stood and offered a hand to the Crafter.

Rae hesitated but took it, baring the scratch to the gathered crew. Cheers and clapping sounded around the deck and in the rigging above them. Cleo discreetly motioned for the sailor closest to her to retrieve Rae's fallen dagger. It took a minute, but eventually, the blade made its way back to the Captain.

Cleo presented it to Rae and said, "This landlubber fought bravely when she didn't stand a chance." The Captain winked as Rae rubbed at her cheek, gratefully taking the dagger offered. "Give her the respect her bravery demands or you'll have to deal with the consequences. Your Captain has spoken, now get back to work."

"Aye, aye, Cap!" The crew gave other various affirmations as they scurried back to their various tasks.

Cleo gave Rae a pat on the back and turned to one woman in the rigging. "Hey, Mouse! How many bet against me?"

The woman showed her teeth, her cracked lips pulling into a grimace. "Only three, Cap!"

"How much for their names?"

Mouse licked her lips as her eyes darted across the deck. "Same price as usual."

Cleo's grin turned feral. "See me after your shift, and I'm sure we can arrange something."

The woman saluted and scurried up the mess of rope and knots attached to the mainmast.

As the crowd dissipated, George shouldered his way to the two women barely recovered from his earlier ordeal. Rae scowled when she saw him, using the pretense of sheathing her daggers to avoid acknowledging him. Cleo's eyes danced with delight when she saw the tall young man.

"Scally! Got your sea legs, yet?" she asked cheerily, swinging an arm around his shoulder.

"Cut the crap, Cleo. What the hell was that?"

"Whatever do you mean? We were just having a bit of fun," she pouted.

"You had your sword at Freeman's throat. How is that considered fun?"

Cleo's eyes hardened, and she placed one hand on her hip. "You walk on a razor's edge, Scally. It's not up to you to question the Captain. Take care to remember I saved all your asses back there." She glared at the man who was close to insulting her in front of her crew.

Rae straightened with shock on her face. "I didn't think I heard that right before. You're the Captain of this ship?"

Cleo rolled her eyes. "Aye, lass. I'm the Captain. What were you expecting, a man?"

"No- you're just so young."

Cleo winced. "Comes with the territory. Most of the old folks retire early in this type of business. That or the Prophetess decides she has better use for them on the other side." She flashed a feral smile. "Plus, I'm as cutthroat as they come. Ambitious by nature, I fear."

Cleo didn't miss the glance Rae shared with George. She knew they were surprised to hear her invoke the face of the Goddess that was the least worshipped, but the Prophetess protected those at sea, or in this case, on the river. Or they were trying to figure out how far they could push her.

"Why did you want to fight me? Did I do something wrong?"

Cleo gave her a quizzical look before bursting into booming laughter.

Rae again looked at George. He shrugged, furrowing his brows.

Rae sighed and looked at the woman, still lost in a fit of humor. "I'm sorry, but what is so damn funny?"

Cleo clapped her on the back as she got ahold of herself. "I like you, lass. You've got the moxie of an excellent sailor." She cleared her throat before continuing, "Come by my quarters for dinner tonight. Both of you. There is much to discuss before we make it to Lockewater."

Chapter Five

Zeke and Bane were lost in their workout while Cleo and Rae took swings at each other. They paused when they heard the shouts and cheers coming from the middle of the ship, looking towards the gathering crew.

"Should we see what's going on?" Zeke lifted to the balls of his feet and craned his neck, trying to get a better view.

Bane gazed at the crowd and frowned. "Best to leave it alone. The Captain can handle it." He turned back to the prow to resume going through their exercises.

Zeke gave a lingering look at the commotion before following the Shifter.

Soon, both men were covered in sweat as they ran, jumped, and rolled across the deck. They switched from strength training and cardio to moving through a series of defensive moves, sparring imaginary opponents. By the end of their session, both were breathing hard with muscles singing from use.

Zeke still couldn't believe the variety of ways Bane imagined to torture their muscles. *I will never complain about Luc's cardio workouts again.*

Bane went to the side of the ship, peering intently into the forest, while Zeke leaned down to put his hands on his legs, trying to catch his breath. Bane looked back at the lithe young man and scrunched his eyebrows.

"Aren't acrobats supposed to be in better shape?"

Zeke took a couple of deep breaths before straightening. "I'm in perfectly good shape. You're just an animal." Zeke's eyes widened as he realized what he said. "That's not—I didn't mean—You're just intense." The acrobat blurted, his face flushing.

Bane's expression remained stoic as he grunted. "Funny, Crafter. Real funny." He watched Zeke's face fall and turn even redder. In his embarrassment, Zeke didn't catch the small smile Bane sent his way. Before the acrobat could respond, Bane covered his smile with a smirk and punched the other man's shoulder. "Relax, it'll take more than that to ruffle my feathers."

Zeke stared at the Shifter before the tension in his shoulders eased and he let out a breathy laugh. Bane's low chuckle joined Zeke's a beat later. Zeke rolled his shoulders and put one leg on the gunwale, stretching his sore muscles.

Bane gazed back at the forest. "We need to figure out if Duncan got everybody out."

"I'm sure he did. George bought them time when he took out the bridges." Zeke winced as he stretched his other leg.

Bane narrowed his eyes. "We need to be sure, though. How do we reunite with them if we don't know where they are?"

"Okay, but how?" Zeke drew out his vowels as he straightened into a standing position.

Bane didn't answer him, keeping his focus on the riverbank. He pursed his lips before giving a short whistle. The Shifter lifted one arm as two birds barreled towards him. The birds banked at just the right time, gracefully alighting on Bane's outstretched arm.

Zeke stared at the larger of the two birds, with its striking dark bands covering its face and the underside of its wings.

"Never seen an osprey before?" Bane asked with a knowing look.

Zeke shook his head, murmuring, "She's beautiful."

"Yes, he is," Bane corrected gently. "Brace your arm and hold it out. You may be surprised by his weight."

Zeke's eyes widened as he did what he was told. The bird looked at Bane and cocked his head, confused by the directions the Shifter gave him. He chattered lightly before reaching a taloned foot towards Zeke's offered arm. Zeke gritted his teeth as first one set of talons and then the other dug into his forearm. The bird's claws were long, but they held tight to Zeke's arm with an unnatural gentleness. Bane pursed his lips and kept his focus on the bird. The osprey seemed to be challenging Bane's directions through the bond between them. With a frown, Bane kept the impressive predator at bay.

The osprey's large, yellow eyes studied Zeke with unwavering intensity. The bird spread its wings, showing off the speckled pattern underneath before settling back on Zeke's arm.

"Ospreys are sometimes called fishing hawks. Their long talons allow them to snatch fish from the water with ease." Bane gently traced one of the bird's claws, letting it brush the Crafter's arm briefly before pulling away. "I'm going to send him ahead to scout the river."

Zeke started. "You're not doing the scouting yourself?"

Bane's gaze never left the bird. "No. I'll be able to see through his eyes. I need to check behind us, see if the mayor could muster a force to come after us."

Zeke nodded and asked, "What's the other bird for, then?"

"Falcons are known for their speed. I'm counting on her to find the rest of our people. She knows where the city is and can start there before going into the Forest." The Shifter stroked the falcon's gray head, causing the bird to close her eyes and lean into his touch.

"It's amazing how they respond to you."

A soft smile formed on Bane's lips as he continued stroking the bird. When he caught Zeke's silver eyes, his own dark avian ones hardened. "The more respect you give them, the more likely they are to share their secrets with you. Magicae and Mortals are no different in fearing and hating the other animals in this world." He rubbed his free hand roughly on his chin before gesturing to both birds. "These creatures are elegant, powerful, and deadly, but the only thing that matters to most people is how dangerous they can be. People look into my eyes and see something unnatural, something they don't understand, but these birds don't care. They see me and I see them. They understand me unlike anyone else, and vice versa."

Zeke's metallic eyes softened as he met Bane's unnatural gaze, the dark irises that filled his eyes, leaving no white space and the emotions swirling within.

Does he know what I think about every time I close my eyes? A vision flashed in his mind, his fingers tracing the other man's jawline and leaning in to capture Bane's lips with his own.

Zeke chased those thoughts from his mind and placed his free hand on the other man's shoulder. "I know what that's like. So many people have looked me in the eye only to make me watch as theirs fill with fear and hatred." He turned his head, breaking eye contact to mask the emotions he could barely keep hidden. "I've never lived in a world where I'm not judged by the power in my veins. But I get it. You're right to say we've never given these guys a chance." He gestured to the osprey on his arm. "It's like what Abuela said about the wolves. They're not the villains we've always made them out to be."

Bane grunted and turned to the falcon on his arm. Shifter and bird sat in still silence, staring into each other's eyes. Bane nodded and tied a slip of cloth to the bird's foot before lifting his arm. The falcon gave a cry and bolted into the forest, presumably to find the rest of their people.

Bane focused on the osprey next. He held his arm out next to Zeke's so their bare skin touched, and the bird gladly moved to it. He kept eye contact with the raptor until the bird gave a chirp and took off, following the river. Bane watched the beautiful bird soar just above the water, dipping one foot into the current. He leaned against the ship's hull and sighed, closing his eyes.

Zeke joined him at the wall of the ship, waiting for the Shifter to talk. While they stood there, the crowd in the middle of the ship dispersed. Zeke's eyes were drawn to the scuttling crew and the shouts of the Captain. He thought he saw Rae and George but quickly averted his gaze, turning to the riverbank. Bane watched him with a frown, following Zeke's sight line.

"What happened between you and Rae?" Bane asked, avoiding a response to Zeke's insight.

Zeke sighed and kept his eyes on the forest. "That's between me and her."

Bane studied the Crafter's tense jaw with surprise. "Aye. As it should be." He rubbed the back of his neck and looked at the sky. A wind blew across the ship, causing goosebumps on Bane's bare chest. "I should go now before the storm gets worse."

He clapped Zeke on the back, his hand lingering for a moment, and took off at a run. Bane Shifted as he went, jumping once he reached the prow of the ship, his shorts dropping to the deck as his falcon form catapulted through the air. He cried for the Crafter below before following the river behind them, looking for any signs of pursuit.

Zeke watched him leave, thinking, *Huntress, help me.*

Zeke sighed when Bane flew out of view. *Huntress, I need to grow a backbone. What would Rae say if she knew I botched a golden opportunity like that?*

He chased thoughts of his best friend away, wiping at his face. His feelings regarding his trapeze partner were complicated. In his heart, Zeke knew Rae hadn't meant to hurt him, but that didn't erase what happened. Using him because she was desperate to get her flames back would never sit right with the wind Crafter.

But what if you were in that position? A small voice deep inside asked the question he was terrified to face. Zeke turned his attention to the hurricane in his core, trying to ignore it. He marveled at the power within before returning to the present.

I need to blow off a little steam. Casting a cursory glance at the crew members mulling around, Zeke did his best to stay at the bow, as out of sight as possible.

He twisted his arms so his palms were facing up and called the wind towards him. His eyes swirled with emotion as the winds from the storm gathered around him. He felt ice in his veins as his blood sang with power.

Zeke felt trapped on the ship, in Rae's betrayal, and with his feelings for the avian Shifter. He relished the release he felt from all three as the wind whistled around him. He played with the wind, spinning and twisting with it before throwing it into the trees.

He whooped in delight, jumping up and spinning one last time. His blood roared in his ears as he panted. He let the wind slip through his fingers and settled onto the balls of his feet.

A crowd gathered in the rigging as many of the crew watched the wind Crafter using his power. They were drawn in by his precision and the joy he emulated as he spun with the wind. There was a renewed feeling in the crowd since their Captain battled and won against Rae. Tensions weren't as high, and they were more curious than anything else. Some looked to the sky, taking in the dark clouds brewing in the distance.

It was a comfort to have two powerful Crafters aboard should the storm prove too powerful.

A call from Adams had them scurrying back to their posts to prepare for the storm coming their way.

Zeke leaned against the gunwale, unaware of the commotion he caused, and catching his breath when he saw Rae motioning him to her.

His heart twisted, but he got up sluggishly, his muscles screaming, and made his way to her. *I'll find a way to forgive her.* He winced as he trudged across the deck toward his trapeze partner. Zeke caught Rae's gaze and noted the concern in their golden depths. *But I don't have to make it that easy for her.*

He flashed her a smirk as he deliberately slowed his pace. Rae couldn't resist rolling her eyes, but the tug at the corner of her lips gave her away.

We'll be okay. Zeke's expression softened despite the resolve within not to bestow forgiveness quite yet.

A boom of thunder raised his face to the sky, just in time to catch the first of the pounding rain.

Chapter Six

Tyee crossed his arms, waiting for the caravan to finish packing. He lost his footing as Koko nudged him with his head. Tyee chuckled and rubbed the stallion's midnight-colored face.

"I know, I know. We'll run again soon." The horse bobbed his head and nudged his rider yet again. Tyee shook his head and pushed the horse's nose away from him. "Now, now. Knock it off, you brute. We have to wait for everyone."

He swung into the saddle and directed Koko to follow the perimeter of the caravan. Eventually, he made it to the colorful wagon he'd been avoiding for some time. The old woman inside held the answers he wasn't sure he was ready for.

Her story was so familiar, though. She has to know. Tyee absentmindedly rubbed Koko's coarse mane through his fingers. His gaze wandered to the sounds of children playing while overwhelmed parents packed the little they had. Tyee was struck yet again by how impossible this community he found himself in was.

Tyee's childhood had been an ugly one, growing up in the poor village of Aston, just north of Tiva. His mother spent her days working at the local tavern, waiting tables and washing dishes as she was needed. Nights were spent working the streets and attending to the needs of men not met by food and drink alone.

Tyee was the product of one of those men's needs.

His mother loved him in her own way, sending him to the streets, begging for food and coin. Anything he collected was proudly presented to the bitter woman, only to be snatched up without so much as a thank you. Most of the time she complained it wasn't enough and that he should steal, taking that which wasn't freely given.

Tyee still remembered the first time he brought her an old man's coin purse. She finally gave her son the love and affection he yearned for.

He was four years old.

His mother's love and praise were like drugs, and his mother, the drug lord. The next several years were dark.

Tyee regretted it all.

The begging, the stealing, the swindling; it all ended when Tyee found his mother trading his coin for a room at the inn. He worked his ass off, feeling useless and shameful, under the impression his mother worked night and day to keep the hovel they called home. Turned out she was living the high life while her son slept alone and hungry in the dirt.

He left that night and never looked back. He moved a couple of towns over to the larger city of Briar, finding the new streets a welcome refuge as he quit his drug of choice.

Withdrawals were no joke.

He toyed with returning to his old ways, desperate for food and a safe place to sleep. Luckily, one of the stable boys stole his pack that day. Chasing the thief led him to his first encounter with the creatures that meant so much to him. Stepping through those dusty doors, he was transported to a whole new world.

He was right on his aggressor's heels but came to a sudden halt as he took in the sights and sounds of a bustling stable. His nose was assaulted by the rich aroma of horse flesh slathered in sweat, mixed with the sweet taste of hay and the pungent tones of feces. To most, the smells were overwhelming, but Tyee found them to be a balm to his soul.

He was almost ten by that time and more sure of himself than most men. He walked up to the man barking orders and asked him what he should do next. Whether the man was distracted or didn't care, Tyee would never know. The man gave him chores and Tyee got to work. He owed everything to that stable master and often wondered what had happened to the stern taskmaster when he left.

Tyee winced at the thought of his old mentor.

Shame flooded his cheeks as his thoughts turned to the events leading up to fleeing the place he once felt safe. There had been a woman, trouble seemed to always follow them, who had insisted he train the midnight colt she just bought. What followed was several years of forming bonds with the animal and woman both.

Until she gave him an ultimatum: steal the stallion or never see Koko again. Tyee took what she offered without looking back and betrayed the people who had offered an orphan the opportunity for a future.

Tyee ran a hand through his hair, staring at the colorful wagon.

The irony wasn't lost on Tyee that this community accepted and gave homes to outcasts, offering them a place and people to depend on, even a criminal like himself. No one in the Circus knew his story, nor did they pressure him to do more for their people. Tyee's tendencies to recluse himself had isolated him for as long as he could remember. He didn't know how to come clean or be part of the community he felt was too good for him.

Coward.

The word permeated his being and set his hands to sweating. He rubbed Koko once more, before dismounting and unwinding the rope attaching Koko's halter to his saddle. He let the rope drag on the grass, effectively ground-tying the impatient stallion.

"There ya go, old friend. Eat your heart out. I'll be right back."

He turned around and ran into someone.

Out of reflex, he reached out and grabbed the slightly built individual by the forearms to steady them. The person let out a shriek of surprise, trying to pull away, but lost their balance. Tyee kept his hold on the assailant, making sure they stayed on their feet.

He inhaled the faint smell of mint and quickly let the individual go, recognizing her to be a woman.

"Tyee! Sorry to give you a fright. I was coming to let you know Zalia finally woke up," Luc said in a rush.

Tyee gave her a puzzled expression. "Why would I want to know that?"

Luc's eyebrows scrunched together. "Uh, the other two fire Crafters said you took charge after the attack. They said you were the one to tell them to get her to Abuela's wagon." Her eyes searched his face, taking in his tense posture. She gave a sly smile. "I offered to bring you the news since I was headed for Abuela's wagon, anyway. It seems you have a thing for fire Crafters." She gave him a wink.

"You caught me. They get me all hot under the collar." Tyee's shoulders relaxed slightly.

Luc laughed and said, "You should ride with me and Damien today. We can fill you in on all of Rae's most embarrassing stories from when we were younger." She tucked a piece of hair behind her ear and ducked her chin. "Maybe that'll keep us from missing her so much."

"You four have been tight for a while, yeah?" Tyee asked, trying not to let his misgivings about spending time with the two remaining acrobats show.

Luc's eyes looked into the distance. "A long, long time. It feels like pieces of me have been missing ever since they left." Luc turned to the horseman. "This doesn't feel real, does it?"

"What do you mean?"

"It feels like my world's been flipped upside down and I still don't know the rules. Three days ago, all I had to worry about was not losing my grip and control while in the air. Now... Tyee, I've never had to fight someone before. Sure, we've all taken basic defense classes, but I've never wielded a sword or shot a bow. How do I find a place in this new reality?" Luc hung her head.

"You make one."

Luc's head whipped up and one eyebrow raised. She motioned for him to continue.

"The world is always changing. It's our job to eddy the changes and face the waves. Look around Luc, most of these people are in the same boat as you. You're right, you don't know how to fight, but you can learn. You can take those skills you've gained from being an acrobat and hone them into something deadly."

Luc pursed her lips into a straight line. "But how? We don't have weapons or training protocols." She sighed. "Tyee, I felt so useless yesterday. All those Shifters... I just kept praying the fire Crafters could keep them at bay. I can't do that again. I need to prepare better."

Tyee studied the acrobat in front of him. He had never given the dark-haired woman a second thought, always assuming she was stubborn, demanding, and an infuriating perfectionist. He couldn't keep track of the number of times she insisted the acrobats redo their run-through or critique the other acts before the burlesque show. She was unyielding and seemed to only see in black and white. There was no room for grayness in the way the Black Swan presented herself to the world.

But this was a different side of her.

"I'll talk to Duncan. I'm sure more people than we know have military or combat training. You should talk to Jess about having the Forgers develop some weapons. We need more if we want to stand a chance against Vincenzio and anyone else that wishes us harm." He really looked at the Mortal acrobat, taking in her flushed cheeks and the tense set to her shoulders. "It's okay to have moments of inadequacy, Luc. They're pivotal in determining whether we have the grit to better ourselves or if we crumble under the pressure. Either way, we'll learn a lot about ourselves as the changes keep coming." Tyee rubbed the back of his neck. "I'll catch you later."

Tyee walked back to his steed, mounting in one fluid motion and directing Koko towards where he saw Duncan last. He gave a nod to Luc as he passed, his intentions of getting answers forgotten as the magnetic pull of action propelled him forward.

"My friends! Please, pause your packing and gather to the side here. Quickly now! The sun has risen in full, and we need to be on the road shortly. I wish to address yesterday and our plans for tomorrow," Duncan said, his hand cupping his chin, projecting his voice to all in the camp.

He sat astride his bay mare on the edge of the clearing they sheltered in for the night. Conrad and Nymeria returned late in the night, reporting that all traces of the Shifters had disappeared as quickly as they came. With that intel, Duncan let his people rest longer than previously intended. They still had leagues to go, but the Ringmaster knew the toll yesterday had taken on the caravan.

Adrenaline kept them going through the night, their levels only heightened by the sudden onslaught of the Shifters. But the crash came hard and fierce after the attack. His people were drained, and it showed. Disheveled clothes, hair askew, and drawn faces abounded throughout the growing crowd.

"Our worst fears were realized three days ago. Heimat has burned." Duncan paused and made eye contact with those around him. His eyes met fire when he came to the woman who challenged him at breakfast before Heimat descended into chaos. She refused to break eye contact and held her chin up high. Duncan inclined his head towards her and continued, "All is not lost, though. We will persevere as we've always done. We will keep going until we find someplace safe for our people." His purple eyes glinted while his lips pressed tightly to form a thin line. "And then we return to take back our city."

Grumbling mixed with cheers came from the caravan of crew and performers.

"We received word late last night that the Shifters of the Forest have left without a trace. We will be on high alert for them, but I am confident they no longer pose a threat to us." Duncan licked his lips. "It was brought to my attention that some people want to train for combat sooner rather than later. I intended to begin once we reached our new camp, but yesterday proved there's no time like the present. Is there anyone confident enough to lead training exercises with the few weapons we have at our disposal?"

The crowd stayed quiet, but individuals eyed their neighbors, trying to guess who could head such a task.

"I would say I know my way around a bow pretty well." Gar, the falconer, spoke up. "We coul' use the ones the hunters take to get game. Just need to coordinate with Betsy and Mac to make sure we don't use them when meat is getting scarce."

Betsy spoke up. "Absolutely! Maybe I'll try my hand at one myself."

Nods of affirmation came from the individuals who usually led hunts while the caravan was on the road. The air surrounding the members of the Circus started thrumming with energy. Crew and performers felt some of their tension dissipate at the opportunity to shed their feelings of uselessness in a fight.

"I can teach basic hand-to-hand combat moves. I think almost everyone's taken my self-defense class, but I can come up with ways to teach more advanced moves." Conrad offered.

"Kaiser and I can help with those too," Nymeria added, a hand on her son's shoulder.

Kaiser nodded and gave his feral grin. "We'll see how many of you can keep up." His grin turned into a smirk.

Many people laughed and a couple of brave kids rushed the big cat specialist, trying to tackle him to the ground. Kaiser sidestepped them and chuckled when their momentum left them face down in the dirt. He used a hand to grab both of them by the backs of their shirts and pull them into a standing position. He helped brush them off and had a quiet conversation with them.

While Kaiser talked with the kids, J stepped forward in human form. "I spend my mornings going for runs. Anyone is welcome to join and start building up some endurance. We can throw in some strength work too in the evenings."

Eva and Wren flexed their wiry arms and held them up to the elephant Shifter, showing off their nonexistent muscles. The crowd chuckled as J smiled and shook his head before returning to his young charges.

A hush settled over the gathering of performers and crew. There was one more person on everyone's mind that could teach basic swordplay or knife throwing.

Duncan waited to see what would happen. The silence stretched on as people started shifting from one foot to the other and anxiously checking their surroundings.

It didn't seem like Tyee would offer his expertise to the group.

Duncan took note and continued, "That is a great start. I will discuss this with the leaders and come up with a basic schedule. Listen during tomorrow morning's announcements for more information." He clasped his hands together. "Onwards and upwards, my friends! Finish packing and meet back here. We will leave shortly, so make haste!" He sent a wind through the caravan, rustling clothes and hair, urging his people forward.

Luc and Damien rode in the back of the caravan. Luc insisted they volunteer to ride in back to make sure they monitored her Abuela's wagon and the old woman inside. It was doubling as the med wagon and traveled towards the back on account of its size. It was the largest of the dozen wagons they forced through the trees, and thus able to hold the most amount of people should the need arise. One other wagon carried medicinal supplies and herbs but wasn't big enough to treat patients in.

Two wagons carried the elderly and young children, while the rest carried food and supplies for the caravan. The food stores they had wouldn't last long with the hoard of people that followed, but strict rationing and supplementing their stores would give them the best chance of feeding their people until they found a place to settle.

The thought on most people's minds was whether they would be pursued by Vincenzio or his men. The caravan kept a steady pace, not as clipped as the previous night, but faster than their normal pace on the road. They hoped to stay ahead of any pursuers, pushing as hard as they could through the mass of trees.

The colorful wagon traveled in the back of the caravan, with only a handful of Forgers on foot and a few riders behind. The Forgers were the most efficient at getting the wagon unstuck as they traversed tree roots, rocky terrain, and uneven footing. They could lift the wagon with ease and coax it to fit through small spaces, thanks to the silver magic coursing through their veins.

The riders were the fail-safe and shielded the Forgers and med wagon from any attack from behind. They could evacuate the wagons should things take a turn for the worst.

"Have you talked to Tyee much? Like since he's joined the Circus?" Luc asked.

"Not really. Why do you ask, my love?" Damien brushed his leg against hers while they rode side by side.

Luc scrunched her brows. "I just wish I knew his story." She scratched her mare's mane and sighed. "And why he wouldn't offer to help train our people. I had a conversation with him about how helpless I felt last night and it struck me how easy it was talking to him." She hung her head as her lack of ability threatened to overwhelm her. "He was the one to suggest we talk to Duncan and Jess about getting training and weapon making a priority. He was so kind."

Damien bumped her leg again until she looked him in the eye. "You have a beautiful soul." She shot him a quizzical look. "Seriously, love. You can't even comprehend not helping others." He gave her a wistful look. "Most people don't put themselves out there as you do. You are the definition of a bleeding heart; I've met no one as compassionate as you." His smile was dazzling as he looked at her. "I don't know Tyee's story, but I know he's gone through a lot. Simeon told me once that Tyee told the other riders he grew up on the streets, stealing and conning to get by. I think the idea of community is foreign to Rae's rogue," he said with a wink. "It doesn't sound like Tyee's ever had anybody to support him. How can we expect him to support the community when that was never modeled for him?"

Luc pursed her lips, frustration sparking at the easy way Damien dismissed her expectations for the horseman. "I guess. But he's been here for years. You can't tell me he hasn't seen it modeled since he's been here."

Damien held up his hands. "Easy, tigress. I—"

"Tigress? Sounds like you need me to step in and handle this." Kaiser leered, bringing his horse closer to the pair.

Damien and Luc shared a look.

"Get lost, Kaiser. Everybody knows you're all talk and no substance." Luc hissed through her teeth.

"Ow, ow, kitty's got claws." Kaiser flashed a smirk at the raven-haired woman.

"Kaiser, you're not part of this conversation. Leave," said Damien forcefully, raising his eyebrows at the contentious young man.

Kaiser shrugged, the smirk still on his face. "Suit yourself. You know where to find me if you change your mind." He threw a wave at them as he urged his horse towards another pair of riders.

Once he was out of earshot, Luc gave herself a shake. "Ugh, that guy always gives me the creeps. What's his problem?"

Damien's eyes followed the inappropriate performer. "I think he overcompensates for not being a Shifter."

Luc shot him a look before throwing up her hands. "You're a terrible person to commiserate with. Where's Rae when you need to complain about people?"

Damien clutched at his chest. "Oh, vixen! How you wound a poor Mortal!"

Luc rolled her eyes, feeling herself prickle with impatience. "Dramatic much?"

"'Tis you that causes so much drama!" Damien winked at her, trying to distract her from touchy subjects.

Luc chose to let go of her annoyance and gave him a playful shove before striking up a conversation about what type of combat they would be interested in learning.

The caravan kept up its determined march, only stopping once to get a couple of wagons unstuck. The skies were gray above the canopy of trees. Small flakes fell gently as the afternoon continued. The first snowfall spurred Duncan and his Circus faster, knowing winter was upon them.

The Circus needed to find a place for a settlement quickly.

Chapter Seven

The river raged like a child deprived of their favorite toy. Enormous waves rocked the *Vengeance* first one way and then the other as the wind changed directions, buffeting the ship and crew alike.

Cleo struggled at the helm, trying to keep the unwieldy vessel on a straight course. The rain came down in droves, plastering her hair and clothes to her skin, and driving the warmth from her hands.

"Adams! Get those sails secured!" She yelled as loud as she could, trying to be heard over the storm. Another gust of wind pulled the main sail loose again. "ADAMS!" she screamed. Her first mate's head whipped towards his Captain and she pointed to the loose fabric.

He stared at it before locking eyes with Cleo. Adams nodded, striding across the deck and bellowing orders to the crew.

The winter storm had come in fast and furious. The rain was so cold it bordered on being frozen. These conditions were dangerous for Cleo's crew to operate in. She bit the inside of her cheek as she scanned the ship, keeping her hands on the worn spokes of the ship's wheel. It spun hard to the right, but Cleo kept ahold of the wheel, wrenching it to the left, and keeping the ship straight.

Her eyes darted to the crow's nest, barely making out the wooden basket in the rain. She prayed their lookout held on tight as another wave caused the ship to plunge down and to the left.

Cleo banked hard to the right, throwing her weight into pushing the wheel. *Fuck.* Her eyes darted back to the prow of the ship but saw little through the pounding rain. The lithe woman's pulse quickened as she went through the options in her head.

Her lips formed a grim line as she ran out of options. Miriam was useless in the crow's nest, and Cleo would tire if the rain and wind kept up. She was barely keeping it between the banks as it was; she couldn't imagine what it would be like when her muscles gave out. There needed to be another way to get through this.

She saw Adams approach out of the corner of her eye.

"Captain!" She looked at her first mate before turning her gaze back to the task at hand. Adams was at her side moments later. "Cap, I think we should call it. This is too dangerous." He laid a hand on her shoulder.

Cleo clenched her jaw to keep her teeth from chattering. "I have an idea, Adams." Her first mate shot her a look.

"Captain... is it worth risking your ship? Your crew?" Adams raised his eyebrows.

"Hear me out." Cleo glanced at the broad man. "I know it's dangerous, but if we keep going, there's no way the mayor catches up to us. Even Bartholomew wouldn't dare sail into this beast."

Adams searched his Captain's face. "Cap, there's no way even Bartholomew could catch us now."

"He was the first to make it through the Teeth unscathed. He could do it blindfolded and you know it. If he's the one that pursues us, we need as much of a buffer between us as possible. Besides, a little danger always leads to better sex." She winked at her first mate before pulling hard on the wheel as another powerful wave rocked the ship.

Adams sighed, bending his knees to absorb the pitching of the deck. "Okay, say we keep going. How are we making it through this cursed storm?" He raised one eyebrow.

Cleo gave him a wicked grin and told him the idea that sprang to her mind moments before. He shook his head at her but agreed to her plan despite his concerns, leaving to give her orders to the crew and civilians on board.

Tamara sat with George and Reg in the ship's berth, where the crew and civilians had their hammocks. She sat brooding while the other two complained about the pitching of the ship. The glass Forger narrowed her eyes and put a hand to her temple.

"You two are giving me a headache. If you're going to bicker, do it somewhere else. Preferably where I can't hear you." She raised an eyebrow at the two.

"No, no, no. We'll stop, Tam, jus' give us a chance." Reg threw an arm over her shoulder. He tilted his head and gave her a hard look when she brushed him off. "What's up, lass? Yer not yer normal self. Yer usually not this short."

Tamara sighed, rubbing her arms in an attempt to warm herself up. Eventually, she said, "I feel so useless down here." She studied the tattoos on her hands, trying to swallow the lump in her throat. "And when I look at our people, all I see are ghosts." Her mind conjured up the faces of those they lost in Heimat.

She rubbed her eyes roughly, trying to keep the tears at bay. *This grieving thing is shit. Pull it together, Tamara.*

All three stumbled to their left as the ship rapidly changed directions on them.

Tamara heard George curse under his breath before turning to her.

"I get where your head's at, Tam. I've felt useless since I stepped foot on this Goddess-forsaken ship." He put a hand on her shoulder. "You can never outrun the grief, or change the past, but we can be grateful for the time we had with them."

Tamara's shoulders drooped with what felt like the weight of the world. She gripped George's hand and squeezed. "It's the holes in my heart that I'm struggling with. It'll be easier once there's something to do and I can keep my mind occupied." She flashed a smile that didn't quite reach her eyes. "Maybe a visit to the kiddies is the distraction I need."

George gave her a nod, understanding shining in his eyes.

"Yes'm, the kiddies are the best kind of medicine. We're always here to talk, lass. Don't forget that." Reg patted her on the back as she got up to leave. Tamara gave them both a look of gratitude before walking away.

She left the two men sitting on their hammocks to make her way to the cabin set aside for the women and youngest children. The *Vengeance* had two cabins for her officers. Cleo had offered her cabin to the children, but Adams swiftly intervened, settling the young civilians in his.

He insisted the Captain take what was rightfully hers, reminding her half of the job was flaunting her power and status to keep their crew in line.

Tamara knew both of them were good people but worried the move was more than just a considerate offer. She kept her eyes on the boards in front of her, keeping her hand on the wall to stay steady despite the swaying of the ship. She left the berth, the section belowdecks where the crew kept their hammocks, and entered the galley, where meals were served. So focused on her feet, Tamara missed the large man striding towards her.

She started when broad hands clasped her shoulders, preventing her from moving forward. She tensed, looking up at the owner of such hands.

"Excuse me, I'm looking for the two Crafters and the Shifter. Do you know where they would be?" Adams asked, dropping his hands once he was sure she wouldn't run into him.

Tamara raised an eyebrow. "The ones from the Circus? They might be in the hammock room." She pointed back the way she came when she noticed the first mate's frown. "Or they could be checking on the kiddos. I'm heading there now. Want me to send them your way if I find them?"

Relief filled the officer's eyes. "That would be an immense help. The sooner the better."

As quickly as he had come, the first mate was gone again, all but running back towards the berth. Tamara shook her head at the quizzical interaction but quickened her pace. She hurried through the galley, past the infirmary, and came to the narrow stairs that would take her up to the cabins boasting larger, more private living quarters.

She rapped three times on the door, the code from Heimat still ingrained in the Forger-turned-glassblower. She tapped her foot while she waited, throwing a hand out when the ship heaved to the side once more. Water spilled into the corridor from the opening above. Tamara shielded her eyes from the spray with one arm. Even belowdecks wasn't safe from the pounding rain above.

The door opened as one of the young mothers pulled from behind with a baby on her hip. She smiled when she saw Tamara, despite her pale skin and gaunt eyes. "Miss Tamara, good to see you." She motioned Tamara inside while bouncing the now-fussing baby. "Poor thing hates the pitching about. Oh, I know. You are just so upset," she cooed at the little one.

"For the hundredth time, Luna, call me Tam." The woman nodded but kept her focus on her fussy charge. "Have you seen any of the performers around?"

"From the Circus, you mean?"

"Yeah. I need to send them up to the first mate."

"Hmm. I think the Golden Eagle went to check in on the Captain's brood."

Tamara furrowed her brows. "The Captain's brood?"

"Aye, last night, the Captain came by and ordered some of us to be brought to her cabin. She claimed stuffing twenty-some people, even children, into an officer's cabin was too much. She's very generous, that Captain of ours." The woman nodded towards the door Tamara entered by, as it was the only way in and out of the first mate's cabin, and led to the stairs to the Captain's quarters.

Tamara squeezed the baby's foot before waving to his caretaker and the rest of the inhabitants in the cabin. She left and hurried up the stairs to the largest cabin on the ship. Once more, she rapped three times on the door. There was no hesitation this time, and the door swung wide open.

Rae stared back at her and smiled once she recognized the glassblower. "Hey, Tam. Checking in on these ragamuffins?" she asked.

Protests sounded inside, while mirth glinted in Rae's eyes. She shook her head, waiting for Tamara's response.

"Actually, I'm looking for you." Rae cocked her head in question. "Adams, the first mate, wants to see you."

Rae bit her lip and gave her a shrug. "You're gonna have to help me, Tam. I'm still trying to figure out who everyone is since escaping the infirmary." Her golden eyes hardened as she continued, "My first encounter with the Captain was a duel until first blood."

Tamara gave her a concerned look. "I heard about that. George said you held your own despite leaving the infirmary hours before. I'll help you find the first mate." She turned away from the fire Crafter, heading back down to the galley.

Rae shouted her goodbyes to the flock of children inside, closing the door behind her before any of them could slip out.

She followed the townswoman down a couple of flights of narrow stairs, using a hand to steady herself as the ship pitched one way and then the next. Water dripped sporadically from the boards above, sending shivers across Rae's skin when they found their way beneath the thin coat she wore. They reached the galley and found Adams talking to Zeke.

Rae kept her features neutral as she remembered the last interaction between her and Zeke. The wind Crafter had taken his time to get to her when she motioned him over, at least until the rain started, but something still felt off. She'd tried asking about his workout with Bane, trying to glean any details of a blossoming relationship, but Zeke only responded with cryptic answers. She was frustrated with the way he held her at arm's length, but time was most likely what would determine when Zeke was ready to forgive her.

Once Zeke made it apparent the conversation was over, Rae left to check on the kids to keep her misery and frustration at bay. The two hadn't spoken since.

She observed Zeke's change of clothes but quickly averted her gaze before meeting his eyes, studying the first mate instead.

He dipped his head in recognition. "The Golden Eagle. A pleasure to meet you." He held out a broad hand.

Rae shook the man's hand, noting his firm grip, medium build, and the air of authority he wore like a cloak. Her heart twinged as she realized he reminded her of Duncan. Huntress, she'd give anything for his advice right now.

"Please, call me Rae,—" she waited.

"Adams, call me Adams. First mate to Captain Cleo."

"Please, call me Rae, Adams. A lot more lovely to meet you than your captain," she repeated, ignoring the look Zeke shot her.

Adams narrowed his eyes. "The Captain has a particular way of doing things. She has her reasons, though."

Rae inclined her head, leaving the matter be. She would have words for the Captain after this storm was done. "I'm sure she does. What did you need us for?"

"The Captain requests your help at once." He explained the plan to the two Crafters, emphasizing their importance in it before asking about the missing Shifter. Zeke informed the first mate Bane had left to scout for any pursuers.

Once he finished with the Crafters, he turned to Tamara. "Gather all your people and head to the cabins. I was informed the captain invited them to use hers as well?" He waited for Tamara to nod and sighed when she did. "She's so stubborn," he mumbled before looking back at the dark-skinned glassblower. "Split them between the two then, do it discreetly, though. I don't want the crew to know about your... arrangements with the Captain. It's going to get rough, be ready for that and anything else that comes our way. It should give you easy escape access should the worst happen."

A gigantic wave suddenly pitched the *Vengeance* to the right.

Adams rolled with it, placing a hand on the wall effortlessly. The other three stumbled into the wall and each other, barely keeping upright. Adams left towards the stairs that would take him to the main upper deck, not bothering to see if the others followed him.

Rae shared a look with Tamara and clasped the woman's forearm before exchanging goodbyes. Zeke nodded to the Forger before following Rae up to the main deck. Tamara gathered everyone from the berth, or hammock room as she called it, and returned to the cabins, helping everyone prepare for the storm as best they could.

Rae felt a tug on her coat just before she reached the deck. Icy rain fell in sheets, soaking her hair and clothes as she stood in the stairwell, open to the air above her. Her blood ran warm as the fire entered her veins, keeping the chill at bay.

She turned to look into Zeke's concerned eyes. She bit her lip but turned back to the task at hand. Taking a deep breath, she took another step towards the deck.

Zeke gripped her arm and turned her towards him. He searched her face and asked, "What happened with the Captain?"

Rae scowled. "Not now, Zeke. We have a job to do. Let's get through this storm and then we can talk." Catching his hurt expression, Rae added, "Hopefully, you'll have dried off by then."

Zeke snorted. "Good one, Sparks. Ya really got me there."

Rae couldn't help the smile on her face when she heard Zeke use the name from when they were kids. She finished climbing the stairs and faced the icy winds and rain from above.

Chapter Eight

Zeke cursed as the rain soaked his clothes once more. His teeth were chattering as he followed his trapeze partner onto the deck. Things were still rocky between the pair, but they had reached a turning point. After the storm, they would make up and their worlds would be righted once more.

They only needed to get through this storm first.

The ship threw him into one mast, almost causing him to topple over it as it battled another wave.

The crew ran in every direction on deck and in the rigging, leaving the two Crafters to only guess what they were trying to accomplish. People shouted, struggling to be heard over the pouring rain and roaring wind. Cleo and Adams stood at the helm, the Captain holding tight to the wheel while Adams bellowed orders to keep the sails tied. The entire deck was slick with a thin layer of almost frozen water. Most of the crew wore ropes connected to a mast, a fail-safe should they lose their footing or hold on the rigging.

Rae and Zeke made their way to the prow of the boat. Mouse was waiting for them with their own ropes to keep them on the ship should disaster strike. Mouse quickly knotted the ropes securely around each of their waists, making sure they had enough slack to do the Crafting that needed to be done. She bounded back into the rigging as soon as her task was done, sending word back to the Captain through their network of people aboard the vessel.

Rae shouted to make sure Zeke heard her, holding onto the gunwale as the ship rocked with each crashing wave. "Okay Z, you focus on the wind. Try to get it to shield the ship from the rain if you can. The more visibility we give the Captain, the better. I'll do my best to calm the waves." She bit her lip.

Zeke gave her arm a squeeze, using the wind to make his voice heard. "You can do it. I'll take care of the wind." The silver-eyed Crafter dropped to a crouch, calling the wind and using his arms to direct it. He moved through different positions, bending the raging wind to his will. He sent it towards the rain, spinning the wind to form an epicenter of calm around the ship.

He kept moving, guiding the wind higher and higher, spinning in tighter and tighter circles, aiming for the direction the rain fell from. Slowly, but surely, the rain lightened until it no longer battered those on the ship.

Gasps and cheers sounded as the rain lightened until completely ceasing on the ship. They felt the tug of the residual wind on their clothes and hair, but it was nothing compared to the gale it once was. Crew members scratched their heads in wonder until others pointed out the drops hitting the river just beyond the vessel.

Zeke took shuddering breaths but kept his hands moving, using the winds from the storm to shield them from its downpour. Sweat beaded on his brow as he concentrated, keeping in mind the slickness of the deck. Crafting using the wind and energy of the storm differed from using the wind in his core. It required greater concentration to keep control of the winds that weren't his own. They had never been bent to anyone's will but their own, following the storm and blowing whichever way they pleased. No, Zeke wouldn't run out of life energy, he would run out of mental willpower long before that.

The trick was adding a bit of his own wind to make the great gales more pliable. He was careful not to overdo it, otherwise, he'd run out of life energy, anyway. The other problem was he had to keep moving. The wind was the energy of thin air, and it couldn't and wouldn't remain still. He had to keep his hands or body moving at all times to keep up with the winds of the storm.

Zeke did what he could, keeping the rain and winds at bay. He spoke gently, sending a message to Cleo, telling her Rae was working on the waves, but her lack of experience with her water Craft meant it might take a bit to strongarm the waves buffeting them.

Zeke kept his eyes on Rae, ready to help as best he could should she need anything. The thought that she had been in the infirmary just the other night weighed on his mind. She hurt him when she took advantage of him, but he knew how awful she felt about everything.

Huntress help us out of the storm so we can put this mess behind us. He whispered a prayer to the face of the Goddess he knew best before concentrating on the task at hand.

He gritted his teeth and worked against the wind. His focus had faltered, letting the gales from the storm escape slightly, leaving cracks for the rain to get through. He used more of the life energy he was trying to conserve to regain the upper hand.

He couldn't lose focus again.

Rae stood on the opposite side of the prow, giving both of them space to Craft. She was trying to grasp the waves below like she had the winds this morning, but they fell through her fingers every time she closed them around one. She let out a frustrated cry and pushed at the waves angrily. Her ears perked up when she felt the waves below respond to her outburst.

Maybe the waves are more like flames. She bit her lip and closed her eyes. All Crafters learned to use the power running through their veins and the elemental power found in nature. Rae knew how to calm a raging forest fire or a campfire gone wrong. She knew how to add some of her own power if the wild blazes were too much. It was as second nature as breathing. She focused inward, looking between the three plaits of power at her core. The fire, wind, and water Crafts had responded when she drew them into strands and braided them, keeping their intensity under control.

Rae thought the currents of the water felt more like the winds than the flames when she originally plaited them.

But maybe she was wrong.

She studied the water plait and noticed how it danced within its confines, just like her flames. She took a deep breath and returned to the present, expanding her consciousness to where the waves rocked and threw themselves against the hull of the ship.

She focused on those waves and tried an alternative approach. Rae pushed and prodded at the currents beneath, using their energy to create a wall around the ship. She had to be clever though, because simply spinning the currents around it would cause the ship to stall. She had to redirect the motion and energy of the waves for their own advantage.

She prayed to the Huntress for strength and pulled a small string of power from her core. She felt the coolness enter her blood, not as biting as the ice she felt from her wind Craft, but not warm like her fire Craft. This felt refreshing and soothing at the same time. A farce for the strength found beneath the waves or in the powerful persistence of single drops eroding rock over time.

Water was a force to be reckoned with.

Rae rubbed her sleeve across her brow, trying to prevent sweat from dripping into her eyes. Using the power from the currents within, she forced the waves to form a wall in the shape of a v, the prow of the ship fitting into the angle it formed. As more waves hit the wall, she directed them to the back of the ship. Once there, she pushed them under the keel or bottom of the boat, propelling them forward.

The Crafter used her arms to keep motioning the waves to the back and under, keeping her feet planted to ground the watery columns protecting the ship from the beating waves. Rae gritted her teeth, having to use more life energy as she used her water Craft to keep the waves at bay. She knew she wouldn't last long if she kept going at this pace.

Her arms and legs trembled as she held her position, continuously moving her arms. She took deep breaths, trying to ground herself, frantically checking the braided currents within and how much more energy she could spend.

A falcon's cry came from above the boat.

Rae and Zeke turned towards the noise, seeing the bird stuck just beyond Zeke's barrier of wind. The wind Crafter gritted his teeth, letting one gale loosen enough for the bird to slip in. He immediately closed the gap before the wild winds could get out of control again. Bane Shifted quickly, grabbing a soaked piece of cloth to tie around his waist.

"How can I help?" He looked between the two Crafters, assessing both of them.

Shifters had the Sight. They could read the auras and emotions of those around them. Bane quickly realized the distraught feelings Rae exuded were because of the power trickling out of her. She wouldn't last long under the current circumstances.

He stepped toward her before either of them could answer him, still focused as they were on the motions needed for their task. Bane needed to touch Rae's bare skin to pass the energy to her. He didn't want to hinder her motions, so he studied what she was doing. Her arms and shoulders moved the most, with her legs staying still, and more importantly, her ankles were bare, not covered by a coat.

Bane lay prostrate and gripped her ankle with one hand. He let his energy trickle into her, enough to sustain her from burnout, but not so much that his stores were depleted too quickly. All the Magicae depended on the life energy in their blood to fuel their Gifts. Every living form had life energy, including Mortals, but only the Magicae could take and use it to fuel their magic. Mortals could offer their own life energy, but it wasn't as strong as the energy from other Magicae, infused with their inherent magic. Bane needed to make sure he didn't overwhelm her and waste the energy he had left.

The deck was cold and wet on his bare chest and carried a musty smell, infused from years of traveling the river and coastlines. Bane clenched his jaw and closed his eyes, his feet struggling for purchase on the slick wooden boards. He needed to keep from sliding to make sure he didn't distract Rae from her Crafting. Using his free hand and legs, he clung to the deck, sharing his energy with the Crafter.

Relief washed over Rae when she saw Bane step towards her out of the corner of her eye. Keeping her feet steady and her arms moving, she felt a chilly hand grip her ankle, followed by the warm, heady sensation of the Shifter's powerful energy entering her veins.

She took a deep breath, centered herself, and continued her motions with renewed vigor. Rae used Bane's energy to direct the waves, finding them even more pliant using the Shifter's power to subdue them. She let a small smile grace her lips, hope building that they may pull it off after all.

Rain splattered on the boards of the ship.

Rae sent a panicked look at Zeke, fearing the worst. His hands were tightened into fists, shoulders tensed as he fought to continue the motions, keeping the winds as a shield above them.

"Bane!" Rae shouted, "Help Zeke!"

The Shifter looked up and gave her a questioning look.

"HELP ZEKE!" she yelled louder and pointed.

Bane looked at the wind Crafter and nodded. He let go of Rae, taking the power in his veins with him. Rae gasped as the waves rebelled instantly, raging against the confines she forced on them. It took all of her strength to will them into submission, letting more of her inner currents leak out of her veins. She saw spots at the edge of her vision, but clamped down, refusing to let unconsciousness take her into its sweet release. She just had to hold on a little longer.

Zeke was struggling. The gales had become unwieldy, their energy building and refusing to be redirected. He sank to one knee, spinning tighter and tighter circles with his hands. Icy fingers gripped his ankle and power flowed fast and fierce into the wind Crafter's being. He quickly dispatched it, quelling the anger of the gales and coaxing them back into their shield.

The deck became dry once more.

Zeke knew Bane needed to get back to Rae. She wasn't used to the currents of her water Craft and he could only imagine the strain it was putting on her.

He clenched his jaw and directed his words towards the Shifter. "Go back to Rae. I'm good."

Bane looked up, saw the determination in the wind Crafter's gaze, and gave a nod.

Zeke braced himself for the absence of power and kept a tight hold on the winds above them. He felt the power leave and the cold around his ankle disappear as an enormous wave slammed into the *Vengeance*. Zeke crashed against the gunwale, losing his grip on the winds above.

The gales whistled as they whipped across the deck, catching crew members hanging by their rope ties, dislodged by the sudden violence of the waves, and spinning them back and forth.

Zeke watched in horror as another wave crashed into the hull, sending Bane straight into the opposite gunwale, head first, and tumbling over the edge.

Rae's unconscious form sat slumped on the deck, the rope around her waist keeping her tethered as she swayed with the deck.

He barely registered the screams as his body's momentum heaved him over the prow, the ship crashing into the rocks on the riverbank.

The *Vengeance* had gambled with the storm and lost.

Chapter Nine

The city of Heimat was in mourning. Buildings were blackened and homes were broken. Families and friends mourned their loved ones, while the mayor and his soldiers did nothing to help the city or its citizens.

Rich walked the cobblestone streets aimlessly, his thoughts plagued by memories. Melody running across the uneven streets, only stopping to tell him to hurry. Dropping Melody off at school for the first time, taking Melody to a play date, Melody greeting everyone on the street.

Tears welled in his eyes as he continued his slow march.

Melody introducing him to Rob, Melody on her wedding day, Melody presenting her first daughter to him. His face was wrought with agony, not seeing any of the other lost souls passing by.

Tommy had discovered Melody's body when he went to check on Tamara's shop a few hours after the chaos ended. He'd been in shock and disbelief at the death of his friend even as he brought her body to the bakery.

Ever since Rich touched the stiff body of his baby girl, he'd been floating somewhere between fantasy and reality. He and his wife hadn't stopped crying since Tommy laid their little girl inside the bakery she loved so much. He couldn't come to grips with the thought of never hearing her laugh or seeing her in his doorway ever again.

There was a hole in his chest that would never be filled again. The loss was as real as if it had been a limb.

Nothing would ever be the same again.

Rich wandered the town until dark, unable to be in the bakery during the daylight.

Tommy and Sara moved their kids from their place in the city to Tommy's mom's place as soon as they could. His mom welcomed them with open arms, as comforted by their presence as they were by hers.

A staggering amount of people were killed or injured during the ransacking and burning of the city. The chaos that ensued was worse than anything Tommy had ever seen. The Barracks, where he'd grown up, were rough. Tommy knew he saw more crime and violence as a kid than most in the city. He learned how to dodge cutpurses, avoid groups of older children, and to leave nothing he didn't want to lose at home. He could count on one hand the few times their house hadn't been broken into.

But losing Melody...

She and Sara were always close, even in motherhood. It got to where they lost track of whose turn it was to host and simply made it a point to have each other over frequently.

Rob, Melody's husband, was like another brother to him and her two girls, like two nieces. His heart throbbed for the three of them. He couldn't imagine losing Sara, the pain and grief it would bring, not to mention the heartache it would bring their children. No, those thoughts were too much.

Tommy made the trek to Rich's bakery carrying a pot of his mother's vegetable stew. Rob and the girls were staying with Rich and his wife Anna while they still reeled from the loss of Melody. Sara wanted to come with him, but he convinced her it was still too dangerous. He refused to put his pregnant wife at risk with a madman in charge. He'd reassured her he would tell Rob and the girls they were always welcome to come stay at the farmhouse whenever they wanted. Tommy was also instructed to let Rob know they could take the girls or him out whenever he needed a break.

He walked quickly, feeling unnerved by the quiet of the city. Gone was the hustle and bustle of children running to school, gossiping women roaming the streets in packs, and the steady clip-clop of hoofbeats sounding on the cobblestones. The streets were empty save for the few soldiers who eyed him as he passed by.

After a while, Tommy slipped into the maze of alleys, taking comfort in the shadows. Normally, he wouldn't let anybody deter him from walking in the sunshine down roads he knew like the back of his hand, but today felt different.

Today, Tommy wanted peace.

He was the opposite of his brother in nearly every way. George had always been quiet, keeping to himself, and blending into the crowd whenever he could. Tommy was boisterous, constantly seeking attention or putting himself in the limelight.

At least in his younger days, he would.

Becoming a father made Tommy's appearances at parties and gatherings seldom and far in between, but he wouldn't have it any other way. He'd give his life for those munchkins and theirs was the only attention he needed these days.

Tommy was the outgoing one, while George was the introverted one. He knew most people compared them and assumed he was the more successful one, but Tommy learned at a young age not to judge a book by its cover. His brother was quiet, but he was also observant.

Tommy knew just about everyone in town, but George knew *everything* about everyone in town, even those in charge. George was the perfect one to get those kids where they needed to be. Tommy hoped he would come back soon.

The bakery loomed above him as he left the dark alleyway. It was no longer the cheery place it once was, with no customers going in and out of the doorway, and an awful stillness clinging to it like the dust that gathered on top of the tallest cabinets. The delicious smells coming from the ovens were gone, overcome by the scent of charred wood that permeated through the town. Tommy had secretly hoped the smell of bread baking for years and years would've won out, but even here was a reminder that Heimat was a shell of its former self.

He shifted the pot to one arm, grunting with the effort, and knocked on the door. Someone called from inside, telling him it was open. He let himself in and was met with inky darkness. The few windows of the bakery were shuttered, leaving the only light in the room that which trickled down from the stairwell above.

A sinking feeling entered his stomach.

He never imagined this place could be so unwelcoming. Even when they met in the basement, in the dead of night to discuss their plans of evacuation, the bakery above had been warm, the coals in the ovens raising the dough for the morning.

Tommy swallowed hard, willing the tears flooding his eyes away. He couldn't look at the side door he'd entered through days ago. Deciding to come through the front door was an act of rebellion and cowardice. He couldn't bear the memories of the side door, of the last time he gave his friend a hug and spun her. Tommy needed to show his city their community was still intact despite the horror brought down around them.

With a shuddering breath, Tommy started ascending the stairs to the living space above. His feet felt like lead but he kept going, holding the pot of stew close, careful not to spill a drop, as if it was the key to dispelling the grief that clung to every part of the bakery. The young man steeled himself as he reached the top of the stairs.

They opened into a modest dining area. The small table in the center of the room held four chairs, only one of them filled. Rich had his elbows on the table, his head in his hands, and a hollow air about him.

Tommy silently walked past him, through one of two doorways, into the small kitchen and set the pot by the hearth, embers cold. Tommy grabbed a wrought iron fire poker and stirred the coals, willing them to give off a little heat. He spied a pile of wood and placed one small piece on the coals, watching it ignite into flames. He placed the grate across, hoping it took some of the chill out of the air as it kept the stew somewhat warm.

Tommy stepped back into the dining room and took a seat at the table. He stayed quiet, offering his presence and nothing more, waiting for the older man to acknowledge him. Rich was like a statue, holding his head in his hands and staying completely still.

Gradually, Rich's shoulders shook as sobs racked the older man's body. Tommy reached out and gripped his hand hard, relief and despair flooding him, warring emotions at knowing the old man felt comfortable enough to break down and feeling helpless to make the pain go away.

Rich squeezed Tommy's hand and struggled to compose himself. After a while, the tears stopped and the old man swiped at his face.

"You're a good boy, Tommy." Rich raised his head from his hands to look at the young man in front of him.

Tommy nodded and moved his hand to the old man's shoulder, alarm flaring within as he noticed how frail the man was. Rich was one of those people who was a pillar in the community, and trying to imagine Heimat without him was like trying to imagine life without an arm or a leg. Tommy kept the shock and concern from his face, saying, "All because of my Ma, sir."

Rich nodded. "Aye, your Ma is a kind woman. You were right to move her when you did. She still at the farmhouse?"

"Aye. Sara and I and the kids are out there, too. Keeping Ma company and trying to get away from everything." Tommy stumbled over his words, trying not to offend the old man or dredge up painful thoughts.

"It's for the best." Rich's eyes seemed to glaze over as he stared into the distance above Tommy's head.

Tommy gripped the old man's forearm, jarring him back to the present. "Come, stay with us." Rich shook his head but Tommy continued, "Seriously Rich, grab Anna and Rob, the girls, and just get away from it all."

Rich furrowed his brows but said nothing.

Tommy tried again. "Rich. I'm worried about you. Johanna said she saw you walking the streets again. It's too dangerous to be pulling stunts like that. The cobblestones are still teeming with soldiers."

A dull fire lit in Rich's eyes and he spat on the floor. "I'd like to see them try me. I've got nothing left to lose." The baker gestured wildly about. "Do they want this? Tell them they can have it. This house, my bakery, it doesn't matter anymore. They can take it all and nothing will hurt like losing Melody." Tears streamed down his cheeks as the anger flared.

"Richard Johnson. How dare you?" A voice sounded past the other doorway leading to the dining area. Movement caught Tommy's eye as a robust woman stepped into the room.

Rich dissolved into tears, dropping his head into his hands once more.

"For Goddess's sake, get up Richard. Crying won't bring her back." Anna, Rich's wife, and Melody's mother, gave the old man a shove before making her way into the kitchen. She checked the stew before rejoining them at the table, preferring to stand instead of taking one of the unoccupied chairs.

Tommy stood up, as was proper, when a vice-like grip took hold of his shoulder and held him in place.

"No need for that, Thomas. Is that stew in there from your mother?"

"Aye, Mrs. Johnson. I was already on my way over, so she sent it with me. She told me grief has a way of making the body forget itself and insisted that sending a meal would warm your bones even when the worst was upon you. She sends her love and condolences as well." Tommy sat up, keeping his shoulders back when addressing the older woman.

Anna had a reputation for being prickly, but losing her daughter seemed to have made her downright combative.

"Send her our thanks. Why were you making the trip out here in the first place?" Anna was more shrewd than most gave her credit for.

Tommy looked at Rich, willing the older man to pull it together. Hearing his wife's question, Rich's ears pricked up and once again, he lifted his head to stare at the young man.

Once Tommy had the baker's attention, he answered, "I came by to give Rich a heads up. I've checked in with all the leaders left in the city and their information is all the same. Most of the kids got out. Reg lost half his group and Mikel's lost one, but otherwise, they all got on that boat set up by Eddy. We just have to hope they meet up with the rest of the Circus as quickly as possible." Tommy took a deep breath and launched into the last of it.

"We're meeting tonight to draw up plans going forward. It's essential we have a way to check in with the rest of the Magicae here in town and decide how we undermine the mayor and his lackeys." The fire of defiance lit in Tommy's eyes. "I wanted you to know what we're doing, but hope you don't feel obligated to come. You're welcome to, of course, but we didn't want to take you from your family. You've lost a lot and we are not about to ask you to give more."

Rich stared hard at the man sitting next to him, realizing the grace his fellow townspeople offered to him. Tommy willed the older man to understand their reasons for leaving him in the dark and to consider his options moving forward.

Anna stepped closer to her husband, placing a hand on his shoulder. "We'll be there, son. At the farmhouse?"

Tommy shook his head. "We're meeting in Tam's glass shop. It's out of the way and big enough to hold a sizeable crowd when the time comes." He inclined his head to the pair. "It would be an honor to have both of you there. We're meeting once the sun sets, per usual." He hesitated before asking, "Do you know where Rob and the girls are? I find it hard to believe those two haven't made their presences known yet."

Anna and Rich shared a look. "The girls have been very subdued since everything happened. But, you're right, Rob took them for a walk, figured the fresh air would do them some good. He was going to walk down by the river," Anna said, a slight tremor in her voice.

Tommy gave a nod and stood up. "Come to the farmhouse. There're beds a plenty and Ma would love to have the company." He shook Rich's hand and gave Anna a stiff hug. "Both of you and Rob and the girls are welcome. Sometimes a change of scenery is the best medicine for a broken heart." He quoted his mother with that last statement.

"You're too kind, Thomas. We'll consider it. Just make sure you leave Rob and those girls out of all this. They've already lost a mother; don't make them lose their father, too." Anna gave Tommy one last hard look as he walked back down the stairs to the gloomy bakery below.

Tommy couldn't leave the broken home fast enough. Anna didn't want him to find Rob, but Tommy had never been that good at following directions from anybody but his Ma. He took the most direct route to the river, not caring who saw him while running through what he'd say to his friend.

"What's the rush, T?" A voice came from his left.

Tommy started, not expecting to come across someone in the empty streets. Seeing the brunette with almond-shaped hazel eyes brought a slight smile to his face. "Hey, Jo. I'm on my way to find Rob." He didn't miss the sorrow that filled her eyes and the way her shoulders drooped.

"Tommy, I know how much Melody meant to you and Sara. She didn't deserve to die." Johanna dropped the cart she was carrying and enveloped Tommy in a warm embrace. "I didn't offer my condolences the last time we spoke. Please know that I'm here if you need anything."

Tommy leaned into the woman's embrace as tears pricked his eyes. He swallowed, trying to get a hold of his emotions before replying, "Thanks, Jo. The grief comes in waves."

Johanna pulled back to meet Tommy's eyes. "As it always does." She gave him a pat on the back. "I'll see you later tonight."

Tommy watched the Forger return to her cart, bending down to grasp both handles. He furrowed his brows. "Do you need help, Jo?"

"Don't be silly. I've taken heavier loads before." Johanna waved him off with one hand.

"Let me help," Tommy insisted.

Johanna rolled her eyes but repositioned herself from between the two cart handles to one side, leaving the other for Tommy to grasp. The pair lifted the cart as one and trudged back the way Tommy came from.

"What is all this, anyway?" He asked.

Johanna took a couple of sideways glances before responding. "I'm trying a new technique with the skins. I'm hoping to create something new."

"That's a cryptic answer," Tommy said with a chuckle.

"One can never be too careful these days." Johanna's tone was somber.

Tommy pressed his lips together but didn't reply. He knew he could never understand the feeling of being persecuted because of the blood in your veins. The young man was confident he could talk his way out of any situation should it come to that. But being one of the Magicae meant living with undeniable proof that you were different.

Most Mortals assumed Forgers could work with materials from the earth such as rock or metals. That meant most blacksmiths and quarry workers were given extra scrutiny should they turn out exceptional work. For this reason, most Forgers with those Materials avoided the trades like the plague.

Johanna wasn't like most Forgers.

She was one of the few that worked with their Material as a trade. Her Material was animal hides and the leather that could be made from it. She risked a lot by staying in her position when Vincenzio came to power, but Johanna was as stubborn as a mule.

Tommy knew her tannery meant more to her than anything, and she wouldn't let a tyrant like Darren Vincenzio take that away from her. He cleared his throat.

"He won't get away with this. The Magicae belong in Heimat just as much as any Mortal." Tommy's tone was decisive.

Johanna shot him a look but didn't respond. They continued on in silence, walking the cobblestone streets past the Barracks and into the Fringe where her tannery resided. They kept to the alleys as much as possible until they were in the Fringe proper. Neither of them willing to risk running into soldiers on their way to the bars and brothels of the Wharf.

Tommy's frown deepened as they moved further and further into the Fringe. This resembled where he'd grown up, and seeing the humble hovels made him grateful for his older brother's sacrifices. His heart twinged at the thought of George. They had always been opposites of each other, but living with almost nothing had bonded them unlike anything else. His older brother had always looked out for him and it hurt knowing there was a possibility he would never see him again.

The young man shook his head and the despairing thoughts inside. He couldn't let himself think about that right now, not when they had troubles of their own to figure out.

"We'll go around back," Johanna said as they neared the tannery, speaking for the first time in a while.

Tommy followed her lead, bringing the cart to the back entrance and the door that was just wide enough for the cart to fit through.

"I don't think I've ever been to the back entrance," marveled Tommy. "I always thought you carried in the hides one by one."

Johanna chuckled. "Now that would be highly inefficient."

"Well, we both know that's not what you're about," Tommy said with a smile.

"Aye, I've been called many things in this lifetime, but inefficient isn't one of them. Thank you, Tommy. I could've done it myself, but the company was welcome." Johanna shot him an appreciative glance before emotion filled her eyes once more.

Tommy clasped her shoulder. "These are the days when we need the company the most."

"When did you get so wise?" Johanna asked with one eyebrow raised.

"Fatherhood. Nothing makes you grow up faster than being responsible for your own little ones. They've taught me everything I've learned." Tommy's eyes filled with warmth at the thought of his three little ones and the fourth one on the way.

Johanna patted his cheek before shooing him out the door. "You best get moving, then. Go find Rob and then go home to your wife and kiddos. Thanks again and I'll see you tonight."

Tommy sent her a salute before slipping out the back door and making his way to the river. He would have to hustle to find his friend but knew what to say to convince him to relocate his family to the farmhouse. Using Johanna as inspiration, Tommy would not take no for an answer.

Chapter Ten

The small, soft flakes of white dusted the forest floor as more and more snow made it through the canopy above. The people and animals of the caravan blew puffs of smoke into the chilly air with each breath. As the day wore on, the road became harder to navigate with the onslaught of snow mixing with the mud beneath their feet.

Once again, they paused to wrench the wheels free of one wagon carrying the young and the elderly. Duncan sent Conrad and Nymeria to scout ahead in their feline forms for a place to rest for the night.

The section of forest they were in held the oldest trees many had ever seen. There seemed to be an order to the pattern of different trees and plants surrounding them. The path they followed became more pronounced, suggesting heavier foot traffic, yet they remained the only ones using it.

Duncan sat astride his mare, his hands stretched wide as he concentrated on keeping the wintry winds from the north at bay. His people huddled for warmth, many only wearing thin coats and pants or skirts. Midge was working day and night in the wagon, devoted to creating clothes, blankets, and cloth out of the hides brought back by the hunters.

She was a Forger, using the cloth she was so fond of to create magic. The saying was if Midge couldn't make it, it couldn't be done. She was unique for a Magicae because, on top of the magic in her blood, she was an accomplished seamstress in her own right.

When she made costumes for the performers, she used her Gift to coax the cloth into the shape she wanted but added feathers, stones, and shimmering bits using a needle and thread to make the costumes stand out. The onslaught of winter had her working furiously, trying to create as many warmer coats and blankets for her people. Luckily, two of the new recruits, including the woman brought in by Eva's dad in Windemere, worked alongside her, racing the clock as the cold settled into the bones of their people.

Eva herself rode in a wagon, Wren burrowed into her side for warmth. J walked behind their wagon, keeping tabs on the two girls in his care and thinking about the classes he would offer to the rest of the caravan. Conditioning was something J took seriously when he had the freedom to be in his human form. His elephant form was powerful and could reach pretty high speeds, but it wasn't agile. That's what he missed most when they traveled for weeks on end to reach the next town, being able to run through a crowd without a second thought or climb a tree just because. The power was nice, but the freedom was better.

He had offered to help get the wagons unstuck several times before, but the Forgers insisted on taking the time to experiment while they had the chance. The wagons were made with different materials, requiring multiple Forgers to work together to lift and propel them forward. Getting it right was taking less and less time, as the Forgers adapted to each new situation with more and more ease. They knew J could help in a pinch, but should he fall, they needed a failsafe. J understood, knowing he could use his commanding form regardless of practice or not. Not to mention the elephant and her babe that followed behind him. They could also help should it be deemed necessary.

He reassured his young charges as they waited for the wagons to get unstuck once again.

Duncan was deep in conversation with Jess, discussing what supplies could be allocated to building weapons and which Forgers would be up for the task. They called Betsy over to join the conversation and provide insight into the status of the bows used by the hunters. The equipment was returned to the back of her chuckwagon along with any game shot that day. She knew how many bows and arrows were in the caravan's stock and which ones could do for some replacing.

Nan sat next to Javie on the bench seat at the front of her brightly colored wagon. She pulled the blanket around her shoulders tighter as a rogue wind got past Duncan, soaking in the warmth it brought to her old limbs. Midge may be behind, but she kept a special eye out for the young and elderly of their caravan.

"You could ride in the back, Abuela." Javie offered, pulling their oxen to a stop as they caught up with the wagon stuck in the mud. "It's at least sheltered from the wind, and would probably be a little warmer." He spared a glance towards his grandmother, worry lines forming on his brow.

Nan pulled the blanket up slightly and linked her arm through her grandson's, pulling him close. She patted his hand, saying, "You're worse than your sister. I'm fine, nieto. The fresh air does me good." She smiled at him, the corners of her eyes crinkling.

Nan hadn't been the same since her episode outside of Windemere.

Her mind and spirit were strong, but her physical body still hadn't recovered fully, needing a cane or person to lean on when she walked. The whole caravan still treated the fortune teller as if one wrong move would shatter her. Nan was determined to convince her people this spell would pass, but deep down she knew her age was catching up with her. The day would come sooner rather than later when she would need to pass on from this world to the next, and join her daughter, mother, and grandmother before her. The Magicae tended to live longer than their Mortal counterparts, but not by much. Their lives expired all the same, proving the two were more alike than many wanted to admit.

Her heart squeezed at the thought of seeing her family again, smelling the faint pine and sage clinging to them all and throwing her arms around the three of them. Sadness clouded her eyes as she imagined that moment. *A bittersweet reunion, to be sure.* She thought to herself, staring into her grandson's striking blue eyes. Seeing the ones she missed meant she would have to leave so many behind.

Nan shook her head, chasing the ghosts from her mind. Her time wouldn't come until she saw her people free again.

She bumped her grandson's shoulder. "How are the lessons going with Solomon?"

Javie rolled his eyes. "As well as an iron Forger in a forest," he snorted.

Nan chuckled. "That well, eh?"

"Abuela, how am I supposed to learn from someone with a stick shoved so far up his a—"

"Nieto! Do not speak about your mentor like that. Show some respect." Nan frowned and contained the burst of laughter she almost let out. "I raised you better than that."

"But Abuela! He wants me to call him 'Master Thorne' like he's some sort of academic progeny. He is the most pretentious bastard in the whole caravan!" Javie threw his hands in the air to punctuate his exasperation with the middle-aged man.

Nan clucked her tongue at the seething teenager. "Javier Santiago. Watch your mouth before it gets smacked." She raised one eyebrow.

Javie hung his head and apologized. "Aye, Abuela. Lo siento." His hands clenched with suppressed frustration.

Nan placed a hand on his cheek, guiding him to look into her eyes. "Mi nieto apasionado. You have a fire within only matched by the Huntress herself. But you need to learn when to keep it in check. You only have the excuse of youth for so long. Best to use it wisely." Javie sighed, but the anger in his eyes dulled. Nan studied his face a moment more before saying, "Solomon can be dreadful, but he is the most accomplished Grower we have. Learn what you can from him and then push yourself further." She winked at her grandson, coaxing a small smile from the young man.

"I knew it! I knew you didn't like him either!" He raised his voice as he shot her an accusatory glance.

Nan chuckled once more, unable to stay upset with the boy she'd raised since he was a toddler. Luc still had memories of her mother, but Javie was too young when she passed. She shook her head. "Hush, now. That's between you and me." She flashed him a conspiratorial grin, earning a genuine smile from Javie. "But regardless, he is your teacher and deserves respect."

"Aye. It's so hard though, Abuela."

"Being his student or the magic itself?" Nan studied Javie. Nan and her daughter, Luc and Javie's mother, were Healers, the type of Herbalists that could sense the properties of certain plants and use them to create tonics, creams, and medicine for their people. Many Healers helped in the med tents since treatment came easy once symptoms were identified.

But Javie was a Grower. Growers could coax plants into blooming or climbing higher. They were skilled at finding plants in the forest and foraged while the Circus was on the road. They kept a library of seeds for growing in the wagon converted to an open-air greenhouse while on the road. Winter in Heimat left little room to experiment, but the Growers did the best with what they had.

The power running through the veins of the Magicae was a fickle thing when it came to inheritance. Magic ran in families, but unions between Magicae and Mortals and even between Magicae of different Gifts made inheritance difficult to predict. The magic could lay dormant for generations and rear its head to the surprise and perplexity of unsuspecting parents. Every child was unique, and even siblings could be born with or without magic in the same family.

For a long time, magic was dominant, meaning a single drop was all it took to give power to the next generation. As years went on, that became less and less the case. It seemed the more surefire way of predicting was how powerful the Gift was. Two parents with strong Gifts almost always passed one or the other Gift down to each child. One strong Magicae and one Mortal gave Gifts to about half of their children, and one or two weakly Gifted parents rarely passed their magic on. In these cases, more often than not, the Gift would reappear later down the road in subsequent generations.

It was as if the Gifts would run dry and need to consolidate for a spell before they could show up again.

Javie struggled to find the words to answer his grandmother. He wasn't an extremely talented Grower, but more than that, he had never wanted to explore his Gift like Rae or Zeke or Freya. He had trained when his Gift first presented itself and then slowly stopped attending the lessons, spending more and more time with the Forgers. Javie was fascinated with the way they could coax metals and wood and cloth into beautiful works of art or functional items that made life easier for their caravan.

With the disaster in Tiva, Nan insisted he take up lessons again. Her constant nagging made him oblige, but it was no secret how much he disliked his teacher and the way the man conducted his lessons. Javie struggled with finding the beauty of making a bunch of plants grow when they could do it just fine on their own.

"Both. The man is awful, but the power in my veins..." Javie trailed off as he held his hands in front of him, gazing at them as if his answers laid just beneath his coat. "It takes so much to make one little plant grow. I draw almost all my power and get one bloom or one fruit. At that rate, why bother?"

"Nieto," Nan gripped his chin in her hand, making him face the steel in her gaze. "Practice is what you need. Your magic is like a muscle. The more you exercise it, the stronger it will become."

"Aye, Abuela. That's what everybody says, but it doesn't feel right. I can't—"

The cry of a falcon pierced the air around the caravan. Nan and Javie turned to watch silver wings flash as the bird searched for one person. They shared a look, knowing who the bird was looking for. Javie coaxed the oxen to move closer to the bowman astride a horse, with a hawk on his shoulder.

Gar had his favorite hawk on his shoulder. The rest of the birds traveled on the shoulders of some others in the caravan. They hunted small game in the forest, bringing back food for themselves and supplementing the diets of the other carnivores in the nomadic city.

The hawk stayed with him, though. It was the first bird he'd raised with his son and no matter what he did, he couldn't bring himself to risk losing that last tie to his absent boy. Gar didn't consider himself sentimental, but under the circumstances, the hawk gave him hope he'd see his son again soon.

The older man let his horse nibble on some leaves and grass at the edge of the path while they waited for the wagon to get unstuck. He watched their progress, stroking the hawk's head, his thoughts with his son.

Raising a Shifter without being one himself was an exercise in frustration most days. A small smile crept onto his face as he remembered running after a young boy covered in feathers, snapping a mouth that was more of a beak, and scratching his arms with nails more like talons. They'd had their growing pains, as fathers and sons did, but he couldn't deny how proud he was of that fine young man.

A falcon's cry pierced through the his train of thought.

Gar's eyes widened as he imagined the impossible.

There was no way Bane would leave without those kids.

But what if?

He held out his arm and let out the breath he was holding as the falcon lighted on his outstretched forearm. The hawk sat on the opposite shoulder and studied the newcomer intensely.

The falcon wasn't Bane.

Bane went for his shoulder every time, and this bird was just following directions. She let out another cry and offered one of her taloned feet to the man she perched on.

Gar had inquired several times how Bane could send the raptors to find him when he was hunting and needed to update his father on his progress. Bane would give him a look and tell him he was overthinking things. He always insisted Gar didn't need to know everything about his Shifting abilities.

Gar knew it was more likely Bane didn't know those answers himself.

He focused on the beautiful bird on his arm, gently accepting the note tied to the falcon's outstretched foot. He cooed quietly to her, using his other hand to transfer her to his free shoulder. The bird nibbled gently on his ear, hungry from the long journey. The old man held a piece of meat towards her, which she devoured.

"Hush, now," he said to the hawk chattering in his ear, complaining about not getting a piece himself. Gar threw a piece to the left for the hawk to grab in mid-air. He did so and carried it to a branch, out of reach of the competition. Gar shook his head at the hawk's distrust of the new bird. The falcon was content on Gar's shoulder, keeping her piercing gaze on the surrounding environment, watching for potential threats.

Gar turned his attention to the scrap of cloth in his hands. He spread it wide to reveal cuts and holes that formed a pattern. This was something they devised years ago, more reliable than any code should it fall into unwelcome hands. He just needed to find the—, there. The distinctive three dots in a triangle always marked the upper left corner.

Gar turned the cloth and his eyes darted across it, taking in every rip and tear, holding his breath as he interpreted his son's message.

A hand on his free shoulder wrenched him from his focus. His dark eyes met kind sapphire ones, Nan leaning as far over her seat on the wagon as she dared.

"What does he say?" Concern coloring her words and betraying her worry.

Gar glanced back at the cloth before meeting the fortune teller's gaze again, a slow smile forming on his face. "They're okay. Everyone made it."

"Thank the Huntress." Nan squeezed his shoulder before brushing some dirt from his coat.

"He wants me to send word once we settle somewhere." His eyes traced the patterns one last time. "Looks like I have a new friend for a while." He stroked the falcon's head gently, avoiding her beak. She would be the only way to send word to Bane and the others, as Bane had no doubt impressed upon her the need to return to them once bidden. Gar sighed, wishing once more he had the abilities his son did. "I better find Duncan and let him know. 'Scuse me, Nan, I'll catch up with you later?"

"Of course, dear. I'm so happy Bane could send word. You make sure that bird gets as much meat as she wants. Anything for the brave soul that brought such wondrous news."

Gar inclined his head and urged his horse towards the Ringmaster. Duncan was helping troubleshoot better ways to keep the wagons from getting stuck with Jess and some of the other Forgers. By his expression, it wasn't going well.

Once the falconer reached their group, he hailed the wind Crafter, who was still trying to keep the wind at bay while he brainstormed. "Hey, Dunc! I got some news you should hear."

Duncan's eyes lifted before he excused himself from the Forgers, making his way to where Gar waited.

Gar dismounted, careful not to displace the bird still on his shoulder. He clasped the ringmaster's forearm. "I know you're busy. These conditions are worse than that rainstorm in Maya City years ago."

Duncan chuckled despite himself. "That mud was more like quicksand. The fools that we were, we kept going anyway."

"Aye, we had another city to get to." Gar shook his head, his chest bouncing lightly with the laughter deep in his throat. "The ego knows no bounds when you're young."

Duncan raised an eyebrow. "We weren't that young."

"Wisdom comes at all ages." Gar held up the cloth, displaying the pattern of rips and tears. Recognition flashed in Duncan's eyes, but he motioned for the older man to continue. "Bane sent me a message. They made it out okay, and everyone is accounted for. The kids, our people, everybody escaped."

"Thank the Huntress." Duncan sighed in relief, looking like a weight left his shoulders at the news.

"Aye. Eases a lot of worry, it does." Gar inclined his head to the falcon dozing on his shoulder. "I'm supposed to send word back when we settle somewhere."

Duncan's lips pursed into a thin line, anxiety flooding back in. He gave a terse nod before clasping Gar's forearm. "Thanks, Gar. Keep me posted on whether you get word of anything else. If you need anything, don't hesitate to ask." He stared at the bird on Gar's shoulder before meeting the falconer's gaze. "Don't let that bird out of your sight." Gar's eyes hardened into steel, knowing he would do anything to protect the chance of seeing his son again.

A cheer rose from around the wagon stuck in the mud as it finally rolled free from its sloppy clutches.

The men mounted their horses, and the caravan continued its solemn march to somewhere safe.

Chapter Eleven

Johanna checked behind her for the third time before crossing the street. Tommy may have been bold during the day, but the streets at night were a different beast. Their city was in shambles as chaos ruled the day and order took a backseat. The unassuming, brown-haired woman wouldn't allow anyone to catch her unaware.

She sped across the cobblestones, melting into the darkness of the alley that would lead her right to the doors of Tamara's glass shop.

Goddess, keep that woman safe. She rubbed at the tattoo on the inside of her wrist. Tamara offered the tattoo as a way for Johanna to pay homage to the mentor who had taught her so much. It was a sweet reminder of her friend and the mentor who taught her everything she knew about Forging.

Tamara needed to return to Heimat, or else nothing would be the same.

Tommy had called a meeting to talk about undermining the authority and plans of their mayor. They needed to bring life back into their city, and this was the first step. She just had to keep putting one foot in front of the other and they would get through it.

Johanna was just glad Eddy set up that damn getaway boat. It stroked his ego and made him even more huffy and hard to deal with, but it saved those kids. That's all that mattered. When Eddy told her Cleo was championing the vessel, her remaining fears were assuaged.

Well, at least they were when the news broke that the *Vengeance* was the only ship to make it off the docks in one piece. The others were sent to the shipyard for repairs.

Johanna knew there was no way Cleo would let anyone or anything catch them with that much of a lead on their enemies. Cleo had been hammering for her own ship and crew ever since she came to this city. Now that she had it, she wouldn't let them slip through her fingers.

Some people may have been worried about the woman's ambition, but Johanna knew a kindred spirit when she came in contact with one. A woman trying to prove her worth beyond the influence of others was a force to be reckoned with. Those kids were in the best hands possible.

Now they needed to figure out how to make it safe for all of them.

She had to give Tommy credit; the youngest of the town leaders, and he was the one to step into Rich's shoes while the baker grieved his daughter.

Johanna felt her heart twinge at the thought of the old man. He hadn't deserved that loss. The leaders were rallying around the man who had made safety a possibility for so long.

Johanna was a Forger herself, her blood as silver as the jewelry adorning many of the highborn ladies at the Capital. Her Material was unconventional in that it didn't come from the earth like most substances able to be manipulated by Forgers. Her Material was leather, and the hides used to make it. She owned the tannery in town and put up the front of using conventional methods to get the results she did.

She learned about the magic in her veins at a young age, and apprenticing in Heimat had been an advantage as she developed her Gifts. As with other Forgers, her abilities of manipulation were limited to one Material. Johanna could work the skins and pelts brought in by hunters and trappers until they were beautiful leather, taking half the time needed compared to conventional methods. She could skip all the processes of soaking, taking the hair off, and rubbing with fat or grease and simply coax the pelts into their desirable, preserved forms.

Once the hides were made into leather, she could use them to create various tools and goods. A single touch had the firm but supple textile forming a waterskin or a pair of shoes or even the shape needed to cover a saddle.

The possibilities were endless.

Everyone in Heimat wanted to commission work from her, but Johanna refused most of them. The coin was nice, but Johanna placed more value in creating the essentials for the families in Heimat and the neighboring towns. There was beauty in creating a sling for a new mother to carry her baby, a new, warmer coat for the old woman that couldn't quite get the chill out of her bones, or a leather sheath for a child's first hunting knife.

The silver running through her veins was easily concealed, but the way her hands interacted with the pelts and the resulting leather couldn't be. This was never a problem before the mayor and his soldiers of destruction and Johanna had delighted in helping some of the young Forgers develop their skills, running them through the drills her mentor had put her through.

Crafters needed movement to control their various Crafts, learning body positions that could be moved through, and adding their Craft as they mastered each position. Forgers used drills similarly to master the ways of manipulating their Material.

They first practiced letting their power wash over all or part of a piece of their Material, as control was the difference between creating something beautiful and creating a mess. Once they mastered washing a Material in power, they could focus on manipulating it.

Matter couldn't be created or destroyed, but it could be changed.

Physical manipulation was easier and didn't require as much power. This could mean changing its shape or thickness, getting a Material to break into smaller pieces, or hold a form. Chemical changes were more advanced. Examples of these included changing the color, weight, or texture of a Material, and joining two smaller pieces together, coaxing them to bind to one another.

Only the most advanced Forgers could make chemical changes permanent to the Material they worked with. It was harder to entice it to keep the manipulations to the very atoms that it was made of.

Johanna shook those thoughts from her head.

It was no good to dwell on what was or what could've been. Forgers like her were the most prevalent Magicae left in Heimat on account of how easy it was to pass as Mortal. All Magicae had their tells, Forgers had silver blood, Crafters had metallic eyes, Shifters never lost the eyes of their animal forms, and Herbalists had viny birthmarks somewhere on their skin. Other than those tells, Magicae and Mortals were indistinguishable from one another. Only Shifters with the Sight could tell the difference with just a look; everybody else relied on the tells.

The youngest Forgers were sent with the Circus since their youthful recklessness could not be contained and scrapes and cuts gave them away almost daily. None of the adult Forgers, besides Tamara, left the city, fighting for their place in the community.

But time was ticking. At any moment, Vincenzio could decide to make good on his promises to rid Heimat of its Magicae. Soon, he would be knocking down doors and nobody would be safe. Determination to save her city spurred Johanna on as she reached the end of the alley.

A quick glance around the back door revealed someone beat her to it. The soot and dirt around the bottom of the door looked disturbed, suggesting someone had already opened it using the hidden key.

Johanna gave a wry grin. She knocked three times on the door in rapid succession, knowing full well who would open it for her.

Her grin widened when the door opened to reveal a curly-haired redhead she considered a sister.

Simone gave her a fierce embrace, guiding her into the deserted place and closing the door behind her. "It's so good to see you, Jo. I would've stopped by the tannery, but there was too much to do in the Lower Districts. The south side got hit hard, and we had to organize a cleanup and soup kitchen for those that took the brunt of it." Simone stepped back to look into Johanna's face but kept her hands on the other woman's shoulders. The redhead cocked her head and moved her hands to straighten the collar of Johanna's coat, giving her a satisfied grin.

Johanna rolled her eyes and swatted her hands away. "Of course, you would organize all that." Johanna continued before Simone could interrupt her. "Trying to show us all up again." Johanna put a hand on her friend's shoulder and squeezed. "Relax, I'm kidding. You're just too organized. Those in the Lower Districts don't know how good they got it. The Fringe is stuck with someone like me, unorganized and a procrastinator to boot." She winked at her Mortal best friend.

"Shut up, Jo. The people of the Fringe *adore* you. You might not like to organize events and things, but you definitely serve the people of your district. Remember all those apprentices that would never leave your shop? They stayed there well past closing time almost every night, didn't they?"

"Yeah, but that was because they had a schoolboy crush on me." Johanna winked again.

Simone chuckled, eyes dancing with mirth. "Of course, of course. How could I forget?" Her curls bounced slightly as she laughed. A few fell into her face that she roughly brushed aside. She growled, "Damn hair. Never wants to cooperate." She brushed her fingers through her mane, sweeping it all into a tight ponytail, and tied it with a string. Her eyes narrowed and Johanna could feel her friend's anxiety rising.

"You did great, Simone. We'll figure this out. Tommy was right to hold a meeting." Johanna rubbed her friend's back, recognizing the panic building in her eyes. "Four heads are better than one or two."

Simone's upper lip trembled slightly as she muttered. "There's so much to do, Jo. How are we going to get it all done? What happens to the other sectors, the Barracks? The Upper Districts? Artist's Row? All those people..." Her hand shook as she brought it up to hold her head. She clutched at the Forger's sleeve. "We can't let them get away with this. This is *our* city." Her voice gained strength and Johanna saw a blaze ignite in Simone's green eyes.

Before Johanna could respond, three raps on the back door sounded throughout the abnormally quiet glass shop.

The women shared a look before Simone rushed to the door. She waited a moment, taking a discreet look out a side window to confirm it was one of theirs. Seeing who it was, she opened the door and rushed an uncomfortable-looking

Eddy into the shop.

Johanna studied the tense-looking Wharfman, asking, "What happened, Eddy?"

He turned hollow-looking eyes to her, a shudder passing through him. "Nothing happened, lass. I'm just still trying to wrap my head around it all." He tried a smile but threw Johanna more of a grimace. "Even the Wharf feels different."

"Were there many soldiers on the streets still?" Simone asked, trying to get a glimpse from the window.

Eddy raised an eyebrow at the woman's gruffness. "Same Simone as always, eh, lass? Artist's Row is pretty quiet, gets more dicey when you get down by the Barracks or the Wharf. Tommy not here yet?" he asked, looking for the man who called them together.

"Not yet. He's always late, though." Johanna answered.

"Aye, those little ones are a handful—"

Three knocks once again sounded on the back door.

Simone immediately threw it open, having seen who it was through the window. Both Tommy and Rich stood in the doorway. She motioned them inside and threw her arms around Rich, pulling him into a tight embrace. Johanna put a hand to her face and was surprised to find her cheeks to be wet, her body having a visceral reaction to seeing the baker for the first time since hearing the news. Eddy shook Tommy's hand, pulling him aside for a quiet conversation.

Johanna waited for Simone to release the older man before stepping up to embrace him. She squeezed hard, noticing how thin he had become and the bones poking through the back of his shoulders. She didn't let him pull away, whispering fiercely, "I am so sorry, Rich. Your Melody didn't deserve to die. We'll make him pay for what he did."

He patted her cheek when she pulled away, not trusting himself to say anything.

"Thanks for coming everybody, let's head upstairs." Tommy beckoned, heading to the stairs leading to Tamara's workroom, where their friends planned their escape route just days ago. The rest followed him up the old, creaky wooden stairs, not saying much.

The workroom sat above the forges, where glass rods could be fired and molded into beautiful shapes and forms. It had giant tables able to hold massive stained glass windows, as they were put together with different colors and sizes of glass. Johanna's eyes caught on a large map in one corner of the room. It was a massive map of the city, detailing the spiderweb of alleys and streets. She wandered over to it, stroking the textured paper and tracing the lines across it.

"Jo, you with us?" She looked to find Tommy looking at her, his smile not quite meeting his eyes and shoulders drooping.

She nodded, thinking to herself, *He looks so tired.*

"Good." Tommy looked at the four other people gathered there. "I asked you all to come tonight so we could decide our path forward. We've all lost someone we loved to the unnecessary brutality caused by that devil in the Barracks, posing as the mayor. I've had conversations with all of you and correct me if I'm wrong, but I think it's safe to say we're all ready to fight back."

Johanna nodded along with Eddy and Simone, but cast a curious look at Rich, who was standing silently in the corner, rubbing his hands and keeping his eyes on the ground. Her eyes flashed to Tommy's, and she raised an eyebrow, discreetly nodding her head toward the baker.

Tommy shook his head, not wanting to answer the questions in her eyes.

"Aye, lad, we're all ready to fight. The Wharf is in chaos. Those bombs did the trick and wrecked all the ships on the docks. The sailors, dock crews, and shipyard workers are wound up tighter than a laundry woman on cleaning day with those soldiers breathing down their necks. It's as tense as a tinderbox near a spark in a drought. We need to do something quick before the riots start. Even the brothels and bars can't handle all those people for long." Eddy said with a frown as he clenched his jaw.

"We also need to figure out what to do with the other sections. I can take the Upper Districts and maybe Eddy takes Artist's Row while Johanna takes the

Barracks. That way, Tommy can focus on his district and strategies for taking the city back." Simone tapped her chin and gestured to each of them as she thought out loud to the group.

Johanna swallowed. The Barracks sat just north of her district, the Fringe, but it was also where Vincenzio kept his seat. She would have to be careful when she went to check on the people formerly in Reg's district. Her eyes hardened as she resolved herself to what needed to be done, absentmindedly brushing the ax tattooed on her wrist.

"And what would you have me do, Simone?"

The four started and looked to the corner where Rich's gravelly voice came from. Simone's eyes widened as she was lost for words.

"Rich—, I—I didn't want to assume anything. We weren't sure you were even coming."

"Neither did I." A voice interrupted from the top of the stairs, making its way towards the conspirators.

Five heads whipped to the doorway where Anna Johnson stood, glaring at her husband.

"And I do say, terrible, terrible place to hold a meeting such as this. Richard failed to inform me he was leaving for this disaster in the making." She shot a look at her husband, no warmth in her voice. "I thought we had agreed to stay out of it and focus on our granddaughters, but it appears I was mistaken." Her voice sent daggers to her husband and the others in the room.

Rich was silent, refusing to look at the woman projecting her pain and grief on him. When a child dies before their parents, the results are usually polarizing. Either the parents come together and become stronger, or they're ripped apart, the damage to their relationship irreparable. There was never any middle ground for such a tragedy.

Anna and Rich had always loved each other fiercely, trading shy glances and love notes like love-sick teenagers years and years after tying the knot. Dancing in the kitchen, laughing in the rain, kissing in the moonlight, all of that and more, undone in an instant when they laid eyes on their daughter's unmoving form.

Simone's green eyes darted between husband and wife while Tommy kept his head down, hands in his pockets, and a guilty look on his face. Eddy sat dumbstruck, shoulders tense, and looking like he was ready to bolt.

Johanna sighed, realizing she needed to be the one to say something. She held her hands up in a gesture, communicating she came in peace, and looked at Rich's wife. "You're hurting. Anna, and only Rich can understand what you're feeling right now. I won't pretend to sympathize with you, but I can empathize with you. We all loved Melody. You would be hard-pressed to find a kinder, more thoughtful soul in all of Kamore. And we're angry." She looked at the other three leaders in the room. "Our lives have been dictated by losing people close to us over and over again. Heimat and what it stands for deserve to be fought for. We lost Mikel, and Reg, George, Tam? They're in the wind and could be shipwrecked for all we know. Which is why we have to move forward." Her hardened gaze locked with Anna's, echoing the power in her veins as she clenched her fists. "I don't care about how little you think of us or where we met, but this place means something to all of us. It gives us the motivation to do what's needed for those not here. My question is, why did you come if you didn't plan on helping?" Johanna lifted her chin in challenge at the abrasive older woman.

Anna studied the only Magicae in the room closely while the others held their breath, waiting to see if it would come to blows. Anna inclined her head. "I appreciate your words of praise for our daughter; she had a way of making everyone feel loved." Unshed tears welled in her eyes but didn't fall as she sighed, the tension and combativeness leaving her body. "I still think this is foolish," she glanced towards her husband again, "but more is at stake than ever before." She drew herself up to her full height and crossed her arms. "What can I do to help?"

Johanna shot her a tentative smile and launched into her idea, the others chiming in as they created a blueprint for getting back at the man they hated most.

Chapter Twelve

Tyee directed Koko to keep trudging through the mud as the caravan started moving again. He patted his trusty steed as thoughts raced through his mind.

He had stopped to watch when Conrad and Nymeria started an impromptu combat class after they returned from scouting, hoping to pass the time while they waited for the Forgers to free the wagon. They invited anyone to come join regardless of age or ability, hoping to provide a distraction for as many as possible. Kaiser was nowhere to be found, but the two managed without him.

Tyee had monitored their progress, noticing Luc and Damien join the fray of bedraggled bodies. The acrobats had impeccable form, using their stances effectively to ground their punches and kicks.

Tyee's lips formed a thin line before down-turning into a frown. He knew they would all have to come a long way if this talk of the Resistance were to materialize into something serious.

He rubbed the back of his neck and sucked on his teeth.

Huntress, I hope Duncan knows what he's doing. The Ringmaster deserved his respect, but turning these performers into fighters was going to be practically impossible. Tyee wasn't convinced it could be done.

The members of the Circus had lived lives full of tragedy and mourning, to be sure, but fighting was foreign to most of them. Instead of learning to use their Gifts in combat, the focus was always on control, ensuring they could stay hidden in plain sight. Tyee hoped that control wouldn't hold them back from doing what was necessary when the time came.

There was potential in the caravan for greatness, but the number of young and old was concerning to the equestrian. Once they settled somewhere and left the vulnerable, their numbers would dwindle. The Resistance would end before it started unless they unlocked the young leadership, hungering for vengeance.

But Tyee knew it would be a long road to taking Heimat back. Especially with Rae, Zeke, and Bane missing, their absences leaving gaping holes in the community.

Tyee ignored the pang in his heart at the thought of the fire Crafter. She was alive, and that should be enough for now.

Duncan announced the news shortly after the wagon situation was taken care of. The pit deep inside abated slightly at the news, but his feelings were still a tangled mess. He knew she was the reason he still traveled with the Circus. The reason he stayed with a community he still didn't feel part of. Without performances, he felt adrift without a purpose, and the only thing keeping him tethered were thoughts of the golden girl.

Tyee's hand drifted to Koko's neck, stroking the horse's coarse, dark hair, thick to keep out the chill of winter. He knew there would be another decision to make sooner or later. He had to weigh whether this fight was worth his efforts. Tyee had felt the unseen pressure to lead training classes when Duncan suggested it to the group. He wasn't interested in teaching a bunch of people how to fight, giving them hope when he didn't believe their efforts would be worth it.

He combed a hand through Koko's mane. These people welcomed him with open arms, but he couldn't shake the feeling they valued his skills over everything else. That's the way it always was and always would be. His worth would forever be tied to what he could do for others.

His head whipped up when he heard a commotion at the front of the caravan.

Tyee quickly maneuvered Koko towards the disturbance, individuals getting out of his way despite their curiosity.

The big, black horse moved swiftly, not balking as the sights and sounds became louder and more chaotic. Conrad and Nymeria had Shifted into their big cat forms, low growls in the back of their throats as they faced the woods to the left of the path. Jess and a group of Forgers took up positions beside them, guarding their flanks. The horses and oxen pulling the wagons closest to the front became skittish with the growling cats and shouts of their people.

"What happened?" Tyee asked Duncan, pulling Koko beside the man's bay mare.

The Ringmaster pressed his lips into a thin line. "Conrad and Nymeria caught wind of something. We don't know what it is."

Tyee raised his eyebrows. "What do you mean?"

"Duncan! Something's not right. We need to go back." J interrupted, making his way on foot to the two men winding through the crowd.

Tyee felt a jolt go through him at the elephant Shifter's words. He looked to their Ringmaster for guidance.

The wind Crafter narrowed his eyes and said quietly, keeping his words low and out of earshot of those nearest them. "You feel it too, J? Nymeria told Jess she sensed a presence in the trees, but couldn't get a read on whether it was animal or human, Mortal or Magicae."

J's eyes widened as he peered into the trees, a hand lifting to his temple. "Huntress... my head. Duncan, there's more than one in the trees. Send everyone back to that last clearing." J took off towards the line of Shifters and Forgers, Shifting as he did so, growing in size and bellowing at everyone to get back.

"Shit." Tyee gritted his teeth before bounding into action, urging Koko to head back the way they came, yelling directions to everyone they encountered.

Duncan dug his heels into his mare's sides, guiding her forward to the wagons just behind the front lines. He stayed calm but commanded his people to gather behind them as best he could. He pulled a couple of young people onto his horse before sliding off and sending her back to where everyone was trying to congregate.

Duncan made his way to the line of fighters, calling the wind to his hands, and preparing for battle.

Hooves thundered behind as Luc and Damien sped towards them, Tyee and Koko hot on their heels.

They took defensive stances as other Crafters, Forgers, and a few Mortals made their way to help protect their people. The rest of the caravan gathered behind as best they could, putting up barriers around their most vulnerable. Fear ran rampant as people struggled to understand what was happening. These new threats made the adults more uneasy than anything else. If it had been the band of Shifters, at least they would've known what to expect and how to fight them. This unknown foe made most people's hair stand on end.

The fighters at the front tensed, weapons and Gifts at the ready, eyes scanning the trees for any movement, ears straining for the faintest of sounds.

Gar's hawk scouted above, finally letting out a cry and rocketing from the sky towards a break in the trees.

All eyes locked on the spot as a shadowy figure appeared between the trees.

The figure stepped out from the cover of the canopy, forearm raised as if ready for attack.

Gasps sounded as Gar's hawk alighted on the mysterious individual's raised arm.

The woman moved without so much as a rustle of leaves. She was dressed in leathers that matched the colors of the forest, fur covering her hood, cuffs, and boots to protect her against the chill in the air. Her long dark hair was gathered behind her, accentuating her high cheekbones and narrow ears. Her almond-shaped eyes glinted as she raised her arm, propelling the hawk towards a tree branch.

She flashed the fighters a dangerous smile. "Well? Let's see what you got."

She dropped to a crouch, holding her wooden staff in one hand. She raised one eyebrow as Conrad stalked towards her, growling. With glittering eyes, she held her free hand in the air and snapped her fingers.

Conrad, Nymeria, and J dropped to the ground in an instant.

Dread coursed through Tyee's body, a memory tugging at the edge of his consciousness. He readied his knives, waiting for Duncan's signal.

The Ringmaster let out a cry and charged the strange woman, punching the wind forward with him and signaling his people to attack.

It was chaos as the lines of fighters aimed for the only assailant they could see. More fighters watched stoically from the trees, waiting for the signal from their leader.

The woman's staff was a whirlwind, strange symbols glowing faintly as the wind dissipated around her. Without missing a beat, she knocked Tyee's knives from the air and sidestepped a group of Forgers rushing towards her. Jess tried hurling one stake used for the big top at the woman, hoping the weight of it would catch her unaware.

The woman let out a laugh, twirling out of reach of the heavy iron.

Her eyes glinted as she mocked the Head Forger. "You're going to have to do better than cheap parlor tricks if you want to stand a chance against me." She swiped her staff out in front of her and let out a cackle as Jess's legs were swept out from under her.

The Forgers, enraged from the treatment of their Head, rushed the woman again. The strange woman's wide eyes were the only indication they caught her by surprise and she nimbly spun from their grasp once more. Without a second glance, she knocked Tyee's second set of knives from the air, sending them flying at Duncan.

Forced to deal with the throwing knives, Duncan missed the woman turn into a whirling dervish, catapulting herself into a spin with her staff aimed outwardly. She kept twirling until she reached the Ringmaster, striking him in the back of his knees, causing him to fall face first. Positioning herself behind him, she placed the staff against his neck and made him rise with her into a standing position.

The fighters stopped, realizing this woman could kill their leader with the flick of a wrist. They had been outmatched and outmaneuvered by one woman, making them seem as incompetent as children. An air of dismay settled on the inexperienced members, trembling with fear at this woman that seemed invincible.

"Release him!" Jess raised her voice. "We seek a place of refuge. We did not mean to trespass. Let him go and we'll head back the way we came."

The woman cocked her head but ignored the Forger's pleading. Her eyes snapped to Tyee's, a cruel smile on her face.

So we meet again, Stableboy.

The voice inside his head was like sharp glass, ripping through his consciousness as easily as flesh. Tyee's hands flew to his head, trying to ease the pain. He felt cold fingers brushing against his mind, tearing a scream from his throat, his remaining knives dropping to the ground.

Luc beelined for the horseman, Koko dancing in distress, worried about his rider. She gripped his shoulder from atop her mare and murmured words of comfort, throwing a glare at the woman still holding Duncan by the throat.

The woman smirked before addressing the company. "Welcome to the Great Northern Forest."

With her words, more figures made their way out of the trees, becoming a force of lithe fighters, dressed in matching leathers, dark hair pulled behind them. The members of the Circus were surrounded.

Chapter Thirteen

Darkness blanketed the town of Heimat. The last remnants of smoke and the faint smell of charred wood permeated the cobblestone streets and dirt alleyways. The people still hid in terror, mourning the people they lost and the city they once called their own. It had been a couple of days since the meeting between the daring city leaders, but not much had changed.

The groundwork was being laid to undermine the unwanted mayor, but their plans would take time. The city leaders went door to door, offering condolences and support to those who needed it before asking for help in the plans to come. Slowly but surely, the people of Heimat were preparing to overthrow their tyrant.

While Tommy and his friends roamed the streets, Darren Vincenzio paced in the chambers of city hall. It was the biggest building in the city, situated in the middle of the Barracks, at the heart of the northern trading hub. He had sent messages by carrier pigeons and riders to the Capital with an update on their losses and the events that led to the burning of the city. He'd asked permission to send troops after the performers and requested more soldiers to bolster his ranks.

He expected a response at any moment, knowing the military commander would send word by pigeon only, not wasting a rider if she was sending reinforcements or deemed it unnecessary. He doubted she would risk letting such a collection of Magicae and their sympathizers slip through her fingers, but he wasn't sure he should take that gamble.

He stopped his pacing to look out the window once more.

The risk was if he sent the soldiers before getting permission, there would be no way to call them back. He chewed on his lower lip, running the scenarios in his head, knowing he would decide tonight, bird or no bird. Vincenzio continued pacing, letting the steps focus his energy as he turned his options over and over in his head.

Vincenzio was a massive man. He was the kind of general you would expect, clean cut, with short dark hair, broad shoulders, and a toned figure. His physical prowess made him intimidating in any room he entered. He had strict expectations for his soldiers, clarifying that when they were on the clock, they belonged to him. Break the rules and there would be hell to pay, collected by the general himself. The understanding was the self-imposed mayor turned a blind eye when the soldiers took leave every few days.

This setup attracted some of the cruelest, most menacing brutes to Vincenzio's ranks. Toe the line until leave and soldiers could get away with murder. Their comrades would never turn against them, and even the women in their ranks had hearts of ice and fists of steel. It was a fight to the top, but once you came into Vincenzio's good graces, the treasures knew no bounds.

A knock on the door interrupted the general's thoughts.

"Enter," he commanded, moving to stand in the middle of the large room lined with benches once used for the assembly meetings of Heimat's former government.

His head steward entered, his nose scrunched as if he smelt something rancid. "Your wife wishes to speak with you, sir."

Vincenzio narrowed his eyes. "And why would she think she has the right?" He clenched his fists and gritted his teeth. "Tell her she will have to wait until tomorrow. Let her know not to wait up. I'll have company late into the night." He shot the steward a predatory smile.

The head steward ducked his head before returning the smile. His favorite pastime was watching the general's wife crumple with fear and dread after receiving word from her husband. Mirabella was beautiful, but beauty paled compared to power. Her husband reminded her of that as often as he could.

Vincenzio watched the man leave, his thoughts turning to the daughter he lost.

Gemma was the only thing he loved in this world. He would do anything to get her back. Copper curls, dimples, and a radiant smile filled his mind's eye.

With a cry of frustration, he hurled a fist through the wooden lectern sitting next to the main table in the middle of the room, smashing it in two. Blood leaked from his knuckles, the pain a dull throb he barely felt.

When he found those responsible for this mess, he would make them beg for mercy, beg for death. That was the only comfort he could find as he resumed pacing, rubbing his bloody knuckles on his trousers.

His head whipped to the window when he heard the beating of bird wings outside. He opened the glass, letting the pigeon land on what remained of the wooden pulpit.

He stroked the bird's head as it cooed quietly. He quickly slipped the letter from its leg, his eyes darting across the page. A slow smile tugged at the corner of his mouth.

Vincenzio stroked the bird one more time before bellowing for his steward. "Zander!" He waited for the man to open the door to the chamber. "Send my wife in. There's been a change of plans."

"Yes, sir."

"And grab a runner to bring this pigeon to the coop." He gestured to the bird on the table.

"Right away, sir." Zander gave a half bow before shutting the door again.

Vincenzio leaned against the long table in the middle of the room, facing the door. His hands gripped the table, knuckles still bloody from hitting the lectern. His features settled into a smirk, satisfied with this turn of events. Myra had supported his suggested course of action with vigor, promising to double the amount of troops he had.

More than that, she also sent an execution order for the Ringmaster himself, identifying him as an enemy of the state. An execution would keep the scum in this sad excuse for a city firmly under his boot.

His eyes went to the top of the row of benches as the door swung open, his demure wife stepping into the space. He noted the way her hands trembled before she hid them in her shawl, her chin held high as she walked purposely toward him. He raised an eyebrow, his smirk taking on an edge as he continued leaning on the table.

"And what can I do for you, Mirabella?" He drawled, crossing his arms in front of him.

Mirabella hesitated, looking at the man she once adored, the man she gave up her family for, and the man who forced her to give up her daughter. Ice filled her veins as hatred filled a heart once full of love. Her lips pursed in a thin line, armed with the knowledge he would never suspect such treachery from her.

"They still haven't found Gemma." Mirabella let her voice shake, adding to the illusion of a distraught mother.

"And whose fault is that?" The general spat, anger, and disgust filling his eyes. "You were the one here with her. You were the one that let her be taken."

"Darren! You know I couldn't let her sleep in my bed again. She was getting too old for that. I was following your wishes!" She willed fake tears to her eyes.

Vincenzio stood up and strode to the slight woman, so they now stood toe to toe. "How dare you? You lost the privilege of using my name when you lost our daughter. And now you suggest it's my fault? You stupid woman." He moved his hand to slap her but stopped centimeters from her cheek. "You're lucky I'm not that kind of man," he growled, dropping his hand. "I thought you had learned to mind your tongue, but I guess I was mistaken." He whirled around, giving her his back in an obvious dismissal. He threw a pointed look over his shoulder. "Is there anything else pressing enough that you thought it necessary to interrupt your husband's affairs?"

Mirabella had caught sight of the pigeon on the desk, sitting next to a letter she surmised to be word from the dictator herself. She needed to tread carefully. Her husband was shrewd enough that he might catch on to her if she pushed too hard. "Did you get word from Myra? Is she going to help us get our baby back?" She let her voice drift into a whisper, staring at the letter on the table, wringing her hands, and keeping her eyes downcast.

Vincenzio narrowed his eyes, turned towards her, and gave his wife a once-over. "I sent Bartholomew after that ship days ago. He commandeered the merchant ship that showed up after the docks were destroyed."

Silence followed as the general stared at his wife.

Mirabella felt sweat bead down her back. She murmured a silent prayer to the Goddess, something she hadn't done in years, for the words she said next. "But what if she was with those vagrants across the river? Darren... what if they took her across in the night and swept her into the forest?" She let her voice crack with hysteria as she murmured the last bit. Inwardly, she winced, knowing the danger it would bring to Duncan and the Circus performers, but Gemma needed protection.

The general snorted. "You fool of a woman. That is precisely why I contacted Myra to begin with. She gave us her blessing, promising more troops are on their way to fill our ranks. Not that we need them, but power is power." He shot her a predatory smile. "Even better, she sent an execution letter for the Ringmaster himself. It's finally time to put these people in their place." Vincenzio turned his back on her again. "Go back to the house, Mirabella. Don't wait up and be ready for the announcement to the troops tomorrow. Wear the green dress." He waved his hand in a dismissive gesture.

Mirabella's heart stopped when he mentioned the execution order. Inside, she was panicking, but she needed to get word to Duncan. She balled a fist in her dress and turned stiffly towards the door, walking away from the cruel man.

"Mirabella."

She stopped and turned back, realizing her mistake too late.

"Of course, sir. The green dress will be perfect for that. Should my hair be up or down?" She lowered her chin and tried to make herself as small as possible. Anything to acquiesce her narcissistic and egotistical husband.

He glared a moment longer before saying, "Down." He kept his gaze on her, the weight of it crushing down her shoulders.

"Thank you, sir. I will be at the ceremony tomorrow." She gave a curtsy, praying he took her pliancy at face value. The facade she had created would be useless if he didn't believe it when she needed it most.

"You're dismissed." He turned around again, satisfied with her show of deference.

It took all Mirabella had not to sprint out of the chamber doors.

She needed to warn the Ringmaster before it was too late.

Chapter Fourteen

Rae felt a line of pressure across her waist and a pounding in her head. There was a large mass at her back and rough wood beneath her cheek. Her mind felt sluggish as she slowly regained consciousness, gathering more details about where she was.

The feeling came back into her limbs, and she groaned. It felt as if she'd been run over by a wagon.

She tried to curl into herself, but the throbbing in her head and muscles made it hard to move.

The metallic tang of copper filled her mouth when the boards beneath her rocked unexpectedly, knocking her chin. Her eyes fluttered open as she tried to take control of her body, the taste of blood in her mouth the spur she needed.

Rae realized she was on her side, with her back to the hull of the ship. She moved her arm to rest beneath her head, using it to create a barrier and stop it from hitting the deck again. She propped herself on her elbow as the ship rocked once more. Her head spun as she brought her other hand to the deck and rolled onto her knees.

Rae stopped, resting her head on her hands, and took a deep breath, exhaling with the gentle roll of the boards beneath her. Grunting, she pushed herself off her hands and rocked back, sitting on her heels. The fire Crafter gripped the edge of the gunwale, noticing the rope still tied around her waist.

Memories flashed as she recalled the storm, controlling the tides, and the inky blackness that took her as the water inside ran dry.

Her head whipped up, looking for Zeke or Cleo or anybody, but she was met with silence. She put a hand to her forehead, shielding her eyes from the mid-afternoon sun.

Bodies littered the deck and hung from ropes attached to the masts. Everywhere she looked was destruction.

A wave of nausea had Rae stumbling to the side of the ship. Holding tight to the side of the ship, Rae emptied her stomach into the water. Once she couldn't retch anymore, she wiped her mouth with her sleeve and leaned on the gunwale, her eyes closed. She took a couple of shuddering breaths to collect herself before facing the ship and its destruction. She leaned her back against the side of the ship, letting her body sway with the gentle rocking beneath her.

Taking one last breath, she forced her eyes to open once more and take in the nightmare she knew was waiting.

Barrels, ropes, and crates were strewn around, half of them broken. The boards nearest the prow were splintered, as was the gunwale, like it had been smashed inward.

Rae winced when she looked at the spot where she'd lain. It was mere inches from a spike of wood, so close to impaling her. A groan shifted her attention from the ship to what was beyond. She gave a jolt when she noticed the proximity of the trees.

We must have crashed on the riverbank. Rae shook her head and clenched her fists, clearing the thoughts of screams and raging water from her mind. The past was the past and all she could do now was keep moving forward.

The sound came again from the opposite side of the ship. Rae started when she noticed a rope, tied to the front mast, pulled taught, right over the ship's hull.

A breeze blew gently, tugging the stray hair from what was left of her braid. Rae gritted her teeth and pushed off from where she still leaned against the side of the ship. She struggled to untie the knots tethering her to the mast, bending her knees and swaying with the ship as if it was second nature. As she worked, she took halting steps to the foremast, giving the rope around her middle more slack.

When she reached the middle of the deck, Rae allowed herself to rest, leaning one shoulder against the solid pole of wood. Her fingers worked frantically despite the cold as she willed them to finish the job.

Finally untying herself, Rae stumbled to the opposite side of the vessel. It was one of the longest walks of her life as she gripped her side and maneuvered around the devastated ship. Her heart pounded and her legs trembled with the effort. Each step was a struggle, but they got easier and easier as Rae kept going.

She did her best to keep the hope blooming in her chest at bay. Zeke was the only other person tied to the foremast as she had been, but there was no guarantee she'd find her friend alive. Rae could feel the shame and disgust with her actions rising. Her hands shook while she edged closer, still not sure whether she was ready to learn the fate of her performance partner.

A loud moan pierced the air.

Rae's heart clenched, and she threw herself toward the wall of the ship, murmuring prayers to the Huntress she wouldn't be too late. With trepidation, Rae peered over the ship, curling a hand around the rope still attached to the mast at the front of the ship. She choked back a sob when she saw Zeke dangling from the rope, spinning as he struggled against the loop around his waist.

Rae's throat was raw from the saltwater she swallowed during the storm. It hurt to use her voice, but she did it anyway. "Zeke!" She tried to pull on the rope, muscles straining, but she could do little in her weakened state. Her eyes shifted to the bank, noting the huge rocks that held the ship in their grasp like teeth. Zeke was above the sandy bank, just a couple of feet up. She swiveled her head, looking back to the mast Zeke was tied to.

"Zeke! Hold on! I'm going to try lowering you down!" Rae yelled, but it came out in a rasp. She stumbled back to the mast, willing her fingers to work as they scrambled across the knots holding her friend in place.

But the knots wouldn't come undone. Rae's mind whirred, searching for a solution.

She closed her eyes and reached within, looking for the power that could help her save her fellow Crafter.

All she found was chaos.

Her water Craft was an endless ocean, the tides and waves dwarfing the rest of the Crafts within her core. Rae knew she would have to get her power in check, but for now, she would focus on helping Zeke. She moved back to the side of the ship, reaching into her boot and pulling out a dagger. She held it in one hand, letting the other direct the waves.

She drew the water from the river up into a stream, raising it to Zeke, the power of the water working against the gravity pulling him down. Rae furrowed her brows, keeping her concentration as she lifted her hand with the dagger, bringing it down in one swoop. The rope holding Zeke to the mast released in an instant, surrendering the acrobat to the mercy of the water. She used her hand to guide the stream down slowly, lowering him to the shallows of the riverbank.

Sweat beaded on her brow as her body slumped against the side of the ship. That small use of her Craft left her exhausted, still bruised and broken from the night before. Her eyes stayed fixed on Zeke as he dragged himself to the riverbank, the tension in her shoulders dissipating as she watched his chest heave up and down.

Both of them had pushed their Gifts to the limit. The elements they felt in their veins were wild and unpredictable, bowing to no one. It would take a day or two for the pair to feel in control and be able to exercise the amount of power they were used to. It would take baby steps to reclaim the endurance they once had.

Zeke lifted a hand weakly in thanks to the fire Crafter. Rae snorted at how pathetic he looked, dripping wet and unable to stand, but pain shot up her side. Wincing, Rae pressed one hand to it, taking shallow breaths and hissing through her teeth.

Her attention shifted to the deck as movement caught in the corner of her eye. More and more of the crew were regaining consciousness and stirring. Her eyes found the colossal form of the first mate, limping across the deck, gently shaking or talking to those on deck.

Rae took a couple more shuddering breaths before pushing away from the gunwale. She needed to find Bane and check on the kids. Zeke was alive and breathing, and she would go to him after she knew the status of the others.

She kept her hand on the side of the ship and used it to pull herself to the middle of the ship. Adams intercepted her before she could get there.

"What the hell happened out there, *Magicae*?" He spat the last word as if it was poison.

Rae stiffened at the way he labeled her. She felt eyes on her as her hands trembled with rage. "Don't you dare. We did everything we could. It wasn't our fault your Captain bit off more than she could chew." She clenched her fists and stood straight, forcing herself to show strength.

The surrounding crew watched with interest to see what the first mate would do with such blatant disrespect towards the Captain.

"Excuse me?" Adams's voice turned icy as he stepped closer to the Crafter, drawing up to his full height.

"I said—"

"She spoke the truth." Cleo walked with a slight limp as she reached her first mate, one arm unmoving at her side, hanging uselessly. The Captain winced every time she bumped it but held the stares of those around her. "I gambled with the storm and I lost." Her green eyes filled with sorrow. "We all lost, some more than others." She gestured to the bodies lining the deck. "Tonight, we will send our deceased to the Prophetess as they deserve. But tomorrow, decisions need to be made. Do we abandon ship or fix her up enough to get her to Lockewater?" She raised one eyebrow in challenge to her crew.

Rae stared at the woman with wide eyes. She hadn't expected the Captain to own up to her decision to continue into the storm. Not after she challenged Rae mere hours after her recovery from the ordeal in Heimat. Nobody said anything, just whispered to each other.

Cleo's eyes softened, and she lowered her brow. "I'm a proud woman, but only fools let pride keep them from admitting what's true. When Adams and Mouse raised their concerns, I didn't listen. I'm the Captain of this ship, and I will take responsibility for my choices. Tomorrow I will hear everyone's thoughts on our next steps before I make my decision. Until then, rest, see the Healers, and grieve for our people. We lay our dead to rest at nightfall." She waved a hand to dismiss everyone. Her eyes found Rae's as she winced with pain, shifting her shoulder into a better position. "Rae, Adams, a word?"

Rae nodded and followed the Captain and Adams to the ship's bow, careful to avoid the splintered wood.

"I will not have that kind of discrimination on my ship, Adams." She gave her long-time friend a hard look, keeping her voice low. "You're better than that. You felt that storm as well as I did. Those two Crafters gave us a chance, and we wasted it. I wasted it." She sighed, looking towards the riverbank. "Put the blame where it belongs."

"Captain, I apologize. It was in the heat of the moment and it was wrong. It won't happen again." Adams stood rigid, his shoulders tense.

"I'm not the one that deserves the apology."

Adams gulped but turned towards Rae. "Please, accept my humble apology. My temper got the best of me." He rubbed the back of his neck with one hand. "You and Zeke did all you could."

Both sailors waited expectantly for Rae's response. She took a step forward, lifting her chin and staring at the muscular man. "I've dealt with hatred and discrimination my entire life. I will not hesitate if it happens again." Her eyes flashed as she continued, "Your emotions shouldn't cause you to fling acid at the people only trying to help."

Adams inclined his head, signaling he understood, then looked to his Captain.

"You're dismissed, Adams. Go check on the crew. I'll be up in a minute." Adams gave her a salute and did what he was bidden, leaving the two women alone. Cleo turned her green eyes to Rae and winced. "You didn't deserve that."

"A lot of people don't." Rae leaned against the side of the ship to hide her fatigue and crossed her arms, waiting for the captain to say more.

Cleo moved to lean against the gunwale next to the fire Crafter, a far-off look in her eyes. "My best friend was a water Crafter." Her voice was almost a whisper, colored with pain. "She kept it a secret from everyone, even me. But I knew. The day she was sent to the executioner's block was the day I left the city and everything I've ever known. My family are good people, but they can't eradicate hate in a city like Fernwen." She looked Rae in the eye as her good hand rubbed her limp forearm. "I do know we can start with this ship."

Rae swallowed. "I'm sorry about your friend. Too many of us know those that have ended up under the blade." She bit her lip and asked what had been on her mind since the other day. "Why did you fight me?"

Cleo sighed but kept her gaze steady. "To keep my crew from mutiny."

Rae started, a look of bewilderment on her face. "What?"

Cleo laughed. "My crew, any crew really, responds to power. They were watching you move through your exercises. If I hadn't seen you in action in Heimat, I would've been in awe just as many of them. A Crafter with multiple Crafts? It's unheard of. I had to assert my dominance to keep the crew in check and doing their jobs." She scrunched her nose.

"My crew tolerates Magicae, but not much more than that. It was a miracle they accepted Hazel in the infirmary, but the Herbalist Gift tends to be the easiest for people to reconcile with. These sailors live in a world where fear and distrust of your people are sowed before most of them could even walk." She held up her hand when Rae started to speak. "I'm not saying it's acceptable, but it's reality, for now. I had to challenge you while you were still weak and I had an actual chance of winning. It wasn't quite the way I wanted to go about it, but when an opportunity comes knocking..." Her voice trailed off as she shrugged her shoulders, grimacing in pain when she was reminded of the state of her bad arm.

Rae furrowed her brows. "Then why admit to being wrong about the storm?"

"Because what do I gain by denying it? My crew respects clout, and transparency is its own kind of power. Mistakes happen, and what you do going forward determines the type of person you are. Now it's up to me to prove my mettle and weather what comes next." She gave a wry smirk. "We can all use a blank slate every once in a while, don't you agree?" Cleo held out her hand, her expression the most open Rae had ever witnessed.

Rae clasped the captain's hand, saying, "To new beginnings."

"And a better future," Cleo added, shaking the Crafter's hand in solidarity.

George woke with a start. He bolted upright, realizing his mistake too late. His head spun as he reached for the wall of the ship. As he came to, the surrounding room steadied into focus, as did the memory of where he was. He had joined Reg in the Captain's quarters, along with a little more than half their people.

The room was pure chaos. Boxes, clothing, and supplies littered the space around him. It looked like they had been through a war zone and, by the bruising running up and down his side, George felt like it, too. The room itself was at an angle, as if the ship was listing forward.

He scanned the room, looking for the people in his charge. His eyes caught on Reg's jacket, and the man slumped on the ground a few feet away. George stepped gingerly around the debris and leaned next to his friend. He shook him gently, the man groaning in pain.

George breathed a sigh of relief and looked around the cabin. Children were crying, bewildered by the surrounding chaos. But they were alive, scared and traumatized, but alive all the same. He went around checking on the adults, shaking them gently, and checking for a pulse if they didn't stir.

A knock on the door had all eyes on him.

He shook his head and went to answer it. The resident Healer of the ship asked to check on the children. George let her in, asking if he could help.

The Healer leaned in to whisper to him. There was an incident in the other cabin and she asked him to go help calm his people. Her expression was grave, but she didn't elaborate further, moving into the room to care for her new patients.

George's heart thumped in his chest as he hurried from the room, fearing the worst. He didn't knock before pushing the door to the first mate's cabin open.

The scent of blood hit him like a wagon.

The color drained from his face as he took in the scene before him. The room had been cleared, leaving the Healer from Heimat caring for the injured.

The mother of the baby Shifter lay on the ground, blood pooled beneath her head. George stepped in quickly, noticing the silent tears on the Herbalist's face. He assessed the scene before lowering himself next to the young woman. He squeezed her hand, and she buried her face in his shoulder. George patted her on the back, letting the woman take the comfort she craved.

"What happened?" He asked gently.

The woman leaned back, wiping roughly at her face. "She cracked her head open... there was nothing I could do. She was cold when I arrived." The Healer let out a sniffle but kept her composure.

"And the baby?"

"Tam took him. Bruises covered one of his sides from the fall, but he must have landed on her, as there was no serious damage to the poor thing." Her chin wobbled and tears pooled in her eyes. "I thought we were done with this, George. I thought we had made it."

George squeezed her hand. "I know." He looked at her face. "But the road to peace is never-ending. It's going to take a long time before we're all safe." He reached over and closed the woman's clouded eyes. Turning back to the Healer, he said, "Go, you've done all you can for her. Head to the Captain's quarters and help the other Healer check out the rest of our people. Send Reg down here to help me." He gave her a quick embrace before helping her to her feet.

She left to get Reg, leaving George alone with the woman. He hadn't known her prior to the escape, but that didn't matter. Her death should have been preventable. He hit his fist on the wall of the ship, relishing the release the pain gave him. He did it a couple more times, letting the pain fill his mind. Taking a deep breath, he looked for a blanket. He spied a trunk tipped over in the corner.

George pulled out a sheet of cloth as he heard footsteps thundering towards the room.

Reg came in, panting, a bruise covering half his face. His eyes went to the young woman, and a gasp came unbidden from his throat. He whipped his head to George, but his friend just shook his head, laying the cloth over the woman's lifeless body.

Reg hung his head whispering, "When does 't end, Georgie, when does 't end?"

George's face was full of concern, but he didn't answer his friend, crouching down to gently wrap the woman's body in the cloth. "Help me move her. She deserves better than laying here like this." Reg wiped at his face roughly before kneeling to help finish wrapping the woman. Once that was done, they lifted her as gently as they could, struggling to get the unyielding body through the narrow door. They carried her above deck, crew members crossing themselves as the two men passed.

Once they reached the main deck, they brought her to the stern or back of the ship, unsure of how to get her off with dignity. They set her down gently, making sure the sheet still wrapped around her from head to toe. The crew was also gathering their deceased and making a line of them on the deck. The five bodies were a grim reminder there could have been more casualties, not to mention those lost in the storm when their ropes and knots failed. George's expression was guarded as he gazed at the line of the deceased.

So much loss. He felt the anger simmering under his skin as he looked for the Captain that got them into this mess. They had placed their faith in her and she failed them. He knew his anger was misplaced, but it felt good to direct it somewhere.

He turned his head to watch the remaining crew members as Tamara's words echoed in his head. *And when I look at our people, all I see are ghosts.*

Ice entered his veins as anger turned to shame.

No doubt Cleo and her crew would have their own ghosts to contend with once this was all over. He looked at Reg and asked, "What are we going to do with her?"

Reg glanced at the sheet holding their fallen comrade and sighed. "She woulda been buried in Heimat."

"Aye, burial is the custom, but do we do so here? In the middle of nowhere? We wouldn't be able to direct her son to where she was laid to rest, should he ask for it."

Reg shot him an incredulous look. "We can't keep 'er body, Georgie. Only the Goddess knows when we'll make it back to Heimat." He looked at the body lying next to them. "Her soul deserves rest long before then."

George dropped his head into his hands. Composing himself, he nodded. "Let's go find someone to lower us down."

The two men made their way down to the main deck, beelining to Adams to see about getting help to lower the woman to a place where she could find peace.

The sun was sinking as the crew gathered around the mainmast. The crowd was made of men and women from all parts of Kamore, ranging in color, build, and age. They all looked different on the outside, but their hearts all beat the same. Those that served on the *Vengeance* hungered for adventure and a chance at a better life.

Rae stuck to the shadows along one gunwale, trying to keep a low profile while still being present to pay her respects. She didn't know the crew members of the ship, neither the ones they lost nor the ones still running the ship, yet Rae knew they wouldn't have made it this far without them. They deserved her witness just as much as the young mother from Heimat had.

Shame filled her insides at the thought of the young mother. *I should've tried harder. And then to sleep through the memorial? Despicable.*

Stop. You needed the rest. Rae let out a sigh and glanced toward the river. Both she and Zeke had fallen into the deep sleep associated with life energy restoration. She knew she couldn't change the past, but she could move forward.

As the sun began its finale in its descent, the sky exploding with colors just above the treeline, Rae's head whipped instinctively towards the lanterns hung throughout the main deck.

Clenching her fists and biting her lip, the Crafter closed her eyes and reached within. She had used much of the afternoon wrangling her water Craft into submission, turning it back into a living plait with the currents straining against their confines within the braid. She took a moment to observe the plait, and once satisfied her restraints were holding, Rae looked at the braid containing her fire Craft.

Drawing near to it, she took comfort in the steady warmth and light exuding from the Craft she loved. Using her hands, she coaxed a single line of flame from the plait, gasping as the familiar warmth entered her veins.

Opening her eyes, Rae honed in on the largest of the lanterns on the mainmast. With determination in her eyes, Rae held up one hand, willing a single flame to light the lantern. *Come on Freeman, you can do this.*

Despite her exhaustion, Rae was resolved to prove to herself she still had the skill to light the lanterns without cracking them. Her hands trembled as the memories of lighting the lanterns for the Circus flooded her mind. She winced as thoughts of cracking the glass caused doubt to creep in.

Steadying her hands, she took a deep breath and resumed her focus. Rae bent the fire to her will, letting a small smile show as the main lantern burst into warm light.

Breathing hard, she leaned against the gunwale, letting the joy of victory wash over her. Rae's head pounded, her body protesting the use of her Gift so soon after the storm.

A hand gripped her shoulder, and she looked to her left, meeting Zeke's silver orbs.

"You should slow down before you hurt yourself." His voice was laced with concern.

Rae opened her mouth to respond just as the Captain started. She threw Zeke a look before turning toward the mainmast where Cleo stood.

"We gather tonight to send the souls of our people on their journey with the Prophetess. We lost too many in the storm last night, too many that we loved and depended on. It is time to offer our thoughts and prayers in reverence for their memory and what they meant to us. A moment of silence for the men and women we lost." Cleo bowed her head, pausing for the silence that followed.

Nobody moved a muscle. The only sounds were the creaking of the ship beneath them and the gentle roll of the river. Even the birds seemed to observe the silence for their lost comrades.

The crew and townspeople took a moment to mourn those they lost, their eyes straying to the bodies on the deck.

After a couple of minutes, Cleo continued, "Prophetess, Goddess, and Huntress, three faces for three different sectors of our country. The Prophetess protects those at sea, the Huntress cares for those on the road, and the Goddess Herself takes care of those settled in towns and cities all over Kamore. No matter where you are, you're bound to feel one of Their hands guiding you gently." She paused and made eye contact with some of those in the crowd. "We must trust the Prophetess to protect their spirits on their next journey as She protects us now. Our friends, those from Heimat, buried one of their own earlier today." She inclined her head towards George and Reg. "Prophetess, protect her."

"Prophetess, protect her." The crowd echoed.

Cleo lifted her eyes to the rigging. "We lost Bonnie, Connor, and Jade from the rigging when their ropes failed them. Prophetess, protect them."

The crowd repeated her words. "Prophetess, protect them." A single tear made its way down Mouse's cheek at the loss of her fellow sail tenders.

The Captain's eyes returned to the bodies on the deck. "Leo, Bones, Darren, Lily, and Shark were lost in the wreckage's aftermath. Prophetess, protect them."

"Prophetess, protect them."

The crowd watched as Adams and a couple of other crew members loaded the bodies into one rowboat. Adams and one other crew member joined the deceased in the boat itself before two burly sailors lowered it over the side. Once the boat reached the water, they rowed to the middle of the river, in view of everyone on the ruined ship.

A line of rope kept them from going too far as, one by one, the bodies were gently placed in the river to be swept away.

"Prophetess, take these physical bodies as you've taken their spirits. Take them to a peaceful resting place and give them a home as you did with the others lost from the ship. They worked hard for everything they earned, judge them fairly." Cleo's eyes shifted from the rowboat in the river to the people on her ship. "From the waters of the womb to the waves beneath our feet, the water is where we belong. To the water, we return these wretched souls. So mote it be." She ducked her head in reverence.

"So mote it be." The crowd bowed their heads, uttering the last words for their friends and comrades.

The only sound was the quiet plop of the last body being set in the river. Adams and the crew member sat unmoving, watching the river swallow them whole.

One of the crew members took up a somber melody, an old sailor's tune urging them toward a better place. The melody was haunting, others joining in or remaining silent, just listening.

Rae looped her arm through Zeke's, leaning into his side. Zeke met golden eyes filled with pain. He pulled her close and squeezed her arm, reassuring her they would be okay. Rae felt some of the tension in her shoulders ease a bit with the comfort of her friend. They stood listening as the song ended.

Another minute passed after the song ended, and the only sound in the crisp night was the soft slap of the oars from the rowboat. Adams and the crew member made it to the ship and climbed back aboard, leaving the rowboat in the water.

Rae let exhaustion take over as she slumped next to Zeke. He gently guided her below deck to get the rest she desperately needed.

Chapter Fifteen

Tamara held the Shifter baby in her arms, rocking him and cooing softly. The babe woke several times during the night, reaching for a mother who was no longer there. Judging by the weak light filtering in through the portholes on the side of the ship, Tamara guessed it was just after dawn. Her gaze shifted back to the boy in her arms, fussing despite the comfort she offered.

She sat with the others in the ship's berth, the space below deck filled with hammocks that the crew slept in, still in shock from recent events. Her worst fears had come true and this precious child had no idea how much he'd lost.

Tears welled in her eyes.

It's too much. When will the cycle break? When do the children stop suffering the traumas of the previous generations?

Her thoughts continued their dark spiral despite the promise of new life in her arms. She started when she felt a hand on her shoulder. Whipping her head around, she met Rae's concerned golden eyes.

"I didn't know her very well, but Luna didn't deserve this." The acrobat wrapped the glass Forger in a fierce embrace, careful not to jostle the baby in her arms. "I'm so sorry," Rae whispered, her voice laced with anguish and guilt. Between the chaos and her exhaustion, the Crafter hadn't been able to offer comfort to the older woman.

Tamara hugged her back with one arm, the other holding the little boy. "Don't blame yourself for this. You and Zeke did everything you could to get us through that storm." A tear leaked down her cheek, fire in her eyes. "We never should've kept going. The Captain put us all in danger."

Rae pulled back, releasing Tamara from her embrace, looking the woman in the eye with a frown. "Cleo was doing what she thought was best." Rae's eyes pleaded with the Forger's brown ones to understand. "She didn't want to risk any pursuers catching up with us."

Rae gripped Tamara's free hand. "Tam, the Captain wants to hear what the crew has to say about where we go from here. We should be there even though we're not crew. This is our only chance to influence what happens next. Come with us, and hear Cleo out. She's not as bad as she seems."

Tamara gave Rae a long look, mulling it over in her mind. She gave her a terse nod before rising to find someone to take the baby. Leaving him with one of the other adults, Tamara followed Rae to the main deck of the ship.

The crew was gathered around the quarterdeck, with Cleo and Adams watching from the helm, where the wheel of the ship sat.

George, Reg, and Zeke stood to one side, looking out of place among the sailors. Cleo watched them with hooded eyes, seeming as if she wanted to say something, but deciding against it. She turned her gaze to the crew she loved more like family. Rae and Tamara made their way to their companions as Cleo began.

"Thank you for being here. We gave a beautiful tribute to the ones we lost last night." She stared at the flowing waters of the river and sighed. "The storm took them too soon because I led them and all of you into danger. I gambled with our lives and we lost. I will hold this failure inside my heart forever." She stroked the wood beneath her fingers. "Some of you will always hate me for what happened, but I can't change the past. My decision came down to risking the lives of some or all, should Bartholomew be on our tail. I did what was best for all of us."

Cleo's green eyes were hard as she swept them over the gathered crew. She demonstrated the steel in her spine as she stood under the judgment of those that served her.

"We needed to push ourselves to the limits to ensure we outran anyone pursuing us. We shouldn't have lost the ones we did, but now we need to move forward so their sacrifices were not in vain." She cast a glance at the Magicae and Mortals standing in the corner. "We wouldn't have made it as far as we did without the Magicae battling the storm for as long as they did. Our next step is traveling to Lockewater, where I intend to employ as many Magicae that will join us on the next adventure."

Whispers ran rampant through the gathered crew. Rae shared a shocked look with Zeke while Reg murmured something in George's ear.

"It's time to put prejudice aside and do what's best for the ship. Grumble all you want, but these are my intentions. The only thing left to decide is how to get to Lockewater. Once we get there, you are free to go your separate ways, but until then, you are still part of this crew. And I want to hear your thoughts on whether we patch the ship and limp along until Lockewater, or abandon the *Vengeance* and travel by foot." Her green eyes surveyed the crowd, taking in her crew and the people they transported.

Members of the crew shared looks. Many of them had grown up in Heimat, so adding Magicae to their midst was not unheard of. But those that weren't familiar with the integrated city grew uneasy at the thought of bringing them into their family. They all knew about and tolerated the integration in Heimat, but the thought of doing so on the *Vengeance* was another story. They would need time to process all this.

"Storms happen, Cap. We all knew what we were getting into when we joined this life." Mouse spoke up from her spot in the rigging. "You've always been equitable to those in your service. As long as the Magicae you add are pretty to look at, I'm all for it." She finished with a wink.

Affirmations and chuckles sounded in the crowd, accompanied by the grumbling of the ones still blaming Cleo for losing their comrades. Tensions ran high between those wanting to give Cleo another chance and those ready to replace her with someone like Adams. But nobody could deny her strength in owning up to her faults while making plans to move forward. A captain's vision was the tipping point between a crew sharing a purpose to fulfill it or replacing the captain for a better vision.

The first mate of the vessel stood next to his Captain, knowing some of the crew were whispering about putting him in charge. He thumped his chest and gave Cleo a salute, glaring at anyone that spoke against her.

"I have crewed with Cleo for almost a decade now, and she deserves nothing but loyalty. She's the Captain, and she made a hard call that lost lives, but that will be her burden to bear. And now, she's asking you to be better for the good of all. You don't like it? There's your exit. Get out of my sight before you say something you'll regret." Adams seethed, pointing to the riverbank, his eyes like steel.

Cleo shot him a look of appreciation before moving to lean against the edge of the quarterdeck overlooking her people. She crossed her arms before nodding for her crew to talk. She made Adams go first, sharing his thoughts about what their next steps should be.

While Adams talked about getting the *Vengeance* to Lockewater, Rae placed a hand on Tamara's arm, guiding her to the edge of the crowd. She lowered her voice, asking, "What do you think Tam? You and Reg know our people better than anyone. Would the children fare better on a broken ship or taking the jungle trail?"

Tamara sucked on her cheek as she considered. Her eyes looked tired when she finally answered the fire Crafter. "As much as we'd like to get off this boat, I don't think it would be wise to go into the forest without a direction or necessary supplies." She furrowed her brows as she did a double take on the group of men to their right. "Where's Bane? Is he alright? I know someone said he had been scouting, but shouldn't he be back by now?" She shot Rae a worried look.

A pit formed at the bottom of Rae's stomach as she searched the crowd for the stocky Shifter. Her wild eyes found Zeke, and he immediately moved toward her. Rae put a hand over her mouth and racked her brain for those last moments before she passed out in the storm. *He came from behind us. He Shifted and gave us some of his life energy.*

Rae let out a cry when she realized Bane hadn't been wearing a rope. That was the only explanation she could think of. The Shifter's absence had been explained away as a scouting expedition, but Rae hadn't stopped to think between her exhaustion and the events after the crash.

"Zeke, Bane's still not back," Rae told her friend as he placed a hand on her shoulder. Tamara touched Rae on the back before heading to George and Reg, noting the concerned looks on their faces. She would fill them in while Rae and Zeke talked.

Zeke furrowed his brows as horror dawned on his face. "I didn't stop to think." His face paled. "Sparks, I saw him go over the edge when we crashed. He hit his head…" The acrobat dropped his hand from Rae's shoulder, the gravity of the situation weighing on him. "There's no way he could've Shifted after using all that energy to help us. We need to find him."

Without wasting another breath, Zeke took off at a run for the rope ladder and the man he cared for.

Rae motioned for the three leaders from Heimat to follow before taking off after him. She pushed the guilt down, recognizing all that mattered now was taking action.

She scaled down the ladder as swiftly as possible, knowing she would do everything she could to find the man who risked everything for them.

Chapter Sixteen

Luc brushed the stray hairs out of her face as she walked in silence. She chanced a glance at the men and women on horseback surrounding them. They were stoic in their duty, escorting the Circus and their new recruits to Huntress knew where. Luc took note that none of them cracked a smile or uttered a word.

The woman who attacked them was the only one who spoke. After taking Duncan hostage, she ordered all of them to dismount and make their way into the darkness of the forest. The woman's people flanked Luc and the other members of the Circus as they made their way down a game path hidden by the foliage of the forest.

The young and old were instructed to get out of the wagons and either walk or ride the horses the others had dismounted from, leaving the wagons and their supplies abandoned in the trees. They were ahead of the walkers, separated by a line of the mysterious riders escorting them. Luc's gaze wandered to her Abuela's hunched form, praying she would be okay.

Damien noted the direction of her gaze and bumped her shoulder before squeezing her hand out of the eyesight of their captors. Luc shot him an appreciative glance.

At least Damien is still here. She thanked the Huntress they hadn't separated them further. *And Javie is still with Abuela.*

Javie rode Luc's mare next to their Abuela, having convinced the strange men and women he walked with a limp and needed to ride. Nobody in the Circus questioned the young man, happy to have him among the vulnerable.

Luc had lost sight of Duncan, Tyee, and the Shifters when they dismounted and were herded with the other walkers. She could only hope they were okay.

The strange group of people led them deeper and deeper into the forest, the chill in the air less intense with the increased protection from the wind. Slowly, the trees thinned out as the sun drifted lower in the sky. Anxiety crept into Luc's chest as the shadows grew longer and her fear of the unknown announced its presence. She tightened her grip on Damien's hand and swiveled her head from side to side, trying to remain as vigilant as possible.

Luc couldn't hide her sigh of relief when a soft glow lit the trail up ahead. As they got closer, lanterns now lined the path they traveled. Luc's relief was quickly overwhelmed by her curiosity as the sounds of civilization became louder and louder. She cast a questioning look at Damien as the sounds of crackling fires, children's laughter, and animals making indistinct noises reached their group.

Luc's ears perked up and her eyes widened in amazement as they came upon a row of houses up in the trees, connected by wooden bridges and buzzing with life. They were like giant treehouses made in harmony with the trees themselves. Luc felt her jaw slack as she studied the structures, dumbfounded by their beauty and intricacy.

Each house was unique in its construction. Some were simply structures built on top of the tree branches, with trunks spurting out of the top and bottom. Others looked as if someone had coaxed the trunk itself to widen and form windows and doors.

It was a feat of engineering and architecture that each house comprised different shapes, colors, and sizes. The last one she noticed was covered in flowers and vines, forming a tapestry of color and texture on the modest structure.

Beautiful. That was all Luc could think of as she took in the community that lived amongst the trees.

The people up above went about their lives, only stopping to stare at the caravan of newcomers being led into their settlement. They wore the same mottled leathers as the ones that captured them but showed more varied styles. The people in the trees were not restricted to the tight leathers more suitable for combat, and they wore flowing shirts and dresses, long coats, and slouched breeches.

The people themselves had high-angled cheekbones and were slight in stature. Most were sun-kissed with dark hair, the occasional redhead and blond mixed in. She caught the sound of a strange language on the wind and realized these people were not part of the world she was raised in. Her mouth hung open as her eyes darted back and forth, trying to take in everything they could.

"Damien, what is this place?" she asked, still taking in the city in the trees.

"I have no idea," Damien answered in a murmur, eyeing the strange people with suspicion. "Stay close to me, amor. I have a bad feeling about this."

Still lost in the novelty of living amongst the trees, Luc placed a hand on Damien's arm. "Don't be paranoid, there are children up there. This is an entire world untouched by Kamore and Myra. Damien, look!" She pointed to one tree in particular, her eyes sparkling as she watched a young boy place a hand on it, energy pulsing from him to the tree he touched, causing new buds to form on the branch.

A couple of their captors shared a look and shifted uneasily in their saddles, unsure of leading so many strangers to their door. They never uttered a word, blank looks still plastered on their faces.

Lanterns lined the path and were strung in the trees themselves, twinkling as the breeze blew through the leaves. The path they followed on the ground ran parallel to what became two paths up above. Rope ladders were strung between large and small trees; frequently, the ladders were replaced with handrails, and the limbs of the trees became the path.

Luc craned her neck, trying to get a better look at where the paths converged and formed a platform around the largest oak tree she'd ever seen. It was where the most noise was coming from as people hustled in and out of the massive structure. This building seemed to have elements of both types of architecture. A roof stuck out from the tree's trunk, forming a front porch of sorts around its entirety while the trunk itself widened at the top before devolving into walls made by hand, creating a structure much bigger than the tree could on its own.

Before Luc could satisfy her curiosity, their captors turned in the opposite direction of the central hub of the city in the trees.

The members of the Circus stayed quiet as they were directed to the southern part of the unusual city. The old and the young on horseback were taken to an area of paddocks filled with livestock, and the smaller horses preferred by those escorting them, while the walkers were taken to what seemed like an amphitheater out of sight from the people in the trees.

Rows of wooden benches sat in a semi-circle facing a platform slightly recessed into the ground. Each line of benches was more recessed as they got closer to the center platform. Their captors gestured for them to fill the seats before standing guard nearby.

Luc tried to keep track of where her Abuela and Javie went but lost sight of them when they were sent to the benches. Two men carried a limp form to the platform and dumped it unceremoniously to the ground.

Luc inhaled sharply when she recognized Duncan's purple coat and mop of brown hair. His hands and feet were bound as he lay motionless in front of his people. Luc couldn't look away until she saw the imperceptible movement of his chest rising and falling. Relief filled her veins, knowing their Ringmaster still lived despite the beating he had taken.

"Poor Duncan. We should do something," Luc said as she stood up. Monitoring those standing guard, she moved to the end of her row, only looking back to make sure Damien followed. She met Jess's defeated gaze and jerked her chin towards the unconscious wind Crafter. Jess nodded, moving to the opposite side of her row and waiting for her opportunity. Luc and Damien did the same on their side, hoping at least one of them would make it to the bruised man.

Damien pulled Luc close and tucked her under his arm, whispering for her to trust him under his breath. Luc leaned into him, following his lead. He used a hand to gently lift her chin, giving her a long, slow kiss. Despite the act they were putting on, Luc felt tingles at the emotion behind Damien's lips. She loved him with all her heart, and knowing he felt the same was the most magical thing in the world.

Focus, Luc. She chided herself, turning her ears to the world beyond the two of them.

Their lips still locked, Damien guided them a little closer to the platform. Luc felt him take a glance at the Head Forger before dipping her. Luc laughed in surprise but got cut off as Damien deepened the kiss.

"Wow. Ten minutes in the woods and they're already savages." A cruel voice cut through the air like a blade.

Anger flared in Luc's chest as Damien lifted her back up. *If you want a show, I'll give you a show.* She gripped the back of his neck and held the kiss longer, daring the woman to say something else. Several moments later, she broke the kiss and made eye contact with the woman who put them in this position. She was watching, as Luc knew she would be, so the acrobat sent their tormentor a knowing smirk.

Luc had dealt with the jealousy of others for as long as she could remember. Usually, she ignored it or tried to make the person feel better, but not this time. She wanted to make that woman as uncomfortable as possible. She noted the way the woman shifted from one foot to the other before stalking toward the platform.

Damien pulled Luc with him as he sat down on the closest bench, eyes never leaving the dangerous woman. Luc's smirk turned to a scowl as the woman nudged Duncan's still form with her foot. A groan sounded from the platform as Duncan stirred.

Jess made it to the front while all eyes were on Luc and Damien, but crouched behind the back of the wooden structure when she saw the woman making her way toward Duncan. The Ringmaster's groan awoke her rage and feelings of helplessness. Jess stood and launched herself at the slight warrior with a guttural cry, tackling her to the ground.

The members of the Circus stared in shock, paralyzed by fear. Their guards moved swiftly, aiding their commander.

Jess got a few punches in before she was dragged off of the dark-haired woman, both panting with effort.

"Sylvia! What is the meaning of this?" A booming voice demanded as a hooded figure strode down the middle walkway between the benches.

The woman straightened quickly and adjusted her armor. She kept her chin high but stood at attention. "Ma'am. I found these outsiders on the outskirts of the Farm. They needed to be brought in for questioning."

Reaching the platform, the figure pushed their hood back to reveal a weathered old woman with gray hair tied back into a high bun and a stern look on her face. Her eyes narrowed as she focused on the younger woman. "You are a fool, General. What questioning is worth bringing them to our back door? You led them to our haven with no blindfolds or hoods. How dare you claim them as threats when you do nothing to protect our people from their retaliation." She berated the woman with a hiss while the guards stood stoically. Her eyes glanced at Duncan on the ground. "Is this their leader?"

"I believe so, Your Grace."

The older woman shot her an incredulous look. "You mean to say your reconnaissance is incomplete?" She pursed her lips. "Honestly, Sylvia. This is not a game. When I was your age, I led a single squadron against an entire army and won. Your arrogance is going to get our people killed." She gave the younger woman one last withering look. "You are dismissed. Report to the Barracks and stay there until you are summoned."

Sylvia gave a half bow and marched to the outskirts of the strange settlement.

Luc and Damien shared a look.

Uneasy relief settled on their shoulders, realizing they wouldn't have to deal with the savage general. Luc studied the older woman, noting her unyielding lines and the tension in her shoulders. She seemed harsh but fair, only time would tell.

The older woman looked to the guards holding Jess and jutted her chin towards the front benches. They escorted the Head Forger to a sitting position before returning to stand at attention by their leader. Luc furrowed her brows when they moved to untie Duncan after a look from the old woman. *What the hell is going on?*

Her chocolate brown eyes watched the guards shift Duncan, so he sat next to Jess. The Forger lent her strength to their leader as he came to.

Luc wrung her hands, the anxiety creeping in with the enormity of the situation they found themselves in.

When did it all go so wrong? She thought to herself, thinking back to Heimat and Windemere and Tiva.

Tiva...

That's when everything went wrong. The scouts sent word back to hurry, but we didn't make it in time. Luc pursed her lips before her eyes widened. *That's when Rae lost control, too. Everything started with Tiva.*

Luc was roused from her thoughts when she realized the strange woman was addressing their group.

"—Again, my humble apologies for the treatment you received from my overzealous General. Please, make yourself comfortable until your leader and I discuss where we go from here." The woman on the platform made to turn when a voice spoke up.

"And what of our people that need healing?" Chiara stood from her spot next to Freya and Gar, making her way to the aisle, her steely gaze never leaving the woman.

The strange woman met Chiara's gaze with her own, never flinching. "You have my assurances our healers are looking them over as we speak."

"No, I think we should have our Herbalists look them over." Chiara pushed, lifting her chin and squaring her shoulders. "Just point us to the infirmary. Most of our supplies are with the wagons, but we'll make do with what we have on our persons."

The woman studied Chiara closely. "I take it you're in charge of these Herbalists?" She waited for Damien's mother to incline her head before continuing, "You may choose one other to come with you. I will escort you there myself."

Chiara didn't hesitate, turning to Freya with a questioning look. Freya stood and walked with her mentor down the center aisle to the platform. Both Healers followed the strange woman away from the amphitheater, guards flanking them as they left.

Luc turned to Damien and whispered, "I completely zoned. What did that woman say?"

Damien gave her a look and shook his head, not believing her daftness.

Luc poked his side. "Come on, Dame, I'm serious."

He snorted. "That, my dear, was Queen Ulla, warrior queen of the Elven, and this is their city in the trees, Verdencia."

Luc's jaw dropped in shock.

Tyee woke with a start, jolting against the restraints on his arms and legs. He struggled for a few minutes before relaxing his limbs; the feeling returning to them with prickling sensations. He forced himself to take a deep breath, watching his exhale form smoke in the cold room he found himself in. Pushing again on the bonds, he realized they were too strong to remove by force. He squinted his eyes against the darkness of the room, only a single candle flickering in the corner.

The adrenaline in his body slowly dissipated, lowering his frantic heartbeat and returning the pounding to his head. He closed his eyes as the feeling and soreness came back to his limbs. He took a deep breath, trying to calm the thoughts racing through his mind.

He needed a clear head to think through his next moves. Tyee had been in worse situations before. He could get out of this one with some creative thinking.

If only the pain in his head would go away.

Who the fuck was that woman? She looked so familiar. Tyee looked at the flame from the candle as a shiver went through his body. He could still picture those dark eyes glittering with challenge, the lithe woman sitting astride Koko.

Shit. He remembered exactly where he'd seen those eyes before.

Memories flashed through his mind. Waking up to a dagger at his throat. Sparring in the forest. Midnight gallops on the ridge. Spending all night in the hayloft.

It had to be Sylvie.

Her hair was cut short and dyed blond when he met her, her face a little rounder, but those eyes.

She called me Stableboy. He remembered the voice in his head and the way she rummaged through his mind like a thief scrambling through a rich man's house.

He winced, his head throbbing with greater intensity as he remembered the intrusion. It had to be the woman that changed the course of his life forever.

She was the one that pushed him to take Koko before the sale could go through. She refused to sell him the horse he loved more than anything and then promised the stallion to a man on the other side of Kamore. Tyee had no choice but to steal the horse and flee, shattering the world he made for himself.

Koko.

Tyee struggled against his restraints once more, putting more muscle into it, and cursing the fibers that held him. He raged, thinking about the beautiful horse he'd risked so much for. Koko meant everything to him.

If Sylvie hurt the midnight stallion...

"Just as stubborn as I remember." A voice drawled in the darkness.

Tyee strained one more time, letting out a frustrated cry, before staring in the voice's direction, and trying to see the woman he once knew.

The candle on the desk winked out as symbols glowed on the staff Sylvie used when she attacked them. His eyes followed the glowing symbols as they whirred through the air in a figure eight.

Suddenly a lantern lighted, blinding Tyee momentarily. When he could see once more, the glow from the lantern illuminated the woman's feral smile.

"Nothing to say, Stableboy? So unlike you." She raised her eyebrows at the incapacitated horseman. She smiled wider, showing more of her teeth.

Would you rather we speak like this?

Tyee writhed in pain as claws shredded his mind once more. He screamed and flailed against his bonds until he wore himself out, his throat raw and raspy.

A dark chuckle came from his captor. "Guess not. I'll just tuck that tidbit away for later," she drawled, running a finger down one of his bare arms. She crouched behind his head out of his sight line and put her lips to his ear. "We have a lot to discuss, Ty. Best get ready to talk."

Her cackle was the last thing Tyee heard before he passed out yet again.

Chiara was frustrated. She'd asked three different times when she could see Tyee. He was the last of the injured unaccounted for.

Queen Ulla took her and Freya to the infirmary before disappearing, not staying to answer questions. She understood the Queen had things to do, but taking hundreds of people captive should've been a top priority.

In her opinion, that was.

Chiara sighed. The lessons of hospitality her mother drilled into her as a child still ran deep. Courtesy wasn't what it once was, in this era after the Uprising. If Myra was good at anything, it was spreading paranoia and fear in the hearts of almost anyone.

The Elven in the infirmary were nice enough, just useless in telling her where she could find the horseman. They had offered free rein of their cabinets for any supplies the Healers needed before talking them through what they'd done in caring for their injured.

Nymeria, Conrad, and J were set up in beds, conscious but still weak from the fight with Sylvia. Her forcing them to Shift wreaked havoc on their systems, but their levels of life energy were stable now, thanks to the Elven, and steadily rising. Chiara was hopeful they would make a full recovery by morning.

Her mind strayed to Duncan and the thrashing he received in front of everyone. Chiara's brows furrowed as she sucked on her cheek. He was conscious when she left, and she could only hope Nan would check him out.

If the group of walkers were reunited with the riders, that was.

Chiara shook her head.

Negative thoughts never get you anywhere in life. Another one of her mother's lessons.

There were a couple of children also in the infirmary. One with an upset stomach and another with a gnarly scratch on his forehead. They were being given the utmost care by the Elven and seemed less shaken by a race thought to have been deceased for hundreds of years.

A small smile tugged at the corner of her mouth. Children were amazingly resilient when given the chance.

The sound of crashing feet broke through her reverie. She looked at the door to the infirmary and was surprised to see Eva, J's performance partner and ward, and Wren, the newly recruited Crafter, barreling inside.

"Where's J?" Eva asked, panting, her eyes frantic as she scanned the beds.

She didn't wait for an answer as she started weaving in and out of the rows of beds, looking for the man who had looked out for her since she joined the Circus. Wren tagged along, following right at her heels with brown curls bouncing behind her.

Chiara strode toward the pair. Putting her hands on Eva's shoulders, she gently turned the young girl towards J's bed.

Eva didn't hesitate and lunged for the mentor she loved. She threw her arms around him, sobbing quietly. J woke with a start, but quickly gathered the girl in his arms, patting her back and gently rocking her. He held one arm out towards Wren and smiled slightly when the little girl climbed into his arms as well. The gentle Shifter stroked their backs and murmured comforting words in their ears. The two girls saw him get hurt and were wracked with worry ever since.

Chiara could see the tension leave Eva's whole body as she cried, relieved to be reunited with her protector. It warmed the Herbalist's heart to see them together. She felt some of the anxiety in her chest ease as she watched the three.

She studied the young Crafter. It was clear she also found comfort in J, but their bond was not as close as that of J and Eva. It amazed Chiara the way Wren stuck to Eva from the get-go. Eva was a quiet one, preferring J to the company of the other children. The fact she was sharing the Shifter with the newcomer said a lot about how close the two girls were already.

She hoped they had time to be kids before the drums of war sounded. She wasn't sure what J would do when the time came to decide whether to stay or fight. His abilities would be an asset to either the front lines or the home front. She hoped he chose the home front, looking at the way those girls clung to him.

She cocked her head as she considered Wren. Most of the caravan assumed she was a water Crafter because of her sapphire eyes. No matter how many times you informed the masses, trends would always lead to assumptions.

Water Crafters were rare in the sense that many of them could hide in plain sight with deep blue or green eyes, but more tragically, few were Gifted each generation. The water Craft seemed to only manifest in every two generations instead of every other or almost every generation like fire or wind Crafts. The water Craft skipped two and the earth Craft skipped three generations at a time. Finding Crafters with water and earth Crafts was essential to keeping the collective knowledge of each Craft alive for the younger ones.

Wren could prove crucial for storing the knowledge of controlling the waters of Kamore if she was a water Crafter and had the chance to develop her skills.

Chiara's attention was drawn to the doorway. The guard they pressed for information on Tyee stood in the doorway, locked in conversation with one healer. Chiara watched the Elven healer closely, scanning his face for evidence Tyee was okay. Her stomach dropped as the healer's face contorted, eyebrows drawn, and lips pursed.

She had a feeling this would not go very well.

Squaring her shoulders, she made her way to the doorway, motioning for Freya to stay with the Shifters and children. The two Elven noticed her coming and shared a look before the guard left the infirmary in a huff. The healer met her eyes, but his were filled with apology. She lifted her hand, stopping him before he could speak.

"Let's talk outside," she said, inclining her head towards the open air. The man obliged, holding the door for her.

Chiara stepped outside the massive wooden structure holding almost twenty beds and the corresponding supplies onto a wide wooden porch. Like all the buildings in the Elven stronghold, the infirmary was in an oak tree, high above the path below.

Chiara walked to the railing, taking in the city of Verdencia. The infirmary was on one end of the city, out of the way of most of the traffic, but close enough to the primary hub that Chiara could observe from a distance.

She took special note of the gathering place in the middle of the city. It was the largest structure among the trees and seemed to be the place where the Elven congregated. Chiara could only guess at what the inside of the structure contained, but she surmised it was some sort of market or dining hall.

Children laughing, friends sharing drinks, and singing could be heard as all manner of Elven flitted across wooden walkways and up and down rope ladders. She couldn't help but think, this is what their people needed.

A home.

Somewhere safe they could gather and grow and *thrive.*

Chiara turned when she caught a movement in the corner of her eye. The healer watched her closely, that apologetic and helpless look still in his eyes.

"Do they know where he is?" she asked.

The Elven healer shifted from one foot to the other before hanging his head. "The guard said she didn't find him in the prison cells or at the barracks." He paused as if deciding whether to say more. She raised one eyebrow, motioning for him to continue. He gulped but made his decision. "The General is also missing. She was supposed to be at the Barracks, but the guard couldn't find her."

He took a moment to glance around them, making sure no one was in earshot. Despite them being alone, he lowered his voice and continued, "There are rumors the General has… colorful ways of dealing with certain intruders. If I were to hazard a guess, I would check the northern rock formations. Just follow the game trail at the edge of the trees north and west. There are a couple of caves that can hold prisoners." Pain filled his eyes. "The General is extreme. She's kept us safe for many years, but you can't treat innocent people like this. Don't judge my people by her alone."

Chiara gripped his shoulder and looked deep into his eyes. "I won't." She squeezed, saying, "Thank you. This means a lot. Will you do me one more favor and tell my friend in there I will be right back?"

When he nodded, Chiara hurried to the nearest ladder.

She needed to talk to Duncan.

Chapter Seventeen

Bane's limbs felt like lead.

He laid on the ground with the back half of his body in the water. He knew he needed to get up, but couldn't bring himself to do so. The sweet release of oblivion beckoned as he forced his eyes open. His head spun as he struggled to get his bearings. The Shifter remembered seeing that ship, making it back to the *Vengeance;* he remembered lending his life energy to Rae and Zeke...

Damn, we lost it. My energy wasn't enough for them to control the storm.

He reached for more air, feeling a burning in his chest. He gasped, remembering being thrown into the gunwale and over the side of the ship.

Huntress. No wonder my head hurts and my body doesn't want to respond.

He took a moment to assess his limbs and torso. The young man knew he had Shifted. His life energy always felt different when he was in an animal form. His limbs and body felt different too, but the energy impacted Bane the most.

Shifting into a falcon, being able to fly and escape the shackles of this world, was pure ecstasy. He loved the freedom, the simplicity, and the power he felt in his veins. Shifter energy was purely primal and being in an animal form gave it free rein.

But something felt different about the way his life energy thrummed in his veins.

It was as powerful as ever, but it had an edge to it he couldn't quite place. He moved his focus to his limbs, narrowing his eyes when he realized they weren't wings.

Fear formed a knot in his belly. There were ancient stories of Shifters getting stuck in forms that weren't theirs. Pushing the Gift to do something unnatural always resulted in devastating consequences.

Bane knew it would be several hours before his energy would let him Shift again. If he could.

This restraint kept their power in check, limiting the number of times an individual could Shift also limited the injuries caused by mishaps. Physically changing bone densities, muscle mass, entire joint structures and the like was not for the faint of heart.

Power thrummed through his veins, but it was useless until he had the strength to Shift back into something he recognized.

Bane's thoughts wandered as he waited. It always perplexed him how little other Magicae knew about Shifting. Mortals were a lost cause, being so many of them feared any of those with Gifts, and could not get past the power to recognize the humanity within. But even among the Magicae, not much knowledge was passed between the different Gifts. The Circus included those of every Gift and Bane could count on one hand how many conversations he'd had with others about their Gifts and what it meant to use them.

He blew air out of his nostrils.

He was just as guilty as those he accused of not seeing him for who he truly was.

Bane knew his situation was special, being that the Shifters of the Circus truly had little interaction with the others while on the road. Being a bird made it hard to hold a conversation about Crafting with Rae or creating a Healing tonic with Nan.

Bane let those thoughts and regrets go, exploring the body he found himself in. He ran his tongue along rows and rows of sharp teeth, his snout long and thin. He could feel he had a tail, a large one, full of muscle. Bane thrashed it twice, pushing himself further into the riverbank.

Bane racked his brain for what animal he could be, keeping the panic of never flying again deep inside.

He wiggled his toes and felt five short digits with claws. His eyes were open, but he couldn't make sense of what he was seeing. He adjusted his head but couldn't get a view of himself. He closed his eyelids, shocked when he found he had three of them.

Finally realizing his eyes must be positioned on top of his head, he opened all of his eyelids again, taking in the surrounding scenery. Sure enough, he could see the riverbank in its entirety, a small piece of his snout in his eyesight.

Interesting.

It clicked in his head as he played with shutting different eyelids, one at a time. He moved his limbs back and forth, trying to drag himself further up the riverbank. The sun was starting its descent, meaning he shouldn't have to worry about heat rash before he could attempt to leave the ancient reptilian form he found himself in.

His lumbering body still felt like lead, but the panic in his chest receded a little. Patience was the greatest lesson a Shifter could learn from their animal counterpart.

Nature moved at a slower, more sustainable pace. Emulating that pace, Bane knew, would be the key to unlocking whatever the storm had done with his Gift.

Time would tell whether Bane could leave the form he found himself in, and nothing he could do would change that.

All he could do was wait.

Gemma sat next to some of the other children on the floor of the berth of the ship. She stayed quiet, hoping everyone would forget about her. All she wanted was to disappear and, then, maybe the nightmare would end.

She pictured her mother's face, and the tears started flowing.

The young girl still didn't understand why her Momma sent her away. She had been a good girl and always stayed quiet when the bad people were around.

She wanted to go home.

Why did her Momma give her to these strangers? Why couldn't she have stayed with Momma and Daddy?

She rubbed at her eyes, trying to stay quiet, not wanting anyone to notice her distress. She willed the power inside to stay subdued despite the emotions roiling within.

These people were nice enough, but they were strangers. They weren't her Momma or Daddy nor were they the people her Momma gave her to. She couldn't help but think of the nice man with the ovens and treats.

She hoped he was okay. He reminded her of the Grandaddy she met once, years ago. The baker had the same crinkly eyes as her Grandaddy. That was how she knew she could trust him.

She squeezed her eyes shut, trying to keep the memories of that day away.

It was the worst one of her young life.

The smoke that filled her nose, the screaming in her ears, and the hurt she saw before she closed her eyes and burrowed into the woman's shoulder. It was all imprinted on her brain, chasing her from sleep and threatening to overwhelm her.

But nothing was as devastating as what she knew in her heart to be true. Gemma realized the woman that carried her hadn't made it, but if she pretended, she could act like the woman was still in the bakery with her crinkly-eyed daddy.

Gemma knew about death and had been to several funerals in her life for distant relatives or government officials. But death was a hard concept for anyone to wrap their brains around. The young girl couldn't even fathom losing the light cast by the person who died.

Her heart was hurting. That's all she knew.

The adults were busy with the baby and the other younger children. Some of the older children played games with sticks and stones to one side. Gemma's eyes flew open, a new purpose set behind those blue-gray eyes.

The little girl with copper curls studied the layout of the chamber beneath the decks, determining the route she could take to the ladder that was out of the sight line of the adults.

She'd return to her Momma if it was the last thing she did.

Gemma knew she couldn't make everything right, but she could find her way back to the woman who brought her life. She just wanted to hear her Momma call her wildflower one more time.

She pulled a hood over her head and hugged her coat tight. She melted into the shadows, careful to make her steps silent as she maneuvered to the ladder that would take her above. Gemma knew she'd have to assess the deck once she got there, but she needed to get up the ladder unseen first.

The boards let out a loud squeak beneath one foot.

Gemma froze. She watched two of the older children and one adult look her way, and her little heart skipped a beat. Tears of frustration welled in her eyes, but she stayed still. She was so close.

The Shifter baby let out a wail, turning all attention to him.

Gemma let out the breath she was holding and used the distraction to make it to the ladder. While the baby screamed, she climbed the ladder quickly until she was out of sight of even the older children. She paused when she reached the top, blinking at the sudden sunlight, willing her eyes to adjust.

The young Herbalist peeked her head cautiously over the railing separating her from the rest of the ship. She ducked down when she saw some of the crowd split and run towards the wall of the ship.

Peeking back over, Gemma recognized the people who led them to the ship. They quickly left the ship, haggard expressions on their faces. Her eyes caught on the blond woman, the one who could control the elements.

The little girl was intimidated by the powerful Crafter. Her Daddy always told her magic could not be trusted. That was why her Momma made her stay quiet about what she could do with the plants. She didn't want her Daddy not to trust her, so she kept the secret between her and her mother.

Crafters were the most dangerous, according to her Daddy.

They could lose control as easily as she could drop a dish that was too heavy. But the woman was beautiful. And she saved everyone from the bad men. How could someone like that be dangerous? Gemma shook her head, spilling those thoughts from her mind. She was on a mission and needed to focus. She turned to the crowd around the Captain and her first mate. The adults were engrossed in their conversation.

This was her chance.

Gemma pulled herself over the railing and crouched behind it, poking her head out to make sure nobody was looking her way. Satisfied the crew was busy, she looked towards the forest.

The power running through her veins leaped at the sight of the greenery. Her blood hummed after being stuck inside the officers' quarters for so long. It made her head dizzy, so she forced her gaze from the forest to the beach, searching for the five adults who left in a hurry.

Not seeing anyone, she glanced at the crowd one last time before rushing to the spot the adults used to get over the edge. She lifted herself over, found the rope ladder, and climbed down to the sand.

The tide came in, drenching her shoes and the bottom of her pants.

She clamped a hand over her mouth to stifle the reflexive shriek elicited by the cold water. After the shock from the cold, all Gemma could feel was elation. She did it.

Now she needed to find a way back to the city they came from.

The young Herbalist sprinted towards the trees, water splashing around her as her feet pounded a steady rhythm to where her power called her. With one last look at the ship, Gemma disappeared into the trees.

And crashed into the back of a pair of legs.

Gemma flew, landing on her backside, while the person she ran into turned around.

The little girl looked into eyes of gold and took off as quick as she could to the right, disappearing into the underbrush. Her little heart raced as she pumped her legs, reaching blindly with her power, willing it to help stop any pursuit.

She didn't bother looking back, trying to stay as focused as possible on getting away.

Her ears caught the sound of light footsteps behind her, so Gemma darted to the right again, heading back to the riverbank. If she could run fast enough, maybe she could lose the Crafter running after her.

Gemma reached a break in the trees, her breathing coming in quick gasps while her legs were on fire. She willed them to pump faster.

The little girl lost her footing as she realized, too late, she was at the top of a sandy hill leading down to the river. Gemma tumbled, landing in a heap near the rushing water.

Rae cursed the Huntress as she chased after the little girl. When the first tree branches scratched her face, she recognized the curls of Vincenzio's daughter. She let out a growl and used the wind to move them out of her way.

Shit. She overran, trying to cut in front of the little girl, just to watch the Herbalist cut back to the river. *Clever girl.*

Rae couldn't help but admire the young girl's spirit, despite the wrench it threw in her plan to find Bane. She was supposed to be searching her quadrant of trees but now had to chase after the runaway. The only question being, why was Vincenzio's daughter running?

Rae sped after the little girl, focusing on stopping her. The sooner she caught the Herbalist, the sooner she could go back to looking for her friend.

Rae crashed through the trees, seeing Gemma lose her footing and disappear out of sight. The Crafter caught herself just in time, recognizing the hill for what it was.

She searched the riverbank, relief settling on her shoulders when she found the little girl in a heap, but safe from the roar of the river.

Her heart stopped when she saw the large alligator only meters from the knocked-out Herbalist. Without thinking, she propelled herself down the bank, calling her fire instinctively. She didn't want to hurt the creature, but wouldn't hesitate should it prove aggressive. Regardless of why the copper-curled girl was running, she didn't deserve to get hurt like that.

Rae kept a wary eye on the large reptile while she knelt to shake the little girl. The alligator moved slightly, angling its head towards them but didn't move closer.

"Gemma," Rae whispered, shaking a little harder. "Gemma! You gotta wake up, bud. We need to leave this nice guy's habitat."

Rae's eyes flashed back to the alligator, hearing the beast thrash its tail violently as if it was trying to get her attention. She furrowed her brows as she watched the peculiar creature. She was struck by its size and the way it laid in the sun despite the heat. Most reptiles she'd encountered in her life preferred the early morning sun, disappearing into the mud or water for the heat of the day.

Something seemed strange. She'd never seen one so far north before either, alligators preferred the warm temperatures of the south to the cold winters of the north.

This large reptile was unnatural.

Rae scanned the riverbank and the tree line across the river, looking for danger. Her ears perked to catch the slightest of sounds, she shifted her gaze back to the trees on her side of the river and doused the fire in her hands.

Only the wind blew through the trees as Rae picked up Gemma, an eerie feeling pushing her to get moving regardless of whether the little girl woke up.

A rattling sound caused her to look back at the giant reptile.

He seemed to clack his teeth together, staring straight at her. He held his ground, not making any moves toward her, just chattering his teeth at her.

Rae frowned, trying to pinpoint why the movement was so familiar. Her eyes widened as she remembered.

"Bane?" She called hesitantly, keeping a firm grip on the child in her arms.

She swore the enormous beast nodded his head.

The color drained from Rae's face as she set the girl back down. It wouldn't pay for both of them to get hurt if she was wrong about this.

Rae scanned the trees once more before taking a tentative step toward the alligator, keeping her hands up and her legs bent in case she was imagining things.

"Bane, I don't understand. Why are you in this form?" Rae felt her cheeks flush, still not believing what she was seeing and flustered by the unhelpful questions coming from her mouth. She couldn't expect Bane to answer a question like that in his present form. If this was indeed Bane, it would explain why the large reptile was so far north. Otherwise, Rae should've left as fast as she could.

But if this was Bane, Rae needed to do what she could to help him.

The alligator thrashed his tail as she approached, still chattering his rows of sharp teeth but not making moves toward her.

Rae's mind raced as she tried to determine definitively whether this monstrosity was who she hoped it was.

Okay, yes or no questions only. Rae closed her eyes for a moment, gathering her thoughts.

When she opened them again, only determination blazed in their golden depths.

"Okay, Bane. If it is you, listen carefully. I'm going to ask some better questions." A small smile tugged at her lips while Bane chattered more insistently. "One tail thrash means no and two means yes. Got it?"

Rae held her breath. This was the moment that would prove whether too much time on the ship addled her brain more than she thought.

The alligator thrashed his tail twice. Chattering once again.

Relief pooled in Rae's veins, hitting her harder than the ice of her wind.

"Okay, great. Glad we got that out of the way. You are Bane, right?"

Two tail thrashes.

"Not some random Shifter that's going to attack once I turn my back?"

One thrash and lots of chattering.

"You're right, you already would've tried if you were." Rae bit her lip, struggling to ask the next question. She sighed, trying a different one instead. "Are you hurt?"

One tail thrash.

Thank the Huntress. Rae thought, the tension easing a bit from her shoulders. If Bane was healthy, he had a better shot of getting through this. She knew little about Shifters and their Gift, but everyone knew that each Shifter was limited to one form. Bane should've been limited to his falcon form, or that of another raptor, as he'd demonstrated in the past. Rae's brows furrowed as her mind wandered.

Maybe, just maybe, he's like me. He's Shifted into different raptors before after all.

Huntress, I hope he knows what he's doing. Rae bit her lip and focused on her friend. Going through the what-ifs wouldn't help Bane at the moment.

Shaking her head, Rae asked her next question out loud.

"Okay, have you tried to Shift back?"

One tail thrash, but Bane seemed to hide his head under one leg.

"You're too tired?" Rae waited until Bane gave two tail thrashes before moving towards him. "Do you need some life energy?" She moved to place a hand on his side but lurched back when he snapped at her.

He thrashed his tail violently and started pushing himself into the water.

"Bane! Wait! I won't give you any energy! Just stay here." Rae said.

The alligator calmed, dropping his head on the sand as if to express the relief he felt at her promise.

"Okay, no life energy. What about food? Do you need some meat?"

Two tail thrashes spurred Rae into movement.

"I'm on it, Bane. I'm going to take this little runaway with me and find the others. Zeke, Tam, Reg, and George were searching other parts of the forest for you. I'll let them know where you are and that you need some meat. I think rabbit is your preferred diet." Rae smiled when Bane sent two tail thrashes her way.

She picked up the little girl and made her way into the woods, concern swirling in her mind and clouding her thoughts. She bit her lip, not wanting to think of the ramifications should Bane be stuck in this new body, trapped as a large reptile forever.

Rae needed to find the others quickly so they could come up with a plan to help the Shifter. There had to be some way to aid Bane in overcoming his limitations.

She lifted her chin, whispered her findings into her cupped hands, and used the winds to send them to the others, before making her way back to where the five of them split up.

Chapter Eighteen

Tommy woke before dawn. Dressing quietly to keep from waking Sara, he checked in on their three children, still asleep in their beds. He hated having to leave, but today was the day. Johanna sent word that some of their people witnessed Vincenzio's announcement that his soldiers would march in two days.

This meant there were fewer and fewer soldiers making their way to the bars and brothels of the Wharf and they needed to set their plans into motion.

Tommy had to make sure their plans were in place by the time the soldiers left. He hoped they could time it right, knowing more troops had to be coming. Vincenzio was an arrogant bastard, but you didn't become Myra's right-hand man by being stupid. No, Vincenzio would've made sure reinforcements were coming; they just had to hope he would be cocky enough to send his soldiers into the trees before the others arrived.

Tommy left the children without stepping into their room at his mother's farmhouse, not wanting to risk waking them. He went back to the bedroom he shared with his wife and took a moment to admire her, staring at her still form, hair a mess, and her body contorted in a way that didn't look comfortable at all.

The things one did to get comfortable when pregnant.

Again, Tommy was struck by how lucky he was. He went to their bed and knelt to kiss his wife on the cheek, doing his best not to wake her. He turned to leave, missing the sound of stirring coming from the bed.

"Do you have to leave?" Came a voice still thick with sleep.

Tommy turned back to his best friend, a smile on his lips. He knelt by her side, tucking a stray piece of hair behind her ear. "Say the word and I'll stay."

Sara's eyes stayed closed as she reached a hand to cup his face. She let out a sigh. "If only." She opened her eyes slowly, looking into his deep blue ones. "It's a good thing I'm so selfless, otherwise you'd never be able to leave my side." She closed her eyes as a yawn overtook her.

Tommy chuckled. "You are the epitome of selflessness." He stroked her hair. "I am lucky to be married to such a divine creature."

Sara snorted. "What are you sucking up for?"

"Having to leave you with three hellions on your own."

Sara patted his hand. "Your mom is an enormous help. Don't worry about us, love. Go save our city and send Johanna my regards."

He pulled her hand to his lips, leaving a soft kiss of gratitude. "Will do, darling. Good luck with the play date today. I know you'll dazzle Rob and the girls into staying here. I love you."

"I love you, too. Be careful and stay safe." Sara murmured before turning to her other side, trying to fall back to sleep before their children woke with vigor.

Tommy left his family and headed for the Fringe, where everyone was waiting for him.

"Simone, for Goddess' sake, we don't need to rehash all of this again. Lass, I know you mean well, but we need to take action, not sit here twiddling our thumbs. We'll miss the wind if we don't get the sails down." Eddy said, a frown on his face.

"Don't lecture me, Wharfman. Heimat deserves more than a half-assed plan with none of the details ironed out. It's better to over plan than not plan at all." Simone seethed, her green eyes blazing and her red ringlets bouncing.

Tommy walked in on a battleground.

The two argued while Johanna watched, waiting for them to wear themselves out before stepping in. She sent a look to Tommy when he entered and shrugged her shoulders as if to say, *what can you do?*

Tommy cleared his throat before interrupting. "Hey. It does us no good to keep fighting like this. Preparation is necessary, but there comes a time when we have to act too." He rubbed the back of his neck. "Rich and Anna are ready at the bakery. They reopen today, intending to be the center of operations. We can send messages with what type of bread is on special and which treats are made. Our people are ready. We just need to decide what happens first. Remember, the goal is to undermine and make life harder for the tyrants of our city. We don't have the numbers for a full takeover."

Johanna scowled. "I still think we need to strike while the iron's hot." She held up a hand. "I know we don't have the numbers, but burning the Barracks would send a bigger message than going on strike for a day or flooding the streets to make travel inconvenient. They leave tomorrow, and we can make it look like an accident."

"I'm with Johanna. Let's give them something to talk about." Eddy added. Johanna sent him an appreciative glance.

Tommy chewed the inside of his cheek as the three looked at Simone. The redhead ran a hand through her hair and narrowed her eyes as she thought. She moved her gaze to Tommy's, an apology in her eyes. "I think the fire would be the best course of action. There are plenty of ways to make it look like an accident without needing many people there. Our other plans involve crowds that could be rounded up too easily."

Tommy sighed, and his shoulders drooped. He'd been trying to steer them away from this plan ever since Johanna suggested it in Tamara's glass shop. He didn't think the benefit of striking at Vincenzio was worth the risk of burning the whole town.

But he was outnumbered.

"It's settled, then. I'll go tell Rich they should put buns on special and have everyone gather oil and tinder to be placed around Vincenzio's compound.

We can light it the night after the soldiers march, as long as everything goes according to plan."

Tommy left to head for the bakery as the other three dispersed to make sure their people were ready.

The time for action was upon them.

Vincenzio walked the lines of soldiers running through drills in the makeshift courtyard between the government buildings. His lips were set in a tight line as he watched row after row of men and women practice their formations.

Goddess, they're awful. Good thing they're leaving before anything serious happens. Hopefully, a walk in the woods will weed out the worst of them.

Vincenzio walked to where his officers stood to one side. They saluted him as he approached, knowing full well their recruits weren't up to his standards. They waited to be reamed out by their commander.

Vincenzio flashed them a predatory smile that showed all his teeth. "Slim pickings out there, I guess."

The officers nodded, not wanting to shatter their luck by talking.

"Make sure the worst of them don't come back." His eyes glinted dangerously as he met each of their gazes.

Again, the officers nodded, giving a grim salute.

Vincenzio licked his lips, satisfied his orders would be followed to a tee. Nobody dared to risk losing his favor, given his proximity to Myra.

He made his way to the southernmost building and climbed the steps to the roof. Zander acted as a lookout, keeping his eyes peeled for the fires that would mark the coming of their reinforcements.

Vincenzio didn't think the original inhabitants of the occupied city would fight back, but one couldn't be too sure. He had seized many cities during his military career and it always went one of two ways; either the city surrendered in full, its people broken and bloody, or the city rallied together, united in purpose against a common enemy.

The General hadn't decided which way Heimat would lean.

He underestimated their resolve and dedication to harboring the Magicae in their midst. He knew the Circus was a cover, a way to ferry the fugitives out of his grasp. They dared to mock his intelligence. He would respond with swift and decisive action. The Magicae should tremble whenever they saw him coming. Vincenzio would send his troops after the traveling city and when his reinforcements came, they would purge the city once and for all.

He looked at his steward. "Anything to report, Zander?"

"Nothing but snow and a few message riders."

Vincenzio narrowed his eyes. "We should start intercepting those message riders. Force the Magicae to play their hand. Squeeze the freedom from their allies and they'll sing like the songbirds they are."

Zander nodded, pulling his cloak tighter as another wind buffeted the roof. "Sounds effective, Sir." He gave the man a sly look. "And how do the soldiers look?"

The commander snorted. "Let's just say I won't be heartbroken when not all of them return."

Zander lifted one eyebrow, the question shining in his eyes. "Nothing like our class, then?"

"Hell no. Our class was exceptional and could march in formation. These runts will be lucky to make it back here in one piece." Vincenzio shook his head. "No, I doubt there will ever be a class quite like Myra's first recruits. Remember the way we would meet in secret in the catacombs?" Vincenzio's expression turned wistful.

"Those truly were the days." Zander hesitated, but continued when Vincenzio threw him a questioning stare. "I hesitate to ask, but Heimat is all that's left for the Magicae, correct? Once this sorry excuse for a city is taken care of, we did it. We won."

Vincenzio pursed his lips and sighed. "If only it were that easy. This doesn't end until Myra eradicates every one of them. And with that Circus... With Duncan in the wind? This is far from over."

Zander furrowed his brows, daring to voice his thoughts to the ruthless military man. "And what about the children born to Mortal parents? How do we find them before they spread their filth further?"

Vincenzio's eyes glinted dangerously. "Myra has something in the works. Keep the faith, Zander. We may not have magic in our veins, but we are not without our assets. Keep me posted on any movement."

Vincenzio put a hand on his friend's shoulder before descending back to the training yard. Zander was the only one he trusted to give him accurate and precise information. The keen-eyed steward would send word as soon as smoke rose on the horizon.

The commander would make sure everything was ready for the day when he could finally squash the people who destroyed his country with the power in their veins and lies on their tongues.

The Magicae were not to be trusted at any cost.

Chapter Nineteen

"*That dress will be the death of me.*" *The man whispered in her ear as he pulled her close.*

Naomi felt chills shoot down her spine as his breath tickled her ear and his hands slid lower. She wrapped her arms around his neck and pulled him close, taking in his intoxicating, woodsy scent. A small sigh escaped her lips as his fingers stroked her sides.

"You should see what's underneath this dress." It was her turn to whisper in his ear.

"I take it all back. Screw the dinner. We just made more important plans." His voice was a growl as he leaned down to capture her lips with his.

Naomi laughed and pulled back slightly, relishing the way the arms circling her waist obliged the movement without letting her go too far. She held a finger to his lips. "Andre, we have to go to the dinner. This pregnancy has been so much harder than Rae's. Who knows when I won't be nauseous next?""

Andre grumbled but acknowledged his wife's wisdom. He kissed her finger before wrapping both her arms around his neck again. "As you wish, my love." Hunger flashed in his eyes. "But know that you're torturing this poor man every second we can't be alone."

Naomi beamed as she shook her head, keeping eye contact with the man who captured her heart all those years ago. One hand held her close while the other moved to her chin, gently tilting it back and taking what he'd been yearning for.

All she felt was electricity as she lost herself in the kiss. Andre devoured her, leaving her weak in the knees. Everything he felt for her was in that kiss.

After the first few moments of fireworks, Naomi slowed the kiss down, making sure she matched his intensity and emotion. Her fingers stroked his short blond locks and kept him close. Everywhere their bodies touched was fire.

Naomi felt her heart thundering in her chest as a soft moan escaped past her lips.

That sound broke the spell they were under, and Andre pulled back with reluctance in his eyes.

"Afterwards, my love. I need to show off this dress." She insisted as she read the emotions in her husband's eyes.

Andre looked her up and down slowly, admiring the beautiful and shimmering golden fabric before capturing her hazel eyes once more. His expression spoke volumes about what he would give to change her mind, but he held his arm out all the same, knowing their duties had to come first.

With a hand on the life growing inside her, Naomi donned a smile and took her husband's arm. They just had to make it through dinner and then they could get lost in each other once more.

Naomi woke with a sleepy smile on her face. One arm cradled the baby in her belly and the other reached up to stretch.

Clank.

Ice filled her veins as the sound of chains overwhelmed her ears. She clamped her eyes shut and clutched at her empty abdomen as the tears started. If she could fall asleep once more, maybe she could be reunited with Andre. Maybe the personal hell she was in would disappear for one more hour.

Everything came crashing down around her as the reality of her situation weighed heavily on her shoulders. Her lip was split, and every movement sent pain shooting through her limbs.

There was a time when Myra took her for midnight walks around the castle, and far from prying eyes. Naomi had always dreaded every one of those walks.

Who knew never leaving those four walls could be so much worse?

Naomi licked her chapped lips and tried to clear her throat, thick from disuse. Her eyes caught on the glass of water near the door.

A battle waged inside as she stared at that cup. Two decades was a long time to keep a prisoner, but Myra wasn't one to do anything half-heartedly. For whatever reason, she wanted Naomi alive, no matter the consequences.

The walks kept the bed sores away. They were also risky.

A couple of years ago, the walks stopped suddenly. For a while, Naomi couldn't believe her luck, at least until she realized she would die within the four walls surrounding her.

The water was drugged to keep her compliant. She did her best to avoid it, but sometimes it couldn't be helped.

Maybe she could see Andre again if she let the drugs take over.

Focus, Naomi. A sharp voice sounded in her mind. *Duncan needs you more than ever.*

Rae needs you.

With that last thought, Naomi resumed her position on the cot and clenched her fist.

Andre, help me stay strong. Goddess, I miss you more than anything. Just help me stay strong for our baby girl.

Chapter Twenty

Duncan's head was still pounding when Chiara came rushing up to him. *Huntress, let it be good news.* Despite his silent prayer, Duncan knew it wouldn't be good when he caught sight of her panicked green eyes.

The members of the caravan were herded to a series of guest cottages, below, and on the outskirts of the city in the trees. The accommodations were more than sufficient, providing warmth against the chill of the winter air and stocked with food, water, and linens.

But they also sent an obvious message—their band of nomads was filled with outsiders and not welcome in the trees with their hosts.

Duncan knew he should be grateful they made it through the ordeal with their lives, but he couldn't deny the ache in his chest and the sorrow in his heart. Once again, the Magicae were not welcome in this strange place.

He looked at his dear friend and gestured to the empty bench beside him. Standing for long periods was still beyond the wind Crafter and would be for a bit yet. But at least he was still conscious. He held onto that as he raised one eyebrow.

"Talk to me. How are our people faring?" he asked as the Healer sat beside him.

Green eyes met his lavender ones. "Everyone's recovering Dunc, but Tyee is missing."

Duncan stared blankly before placing his hands on his knees and feeling a punch to his gut. Being missing was dangerous in this foreign land. And as much as Tyee prided himself on being a loner, the horseman needed them as much as they needed him. The young man had stepped up as a leader and was a seasoned fighter with a quiet confidence Duncan depended on. Tyee needed to be found.

Furrowing his brows, he wracked his brain for something, anything, that could give them a clue on Tyee's whereabouts. He looked at Chiara, and judging by the tense set to her jaw and the way her fists clenched, she believed the worst.

But why would the Elven take him? Leaning forward on his knees, Duncan steepled his fingers. He chewed on the inside of his cheek as he thought back to the ambush in the trees. *The woman.* Snapping his fingers, Duncan turned to the Herbalist.

"Does the General have him?" Duncan asked, remembering the predatory way she looked at the horseman. He would bet his right hand the two shared a history.

"That's what one healer in the infirmary thought. He told me she has a cruel reputation and wasn't in the barracks like the Queen commanded." Chiara answered, unfazed by Duncan's knack for guessing the truth. She'd experienced his powerful sense of intuition long enough to know it was just the way he was. "He suggested we look in the caves and I'm going after him."

Alarm shot through Duncan's body as he gripped her arm with wide eyes. "Not alone, you're not."

"Well, you're too weak to come. I'll be okay. Reason and flattery have won more wars than bloodshed and fighting ever has." Chiara pried his fingers from her sleeve. "I can do this, Dunc."

"Do what?"

Chiara looked at her son and felt the familiar uplifting feeling deep in her soul. Damien didn't know it, but he was the reason his mother made it through the Uprising. After she lost Damien's father, her will to keep going wavered, spurred on solely by the need to provide for her son. He had saved her in more ways than one.

Seeing him grow into an accomplished young man with an even kinder soul made the years of heartache worth it.

"Tyee is missing, and I'm going to follow a hunch to find him." She stated.

"Does that crazy woman have him?" Damien scrunched his eyebrows, his frown deepening when she inclined her head in affirmation. "Then I'm coming with you."

"Me too." Chiara looked to see Luc at Damien's hip, having missed the formidable woman while thinking about her son.

Chiara hesitated, giving Duncan an opening. "Take them with you, Chiara. A Healer and two Mortals won't be viewed as threats. They'll cover your back without jeopardizing your diplomacy. Bring him back to us, safe and sound."

Chiara pursed her lips before nodding. She didn't like putting the two young people in danger, but three sets of hands would make the work lighter.

They had a horseman to save.

Duncan watched the three leave with fear in his heart. If anything happened to them, he didn't know what he'd do.

The sound of someone whistling distracted him from his thoughts as Jess made her way to his bench. She smiled when she noticed him watching her and called, "Oy, Dunc! How ya feeling?"

Jess took the seat next to him and stared expectantly.

"I'm worse for wear, but still kicking." He hung his head and let his exhaustion show. Jess was the Head Forger on the Governing Council and acted as Duncan's second in command. She was the one he consulted most often because Forgers were the bulk of the Circus and she was the best at thinking through things logically. She had a proven track record of making hard decisions based on the facts in front of her. Jess was level-headed, stubborn as an ox, and he trusted her implicitly.

If there was anyone he didn't need to hide from, it was Jess.

Her expression softened when Duncan let the mask drop. "You've been through a lot, Dunc. You deserve some rest."

"But rest won't keep our people safe or get them through this mess. Give it to me straight, Jess. How much trouble are we in?" He looked her in the face, a grim expression on his own.

"It's not good, Dunc. Not good at all." She warned, but he motioned for her to continue. "The General took out all of our heavy hitters. One snap and all the Shifters were done for? It doesn't bode well. Our people are tough, but they're not trained fighters. The few practice sessions they got in mean nothing in the face of their soldiers." She looked around and lowered her voice. "You don't extinguish your very existence from the rest of the world without spilling a little blood. Their fighters are well-trained. I watched one of their sessions from the bushes. We wouldn't be able to take them."

Duncan's face fell at the words he knew she would say. At Jess's worried expression, he said, "Thank you for your honesty. It's on me to act as a diplomat, it seems." He scrunched his brows together as he reassured her. "I should get to bed and rest as much as I can before the Queen's summons. Supposedly, she'll be calling on me in the morning. Come find me in the morning and run through scenarios?"

"Absolutely," Jess answered before turning to the left upon hearing her name being called. Turning back to Duncan, she offered, "Need help getting settled?"

"No, don't worry about me. I'll manage. It sounds like someone wants to see you."

She waved her hand at the voice and tsked. "It's only Duke. He can wait until I'm good and ready to go find him."

Duncan chuckled. "I'm happy for you."

"So am I." She smiled and stood, offering the Ringmaster her hands as he made to stand.

Jess helped him into his cottage before resuming her stroll through the makeshift city, picking up the tune she had been whistling prior.

Duncan fell asleep with a small smile on his lips, grateful for little things despite the obstacles he'd have to face in the morning.

"For fuck's sake, Sylvie. I've told you over and over. We weren't looking for the Elven; I didn't even know you were Elven. How the fuck were we supposed to find you when we didn't know you still existed?" Tyee spat blood to the side of his restraints, sending daggers at the woman refusing to see reason.

The general tapped a finger on her chin, studying the horseman with deadly, glittering eyes. "Don't tell me you didn't see right through the disguise I made; it wasn't even that good. I knew what you were the second I laid eyes on you."

Tyee wracked his brain, trying to remember that first encounter with the harsh woman. By the time he met her, he was a man and the stable's head hostler, just below the stable master in terms of hierarchy. She'd whirled through the stable adorned with jewelry, demanding the finest horse they possessed and refusing to take no for an answer. He remembered her then-blond hair had a pixie cut to it with jagged edges that hinted at the cruelty within. At the time, he simply admired her for the physical beauty she presented at face value, unaware of her true nature.

She chose Tyee the minute she laid eyes on him as her trainer, flashing a bag of gold at the stable master when he protested losing Tyee's talents.

She had loved her games back then, too.

Tyee paled as he realized the hidden motives beyond her claims of liking how he looked. The general smirked at him, watching him realize the truth.

She traced one finger down the length of his forearm, giving a dark chuckle. "You didn't think your face was *that* pretty, did you?" Sylvie threw him a pout. "Oh no, you did, didn't you?" Her pout turned to a feral smile. "No, I needed to discern what you knew about your heritage and whether you'd be a threat to our people. A general can never leave her duty behind, you see." She spat the words like acid.

Tyee struggled to follow her train of thought. Something wasn't right about the way she was discussing his ancestors. He knew his mother was a lowlife, but his father... Tyee never met his father or even asked his mother about him, assuming he was some thug who knocked her up.

Tyee tried to discreetly reach for the knife hidden in his sleeve while the woman preened at her own words. He tried to distract her. "So putting Koko up for sale was a test."

Tyee did his best not to wince as a nail traced his jawline. "No, no, no, Stableboy. You're still dense as a board up here, aren't you?" She tapped his forehead with two fingers. "Putting Koko up for sale was to disrupt your perfect little empire. You thought you were hot shit, and I needed to take you down a peg. Forcing your hand ensured you'd run." She gave him a coy sideways glance, pausing his search for his knife. "I never expected you'd find such a band of misfits. Not to mention a new plaything to keep your bed warm at night."

Thoughts of the golden-eyed acrobat filled his mind as he tried to keep his emotions in check. He knew Sylvie had been in his mind and was trying to get a reaction by insulting the woman he yearned for. Rae was a lot of things, but not cruel like the woman before him. His heart squeezed at the thought of never seeing her again. He needed to keep his wits about him and escape this nightmare.

So he could find *her.*

Tyee clenched his jaw, forcing the words from his mouth. "Desperate times call for desperate measures." He wanted to take the words back as soon as they were out, but the glittering of his captor's eyes proved he was on the right track. He needed to play Sylvie's games if he wanted to get out of this mess unscathed.

She chuckled. "There's the man I once knew. So tell me, if you weren't looking for us, for me," her eyes danced as they met his dark ones, "why were you traveling in the Great Northern Forest? My ancestors did their duty in giving this place a wretched reputation. I doubt your caravan of soft hands wanted to come here by choice. They were quaking in their boots when they had to face little old me, not to mention my soldiers." Tyee felt her breath on his face as she leaned in close. "I'll ask nicely one more time. Why are you here?"

Tyee schooled his features, not wanting to give anything away. The years spent lying to his mother prepared him well. "The promise of new land was too tantalizing to ignore. You already know there are Magicae in our group; we need a place to settle peacefully, away from the discrimination of Mortals." Tyee knew Sylvie wouldn't take kindly to the possibility of them being pursued by Vincenzio's forces. It was better to make her think they came here of their own accord, with no outside pressures determining their course. It made the Circus less of a threat to her people.

Sylvie narrowed her eyes and fixated on his face. "You're lying."

Sweat beaded on Tyee's palms as he struggled harder to find the knife hidden in his sleeve.

His stomach dropped when Sylvie held his knife in front of his face.

Looking for this?

She flashed a wicked grin as Tyee writhed in pain, unable to handle the pressure of her mind forming words within his own.

The lantern flickered.

Sylvie's head whipped to the doorway as a figure materialized there.

Queen Ulla lowered her hood with a scowl. "These were not your orders, Daughter." Her voice was as dangerous as a blade. "Why are you not at the Barracks as instructed?"

Sylvie swallowed but held her ground, inclining her head slightly, knowing not to breach protocol despite her mother doing so. "I needed answers, Your Grace. You said it yourself, you led an army at my age, the least I could do is discover the truth about these outsiders."

Sylvie stood at attention, her shoulder-width apart, knees bent slightly and arms tensed for whatever came next.

"Fool. His people are looking for him. I promised them their comrades were safe only to find you torturing the one they're looking for. Three are on their way as we speak."

Sylvie clenched her teeth, trying to keep the frustration from her voice. "I could've handled them. None would be the wiser."

Ulla sent a glare at her daughter before rubbing the skin between her eyes with one finger. "Sylvia, we need to treat these people carefully. The last thing we want is for them to share what they've seen with the wider world. *Secrecy* is our best protection."

"They're soft. We could kill them in one fell swoop, make sure none of them get away."

"Then why didn't you?" The Queen's gaze bore into her daughter's eyes.

Sylvie stammered, trying to defend her actions. "I couldn't—there were children in the group. We never punish children for the sins of their parents."

"Exactly, and why you *should have allowed them to go.* The trail is hidden, your guards are competent and you've trained them well. You need to trust in those below you if you ever want to become a Queen to our people." Ulla's gaze moved to Tyee's still figure.

He'd done his best not to draw the women's attention to him. Hoping they would forget about him. No such luck.

Ulla's eyes widened as they drank in his presence. "This is him? The one you reported on years ago?"

"Aye, Mother, this is he."

Ulla's eyebrows knitted together as she pondered her next move. The two women shared a look, understanding passing between them.

Sylvie left with a flourish of her long coat, disappearing as she moved through the empty doorway.

Ulla undid his bonds quickly before passing her hands over his body, removing the blood, sweat, and dirt staining his skin and clothes.

He made to sit up, but the Queen pushed gently at his chest, easing him back to the cot.

She placed a hand on his forehead and Tyee's world darkened once more.

Duncan sat on the bench outside his cottage, studying the city of Verdencia. It was apparent the Elven had a connection to the trees holding up their city. Upon closer inspection, many of their bridges and structures seemed to be created from the trees themselves, as if the Elven could coax shapes and growths from the tall giants of the forest.

He noted that when the Elven made it to the ground; they wore camouflaged leathers and communicated without words. The only people leaving the walkways in the trees strode with the confidence of years of training.

Only the guards and soldiers leave the trees. I haven't seen a single child even attempt to climb down. Very peculiar indeed. The Ringmaster mused to himself. *A haven that is also a cage.*

Duncan knew his people were impressed by how the Elven used the forest to create a place to call home, but his stomach was in knots as he observed the Elven. The feeling in his gut said this wasn't what his people should strive for. This was a worse kind of fear; the kind that had you looking over one shoulder at all times, restricting everything you did, but pretending everything was fine.

Duncan shuddered. Life on the road was hard, but at least they knew danger when they saw it. He knew he'd never do well in a cage, real or imaginary. Anything was better than that.

He was waiting for Queen Ulla's summons. A messenger brought word the other day that the Queen would send for him in the morning. Duncan was as prepared as possible for his first meeting with royalty, having prepped with Jess during the early hours of the morning.

He rubbed the back of his neck as one of his legs bounced. The wind Crafter debated going for a walk but thought it wise to save his energy until he met with the Queen.

His people deserved answers.

It was fine to accept their hospitality, but Duncan wouldn't let his people become hostages, dependent on these people for their needs. Self-sufficiency wasn't something the Circus lacked and he wouldn't let his people lose that on his watch.

Chiara, Damien, and Luc came home empty-handed late in the night. They reached the caves the healer told Chiara about, but they were empty. More than empty, they looked like they hadn't been used in years. Duncan was relieved when they returned, their safety worth more to him than anything, but the absence of the horseman was becoming more noticeable.

He would demand to know Tyee's whereabouts from the Queen herself if it came to that.

Duncan caught movement in the corner of his eye, at the base of one of the large trees holding the Elven city in its branches.

A messenger made her way through the humble cottages, glancing this way and that as if searching for someone.

Duncan rose to meet her, inclining his head as she approached.

"The Queen is ready for you." Her eyes darted back and forth as if expecting danger from all angles. "Follow me."

She darted off like a rabbit, not waiting to see if Duncan followed.

The wind Crafter strode after her, avoiding the questioning looks from his people. The sooner he got to the queen, the sooner he could answer their questions.

The messenger brought him past the city in the trees to a cluster of tall oak trees with one structure between them.

Ah, these must be Ulla's quarters. Curious they're this far from her people. Privacy must be a priority then. Duncan couldn't help the running commentary in his mind, analyzing everything he encountered. One didn't know when the smallest of details would be useful.

The messenger stopped below a ladder carved into the tree, the hand, and footholds within the bark itself.

"Climb up the tree and there will be guards to announce your presence and admit you to the receiving chamber. No weapons allowed." She gave him one last hard look before darting back to the Elven stronghold.

Duncan watched her leave, observing how she found the hidden ladder that would take her back to the main part of the city. Turning back to the ladder on the tree he stood in front of, Duncan took a deep breath and started climbing.

Still worn from the ordeal the day before, Duncan took longer than he liked to reach the top, but he made it.

Guards helped him to his feet before patting him down for weapons. One of them took a small staff, whispered a few words, and passed it over his clothes, the runes engraved in the wood glowing with a soft light. Duncan recognized them as similar to the ones on Sylvia's staff when she attacked them in the clearing.

Interesting. He was intrigued by where the Elven's power came from, but first, he needed to negotiate his people's safety for their silence. He squared his shoulders and stepped through the doorway indicated by the guards.

Queen Ulla stood behind a large table, studying the documents strewn across it. She looked up when Duncan entered, gesturing to the seat next to her.

"Ringmaster, please, come sit. I'm sure you're still recovering, and the climb couldn't have been easy." She gathered the papers and set them on a small table behind her, before making her way to the round table herself.

Duncan sat in the chair she gestured towards, happy to observe before demanding the answers he sought. The Queen sat, steepling her fingers and looking Duncan straight in the eye. "I will not lie to you, Ringmaster, I'm at a loss on my next course of action, given the circumstances."

Duncan pursed his lips, but remained silent, waiting to see what the woman would say next.

Her eyes narrowed at Duncan's lack of a response, mistaking his quietness for weakness. "I can't let you go with the knowledge of my people you've already gathered, nor can I keep you here indefinitely." She raised one eyebrow in the Crafter's direction. "If you have any ideas, I'm all ears."

Duncan tapped one finger and let his gaze wander. He took in the surrounding room, his mind racing for the words to get them out of this mess. His eyes snagged on a stained glass window looking to the city.

He reached out to touch her but stopped himself before he made it that far, letting his hand drop to the table. Her eyes watched his hand as he studied her. Queen Ulla was all harsh lines and angles; her gray hair was drawn into a tight bun at the nape of her neck, accentuating high cheekbones and the way her chin came to a point. She met Duncan's stare, still waiting for him to proceed.

Duncan cleared his throat. "Your Grace, my people are not a threat to you. We are not familiar with this land. We entered the Forest without knowing where we were going. Our Herbalists found a hidden path, and we followed it, but none of my people could retrace their steps back to where we started." He paused and studied the harsh woman in front of him. "I get it. You fear for the safety of this place and its people, but *we are not a threat.* We will not run our mouths about a lost people in the middle of the woods. No one would believe us, Your Grace. The reputation you've set for this place makes even the toughest soldier quake in their boots."

Duncan looked at the Elven Queen, but her eyes focused on her hands resting on the table. Her lips pressed together tightly and her expression was unreadable.

Duncan swallowed.

He knew he laid it on thick, but their lives could be at stake. The Queen seemed more reasonable than the general that captured them, but you didn't keep a race hidden for decades without making hard choices.

"You talk about not being able to find this city, but how do I ensure your people won't tell others we are in the forest? Just because you can't pinpoint a location doesn't mean you can't do damage."

Duncan's eyes went to the stained glass window again. It contained a border of those strange symbols that were on the staffs the guards and general carried.

His eyes widened.

"The runes. Use the runes." He gestured to the window. "Those symbols. It's how you channel your magic, right?"

Ulla gave him a puzzled look. "How would the runes solve the problem?"

"There must be one that means silence or quiet." He raised one eyebrow at the Queen. She nodded and motioned for him to continue. "If there was a way to activate it with certain words or questions, we could tattoo my people with the rune. Any time they tried to mention your people or what they witnessed here, the rune would activate and prevent them from speaking."

Ulla scowled, mulling over the Ringmaster's words. "And when they try to communicate without speaking? When they write their words on paper or sign it with their hands?"

Duncan frowned. The older woman had a point.

"We could do that, but instead of writing silence, why don't we write forget? Your people will forget about their time in the Forest when they get the rune tattooed on their skin and my city will be safe."

Duncan felt dread in the pit of his stomach. Playing with the strands of the mind was a dangerous game. He needed to tread lightly here.

"Your Grace, I will need to ponder that. It is much more invasive than what I proposed. I will need to consult with my Council before I agree to such things." He kept a close eye on the woman as he prepped his next question. "Queen Ulla, I need to know where Tyee is. He's not in the Infirmary, the cottages, or anywhere else we've checked. Where are you holding him?"

Duncan's keen eyes didn't miss how Ulla tensed at the mention of the horseman or how her fingers curled slightly. Her face remained impassive, but Duncan knew she was trying to hide something.

What do they want with Tyee? Why won't they tell us where he is? Duncan did his best to swallow his frustration.

"I do not know who you're talking about. It's presumptuous of you to assume we took him with no evidence to support your claim. Just because you can't find him doesn't mean we took him." Ulla looked down her nose at the Ringmaster, fingers still curled, giving away her duplicity.

"Your general took him hostage and we haven't seen him since. Do you mean to tell me you don't have control of you people? You don't know what goes on in with your military officers? That's a dangerous game, Your Grace, and how Myra gained power to begin with." Duncan pressed.

Ulla's expression turned frosty. "I think it's time for you to leave, Ringmaster." She jerked her head to the exit as she stood up, dismissing the Crafter. "I suggest you decide about the forgetting rune soon before I make it for you." She spat, returning to the papers she'd been poring over. "It would be in your best interest not to criticize my ways again."

Duncan swallowed before making his way out of Ulla's stronghold in the trees. He needed to go to the general for the answers he sought.

Chapter Twenty-One

Cleo watched her crew make the final necessary repairs to the *Vengeance* to make her ready to limp along to Lockewater. The Captain had done her fair share of the work, letting herself get lost in the physical labor of nailing boards and sanding the splintered ones. After a while, she retreated to the helm, braiding rope while her crew worked. She winced as she took in all that would need to be done when they reached the city's shipyard. They could do some repairs here, with the limited supplies they had below deck, but it would take a pretty penny to make the vessel seaworthy again.

She let a soft whistle escape her lips at the thought of the shipyard in Lockewater. It was notorious for its craftsmanship, and the price tag that came with it.

The Captain hung her head as she studied the wood beneath her fingers. The meeting she held with her crew went about as well as expected. She knew she'd done the right thing and wholeheartedly believed in bringing more Magicae into their ranks but Cleo wasn't sure she was ready to face the repercussions. She could pinpoint almost every single person who would jump ship because of what she said. It hurt knowing so many of the people that were like family could leave without a second glance. She was only doing what was right. If only they would give the Magicae a chance.

But this was the real world.

Cleo saw the way they watched the Crafters and Bane. All they saw was destruction and not the potential good that could come with that type of power on board. Fear and learned hate weren't easily undone once it was ingrained in a person.

Cleo clenched her fists and let out a hiss. *Fools. A ship is only as strong as its weakest board. And the same goes for its crew.*

They would have deserters once they reached Lockewater. The city on the coast would be crawling with captains and merchants searching for fresh crew members to add to their ranks. Those that disagreed with her new ways of doing things would jump ship as soon as the right opportunity came along, no matter what she or Adams said.

Good riddance. Cleo resigned herself to finding as many Magicae as she could to fill their empty positions once they reached the town.

A throat cleared behind her.

She turned and met George's light brown, whiskey-colored eyes. She raised one eyebrow at the lanky man. "And what can I do for you, Scally?"

George ignored the slight dig of a nickname, no doubt remembering those moments stuck at the deck rail when he was heaving his guts over the side. "Captain, Rae found Bane." He paused, looking to see who could be listening. Lowering his voice, he continued, "He's in no condition to travel, though. Rae and Zeke will stay with him and meet us in Lockewater. Tam and Reg are checking on our people now, prepping them for the last part of this journey."

Her sharp green eyes studied his figure. The leader from Heimat looked exhausted, his face gaunt with a tension that never left his body. His muscles seemed as if they were ready to spring into action should danger present itself. She searched his face as she covered his hand with hers.

Prophetess, I need a good tumble in the sheets. And by the looks of it, so does this landlubber. She put those thoughts aside, focusing on the man in front of her as he pulled his hand away. *Guess not. Back to plan Adams, it is then.*

Out loud, she tried to offer the man some comfort. "We're almost there, George. You'll be able to get off this boat and your people will be safe."

George wouldn't meet her eyes as he let out a bark of laughter with no humor in it and blew the air from his lungs. "Getting to Lockewater means we enter the forest. I know you mean well, Captain, but safety isn't a luxury our people will find for a long time."

Cleo's eyes softened. "I'm sorry. That came out wrong." She looked at the running water of the river and sighed, looking back at the man. "I meant to say you could be on your way to reuniting with the others of the caravan and then back to your city. Once everyone is settled, you'll return to Heimat, no?"

"At some point, but the future is only known by the Goddess, as the people say."

"By the Prophetess, you mean." Cleo corrected with a wink, trying to add levity to the conversation.

George snorted. "Don't tell me you believe all that nonsense."

"And what if I did?" Cleo's eyes glinted as one eyebrow raised in challenge.

"I would say you're playing a dangerous game."

Cleo snorted and gave the man a curious look. George met her gaze stoically, leaning against the side of the quarterdeck.

Cleo said, "The faces of the Goddess give people something to believe in, and I would be a fool to deny that to anybody."

"Aye, but your own misplaced belief will only lead to heartache." The man from Heimat studied his hands.

"Good thing it's not misplaced, then." Cleo said with a wink.

George furrowed his brows, changing the subject. "This is my first time outside of Heimat. What should I expect when we get to Lockewater?"

Cleo's eyebrows shot up. "You've never left Heimat? You wound a sailor with those words." Cleo gripped her chest theatrically. "Doesn't the road call to you? Begging you to venture out and discover what you're made of? Everyone needs to travel, even if it only solidifies your love for where you came from." Her eyes strayed to the water again, smiling as a breeze ruffled her hair. "This world is beautiful and wild. You just have to be brave enough to experience it."

George tapped two fingers on the wood in front of him, digesting the Captain's words. He sighed. "Some people only yearn for a warm place to lay their head and safety for their loved ones."

"Poppy cock. You can't tell me you've never yearned for something more." Cleo's tone was dismissive as she searched the man's face for any type of reaction.

George was quiet, wringing his hands as he gathered his thoughts. After a couple of moments, he said, "Regardless, I've always had people I've needed to look after."

"Pft. Those are excuses, Scally. You can't live your life for someone else." She challenged. "Would the ones you look after want you to put your life on hold?"

George adjusted his coat aggressively before turning to the woman. "You make a lot of assumptions there, Captain." He shot her a guarded expression. "You can't judge a person's choices if you don't know their circumstances. Travel isn't the only way to experience the world or its people. Your crew has traveled more than most, experiencing Kamore and its people, yet many of them still cling to unneeded prejudices. But please, keep going about how valuable travel is in changing the opinions of others." George spat.

Cleo raised one eyebrow. "Looks like I touched a nerve with that one. Aye, you're right that travel can't fix everything, but it's a good place to start. There's a place on my ship whenever you get the itch."

George shook his head. "Thanks for the offer, but I'll pass." He sent her a wave and made his way below deck to check in on their people.

Cleo watched him go, still in disbelief at George's lack of desire to see the world. She didn't know his story, but she would. Maybe then things would make more sense.

She turned back to her crew, waiting for Adams to give the go-ahead to take the ship to Lockewater. The sooner they got moving, the better for all of them.

Zeke was sitting on a rock near the riverbank, keeping watch over Bane. Rae was down by the beach, talking with Gemma. The little girl had stirred when Rae tried transferring her to George, screaming and hollering until Rae promised to keep the Herbalist by her side.

The Crafter picked up a rock and threw it across the rushing waves, skipping it several times over the surface of the water. She helped Gemma take a wide stance and throw parallel to the waves.

Rae had always been a natural with the kids, delighting them with jokes and games. Zeke had wanted to clear the air between them since the storm started, but the little girl put a wrench in his plans. She needed Rae more than he did at the moment.

His eyes strayed to Bane in alligator form. Zeke knew a little about the Shifters, enough to know this could devastate the young man.

He'd heard stories about Shifters getting stuck in other forms besides their natural ones from J. The Councilman was easy to talk to and someone Zeke sought as often as he could. Sadness panged in his chest as he thought about J and the others in the Circus. This far away, all he could do was hope and pray they made it out okay. He gave a dark chuckle, imagining how Luc was bossing everyone around, while Damien did his best to contain her. His chest tightened at the thought of his friends, wishing they were together once more.

We'll make it through this. His hands clenched at his sides while he was lost in thought. *We've come too far as it is.* His concern for Bane was overwhelming, and all they knew was that he was too tired to Shift back. Zeke worried part of it was that Bane didn't want to accept the fact he might be stuck in that form indefinitely. The wind Crafter tapped his fingers on the rock. He knew Bane was unconscious when he went over the gunwale of the ship and couldn't have Shifted with such little life energy in his veins.

The question now was how did Bane Shift into a form not his own?

Zeke's eyes moved back to Rae. *If Rae can control all four elements, maybe Bane can use all forms.* His mind returned to the night before arriving in Heimat, to Nan's story of their ancestors with unfathomable power in their veins. The Shifter could take whichever form he wished, as long as he could picture it in his head.

Zeke hoped that was the case.

It would raise more questions about what was going on with their Gifts, but at least Bane could leave the form he was in.

Rae's voice interrupted his thoughts.

"Z! I think they got the ship moving! Come look."

Zeke reluctantly left his perch on the rock, not wanting to leave Bane alone should something happen. The alligator hadn't moved since he'd gotten there, but that didn't mean circumstances couldn't change. He made his way to where Rae and Gemma stood by the river, gazing downstream.

Sure enough, the *Vengeance* was on the move. They could make out the figure of the Captain at the helm, trying to keep the vessel in the middle of the waves, away from the dangers posed by shallow water. Zeke said a silent prayer to the Huntress that they would make it safely. The crew should've left a rowboat on the beach for the four of them to take to town. Rae had suggested it, assuring them her water Craft had recovered enough to guide them where they needed to go.

Rae ran her hands through Gemma's curls as they watched the ship disappear into the trees. The little girl was quiet as she watched the ship.

Zeke didn't know what to make of the little girl with an affinity for plants. Watching her now, it was hard to reconcile the devastation brought about by her father. Another example that children were not their parents.

He shook his head, stopping his train of thought, and turned his head to Rae. "You never told me what happened with the Captain."

Rae gave a jolt, expelled from her reverie, and her hands paused their movement. Her golden eyes met his silver ones. "Oh, with everything that happened, I almost forgot about that. Cleo challenged me to first blood."

Zeke's eyes widened. "Why? Right after you recovered from everything in Heimat?"

Rae shrugged her shoulders as Gemma crouched down to study some plants beneath their feet. "She said it had something to do with reassuring the crew? She needed to hit me before I was at full strength to keep her crew happy or something."

"Huntress. I don't think I'll ever understand sailors. How are you doing with everything?" Concern shone in Zeke's eyes.

Rae crossed her arms and gave herself a squeeze, turning her head from Zeke. "I feel guilty, Z. The crash wouldn't have happened if I had been stronger. I need to practice my Crafts and build up some endurance, but how am I going to do that with water and earth? My fire is mastered, and I know you'll help me with my wind, but what about the other two?" She met his gaze hesitantly, a flicker of hope shining in her eyes.

"Can I be—,"

"I forgive—,"

They both spoke at the same time before bursting into laughter. Rae threw her arms around Zeke and squeezed him tight.

"I'm so sorry, Z. I never want to hurt you again. These past few days have been hell." She murmured against his chest.

"Mission accomplished then, eh?" He teased, a smile in his voice.

Rae punched his shoulder lightly. "Jerk. But yes, your mission was accomplished, and I still feel terrible. I will spend the rest of my life trying to make it up to you." She squeezed again, unwilling to let the moment go.

"About time, Sparks. I had to make sure you were ready to atone for the rest of your life." Zeke pulled back and winked at her.

A noise to their right caused both Crafters to jump apart and land in a ready position, calling on the power in their veins.

Gemma had wandered down the bank and watched in awe as the alligator under their watch started changing. She gasped and ran behind Rae, hugging her leg and peeking out, pointing at where their friend lay.

Zeke ran to the Shifter and watched in awe as it shrunk, scales flattening and snout receding, long teeth becoming dull and boxlike.

After a few minutes, Bane lay face down in the sand in human form, groaning from his efforts.

Zeke went to him, placing a sheet over the man's naked form, protecting bare skin from the waning sun.

Bane coughed a couple of times before propping himself on his elbows and looking to the wind Crafter.

"Well, that was unexpected." The Shifter mumbled before collapsing back to the sand, losing consciousness.

Zeke and Rae shared a look before moving to make Bane more comfortable as he recovered.

Gemma kept out of their way but stared at the Shifter with wide eyes, shocked into silence at seeing such a transformation.

Chapter Twenty-Two

Bane woke with a start, taking a moment to remember he wasn't in his alligator form anymore. Fleshy fingers patted at his face in the darkness of twilight, relief filling his veins as he felt his nose and mouth, no longer elongated. The tension released from his limbs as he relaxed, closing his eyes after noting the three Magicae sitting near where he laid.

His brain had other ideas.

That ship.

Bane's eyes flew open, and he struggled to get up, eyes searching the river for signs of their pursuers. He tried to talk, but it came out as a growl.

Zeke cast a curious look at the Shifter but didn't make to move.

Bane cleared his throat, silently cursing his vocal cords.

"Zeke!" His voice came out as a rasp. "Rae!" He coughed several times, trying to get the remaining gunk from his throat.

The two Crafters shared a look before making their way to the Shifter. Rae gently extricated herself from Gemma, the little girl dozing with her head in Rae's lap. The Crafter bundled up a blanket and placed it under the little girl's head before following Zeke to where Bane was now sitting up.

Bane studied the little girl with alarm, recognizing her from somewhere. He frowned when he realized the little girl was Vincenzio's daughter. He'd met her briefly on the ship when he introduced himself to the people from Heimat.

Things are complicated indeed.

He reverted his attention back to his friends as they approached. Zeke placed a hand on his shoulder and studied his face, waiting for him to say his peace. After a moment, he offered Bane a long coat and some trousers.

Bane took them gratefully, slipping the pants on underneath the sheet and shrugging the coat onto his shoulders. He cleared his throat again and tried once more. "We have problems. Before the storm, I saw a ship." He took a drink of the water Rae offered, gulping at the waterskin and trying to quench the thirst he didn't realize he had. He wiped his mouth and handed the now empty skin back to Rae, nodding his thanks. "Someone's coming after the *Vengeance*."

"Are you sure?" Rae asked.

Bane nodded, eyes drifting back to the river. "I don't know how Vincenzio did it, but he sent someone after us. The storm probably held them up; I doubt they have Crafters aboard to navigate something as nasty as that one. We need to stop the ship from getting to Lockewater."

"Or at least slow them down long enough to give us a chance at flight. The plan was to head into the forest once we reached Lockewater, right?" Zeke asked.

"Yep. George and the others should start prepping for the trip once they set anchor in the harbor." Rae frowned. "Maybe Bane should bring word to spur them into action sooner?"

"What about the girl?" Bane asked, inclining his head to Gemma. Rae bit her lip as she watched the little girl that had become so attached to her. "I can send a bird, but I don't think leaving is the best plan of attack. It's going to take all of us to stop this ship."

Zeke moved to the riverbank, studying the width and depth of the river. He turned to Rae. "Could we block the river?"

Rae moved closer, and the pair discussed how they could work together to stop the ship in its tracks.

Bane studied the pair, noticing the tension that was once between them was gone. Their easy banter and friendly affection were back. Whatever happened during the storm fixed what was broken between them. Bane was happy for Zeke, knowing how the Crafter had felt off while they exercised on the ship.

The Shifter had the Sight, as most Shifters did, and could read every emotion given off by the lithe young man thanks to the power in his blood. Zeke's aura emanated a softer, more consistent glow than on the *Vengeance* and Bane was sure the fire Crafter was the source.

Bane's attention returned to the young Herbalist in the grass. Gemma was snoring softly, unaware of the activity going on around her. His eyes narrowed, unsure of what they should tell her. The little girl was dropped off by her mother, but Bane wasn't convinced she wouldn't do what she could to get back to her father. The little girl had to only be around four or five. There was no way she could understand what was happening to her world.

Bane's heart gave a painful twinge as sympathy and empathy flooded within him. He'd always had his Da to lean on growing up, and despite everything that took place during his childhood, he could always count on his old man. Bane narrowed his eyes, focusing on the little girl's aura and looking for the answers he sought. Using his Sight, Bane saw Gemma's emotions in his mind's eye, noticing her soft green light interjected with angry lines of red and black. The gray color of confusion colored her edges and dark green swirls danced around her.

Bane came back to the present, still watching the sleeping girl. He looked to the grass and flowers below her still form and noted the way they stretched towards her. He surmised they were responsible for the swirls in Gemma's colors. They called her power forth, singing to her very blood.

Bane caught movement in the corner of his eye and turned toward the river. Sure enough, sails appeared in the distance. His heartbeat quickened as he went through their options. They didn't have a plan for the three of them to stop the ship and its crew. Rae and Zeke still discussed the best ways to block the river without causing irreparable damage to its ecosystem.

"We have company." Bane said, inclining his head to the ship in the distance.

"Shit. Okay, we need to decide whether we want to trash the ship or slow it down." Zeke said, his eyes trying to estimate how much time they had before the ship was upon them.

"We can't trash the ship, Z. There could be innocent people on board. What if it's just a ship in the wrong place and at the wrong time?" Rae asked.

Bane nodded his agreement, adding, "I'll send a bird to warn the others. If we don't succeed, our people need to get out. Those children need a head start if they're going to have a chance of staying ahead of them." He sent a whistle into the trees, drawing out a small beautiful hawk. The bird perched on his outstretched arm, peering into yellow reptilian eyes. He ripped a piece of fabric from the sheet that once covered him and looked at the others. "Do we have something to write with?"

Rae and Zeke searched their pockets before shaking their heads.

Bane chewed on the inside of his cheek before looking at the hawk on his shoulder. Murmuring soft words, Bane held one finger out to the bird and sent an image of what he wanted to the hawk's mind. The bird balked before nipping at his finger and drawing blood.

"Bane, you don't need—," Rae started.

"It's the best we got on short notice." He said simply, using his blood to write a single word on the fabric.

RUN.

Bane pulled at the power in his blood, sending his thoughts into the bird's mind while Rae and Zeke directed their attention to the river. Forming a connection between their consciousnesses, Bane asked the hawk to fly fast and find the lanky man with an unassuming face. He sent a picture of the ship and the striking woman that acted as its Captain before tying the fabric to the bird's leg when it was offered.

Bane never forced an animal to do something. It was a common misconception of Shifters that they could bend an animal's will to their own. In reality, Bane could only ask if the bird would do something for him. Sometimes the raptor accepted without argument, while others demanded food or other goods as payment and some refused outright. The ones more likely to refuse rarely came to his whistle, which is why he used the technique.

The hawk blinked once before taking off towards Lockewater.

Bane turned back to the two Crafters, and his jaw dropped. The pair were creating what looked like a whirlpool in the middle of the river. Rae moved her arms in a circular motion, bending the currents to her desired direction. Zeke then used the wind to expand the ripples from Rae's whirlpool in order to move the ship into the bank before hitting the raging current.

The ship was approaching quickly, and Bane focused on what he could do to aid the Crafters. He noticed Gemma watching wide-eyed and went to the little girl.

"Gemma," he called. The little girl wrenched her eyes from the spectacle to look at the Shifter. He noted her fear as he moved closer and crouched next to her. "I need you to do something for me. Are you listening?"

Gemma shook her head vigorously, eyes shining with tears. "Is that a bad man?" She tugged at his sleeve as she pointed to the ship in the distance.

Bane frowned, not knowing how to answer. Deciding honesty was best, he said, "We don't know if that ship is bad or good. That's why Rae and Zeke are going to nudge it to the beach and slow it down a bit. That should give everyone on our ship a chance to get out of town."

Gemma's chin wobbled, but set her shoulders and nodded her head. "My Momma always said safe is best."

Bane's heart broke a little to hear the girl talk about her mother. He gave her a one-armed hug before looking her straight in the eyes. "Your Momma is a smart woman. Now, I want you to give Rae and Zeke some cover with some plants. Can you do that for me, kiddo?"

Gemma scrunched her eyebrows together, reaching to touch the ground beneath her. Closing her eyes, she tapped the ground, and a bush sprung up. Opening her eyes, she clapped her hands and smiled, proud of her efforts. She turned to Bane with a questioning look. "Like that?"

"Just like that." He guided her in front of the two Crafters, positioning her between them and the river. Bane ignored the curious looks from Rae and Zeke, giving the little girl a nod. "Do it again, right here. If you get tired, stop and let me know."

Gemma got to work, giggling as she called forth bushes and small trees, making a game of trying to guess what would spring forth from the ground beneath her.

Bane's attention flickered between the young girl and the ship approaching their part of the riverbank. He noticed Gemma fading and guided her to a spot in the trees, hidden from all sides. He touched one of her bare arms and let some of his life energy trickle slowly into her blood.

Gemma's eyes fluttered as she felt the power enter her. She let out a slight giggle. "That tickles," she said, pulling her arm back.

Satisfied the girl wouldn't lose consciousness, he went back to the Crafters.

He closed his eyes, reaching inside to pull forth his falcon form. Bane hesitated when he saw the two strings of power in his core. He ran a hand over both, overcome with different emotions as he touched. The first was as familiar as a second skin. He felt the whip of the wind, the joy that came with flying, and the power of sharp talons and a deadly beak. In the past, there was always just one string attached to the form of any raptor. Just a thought would change the feeling and he could become a hawk or an eagle or an owl.

But the second string. It felt unyielding to his touch, rough like scales but cool and refreshing like water. He felt power and hunger and the quiet confidence of an alpha predator.

So the alligator is permanent. Bane thought as he questioned what to do. His wings would give him the mobility he needed to maneuver around the masts and rigging of the ship, but the alligator was a tempting alternative. He didn't know if anybody on the ship would recognize his falcon form, another reason the alligator may be beneficial.

As Bane wavered between the two, unsure of which would provide the best assets, the ship got closer.

Rae and Zeke had started the whirlpool when they saw the ship, then slowed their Crafting down to conserve their energy. They quickened their movements as the ship loomed closer, causing the whirlpool and perimeter waters to rage. They were mostly hidden from view thanks to the young Herbalist and Bane's quick thinking. The two did their best to stay behind the foliage while monitoring the waters below them.

The ship was now only yards away, and the crew could be heard yelling and scrambling to do what they could to avoid the spinning waters they were headed to.

Bane reached for the string that would give him wings, modifying it to give him the strength of an eagle when a flash of light blinded his mind's eye. Bane tried to clear his vision, searching desperately for the line he wanted when his eyes alighted on a third string.

On instinct, Bane grabbed it and felt himself get swept up into the Shift. Power, anger, and a fierce urge to protect overcame him as he leaned into it.

He felt his body fall forward, so he was on all fours, his shorts ripping quickly as thick, brown fur covered his limbs and torso. His muscles and body structures felt like they tripled or quadrupled in size as Bane fought for control of his unwieldy new bulk.

He blinked small eyes, trying to get a better sense of his surroundings as his nose and jaw elongated. They weren't nearly as long as the snout his alligator form had, but the smells he encountered were otherworldly. His eyesight was shit, but his sense of smell painted a picture of the same, if not better, caliber than that of his human sight.

Bane let out an experimental noise and almost jumped when the deep guttural sound came from his vocal cords.

He took in his surroundings, noting that Rae and Zeke still Crafted beside him, not losing a beat despite the intimidating creature next to them.

A deafening crash assaulted his senses as the currents did their job. He waved his snout in their direction before barreling down the slope before him. Bane was pleasantly surprised to find the colossal form could pick up a good amount of speed.

He reached the sand of the bank and took on a steady lope, sending a message down the string within him. It would project his thoughts, the smells of worn wood, the damp air of the river, and the musty scent of the riverbank. He sent the feeling of his paws moving from grass to the packed dirt and sand of the bank, and the break in the foliage a little way from the Crafters and the young girl.

He sent the call as far and wide as he could.

They just needed to buy a little more time.

He came upon the ship as the crew recovered from the crash. Some were thrown overboard, but most kept their hold on the ship, struggling to get upright as they noticed Bane's lumbering form. Bane had to be careful not to draw the force of their arrows or throwing knives. His hope was they would stay on the ship until it was too late. Any other bears that came would be asked to play defense, and keep the crew on board for as long as possible.

Bane just needed to do his part first.

The wind and water still raged along the river, Rae and Zeke providing as much cover as they could, still hidden by the foliage above. Bane prayed to the Huntress they stayed that way. The whole point was to keep these pursuers from realizing Magicae were detaining them, and not a string of random events.

Bane reached the side of the ship and lifted onto his hind legs. He'd only seen a bear once a couple of winters ago on the way to Heimat. He had been in awe of the enormous creature's paws, but nothing could have prepared him for the hefty weight and sheer power behind each of his new, massive hands.

He let out a short growl before throwing all his weight behind one paw and punching it against the side of the ship, shredding the wood with his claws. He used his nose to find where the boards were already cracked and snapped upon impact with a large rock on the bank.

His goal was to widen the hole, not make it irreparable. If these people were indeed not pursuing them, they were innocents trying to make a living. It wouldn't sit right with Bane to screw them over.

Life in Kamore was hard for everyone. Not knowing someone's story wasn't an excuse to disregard their feelings or quality of life.

A thump in his shoulder had him seeing red. The animal instinct within demanded retribution as Bane roared and whirled toward the direction of the arrows. It took everything in him not to charge the unseen enemy. He felt blood trickle down his shoulder as he gave the ship a couple more swipes.

He took off in the opposite direction from which he came, bringing prying eyes and suspicion away from the Crafters' hiding spot. Only the deep huff of another bear caused him to pause his ascent back into the foliage.

Bane quickly sent a warning to the second bear, hoping Zeke would keep the arrows off this bear as he had with the Shifter.

Curse these blasted eyes. Bane raved in his head, trying to see if the crew targeted this bear as they did him. He sent another image to the animal, enticing it to give the ship a wide berth. Hopefully, the crew would leave the massive creature be if it didn't attack the ship.

Bane cursed the way the huge mammal interpreted the world, not used to dealing with sounds and smells instead of pictures. His form was physically an animal, but his mind was still very much human. It was disorientating and unnerving being in a form that could sense so much in such a different way than he was used to. It would take time to get used to this way of interpreting his environment.

The bear lumbered by the ship, taking its time, but not drawing the wrath of the people on the ship. Bane nodded his head as he crashed through the trees to get back to his friends. He sent his thanks to the bear, instructing it to stay as long as it could, keeping its distance and communicating with any others that heeded his previous desperate call.

He made his way to the other Magicae, only giving a huff before reaching the two Crafters.

"Nice work, Bane!" Zeke murmured, patting his flank.

Rae tore her eyes from the ship and gave a concerned look at the arrow protruding from his back. "Come on guys, we better head to Lockewater. They'll be occupied for a while now." She inclined her head towards the ship, needing desperate repair. "We'll have to figure out what's going on with your forms later. I'm just glad you could use it."

Zeke shot him a concerned look, hand still on his flank, and Bane knew he was wondering how this could be possible. The Shifter leaned into Zeke's touch, finding comfort in his closeness.

Rae walked to where Gemma waited, bouncing up and down with excitement at their success. The Crafter soothed her before leading the way to the path leading to Lockewater.

Bane gave another huff and nudged the young woman, holding a paw towards the little girl.

"Bane... I don't know if that's a wise idea. Your shoulder..."

Bane pressed past her and gave Gemma a gentle nudge before lowering his good shoulder toward the ground. She hopped up with a shriek and a little help from a light breeze.

The four made their way to Lockewater, the Crafters following behind Bane's hulking form carrying the young Herbalist; the rowboat forgotten in the aftermath of their efforts.

Chapter Twenty-Three

Mirabella paced the length of her rooms, trying to work up the nerve to go through with her plan. She could stay and play her part if it meant others would live, but gaining information with nobody to pass it on to was a waste. The root of the problem was she didn't trust anybody in her husband's estate, not even the servants. Everybody would sell her out if it meant they could get into the General's good graces.

She sighed and looked to the small window in her bedroom. A glance at the door had her chuckling at her paranoia. The General hadn't visited her rooms since Gemma was born and his infatuation with Myra took hold. Mirabella spent the first few years of their marriage wondering how she'd been so lucky to find a love as pure as fresh snow.

The irony was how damning that love turned out to be.

Mirabella walked to the window and opened it wide, inviting in the winter's chill wind and the light of the moon. The sudden gale took her breath away and sent a pang through her heart.

Such a fool. She thought to herself, thinking of the brother with lavender eyes she abandoned long ago. Vincenzio and Myra filled her head with lies, convincing her the Magicae were dangerous to themselves and the people around them. They convinced her Duncan and the rest would be better off under their control.

She could only hope she still had time to make things right.

Andre and Naomi, Rae's parents, trusted her to their demise. But Mirabella knew she couldn't change the past. The Goddess herself couldn't turn back the hands of time She created. Or so some believed.

If her love for her brother wasn't enough to convince her Myra was wrong, the love for her daughter was. Her heart squeezed as she thought of that little wildflower. A shiver went through her as she straightened her spine and left the window to go to her dresser.

She rummaged through the top drawer until she found what she was looking for. She glanced at the door again before reaching for a glass beside the mirror. The woman poured herself some whiskey and silently raised it in front of her reflection, cheersing herself before knocking it back with one gulp.

Mirabella set the glass down and ran the back of one hand across her mouth. She gripped the sides of the dresser as fire rushed down her throat and into her belly. She met her gaze in the mirror, noticing her pale complexion, the bags under her eyes, and her dark, limp hair.

She let the whiskey do its job, giving her the liquid courage she needed to get out of the hell she was living in. She reached into the top drawer and pulled out a pair of scissors, glancing at the door once more.

With a determined look in her eyes, she took a deep breath and cut her dark locks into a short bob, using the mirror as her guide. She made quick work of ridding herself of what her husband prized most. Mirabella knew this act of rebellion wouldn't go unpunished, not that her husband paid much attention to her these days, anyway. It was the lack of control he would respond to.

The soldiers left at dawn, though. This was Mirabella's best chance at getting out of this waking nightmare. There was no way to get a message to Duncan, so she would go herself. Not having Gemma tethering her to this place made her motivation to leave that much stronger.

The ship with the Magicae would meet up with the Circus at some point. Going after Duncan and his new family would be the easiest way to intercept her daughter.

And then maybe we can start over. Mirabella studied her gray eyes in the mirror and ran a hand through her shortened locks. The phantom feeling of the length she lost made her hair feel shorter than it was. She broke eye contact with her reflection and dipped a towel into the water basin by her dresser. She tried to take the dye from her hair using the wet towel. Some came off, but her hair remained dark.

She sighed and grabbed a vial from one of her drawers, adding it to the water basin and casting a glance at the window. Mirabella needed to accurately judge the brightness of the moon and how much time she had left. Leaning backwards, she dipped her short hair into the basin, using her hands to make sure the liquid covered every inch of her scalp.

The woman winced and let out a hiss as the chemicals burned her skin.

Mirabella grabbed the pitcher of water next to the basin and dumped it on her head, feeling sweet relief as it cooled the burning on her scalp. She used the towel to wrap her hair and wipe the sting from her hands before shedding the thick nightgown from her shoulders.

Reaching into the bottom drawer, she removed the few items in there, including the drawer's false bottom. Inside the hidden compartment was a pair of thick breeches, a long blouse, and a thick unassuming overcoat. She donned her new clothing, stuffing her feet into wool socks and black boots before using the towel to finish drying her hair.

Mirabella had to stifle her gasp when she caught sight of the gray hair she now wore. Having dyed it for years, it was as if a new person stared back at her.

With a shake of her head, she gruffly pulled a winter cap over the shock of gray and put her fingers into her ermine fur gloves. They were the one piece of her usual wardrobe she allowed herself to take.

Grabbing the piece of paper from her dresser, already filled with the words of her alibi, she placed it on the stand next to her bed. She left a note, letting her husband know she walked along the riverbank, looking for their daughter and trying to atone for her mistakes.

Mirabella knew he wouldn't care and leave her to her own devices. He would be silently hoping to be rid of her and free to marry the pretty young thing he constantly threatened her with when she argued or disobeyed his commands.

She blew the candle out, grabbed her pack of supplies, and slipped through her window, scaling a trellis down to the ground. Once her feet felt the earth, she ran as fast as she could, flying over the temporary bridge across the Little Mantaga and disappearing into the forest without a trace.

Johanna woke before dawn with a nervous energy filling her limbs. She drank her coffee on the front porch of the tannery, her eyes straying to the activity buzzing around the Barracks. She knew why Tommy was reluctant to use fire to cause the havoc they wanted.

But Heimat had burned enough for the people that occupied it.

Now was the time for them to take back what was theirs, and make their invaders taste their own medicine. Johanna saw red as she wrenched her eyes from the direction of their problems. Her hands shook with contained rage as she clenched her cup of coffee.

She looked up as footsteps sounded on her front steps. The sounds of arguing reached her as she recognized who was dropping by at such an hour.

"Eddy, I've told you a million times, my red hair doesn't mean I'm predestined to have a temper. You can't base your perception of a person solely on how they look." Simone lifted a hand to Johanna as she headed to the kitchen to get two more mugs of coffee.

It wasn't a surprise to see Simone this early, as the two women had been meeting as such for years. Taking a little time in the morning to reconnect before their busy days was something they both cherished. What was strange was seeing Eddy in tow.

Johanna raised an eyebrow as she met the Wharfman's gaze. He gave her a wink, waiting for Simone to return from the kitchen before giving her a response.

"The Prophetess bestows clues everywhere, lass. You just have to know where to look." Eddy goaded, taking the mug Simone offered him.

The redhead rolled her eyes at him, responding, "The Prophetess? She protects those at sea or on the water, you old codger." She gestured with her free hand to the floor beneath their feet. "Last time I checked, our feet were still dry."

Johanna chuckled, moving a couple of things from her small table on the porch and gesturing for them to make themselves comfortable.

"Gah. I am not old; wise, maybe, but never old. You'd do well to remember that, lass." He sat on the wooden chair with gratitude, recovering from the long walk to the tannery. "As for the Prophetess, she watches over every sailor, current or past, at sea or on land. She is the greatest of the three faces, and the most beautiful." Eddy said with a wink.

"I can see why you never married, Eddy." Johanna laughed. "Your heart belongs to the Prophetess herself. No woman could ever compare." She bumped his shoulder with a hand.

Simone gave the man a wry smile. "You're right, Johanna. That's why he's such an insufferable man to boot! Hard to have a good night in the sheets when your lover isn't made of flesh or blood."

Eddy shook his head as Johanna let out a snort, letting the women compose themselves before saying, "You jest, but the truth is no woman could hold my fancy for that long. The call of the wind and waves beckoned to my very blood for all of my youth."

"And then?" Johanna asked, genuinely interested in how Eddy ended up so far inland.

The older man sighed, "And then, as they say, all good things must end. I injured my leg and hand pretty badly. Couldn't sail anymore, but I had a bunch of knowledge locked up in the kisser. Been working at the docks ever since, helping get boats into shape for the open ocean and identifying shoddy craftsmanship from other ports."

Simone gripped his arm. "Well, I'm glad you're here. Even if you tease me for my hair." Her eyes turned distant as the reason for their visit came to mind. "Jo, we came by to make sure everything's ready for tonight." The woman bit her lip, unable to meet her friend's gaze. "And to see if we could change your mind."

"Not that we think you can't do it, lass. We just don't want to see you do this by yourself." Eddy added, seeing the defiance enter Johanna's gaze.

Johanna stood up, walking to the edge of the porch and leaning against one of the support beams, eyes resting on the Barracks in the distance.

"Jo, please. Let us help you. Having three people light three fires is less risky than one person lighting all three." Simone pleaded, moving to her friend and taking one hand in both of hers.

Johanna's eyes were hard as she looked at her friend. "Simone, the more people involved means the more people there are to get caught. I've studied the Barracks ever since I moved out this way. It's too risky when we don't have a fire Crafter to light it from a distance."

"But what if something happens? What if something goes wrong?"

"Simone, it might. But at least I'll be the only one in danger."

"Bullshit. You put us all in danger with your stubbornness. The people of the Fringe need you." Simone shook with anger as she glared at her friend.

Johanna tucked her fists into her pockets, hiding how they trembled. "Simone, listen to me. Eddy isn't in any shape to help. I don't know how you convinced him, but the guy gets winded from a long walk. He couldn't escape capture, should it come to that." She used one hand to gesture at the Wharfman, going on as if he couldn't hear her. "And you. Simone, you're too valuable. You organized a soup kitchen in half a day. You have the brains and motivation to get our city out of this. I'm not risking either of you."

"Glad to know what you really think of me, lass," Eddy grumbled.

Johanna's eyes blazed as she focused on the Wharfman. "Eddy, it's the truth, and you know it. If we were to get intercepted, you would be the first they'd target. I don't mean to be harsh, but honesty is better than seeing you hurt."

Eddy inclined his head but didn't respond.

Johanna's face softened as she gripped both her friends' hands. "Really, you guys. I appreciate your offers and your concern, but I got this. I'm quick, steady on my feet, and this way we only risk one of us, not all of us. Plus, this way I get all the glory." She said with a wink, trying to lighten the mood.

Simone let out a half chuckle, half sob before pulling her friend into a fierce embrace. "Just remember, you'll have to deal with me if something goes wrong," Simone mumbled before pulling away and wiping at her face.

"Out of the way, Red. It's my turn." Eddy shouldered past Simone to envelop the tanner into a bear hug. He murmured encouraging words into her hair and squeezed her.

Johanna pulled away after a couple of minutes, only determination in her eyes. "I appreciate you both. Now move along." She motioned for them to head out with a wry smile. "Much more of this, and I'll be just as sappy as you lot." Catching the concern in her friends' eyes, she added, "I'll be fine. Get moving before prying eyes see too much." She gave Simone a gentle push and sent a pleading look to Eddy, hoping they would take the hint and understand she was doing it for them.

If Johanna was captured, anybody she was associated with would be in danger. She needed to keep as low of a profile until then, but didn't want her friends to worry more than they already were.

Sometimes it sucked being the realist of the group.

Eddy gave her a nod, saying, "Stay outta trouble, lass. I'll check in tomorrow morning again." The Wharfman left with a wave.

Simone gave the Forger one last hug before following the old sailor.

Johanna watched the two leave before shifting her gaze to the Barracks.

Today marked the day Heimat fought back.

Darren Vincenzio paced the council chambers once more, still enraged by his wife's treachery. A servant brought the letter to him with trepidation while he waited for his wife before addressing the troops. He had ripped the letter in half without thinking, his anger getting the best of him. The ripping sound brought him back to his senses before he could destroy it further. The rational part of him knew it was the only clue that could lead to where his wife had gone. Taking the pieces of Mirabella's carefully crafted letter, he brought them to his quarters for safekeeping before making it out to the balcony.

He was forced to address the soldiers solo, feigning as if Mirabella was sick in bed. The send-off went well enough, but a feeling in his gut made him apprehensive about his wife's absence. Vincenzio had watched his troops march into the forest filled with pride and vengeance, but now he only felt apprehension about the lack of protection within the city limits.

What game is Mirabella playing?

Mirabella had been a force in her younger years. She was only sixteen when the Uprising took place, but full of conviction for the cause. When she betrayed her brother to ensure their success, he'd known he would marry her one day. Between serving as the head of Myra's guard and training new recruits at the Capital, Vincenzio struggled to make time to court the young woman. Somehow, he made it happen, and five years to the date after the Uprising; the couple married with Myra as their officiant. It had been the happiest day of his life, and their relationship had only gone downhill from there. The stress of two miscarriages and months on leave with Myra's forces strained the love between them.

After Gemma was born, their marriage only crumbled further.

He knew Mirabella had been in a dark place after losing two babies, which is why he stepped up and started making all the decisions for her. They had an image to uphold, and she had taken long enough to mourn. It wasn't his fault she never voiced her own opinion; he was doing his duty as her husband, despite her not fulfilling her own as his wife.

Mirabella was an excellent mother to their daughter. She just lost sight of her role as *his* partner. It was no wonder resentment built between them. He was selfless while she took advantage of his leniency.

And now she was gone.

The last rays of dusk splintered through the west-facing windows as Vincenzio stewed. He paced towards the door, still waiting for the squadron he sent along the riverbank to return with his wayward wife. It would be time for a lesson when she was returned to him.

DING-DONG, DING-DONG, DING-DONG.

Vincenzio's blood turned to ice as the bell tolled, warning of danger. He didn't have time to think, only act. He grabbed his scabbard with the sword sheathed inside and ran out the main doors, pulling out his sword and tossing its case to the floor behind him.

Chaos greeted him as marched into the courtyard.

Soldiers and servants ran back and forth while fire raged in several of the government buildings. Vincenzio stood in shock, not believing someone had the gumption to attack their stronghold. He recovered quickly, grabbing one young man by the back of the neck as he tried to run past.

"Get your head out of your ass and do something productive. Organize the others and put those fires out. NOW!" The military man left no room for argument before releasing the young man forcefully. He stumbled slightly before saluting his superior and running to get water.

Vincenzio shifted his gaze to the buildings on fire and caught movement in the corner of his eye.

When he turned to look for its source, a new blaze enveloped the building that housed the pigeon coop, an invaluable resource for communicating with Myra. Vincenzio clenched his fists until they bled, a vein becoming prominent in his forehead. With a roar, he charged toward the building, releasing the pigeons inside. Almost a dozen immediately flew in the Capital's direction, those being the ones slated for sending messages to the tyrant.

Vincenzio could only hope the sudden onslaught of birds without messages would raise the alarm bells in Myra's gut. He moved back to the center of the courtyard, looking for the calculated movement he'd seen before.

His eyes were wide as he took in as much of the scene as he could. He caught another flicker of movement in his peripheral as a loud crash sounded inside the council chambers. Heat blasted the front doors straight off their hinges.

Vincenzio barreled to the left side of the building and stuck his broadsword as far out in front of him as possible.

A figure in mottled furs tripped as they tried to avoid the menacing blade. Moving too fast, they fell in a heap close to Vincenzio. He had to blink several times as the figure seemed to disappear and reappear on the ground in front of him. He focused on the uncovered hand peeking through one sleeve. As long as he focused on that piece of flesh, he could keep the compact figure in view.

Using his boot, he turned the figure over, keeping his sword pointed toward them. The figure's hood slid back to reveal a young woman with hazel eyes and mousy brown hair, a gash on her forehead dripping silver. A predatory smile lit the general's face as he realized what he had in his grip. The woman struggled to catch her breath after having the wind knocked out of her.

He watched her eyes dart in panic, searching for a way out, and noticed the despair that filled them once she realized escape was impossible. When she met his cruel stare, though, only resolve lit the depths of her eyes.

He shot her a smirk and growled, "Not quite according to plan, huh?" He used the tip of his sword to lift her chin up, a pinprick of silver blood visible as his blade pierced her skin. "Roll over like a good dog and nobody gets hurt. Hands where I can see them."

The woman swallowed and waited for him to move his sword so she could comply. He did so but missed the smirk she flashed as she spit in his face and scrambled to get up and run, trusting in the suspicious nature of the long hooded cloak she wore.

Not fast enough.

Vincenzio saw red as he thrust the blade into her side, sticking her like the swine she was.

The manic grin died on his lips as he felt something dig into his thigh. Looking down, he realized the woman had thrown a dagger in one last-ditch effort to wound him.

With a grunt, Vincenzio removed his blade from the Forger's side and silver liquid pooled beneath her. He wiped Johanna's shimmering blood from its edge and left her body where it lay. With every bit of self-control he had, he moved with a slight limp to bellow orders at the soldiers and servants struggling to put the flames out.

Johanna's face still bore the smirk of resistance as she took her last breath.

Chapter Twenty-Four

The Governing Council was meeting in the amphitheater close to the cottages as the sun burned brightly above them. Luc sat with her back straight as she studied its members, while Duncan informed them about his meeting with Ulla. He had called an emergency meeting as soon as he returned from seeing the Queen, wanting to meet while his memory of their interaction was fresh.

Duncan represented the Crafters, as he had for years, Jess represented the Forgers, Chiara the Herbalists, J the Shifters, and she represented the Mortals of their caravan. Her Abuela, Gar, Midge, and Conrad held the four Elder positions, ensuring there would never be a tie should decisions be put to a vote.

This was Luc's first term on the Council, and she still couldn't believe her people trusted her to decide on their behalf. Her position as Head Mortal was unique in that she represented many of the friends and families along for the journey, supporting their loved ones and the Magicae in general. She took her job seriously and tried her best to weigh all their options before casting her vote on issues.

Her eyes caught her Abuela's gaze, and she ducked her head, heat flushing her cheeks at being caught looking instead of listening. Her Abuela sent her a wink before turning back to the Ringmaster.

Luc frowned as he finished, stressing the Queen's veiled threats and suspicious reaction to his questions about Tyee's whereabouts. The group burst into conversation as soon as he finished, each person trying to get their point across first.

Luc toyed with the pendant on her necklace, but stayed quiet, knowing her opportunity to speak would come.

"Okay, okay! Order, please!" Duncan commanded, using his wind to dampen the volume of those around him. "We can't listen when everyone speaks at once. We need to decide on two courses of action. The first one is what to do about the Forgetting rune. Do we agree to the Queen's terms or demand our own? And the second is what do we do about Tyee? They're keeping him, for Huntress knows what."

Jess spoke first, before anyone could interrupt her. "We can't take the Forgetting rune," she said flatly.

Luc watched as concern knitted Duncan's brows. Before he could respond, Conrad spoke up.

"Seconded. We know nothing about those runes of theirs. They could do whatever damage they wanted, and we'd be none the wiser." The tiger Shifter growled lightly, still recovering from the fight but too stubborn to stay in bed. Chiara kept a close eye on the older man to make sure he didn't overdo it.

"That was my reaction to the Queen's counter as well. But I must remind everyone, we are guests in this place, surrounded by a people willing to do whatever they must to keep their existence a secret. Their power and fighting capabilities need to be taken seriously." Duncan grimaced, echoing Jess's points from earlier.

Luc regarded their Ringmaster with shrewd eyes, trying to guess his thoughts. The dilemma resided in that they didn't know where Tyee was. If they gave in to the Elven's demand for the runes, they would be at risk of not recovering their friend. Luc had a sinking feeling that Duncan was ready to put the group's relative safety over finding Tyee. She hoped not, but couldn't shake the feeling that something terrible was coming to pass. Her time to speak would come and she needed to be ready.

"What if we left without telling them? Disappeared in the night?" Midge suggested.

Chiara's face was pained. "I don't know if that would work, Midge. They may see it as an act of aggression and pursue us. I don't think that general would be merciful a second time around." Midge shrugged her shoulders and nodded, accepting the Herbalist's critique. Chiara held her chin high as she continued, "And that would mean leaving Tyee behind. We need to get the horseman back before we agree to any sort of rune. I spoke with one of their healers and he insisted the Elven people would not take kindly to their Queen harming innocent children."

Luc breathed a quiet sigh of relief. She caught her Abuela's gaze again, but this time the old woman simply raised one eyebrow in challenge. Luc knew she was waiting for her granddaughter to say something before she spoke up.

The young woman nodded to her Abuela before clearing her throat. "I echo what Chiara said. We can't do anything until we find Tyee. Some may argue the safety of the group should take priority over an individual, but we need to think about what message that sends to our people. What happens when they are the individual and the group supersedes them?" Her eyes blazed. "We need to be careful about what we communicate with our actions. Tyee deserves to be found just as much as anyone else."

She made eye contact with everyone in attendance, saving Duncan for last. Her fierce gaze communicated what she couldn't say in words. The Mortals in the group would grow untrusting if they failed to do all they could to save the Mortal horseman. A schism was the last thing the Circus needed at a time like this.

Duncan took a moment to study those in front of him before replying to Luc. His kind eyes met hers, the lavender color inviting as he gave her a nod. "I completely agree. Tyee needs to be found first." He hesitated, holding something back.

"What's on your mind, Dunc? What aren't you saying?" Nan finally joined the conversation, proud of her granddaughter's insight and willingness to speak up for the people she represented. She gestured to the group. "We're all friends here."

"Absolutely, I have a hunch, no concrete evidence, though, so I don't want to suggest something that is untrue. The Queen was extremely evasive when she talked about Tyee as if she wanted us to believe he left on his own accord. And I have been wracking my brain trying to figure out how that benefits the Elven. If they were holding him hostage, they would spread the word as far and wide as they could, as is the point of a hostage. But it's as if they'd rather get us out of here and keep Tyee with them."

"Well, the General knew him, right?" Jess asked.

"What? How do you suppose that, Jess?" Gar rubbed the back of his neck and shot a quizzical look at the Forger.

"She ignored me to look right at him and smiled." Jess's face was grave. "And mark my words, it wasn't the happy-to-see-an-old-friend kind of grin, more like a predator-finding-its-prey kind of smile. She took the horse he was tied to once we got closer to the city. I kept my eyes on her the entire time. She has to have him somewhere."

Gar grunted but said nothing else, at a loss along with the rest of them. Duncan's second in command demonstrated her keen senses and attention to detail once again. Everyone shifted their attention back to the Ringmaster, waiting for him to continue.

Luc furrowed her brows as she looked up at the city in the trees. Something about the Elven people and the guards that escorted them seemed so familiar to her. She closed her eyes and ran through the events before they were captured. She remembered Duncan charging the woman, their attacks failing, and Jess pleading with the general to let their Ringmaster go.

And then...

Jess was right. The woman looked right at Tyee before he started screaming. She had gone to him, trying to calm Koko, but the order to dismount came quickly after. Tyee was taken from Koko and tied up like Duncan before being lost from Luc's line of sight.

The acrobat opened her eyes and interrupted what Duncan was saying. "The General was the reason Tyee screamed; she must have done something to him.

He was clutching his head before he was taken from Koko's back." She nodded at Jess, affirming the woman's observations. Noticing everyone's impatient stares, she realized too late she'd interrupted someone.

Her eyes met Duncan's in horror, but only kindness and amusement shone in their lavender depths. He nodded for her to continue.

"Damien and I think they're communicating without speaking somehow. I think the General tried to do the same with Tyee, but it didn't work for some reason." Luc knew her next thought would raise eyebrows, but she said it anyway. "I think Tyee must have Elven blood."

Midge gasped, Nan furrowed her brows, and Duncan's face remained warm, giving nothing away. Luc gauged the reactions around her before plowing forward. "It's the only thing that explains why they want us to leave without him. And he has a similar build and coloring to our reluctant hosts."

The group sat in shock, nobody saying anything for a few minutes. Luc felt butterflies in her stomach as she looked anywhere but into the eyes of her fellow Council members. Most times, she still felt like an outcast on the Council; part of it, but untested and lacking in life experience. That familiar feeling of being in over her head threatened to swallow her until she found her Abuela's eyes. The pride and impressed look in the old woman's eyes settled some of the anxiety in her stomach.

A rough voice sounded. "Or he's dead." Conrad voiced the possibility nobody wanted to consider. He inclined his head to Luc and Jess. "Don't get me wrong, I think the gals are right. There's more going on than we know, but sometimes the simple answer is the truth. Everything you've said could be true, but the evasiveness makes me think they don't want to present a body."

Luc chewed on the inside of her cheek as Conrad said his piece. When nobody spoke up, she said, "That's a possibility. They could keep it from us to get us to comply with their terms, but again, as Duncan said, wouldn't they come right out and say it? Wouldn't they be gloating from the rooftops? No, there's more to the story than that."

"But if they did that, they'd assume we'd want to see him alive. This way, they can get away without risking us asking." Conrad countered before coughs racked his muscular frame.

Luc watched the faces of the others, worry taking hold of her heart. She wouldn't give up on the horseman that easily, but she needed to judge how hard to push the Council. The Mortals in their caravan deserved her voice, Tyee included.

Besides, he was important to Rae, no matter how much the Crafter denied it. Luc had witnessed a change in her friend since the pair became more serious. Rae had always been independent and headstrong; it was nice to see her letting someone else care for her.

Luc would do everything she could to make sure Tyee was waiting for the Crafter when she got back. And she could also admit to herself the horseman was growing on her. She wanted to learn more about his story and where he came from.

Her head shot up when Duncan cleared his throat.

"My friends, we can argue until we're blue in the face, but the reality is, there is no correct answer." The wind Crafter nodded in Luc's direction.

"I think Luc is onto something with her theory about Tyee having Elven blood. It remains to be seen whether they kept him alive or, as Conrad suggested, found a better use for his corpse. Regardless of the outcome, we must heed Luc's words on choosing the message we want to send carefully. Our people deserve the best from us. We need to distract the Elven long enough to find Tyee. Any ideas?"

"What about a Circus performance?" Chiara spoke up, inclining her head to the trees above them. "Win over the people with our acts and showmanship and those of us not performing can spread out and look for the horseman."

"We would need to convince the Queen to let her people come down from the treetops. Which might be tricky." Gar mused.

"Maybe not," Nan said with a twinkle in her eyes. "Gather in, dearies. I have an idea."

Luc gave a silent chuckle as everyone hung on her Abuela's every word. The old storyteller weaved a plan to endear them to the Elven people and force their Queen's hand.

Luc could only hope it worked as well as they wanted it to.

Tyee floated in the dark space of his consciousness, dreaming of stables and tall trees and a golden acrobat. He murmured to himself, reaching for the woman he couldn't forget when his dreams changed. The stables became a dark cave, runes glowing faintly on the wall, the trees became jagged glass, broken and glinting in their glow, and the acrobat... her face became sharp, hair grew darker, and a cruel smile formed on her lips. She reached a taloned hand toward him as she mouthed the words, 'stable boy,' but was drowned out by the screams wrenched from Tyee's throat.

He screamed until his voice grew hoarse, unable to move in the inky darkness. The woman and the cave faded away once his screaming stopped, the feral smile still on her lips.

Tyee felt his heartbeat thundering in his chest as his breaths came in rasps. He blinked, and another scene appeared before him.

This time, it was a memory from his childhood. He was back in the hovel they called home, barely a toddler. He had been of little use back then, other than as a prop for when his mother went begging for coin. But this was a moment at home when his mother wasn't using him or ignoring him.

She was singing to him. Her voice was pretty as it followed a haunting melody, in a language he'd never heard.

The horseman watched with bated breath, eyebrows pulled together as he tried to puzzle out this memory buried deep within his being.

As the last note sounded, he watched as his mother cracked, tears streaming from her face. To his amazement, she pulled him close for a cuddle, taking comfort from having a sleeping baby in her arms.

She whispered something in the baby's ear.

Tyee strained his ears to catch what his mother said all those years ago.

"I'm so sorry, my sweet boy. Words will never do justice to the life I've chosen for you. Forgive me for what your future entails."

As he watched, her face became disfigured, teeth elongating, eyes becoming slits, and ears sharpening into points at their ends. A horrible hiss came from her gaping mouth as she lunged for him, the baby nowhere to be seen.

"Come here Tyee, Mommy has a surprise for you." Gone was the soothing tone from the lullaby; instead, the creature's voice was deep and gravelly, unnatural coming from the form of a young woman. Tyee pulled back quickly, evading the clawed hands just barely. Despite his need for clarity, he turned his back on his mother one last time and fled.

The surrounding darkness became suffocating as he ran, trying to find a way out of this nightmare. Images flashed to the left and right of him, making him pump his legs faster, doing what he could to escape the memories. His lungs felt like they were on fire as his heart thundered in his throat. One wrong step and the nightmare would find him again. A light flashed in front of him, highlighting a lone figure in the distance.

Tyee ran harder, not sure whether he would avoid the mysterious person or engage with them. All he knew was he needed to leave the darkness behind him.

The figure became more distinct, featuring the lithe figure of what he presumed was a woman. His steps faltered in trepidation, praying it wasn't Sylvia or his mother. He noticed golden hair tied in a plait over one shoulder and a golden jumpsuit that accentuated all the right curves.

Hope swelled in his chest as he came upon the woman, his hand reaching out to touch her shoulder, but he pulled back quickly when she turned of her own accord.

"Your blood is glowing." She whispered, her golden eyes never leaving his. The image of Rae hissed the last word before disappearing as if scattered by the wind.

Tyee tried to capture her essence, grasping at the pieces of her image that floated around him to no avail. As the last of her disappeared, Tyee screamed in frustration, dropping to his knees and pounding one fist on the ground as the light glowed around him. Frustration and anger threatened to overtake him as he looked up at the glow ahead of him.

The light flashed brightly, blinding Tyee, and then his world went dark.

Tyee woke with a jolt, still trying to clear the spots from his vision.

When he could finally see, he let out a groan.

Not again, he thought to himself as he moved his hands as much as he was able, a thick cord limiting his movements. The horseman shook his head, trying to make sense of everything he'd seen while in his subconscious.

Nothing made sense. Sylvie, his mother, Rae...

They were like pieces of a puzzle that should fit together but didn't, no matter how hard he tried to force them together.

Growling, he looked around at his new surroundings. He wasn't in a cave anymore, sunlight peeking through the slats of wood above him and to his left. Tyee noted the sun's position, surmising if it moved higher in the sky, that would be east, but if it lowered, he could be sure that direction was west.

He caught wafts of the smoke from a cooking fire, the aroma of spiced meat making his stomach grumble, and the smell of green one found deep in the woods. Straining his ears, Tyee could hear faint laughter and squealing in the distance. He gently lifted his arms, testing the strength of the cord tied to his wrists before running his hands along the wooden surface he was tied to.

The devil was in the details, after all.

The more Tyee observed, the better the picture he would have to mount his escape. Gritting his teeth, he got to work, trying to fray the bonds on his wrists against the table he was tied to. He guessed this was a residence in Sylvie's village, not the cave made for holding prisoners.

He was having trouble keeping his nightmares and the conversation he heard between Sylvie and what must have been her mother separate. The edges bled together in his mind, making it hard to decipher facts from fiction. What he knew was the Elven had him in their clutches and their princess had a vendetta against him.

Tyee paused in running his wrists over the rough wood beneath him as he focused on remembering what he'd learned.

Sylvie was searching for something all those years ago. The horseman chewed on the inside of his cheek.

Not something, someone. His heart raced as he thought back to the half dreams, half memories he was thrown into during his unconsciousness.

My mother.

Tyee's heart skipped a beat as the time he spent with Sylvie came flooding back. All the times she probed about his family, where he came from, and his mother. She was as persistent as a dog with a bone, trying to get any and all details from him. And on that day, when he started the fire in the stables and took Koko, Sylvie teased him. She had claimed she would stop in Aston and get the answers she needed since he was useless in that department. That day was a mess and Tyee never gave a second thought to her words.

The iciness she presented to him when she challenged him to take the horse he wanted had driven any fondness for her from his heart. Sylvie alone knew the true extent of the bond he had with the midnight-colored stallion. The fact she would throw it back in his face so arbitrarily had been the worst betrayal.

But what would the Elven want with my mother?

Tyee was at a loss until the half memories from being unconscious came back to him. His mother singing in a strange language, Rae's words about his blood glowing, and how he didn't remember either of those things actually happening.

The horseman shut his eyes tight, trying to stop his thoughts, knowing the revelation to come wasn't one he was ready to face.

"It seems you've been spending too much time in the dark. Can't handle the sun anymore?" The taunting voice was thick like honey, and just as sickeningly sweet.

Tyee's eyes flew open as his body flailed against the bonds that held him. A snarl ripped from his throat and he glared at the woman he despised. His nostrils flared as his chest shuddered with each breath. Tyee felt rage like he'd never known as he observed the Elven woman.

"Settle down, boy, soon enough you will get your answers." Sylvia made to place a hand on Tyee's forehead but he jerked away at the last second, eyes blazing as they held hers.

"I want answers now," he growled. "Why are you holding me hostage?"

She traced the rips in his shirt from her torturing with one long-nailed finger, keeping her eyes on his as she moved closer to his belt line. She smirked at him but obliged, "To learn all I could about your band of misfits, of course."

"Drop the act, Sylvie. You already did that. What's your reason for keeping me tied up now?" Tyee narrowed his eyes at her, before asking her in a low voice, "Does it have anything to do with my mother?"

Sylvia's face betrayed no emotion but the slight widening of her eyes told Tyee he struck a nerve. Her smirk turned to ice as she answered. "Your mother? What would I want with your deadbeat excuse for a mother?"

"Tell me the truth, Sylvie. You owe me that, at least. My mother was the one thing you never let go of until I finally convinced you I knew nothing or would not tell you no matter what you did. That's why you left and turned my life into shambles. You manipulated me into setting fire to that stable."

"My name is *Sylvia* and I owe you nothing, Stableboy. You ruined your own life. Don't blame it on me when you were the one that lit the match." Sylvia hissed her reply, making to touch his forehead once more.

Before she could, Tyee asked what he was dreading. "Was she Elven?"

Sylvia couldn't hide the emotion on her face this time, dread and disbelief passing across her features. The hand she was holding above Tyee's head dropped as she struggled to make her face a blank mask once more.

Tyee took his chance and grabbed at her wrist, cradling it to keep her from pulling away. The knots in his stomach only tightened, knowing he'd found his answer no matter what Sylvia said. Tyee had Elven blood running through his veins whether or not he wanted to admit it.

Before Sylvia responded, he asked, "Is that why you won't let me go? Because I'm half Elven?"

Sylvia looked down at where his hand held her wrist before wrenching it from his grasp with a growl. She paced in front of him several times and gave him a withering look before leaving the wooden structure and slamming the door behind her.

"Well, that answers that, I guess." Tyee mumbled to the now empty room. He shook his head to clear his thoughts. His blood was irrelevant unless it could help him get out of this mess.

That made Tyee pause.

The horseman knew a little about letting those with Gifts use his life energy to control the magic in their blood. He'd offered it exactly three times in his life, twice were to Rae, but the first time, he offered it to one boy in the stables of Briar.

Tyee knew the boy was Magicae the moment he laid eyes on him. There was always a tingling sensation in his gut when he was near someone with one of the Gifts of the Goddess. It became apparent the boy was a Forger with the ability to manipulate iron soon after he joined the stable staff.

Tyee was the head stable boy at that point and put the boy to work aiding the blacksmith when he came to trim hooves and put shoes on the horses.

It was a mistake. Both Tyee and the boy were too young and naïve to realize a Forger working with his Material daily was a recipe for disaster. Outside of Heimat, all the Magicae avoided those professions that dealt with whatever their blood called for.

The boy couldn't hide his abilities and the blacksmith reported it to Tyee himself, the boy's direct supervisor. Tyee had no choice but to report it to the stable master or risk the blacksmith reporting him as a Magicae, or worse, a

Magicae sympathizer. Before he did, Tyee went to the boy and warned him of what was to happen. The boy panicked after a long day, his Gift exhausted, and could barely get himself to pack his belongings.

That was when Tyee offered the boy his forearm, knowing it was the least he could do since he was the reason the boy was discovered. The gratitude on the boy's face had made Tyee's heart twinge before he almost blacked out at the onslaught of emotions communicated through where the boy's skin touched Tyee's arm.

It was intense. And the boy's panic hadn't helped either. He'd pulled so fast and furious, and then his emotions came flooding in shortly after. The bond between them was like a bridge, giving each of them a glimpse into the essence of the other's being.

It only made Tyee feel even more guilty. Luckily, the boy escaped without issue, and Tyee wasn't suspected of helping him escape. After that, Tyee took measures to make sure he never made that mistake again. When Magicae joined his staff, he observed them until he could ascertain what Gift they had. Once that was done, he assigned them to a position that allowed them to hide their abilities with ease.

It was the most vexing part of his job, knowing he had people that could do magnificent work, but having to make sure they never got close to using those skills.

Such a waste. Tyee thought as his mind turned to the couple of times he offered energy to Rae. He'd offered twice, but she only accepted once. He remembered the surprise on her face when she opened the connection between them, and undoubtedly saw the feelings he already had for her from a distance. Tyee could barely admit it to himself, but offering her his life energy had been the easiest way to let her know he was interested in the woman.

What better way to communicate than sending his emotions to her directly? No words needed.

Huntress, he was a coward.

But there was another time he gave her his energy, the time when she asked if she could take some. He remembered there had been a surprise then too, but they never spoke about what changed between them. Emotions became less and less transparent each time two people shared energy. The mind's ability to protect itself surpassing even that direct of a connection.

I wonder if she saw my blood glow. Tyee mused, wondering if his subconscious had heard her thoughts despite the mental blocks put in place by his conscious mind. A thought came unbidden to him as he remembered when Sylvie found them in the first place.

She had a staff that glowed. The *runes* on the staff glowed.

Maybe there was a way to use his blood to call to the runes. He resumed rubbing the cords at his wrists on the table below him, closing his eyes and trying to find the power in his veins.

He would keep searching inward while outwardly, he took as much action as he could. Tyee needed the cord to fray or his blood to awaken before Sylvia or the Queen returned.

The time to escape was now or never. He silently thanked the golden acrobat for giving him the insight he needed.

He would find her if it was the last thing he did.

Chapter Twenty-Five

The four Magicae made it to Lockewater with little issue. They camped outside of town a bit that night to allow them time to rest and for Bane to Shift. The morning after they beached their pursuers, the four made their way into town, looking for George and their people.

Lockewater was a sailing town through and through. Its inhabitants were fishermen, merchants, and dockworkers. The town used the river to the north as a barrier to the Great Northern Forest and its supply of freshwater, while the coast to its east provided food and a means to live. The shipyard was the most renowned in all of Kamore and brought more traffic to the town during the summer months.

Luckily, winter was the off-season, and the streets were emptying for the long, cold months. Within the week, most of the visitors should be gone. This was the first time Rae, Zeke, and Bane had been in a city without the guise of the Circus to protect them.

It was exhilarating and terrifying at the same time.

The three did their best to draw as little attention to themselves as possible. Especially since Heimat wasn't the only city feeling the effects of Myra's campaign to "civilize the North." Soldiers stood on almost every other corner keeping an eye out for signs of Magicae and their supporters.

The sooner they left the city, the better.

Gemma clung to Rae's arm as they walked the streets behind Zeke and Bane. The little girl regarded everyone they saw with wide eyes. The little girl's hood slipped again, her unmistakable curls peeking out from underneath the cloth.

Rae knelt next to the girl and quickly drew it back up, tucking the stray pieces of hair into the girl's hood. She noticed Gemma's unnatural quietness and chucked the little girl's chin.

"Hey, chin up, Red. Just stay calm and act normal. We've got you." Rae held the young Herbalist's gaze, recognizing the fear in her eyes. Deep in her heart, Rae felt only anguish. This little girl shouldn't have to walk streets lined with soldiers. She shouldn't have had a fear ingrained so deep that walking down a busy street made her petrified.

How do I make this right? Rae thought as she searched the little girl's face. It looked like Gemma wanted to say something, so Rae lifted an eyebrow, saying, "Go on, Red. Say what you wanna say."

Gemma glanced to their left and right before leaning into Rae's side to whisper in her ear. "But what about the bad people?"

Rae kept the anger from her face, schooling her features before pulling back to look into the little girl's face. The Crafter knew the last thing this little girl needed was to think Rae was upset with her. Rae needed to reassure the Herbalist and make her feel safe.

"Look at me, Gemma." Rae waited until the girl's gray eyes met hers. "I will protect you from the bad people; we all will. Stay close to one of us and we will keep you safe. I promise, Gemma." Tears filled the girl's gray orbs, but none fell as she shook her head vigorously, wanting to prove herself to the woman she idolized.

Rae pursed her lips before turning to look for the men they were following. The pair stood a little way off, having realized they lost the other half of their party. Rae met Zeke's falsely colored eyes and nodded once, answering the concerned look on his face.

Bane had recovered enough to Shift into his human form, but hadn't wanted to risk Shifting again into a hawk or other animal form. He wore a hood that obscured his brown, bear eyes containing no whites, counting on Rae and Zeke to do the talking while he played the part of a mute.

Rae and Zeke always traveled with tonic for their eyes. It was a practice drilled into them as kids to ensure they always had protection should they encounter unknown Mortals along the way.

The key was to be present enough in the crowd to blend in. They didn't want to draw attention to their party as they roamed the streets looking for their friends. Rae and Gemma caught up with the other two and all four made their way to one alley that met up with the main road.

"We need a better plan than just wandering around. If they got Bane's message, they may have already gone into the forest." Zeke said, looking between Rae and Bane. "We need to get to the docks." He glanced at the sentinel on the corner. "And away from prying eyes."

Rae bit her lip. "The docks are usually where the brothels and bars are for the incoming sailors, but also tend to attract soldiers. Do you think George and Tam would bring the kids there?"

"No, but I know that's where Cleo and Adams will be. They'll be our best bet at finding a place to start, even if we have to keep our heads down."

Rae nodded. "Fair enough. We need to head east towards the coast."

Bane tipped his head up slightly and sniffed. Even in his human form, Bane's senses were powerful. He motioned for the two acrobats to come closer. "I can get us to the docks, but do we wanna bring the kid that way?" he whispered, keeping an eye out for anyone that might wander into the alley.

Rae shot a worried glance at the young girl before looking at the others. "I don't like the idea of splitting up, but you have a point. Let's all head that way, and I'll walk with her along the coast."

Bane nodded but looked to Zeke, wanting the wind Crafter to weigh in before they left the alley. Zeke looked at the little girl and sighed. "We can't split up. Gemma?" He called, crouching to look the girl in the eyes. "We're heading to the docks to find Captain Starski. We need you to stay close and keep that hood up, no matter what. It's going to be a rougher part of town, but we'll keep you safe, understand?"

Gemma's upper lip trembled, but she nodded. "I can do that, Mr. Zeke. I'll be brave."

Rae's heart broke again, listening to their conversation. Zeke caught the sadness in Rae's expression but responded, "Hey now, none of that. Call me Zeke, little one. And I know you'll be brave. You're already the bravest five-year-old I know."

The Herbalist studied Zeke intently before a small smile broke out on her face. "I'll call you Zeke if you call me Red." Rae let out a burst of laughter before clamping her hand over her mouth, dissolving into silent shakes.

Zeke smirked at the little girl's brazenness, clearly feeling more comfortable with the three Magicae. He stuck his hand out and smiled when Gemma grabbed it quickly and gave him a firm shake. The acrobat shot a glance at Rae and raised his eyebrow at the Crafter. Gemma was besotted with his best friend to the point where she wanted everybody to call her by the nickname Rae coined.

He just shook his head as they made to follow Bane to the docks.

"Read 'em and weep, boys. Bested again by the woman you swore you'd wipe the floor with. Who's next?" Cleo's green eyes danced with challenge as she laid her cards on the table, winning the poker hand yet again and leaning to claim the pot in the middle of the table.

A dagger thunked next to her sleeve, biting into the rough wood of the table and causing her to pause. She flashed thunderous eyes around the room, searching for the interloper. They caught on the burly man next to the table she sat at.

Cleo grabbed the dagger and stood in one fluid motion, her chair toppling to the floor. The tavern went silent as the patrons and employees watched the interaction near the poker table. The captain moved with cat-like grace as she knocked the larger man onto his back on top of a nearby table and held the dagger to the man's neck.

"One wrong move and you're dead. I suggest you explain what you have against a fair win and that you do it quickly." She hissed, keeping the blade against his throat.

The man just glared as Cleo dug the blade deeper, a thin line of blood trickling down his neck.

"The guy's mute, Cap. You're wasting your time." Mouse drawled, her beady eyes darting around the room, on the lookout for trouble. "Let him go and let's get out of here."

Cleo shot her a look. "What do you mean, he's mute?"

"I mean, he can't talk. I've been watching him; he doesn't have a tongue." She stuck her own out to demonstrate and stress her point.

The Captain brought her attention back to the man she held at blade point and narrowed her eyes. Her lips became a thin line as she went through her options. A dangerous smile lit her face as she said, "Is that true, rapscallion?"

The man slowly nodded, opening his mouth and revealing the mess that once was his tongue.

Cleo studied the man, realizing word had gotten around they were looking for a crew. Her winning at poker meant anyone looking for employment knew she could back her promises for payment. This man could be a handful or one of the most loyal men she could hope to find. It just depended on how she handled this interaction.

Slowly, she moved her dagger away from the man's throat and let him right himself. Once he turned his attention back to her, she asked, "Can you tie a knot? Tack a sail? Climb the rigging?"

He nodded three times.

"You're hired. Report to the southern dock at dawn. We sail for the Eastern Islands."

The burly man gave her a salute before leaving out the back entrance of the eating and drinking establishment.

"Was that wise, Captain?" Adams asked, one eyebrow raised as Cleo returned to her poker table and pocketed the money she rightfully earned.

"I think I liked it better when you never questioned what I said or did." She grumbled. "He's perfect. He'll never give up any of my secrets. Perfect for a woman that wants to blow off some steam."

Mouse let out a cackle and ribbed the first mate. "Glad to serve a captain with her priorities straight. I need to find me a smoke. I'll see you both in the morning." She waved a hand at the two before heading to the door.

As Mouse reached for the handle, the door swung open and almost hit the older woman.

Bane and Zeke stormed through, scanning the room for those they sought. Bane kept his hood down, still hiding his animal eyes. Luckily, this was one of the few bars that held out against the onslaught of the military. The two men relaxed slightly upon not finding any soldiers inside the crowded establishment.

Zeke caught sight of Mouse first and inclined his head in apology, recognizing the scowl on her face for what it was. "Sorry, Mouse, didn't see you there. Is the Captain here?"

Mouse glared but pointed behind him before slipping out the door.

Cleo watched the two men approach and shot a look at Adams. Under her breath, she said, "I'm telling ya, Adams, these boys just can't resist me." Adams snorted and shook his head, only causing the Captain's smirk to widen. Her green eyes assessed their rumpled clothing and haggard appearance. *What hell did they go through?* Her eyes narrowed as she realized Rae and the girl were absent. *And where's the fire Crafter?*

She projected her voice, "Come to join my crew? I'm afraid there's no room for landlubbers like you two." Her eyes glinted with mischief despite the drawn expressions on both men's faces.

"Captain, we need to talk." Zeke got straight to the point. He cast a glance around the room, adding, "Somewhere private."

"A man that knows what he wants! Careful acrobat, don't want to get too steamy with an audience around." She waggled her eyebrows.

Zeke glanced at Bane before hiding his reddening cheeks. Shaking his head, he composed himself and said, "Captain, we need your help, please."

"I told you they'd be begging for me." She winked at Adams before turning to the back of the tavern. "There's a room back here. Follow me." Cleo waved at the barkeep as she made her way into the back room of the tavern while the three men followed her. She looked at the two men seated at the table and jutted her chin out. "Clear the room, boys." She laid down three silver coins between the two of them and held the older man's gaze.

Not breaking eye contact, he snatched the pieces and stood. With a grunt he headed out the door they came through, the younger man following shortly after.

Cleo shot a pointed look at Adams and jerked her head towards the door. She waited until he stood guard before turning to the two Magicae.

Raising an eyebrow, she asked, "Well? Why did the two of you come barging in on us faster than a storm at sunrise?"

Zeke shot another concerned glance at Bane, but answered, "We encountered a setback." He looked the Captain straight in the eyes. "There was a ship pursuing us that got stuck in the storm. If you hadn't pressed forward, we surely would've been overtaken."

"You're sure they were pursuing us?" Cleo drummed her fingers on the table, keeping her eyes on Zeke.

Zeke again looked at Bane before continuing. "We don't know for certain. It looked like a merchant ship, but it was moving fast, like it was looking for someone. We beached them and Bane wrecked their hull to slow them down." He nodded to the Shifter, still keeping his hood down low.

Cleo's lips formed a thin line as she moved her attention to the Shifter. He hadn't said a word since arriving, despite Zeke's obvious pleading for him to join the conversation.

Curious. She thought to herself. *The Crafter is pining over that one. Guess I'm out of luck there too.* She sighed quietly, chasing those thoughts away. The real question she should be worried about was whether it was Bartholomew who followed them. She drummed the table as her eyes unfocused. *He'll be looking for the Vengeance if it is him.* She sent a searching look to Adams. It wouldn't do to continue the way they had been if Bartholomew was after them.

Cleo heard Zeke ask a question, but didn't register what he asked. She shook her head. "Say that again, Crafter."

"We need to find George and the others. Did they get the message Bane sent?"

"And how the hell am I supposed to know that, landlubber? Those towns-folk got off the ship faster than we could draw a breath when we landed. The dark-skinned woman said they had to find cover until you four—where are the other two?" Cleo frowned as she searched in vain, reminded that there should've been two more Magicae in their group.

"Rae took Gemma down by the ocean to look for shells."

"On a night like tonight? It'll be too dark to see anything down there." Cleo admonished.

"Better than bringing a little girl into an establishment like this," Bane spoke quietly, monitoring the door that Adams guarded.

Cleo's eyes held a slight glint as they whipped to the Shifter. "So he can speak. I was worried you'd lost your voice with your new form."

"Stay on topic, Cap," Adams called from his post. "There's a lot of move-ment by the poker tables. I think they're looking for you."

"Right, so any idea where they would've gone?" Zeke asked, casting an anx-ious glance at the first mate.

Cleo narrowed her eyes and drummed her fingers one last time. Just as quickly, she snapped them as a smile lit her face. "The Merryweather Inn. I overheard some of the crew talking about how they wished they could stay there for a few nights. I bet Mouse told them to go there." She looked between the two men in front of her. "Keep the sea to your right until you reach the Fisherman's Wife. It's a bakery, and take a hard left. It'll be about four or five blocks down and on your right."

Bane nodded as Zeke clasped the woman's arm. "You're Goddess-sent, Cap-tain. If there's anything we can do to repay you, say the word." The Crafter's tone was genuine as he met her green eyes.

Cleo was taken aback when she noticed Zeke's eyes weren't the glittering silver they normally were, instead gray orbs looked into hers. *So the Crafters had tonics with them. Even more curious that the Shifter is the one hiding.* She still couldn't figure out why the Shifter wasn't in his falcon form but knew there wasn't time to satiate her curiosity.

"The warning about a could-be Bartholomew is more than enough repayment. Now get, unless there's something else you'd like to explore while we have the privacy?" She waggled her eyebrows at the good-looking men, chuckling at the clear tension in their shoulders. She hooked her arms around both of them and led them to the door. "Prophetess, relax, I don't bite. Go find your people."

She pushed them out of the private room, looking at the commotion by the poker tables. With a nod, she and Adams slinked past as quietly as possible, slipping into the night behind the two Magicae.

Chapter Twenty-Six

Rae looked up as determined footsteps pounded down the beach toward them. It was a terrible night for shell-collecting with no moon to light their way, but he gentle roll of the waves made up for the lack of treasures. She pulled Gemma close. Keeping a firm hand on the little girl's shoulder, Rae positioned herself between the Herbalist and the impending footsteps.

The Crafter only relaxed when she recognized Zeke's silver hair and lithe build, accompanied by a still-cloaked, solidly built Bane. She loosened her grip on the little girl and started towards the two men. She frowned when she noticed their drawn expressions.

"Bad news?" she asked when they got close enough.

Zeke searched the area before responding. "Cleo knew exactly who could've been on that ship. She didn't know if the others got Bane's message but had a good guess where they went. We should hurry, though, in case they've already left."

Rae studied her best friend, noticing the tension in his shoulders and how he clenched his jaw. She bit her lip before responding. "What's wrong, Z? You're as tense as a bowstring." She placed her hand on his shoulder and gave it a gentle squeeze, following his gaze across the beach.

Zeke shot a glance at Bane before meeting her searching look. He lowered his voice, monitoring where the Shifter stood with the little girl. "He barely said anything. Even when we were alone with Cleo and Adams. The only time he said anything was to defend the decision not to bring Gemma to the tavern. I'm worried about him."

"I'll talk to him. You take Gemma and lead us to where our people should be. We'll follow behind." Rae gripped both his forearms and waited for him to nod. It was unlike Zeke to be so worried, but Rae knew he was concerned about the Shifter. Bane taking different forms was dangerous, considering the unknown ramifications for the long term.

Rae went to the other two and leaned down to whisper in the young Herbalist's ear. Gemma giggled and ran to Zeke, grabbing his arm and forcing him to run ahead with her. Rae linked her arm through Bane's and led him at a slower pace.

"Walk with me, Shifter. We have a lot to talk about." Her smile sounded in her tone.

Bane cast a look at the Crafter but said nothing as he faced forward, a grim look on his face. He missed the hurt in Rae's expression before she schooled her features.

She knew this wouldn't be like talking to Zeke or Luc or Damien, but she wasn't expecting to hit such a wall. This was worse than trying to hold a conversation with Kaiser. *Even Tyee was never this closed off.* She sighed, knowing she'd have to try harder.

"Come on, Bane. Talk to me. Zeke's worried about you and so am I. I get wanting to keep a low profile, I do, but when it's just Adams and Cleo? Did something happen? Is there something you're not telling us?" She jostled the arm she was linked with slightly, keeping a firm grip so Bane couldn't escape.

After a couple of moments, he gave in. "It feels so strange. As if everything I know about the Gift running through my veins has been upended." He stopped to look Rae in the eyes, ambling his hood back so she could see the deep brown, bear eyes hidden by the rough fabric. "I'm having trouble wrapping my mind around the idea that everything I know and have experienced is wrong." He hung his head and took advantage of Rae's surprise by unlinking his arm from hers.

"What do you mean, wrong?" Rae asked, her eyebrows pinched together.

Bane seemed like he was at a loss for words as his hands rubbed his temples. Finally, he spoke, "It's like my entire perspective has shifted. If I could've done this all these years, my life would be so different. My Ma would still be alive."

Rae's face softened, and she gripped his forearms, forcing him to meet her gaze. "Bane, don't do that to yourself. Dwelling on the past is, more often than not, an exercise in frustration. Aye, things would've been different if you or I knew our Gifts were different when we were younger. And maybe some people we love would still be here, but Bane, their deaths *are not our faults.* It's not fair to put that weight on your shoulders."

Bane sighed. "I know, Rae. I know I shouldn't do that, but I can't help but wonder whether things would be better if I'd tried it sooner." He ran a hand over his short-cut hair. "That's what I'm struggling with most, Crafter. If only I'd tried sooner, so many things would be different. But you're right, I can't change the past. I can only keep charging forward. "

Rae rubbed his upper arms and nodded. "I couldn't have said it better myself." She hesitated for a moment before asking her next question. "Do you ever wonder why me?" At his quizzical look, she continued, "Do you ever wonder why your Gift is stronger than anyone else's? What does it mean, and why do we have it?"

Bane gave a terse nod. "Ever since I realized the truth, I've been wondering that. Do you know much about how Shifting works?"

Rae shook her head. "I know Shifters can take one animal form and there is a limit on how many times they can Shift in a given period, but that's it. Please, I'd love to learn more."

"I've been thinking about how little I know of the Goddess's other Gifts for years. Not having vocal cords for most of the time on the road makes those discussions few and far between."

Rae nodded. "I think having so much to worry about in terms of your own Gift doesn't help either. When I was learning how to use my Craft properly, it took a lot out of me. I didn't have the time or energy to think about anybody else."

"Aye, but that's the excuse for those in their youth. Now that we're older, we need to make it a priority to learn more about others' thoughts and experiences. I don't know how it is with Crafting, but Shifting is found within. When I look into my core, I see a string. On one side is my animal form, and on the other is my human form. Pulling the string in either direction forces me to Shift form. The limits have to do with how hard or easy it is to pull that string.

"As an older and wiser Shifter, I recognize it makes little sense to keep pulling the string when it goes nowhere. So instead of wearing myself out, I wait until the pulling gets easier. But yesterday...

"There's only ever been one string. A thought could make it change color and what raptor form I took, but one string regardless." His face communicated the disbelief his voice didn't reflect. "Yesterday, there were two. The alligator was still there, making me hesitate about what to do. I thought it was a fluke, but that second string meant it was there to stay."

"And the bear?" Rae asked gingerly.

Bane let out a deep breath. "As I floundered, trying to decide which string to pull, a third one appeared. I didn't think, I just acted and when I pulled the string, I was a bear. Rae, I don't... I don't know what this means. I was trying to think about what I could do that would make the most sense for taking down that ship. It was coming in so fast..." Bane paused and swallowed. He looked her in the eyes and said, "Do you remember Abuela's story?" He looked at her expectantly.

"The one she never finished? The one from before the first night in Heimat?" Rae asked.

"Yes, that one. Do you remember the Shifter in that story?" He waited for Rae to nod.

"Ezra, his name was Ezra," she said.

"And Ezra could Shift into any animal he'd seen before. Rae, what if those are my limits too? What if I can Shift into anything I've ever seen before?" Bane's voice was steady as his hands trembled, not quite believing what he was saying.

Rae studied the Shifter intently before nodding slowly, validating his thoughts. "You could be right, Bane. The Crafter, Yana, could control all four Crafts. And so can I…"

The acrobat trailed off. "Something's been going on with our Gifts for a long time. When Abuela was telling her story, you could tell that everybody was getting tense at the blunt reminder of our Gifts not being as powerful as they once were. But you and I are different for some reason. Our Gifts seem just as strong as our ancient ancestors. What does it mean?"

Bane shot her a blank look. "Only time will tell, Crafter."

"It's a relief that I'm not the only one going through this." Rae confided. "Previously, I had little time to reflect on everything. What with thinking I was going to lose my fire altogether, the attack in Heimat, and the escape on the *Vengeance*, I haven't stopped moving. Trying to wrap your head around all of this can be overwhelming. It's still overwhelming." She met Bane's gaze saying, "We were all concerned about you when we found you in an alligator form. Now that it seems like you're going to be okay, I want to make sure you know I'll be here for you if you ever need anything."

Bane's bear eyes, deep brown with no whites, only contained gratitude as he nodded and took in Rae's words.

A call up ahead shifted both their attention towards where Zeke and Gemma waited. The pair had continued running, splashing in the shallows every so often despite the cold, and laughing while Bane and Rae discussed their new circumstances.

The time had come for them to turn left.

"This must be the Fisherman's Wife," Bane said. He continued when Rae shot him a questioning look. "It's a bakery. Cleo told us to turn left once we reached it, and the inn should be four or five blocks down."

Bane and Rae caught up to the other two after a few moments. Rae caught Zeke's gaze and gave him a slight nod indicating Bane was okay, shaken up, but okay.

Zeke gave a soft smile, grateful that Rae could get more information out of the stoic Shifter.

Gemma bounded up to Rae and hugged her knees, her hood slipping back slightly.

Rae tsked teasingly at the little girl, pulling her hood back up to hide her signature curls. "Did you have fun with Zeke, Red?"

The young Herbalist shook her head vigorously. "Yes, yes, yes. Zeke even taught me how to cartwheel, wanna see?"

The little girl was bouncing with energy, clearly excited at her new trick. Rae chuckled, but said, "Let's wait until we're in the woods. We need to find the others first, but I promise you can show me once we have the cover of the trees over us. Maybe I'll even teach you how to do a front handspring."

Gemma's eyes widened at the thought of being able to do more tricks and she happily gripped Rae's arm, content to be close to the Crafter until there weren't prying eyes around.

While Rae talked with Gemma, Zeke nudged Bane's arm.

The Shifter gave a grunt but said, "I'm okay, just reeling from everything that's happened. We need to get out of this town."

Zeke nodded. "I agree. The sooner we find our people and get out of here, the better. I never thought I'd miss the road so much."

"Neither did I." Bane fumbled for something in his pocket before offering a hawk's feather to the Crafter.

Sending the Shifter a sideways glance, he took it and asked, "What's this for?"

Bane's neck flushed slightly as he shrugged. "In case we get separated. This way, I'll always be able to find you."

Zeke didn't press the cloaked man further as he hid a slight smile, staying close to Bane's side.

Before they knew it, the sounds of music, singing, and carrying on reached their ears. Once they got close enough, they could make out a sign that read *"The Merryweather Inn, Where the sun always shines!"* The three adults shared a look and Rae pulled Gemma in closer.

This wasn't what they were expecting. All three adults wondered whether George and the others had stayed at such a boisterous place. There seemed to be so many people, not necessarily the best for trying to keep a low profile.

Rae gave the two men a nod, indicating they should go in as she moved Gemma to one side of the establishment.

But Bane shook his head, "Let me stay with Red. Two women alone in the night only invite unnecessary danger. Besides, you'll be able to talk and better support Zeke."

Rae bit her lip but eventually nodded, seeing his logic. She turned to the young Herbalist, "Stay with Bane, Red, and remember, he's pretending to be mute, so he won't talk to you."

The little girl jutted her chin out and put on a brave face before gripping Bane's outstretched hand. The pair made their way to an alley and hunkered down, playing the part of beggars trying to find a safe place for the night.

Rae looked at Zeke with a twinkle in her eye, always ready to add levity to any situation. She linked her arm through his and asked, "Well, dear husband, should we try to get a room for the night?"

Zeke chuckled. "Of course, my dear, your wish is my command. Happy wife, happy life after all."

Rae giggled, happy she and Zeke were on better terms once again. Their friendship and closeness gave her more courage as they entered the busy inn.

Once they opened the door, they were met with a cacophony of sounds and an assault of distinct aromas. There was a band on stage playing a jaunty tune while patrons sang along or talked loudly, trying to be heard over the music. Servers weaved in and out between the packed tables, bringing drinks and taking orders, while stew and platters of fish made their way out at an alarming rate. Three bartenders worked behind a long wooden bar, never stopping as they filled drinks for patrons at the bar and the servers running between tables.

Rae and Zeke shared a look before making their way to what they surmised was a front desk. The woman standing behind the desk was short and stout, but her presence was larger than life. She chatted with patrons, scolded servers, and called directions to the bartenders, telling them to make sure the drinks were stiff enough. When she caught Rae and Zeke making their way toward her, she gave them a once over, trying to decipher what they were looking for.

"And what can I do for you two darlings?" she asked. "Do you need a table or room? It might be a few minutes for a table, but you're in luck. I do have one room available. Should I pencil you in?"

Rae took charge, knowing they needed to figure out where their friends went as quickly as possible. "I'm sorry, ma'am, we just have a couple of questions for you about some friends of ours. If you don't mind, we would appreciate it."

The woman's eyes narrowed in suspicion. "Don't know where you two are from, but it certainly isn't Lockewater. We're not in the business of giving out our patrons' information around these parts. I'll say it once again. Are you here for a meal or a room? Anything else, and you can move along."

"We meant no disrespect, ma'am. Our group got separated and we're just trying to meet up with our friends. They said they were coming here but we haven't seen them. We just wanted to know if you could give us any information on whether they were here or if you saw them."

The stout woman pursed her lips but remained silent. Before Rae could try again, Zeke spoke up. "Madam, your establishment here is very impressive. It's clear your patrons enjoy being here and we would be fools not to indulge in what you offer. You see, our daughter is with the group." He put an arm around Rae and pulled her close. "My wife got sick, so we sent her up ahead with the others to be safe. Our friends travel in a sizeable group with lots of women and children, and now that my wife feels better, we need to meet up with them for safety. Please, any information you have would help us reunite with our daughter."

Zeke's speech seemed to touch a nerve in the woman as her posture relaxed and her face became less severe. "Aye, I saw them. They were here for a night but left in a hurry. Unfortunately, that's all the information I have. They were good patrons, always polite, and left their rooms almost as clean as they found them. I'm sorry I have no more information."

Rae grabbed the woman's forearm, giving it a gentle squeeze. "Thank you, it helps more than you know."

As Rae and Zeke made to turn around and go back through the front door, the woman called after them, "The night is cold and long. Are you sure you don't want a bit of stew to go?" When they hesitated, she added, "It's on the house. Your friends left the biggest tip I've ever seen. It's the least I could do."

Zeke spoke up. "Your kindness doesn't go unnoticed. That would be wonderful."

"Great, take a seat over there on those empty chairs and I'll have it run right out to ya." The woman left for the kitchen to have a word with the cooks.

In her absence, Rae and Zeke sat in the chairs she pointed out and observed the boisterous tavern. This was the type of place that prided itself on the community it nurtured. The people inside were clearly locals, skin weathered by a life at sea or near the ocean. Nobody was dressed in fine silks or unnecessary jewelry, but instead, they wore humble leathers and cloth suitable for working in the elements. The community was lively, with individuals greeting others, joining conversations, and encouraging friends to get up and dance.

The two acrobats were warm not just physically, but within their hearts, as they watched the working class of Lockewater build the strong bonds of a community.

"This reminds me of Heimat," Rae murmured so only Zeke could hear.

Zeke nodded and inclined his head to the woman running the show. "And she reminds me of Betsy, a mama bear looking out for anyone and everyone in her care."

Rae chuckled. "That's for sure. Huntress, I hope they're okay."

Zeke squeezed her hand. "They'll be okay, Sparks. We just have to have a little faith." Rae looked at her friend, eyes bright with unshared tears.

"What about Luc and Damien? What if we never see them again?"

"Rae, don't talk like that." Zeke scolded. "They're smart, and they'll make it through this. We'll find them."

Rae rubbed at her face roughly. "I know, but it's been so hard. Not having them with us feels like a piece of me is missing. I didn't think about how hard this would be when I ran into that city."

Zeke put his arm around her, pulling her in close. "Nobody knew what they were getting into. We all reacted to what was happening in Heimat. We'll find them and we'll fight for our place in this world. You heard Duncan, the time to choose is now. You can choose to think the worst or you can choose to believe in the ones you love. What's it going to be?"

Rae leaned her head against Zeke's shoulder and mumbled words Zeke couldn't make out.

"Say that again, Sparks."

"Some things cannot be changed," she whispered.

Zeke, barely able to make out her words, shot her an incredulous look, as there was a commotion outside the tavern. Rae sat up quickly, sharing a glance with Zeke as they said in tandem, "Gemma."

The two raced out of the tavern, making their way to where they left Bane and Gemma in the alley. Sure enough, two large brutes were facing off against Bane, Gemma behind him, her hood exposing those damn copper curls. As they approached, they could hear the two men talking.

"Come on, lad. Give her to us and we'll make sure she finds her father," said the first man.

"We'll even give you a cut of the reward," added the second.

Rae couldn't believe what she was hearing as Zeke took a defensive position beside her, crouching down with his fists out. The pair crept closer, keeping to the shadows and staying out of sight of the two thugs. Rae discreetly leaned down and grabbed the daggers from her boots. Zeke still had his fists out, but she shook her head at him. The last thing they wanted was for the thugs to identify them as Magicae.

Zeke frowned but pulled out his short sword from the scabbard at his hip. Once they were close enough, Rae signaled with her hand and threw both daggers at the man on the left, one hitting him in the leg before Zeke could make a move. The man fell to the ground, clutching at where the dagger pierced his flesh. The second man fled as soon as his partner fell, tossing Bane to the side and moving further down the alley.

Bane held his position, keeping himself between the men and Gemma, watching the thug flee down the alley. Using the flat side of his sword, Zeke knocked the man on the ground unconscious until they could figure out what to do with him. Gemma ran to Rae with tears in her eyes, clutching at the Crafter in desperation.

Rae held the young girl close and stroked her curls, but met the eyes of the two men next to her. "We can't let him get away," she said, knowing if they did, word would be out that Vincenzio's daughter was somewhere in the city.

"I'm on it," Bane said as he took off after the man. Zeke made to go with him but stopped when Rae shouted.

"Z, stay here. Let Bane do it. We can't get separated again. Let's figure out what to do with this guy and then we can follow."

Zeke hesitated, saying, "I gotta go after him, Sparks. Hit him with a sleeping draught and come find us." Making up his mind, he turned and raced after the Shifter.

Rae frowned in annoyance as she pulled Gemma close. With a sigh, she studied the alley around her and got to work hiding the poor excuse for a man.

Chapter Twenty-Seven

Tommy watched in horror as the woman's body was hung from the fence. He was still in shock at how wrong everything went after Johanna lit those fires.

They wanted to strike back at the man who destroyed their city, but his retribution was so much worse.

He had been a fool to let her light those fires alone.

Nobody knew the entire story, but rumors were Vincenzio cornered her and instead of being taken captive, she'd chosen death.

Stubborn, stubborn, woman. Tommy thought to himself, but he knew he could never blame Johanna. Those petty thoughts would never make the guilt inside go away. He knew Johanna had been prepared to take whatever action necessary to keep the rebel leaders safe.

He just never thought she'd have to.

The governor called everyone in Heimat to a special assembly in the town hall. Tommy had been prepared for stricter sanctions or a tighter curfew, but not this.

Anything but this.

The leaders were scattered among the people. Only Rich and Anna were absent, not willing to see the man responsible for their daughter's death.

Thank the Goddess they didn't come. Tommy thought as he looked at the body once more. Gasps and soft sobbing could be heard throughout the gathering of people as they realized who it was.

One blood-curdling scream that could have only been Simone's rose high above the sounds of the others.

Tommy's heart clenched, knowing what it was like to lose such a close friend. Nobody deserved that grief.

The crowd waited with bated breath as Vincenzio made his way to the stage, a cruel smirk on his face. "Glad to see I have your attention. Last night, we found this piece of trash trying to attack our stronghold. I'm here to teach you a lesson and remind all of you what's at stake. If anyone thinks of crossing me or attacking my city, there will be hell to pay. I know there're more Magicae here. I know you're hiding them from me, *and I'm sick of it.*" His last few words came out in a hiss as he glared at the crowd.

"We will uproot all of you, even if it means we have to go door to door and test every single one of you in this Goddess-forsaken city. The reign of the Magicae is over. Turn in your friends, turn in your family, and turn in your neighbors unless you want to be labeled a traitor, just like them. I will give you seventy-two hours and then we go door to door." With a flourish, the general turned around and exited the stage, leaving only silence behind him.

The guards finished tying the body before following their commander, Johanna's corpse swaying in the wind.

Tommy's heart thundered in his chest as his mind raced. They only had seventy-two hours to figure out how to save what was left of their people.

He exited with the hordes of people, wandering until he made it back to his mother's farmhouse.

As soon as he saw Sara, he collapsed in her arms, sobbing uncontrollably.

Sara stroked his head and whispered soft words of love and encouragement, waiting for the sobs to subside. Once Tommy stopped crying and took several deep breaths, Sara asked, fearing the worst and knowing they had lost someone else, "What's wrong, love? What happened?"

"Johanna—they—they strung her body up like a swine going to slaughter. They left her in the square for everyone to see. She's—her body's just on display. He killed her, Sara. I can't—what do I do?" Tommy couldn't form a coherent sentence as he struggled to describe what he saw in the town square and the horror of it all.

Sara stroked his hair once more, a slight tremble in her hand as she processed the information that another person close to them had given their life.

"Oh love, I'm so sorry. Jo was one of the best, and she will be missed so much." Tommy broke down into sobs yet again, clutching at her as if she was an oasis in the desert. Sara continued, "Tommy, we need to make some hard decisions, love. I don't think things are going to get any better for a long while. We need to decide right now what we're willing to sacrifice and what we're not. You and I? We're privileged. We have nothing to hide, but we love this community, we love our neighbors, and we can't let them fight alone."

Tommy lifted his head, knowing his wife spoke the truth, but anguish filled his heart all the same. "Sara, I can't risk you. I can't risk the kids. The baby. My mom... I couldn't live if you all weren't here."

Sara looked into his bright teary eyes, hers ablaze with purpose. "Don't talk like that. I could die tomorrow, giving birth to this baby, regardless of what happens with Vincenzio. There's always a risk, Tommy, and you can't afford to talk like that. There are three wonderful babies out there that need you. If one of us or all of us, Goddess forbid, died tomorrow, it's your job to live on without us.

"All of our loved ones that have passed on don't want us to give up living just because they can't anymore. On the contrary, they want us to live because they can't. Losing Melody and losing Jo mean my heart will always be broken, but that's okay. The cracks leave room for their light to shine through and remind me to live up to their memory. So I'll repeat it, Tommy. We have a choice to make. Do we stand for our community or do we flee?"

Tommy never loved his wife as much as he did at that moment. She truly was his better half, blessed with beauty and brains. "Aye, love, you're right. There's only one choice, we choose our community. We choose to fight for those that can't." He paused and let out a sigh, the weight of their odds on his shoulders. "I just don't know how."

Sara gave a mischievous smile. "Well, that's what I'm here for," she said and pulled him close. The two took comfort in their embrace as they took a moment to grieve the woman they loved and admired.

The toll taken by losing one of their leaders was too great to bear alone.

Mirabella winced as another branch scratched her face. Moving through the forest was proving to be more difficult than she anticipated. She grew up running through the woods and playing in the trees on the outskirts of the Capital, but something about this place felt different. It was as if the very trees were a little wilder, and a little more dangerous.

Furthermore, she couldn't decide whether daytime or nighttime was worse.

In the daytime, Mirabella could make more progress through the forest but faced constant decisions on where to go and the doubt that she was traveling in circles. Nighttime was filled with sounds and rumblings that made getting any kind of sleep nigh impossible, but she pressed onward. She knew the only way she would see her daughter again was if she did this one thing, no matter how impossible it seemed.

Besides, she owed Duncan that much.

A memory came unbidden to her mind. It was from that day, the day of the Uprising. Mirabella had only been sixteen, sick of being in her older brother's shadow and the shadow of his best friend. When they were younger, she'd always tried tagging along, only to be shoved to the wayside and deemed too young to keep up with them.

The former redhead grew up primarily in isolation, finding it hard to get over the crippling shyness she felt around others. Mirabella had been hurt deeply by the dismissal from her older brother and his lack of interest in having anything to do with her. He was the one who was supposed to protect her, but when he didn't, she decided she would have to do so herself. It became her mission to protect others just like her, alone and forgotten.

She went into politics to advocate for the Ungifted Mortals like herself and become more like Andre. After seeing how close Andre and Duncan were, she presumed that if she were more like Andre, her brother would finally notice her.

That was the beginning of her downfall.

Young and easily impressionable, Myra had taken her under her wing, paying the teenager the attention she desperately desired. Looking back, it was as plain as day how Myra manipulated her and used Vincenzio as motivation to get her to do whatever the General wanted. Myra played on both of their ambitions and desires to get what they wanted. It was Myra who convinced her to go to Naomi and bring up that bloody lie.

Curse the Goddess, the Huntress, and the Prophetess for leaving her at the mercy of wolves and lions. Curse them all for pitting her against forces too powerful for her to get past.

Myra promised Vincenzio easy and early promotions if he convinced Mirabella to join their cause. He would have the world at his fingertips if he convinced Mirabella the Magicae were better off away from the general populace and that her own brother would be safer in a prison where he couldn't hurt himself.

Between the two of them, they convinced her the Magicae were too unstable and dangerous to themselves and others. They spread lies and fed her poison until she did anything and everything they asked of her.

On the day of the Uprising, she went to Naomi and claimed that Andre had been sleeping with her. While the President and his wife squabbled, Myra made her move.

She isolated the two, pulling her guards and rounding up the servants before inciting the rage of the people just outside the doors of city hall.

Once Andre stormed out of his office, he realized the mob she created at the steps of his front door.

Duncan had been trying to quell the madness, but it was no use; the mob thirsted for blood and wouldn't be satiated with anything else.

Mirabella had watched her brother escape, holding her tongue instead of alerting the other two. She'd felt like she'd made a terrible mistake as she watched her kin run for his life.

Mirabella knew for certain her actions were wrong as soon as she saw Andre lose his head.

But it was too late.

Mirabella's doubt and guilt took root when she saw Andre's head roll, but she clung to the fact that Duncan had gotten away.

Her brother was nowhere to be found after all was said and done, but she was in too deep to get out. Mirabella had been so convinced the Magicae were better off away from the general populace. With the stubbornness of youth, she rationalized her actions despite the lack of fair trial given to their President. The Magicae were still too dangerous to be as integrated as they had been. Myra's actions were extreme but better than leaving Mortals to fend for themselves in a city full of Magicae.

They had to be.

Mirabella shook her head, cursing her naivety and wishing once more she could go back and change everything. If Naomi and Andre hadn't trusted her, things would be so much different now.

She was brought back to the present as she almost tripped over a root in her path. She didn't know where she was going, but she let her intuition guide her.

It was all she had as she walked blindly through the trees.

Mirabella held onto her mother's words about family, banishing the doubts at the edge of her mind, telling her Duncan still wouldn't have time for her. Even as a little girl, her mother had known how desperately Mirabella yearned for Duncan's approval. Her mother always told her that no matter what happened between the two of them, they were siblings and would always be connected.

Mirabella closed her eyes as she attempted to search inside to find it. She wasted no breath on prayers that would fall on deaf ears. Mirabella didn't believe in the Goddess or her other faces, finding long ago there was little solace in praying to a deity that never responded.

No, if the Goddess had ever cared about Mirabella, She would have stepped in years ago.

Mirabella only had herself to rely on as she stumbled through the woods.

Out of breath, she stood near a tree, panting as she leaned against the tall oak and tried to get a hold of herself.

Voices to her right caused her to pause.

"I'm telling you, man, those Magicae are weird. Did you hear they're performing for us? What the hell is that?"

"Oh, shush. The kids will love it." A second voice answered the first.

"Yeah, but I'm not a kid. What am I supposed to do? Watch while they make fools of themselves?"

"Who knows? It might be cool." The voice hesitated before asking, "Do you think this is the Queen's way of making up for her daughter's blunder?"

"Sylvia is going to have to do a lot more than put on a show to make up for this one. There are whispers that the Gilkyn and Sartris families are prepping their eldest children should it come to it."

Just as quickly as they came, the voices trailed off.

Mirabella made sure she stayed hidden as she listened to the pair walking through the woods

A performance, she thought, *performance by Magicae? What the hell is Duncan planning?*

Mirabella tucked her bleached hair behind her ears. She knew she needed to follow the voices to figure out where her quarry resided, but it had been a long time since Mirabella traveled in the woods. Walking silently would be a challenge, seeing as every step crunched a leaf or sent a rock scuttling across the forest floor.

The determined mother made slow progress following the path taken by the voices. After almost an hour, the two voices stopped. Mirabella crouched behind a bush, looking frantically for the two figures she followed. Looking to her right, she saw a clearing where, sure enough, the two figures stood waiting.

Curious, Mirabella crept forward, staying out of sight. Taking advantage of her position in the brush, Mirabella finally studied those she followed.

They were both fairly tall, but extremely narrow in stature, making it hard to tell whether they were male or female after hearing their deep voices. There was a dissonance between their physical attributes and the way their voices sounded. They wore clothes painted a mottled brown and green, allowing them to blend in easily with the surrounding forest. Their long dark hair was pulled sharply away from their faces into high ponytails.

She had to stifle a gasp as the two seemed to disappear before her very eyes.

Something was off about them and she couldn't put her finger on why. Mirabella needed to be careful about what steps she took next to make sure this wasn't a trap. She wasn't sure but had a feeling the pair knew she had been following them. That meant one wrong move could end in disaster. She needed to wait to see what would happen next before making any hasty decisions.

Mirabella rearranged herself into a more comfortable position as she hunkered down to wait, despite still not knowing what she was waiting for.

But once again, Duncan's younger sister trusted her instincts, convinced they were what led her to the voices to begin with.

Vincenzio stumbled into his chambers, finally allowing his weakness to show once he was out of sight from the public and his soldiers. Only his personal doctor knew the extent of the injuries he'd suffered, and he didn't plan on letting that change anytime soon.

With a grunt, he sank onto his bed and let out a sigh. It would be a few days before the wound fully healed, but Vincenzio wouldn't let that stop him from figuring out where his blasted wife had gone. With a groan and a clenched jaw, he moved to the desk a few feet away from the bed. Upon reaching it, he collapsed into the chair behind it.

He picked up the two pieces of the letter Mirabella left one more time, gazing incessantly at them. He knew if he could just read closely enough, he could interpret where his wife went.

Ice-cold dread soaked his insides as he reread her words. He knew it had been wrong to trust her all those years ago during the Uprising. In her youth, she'd let him manipulate her however he wanted, but that hadn't meant she didn't have spirit. Vincenzio rubbed his chin as he reread her words over and over, searching for any sort of clues.

Myra had always found it ironic that Andre's best friend was also his undoing through the man's younger sister, but Vincenzio was worried she would also bring about their demise. She was the only one he'd told about the bounty placed on Duncan's head. If she had gone to find him, his soldiers wouldn't have a chance to act on that order.

But this was the Great Northern Forest they were talking about. One woman alone wouldn't stand a chance at finding the rogue Magicae when up against his legions of soldiers. No, Mirabella wouldn't be that stupid.

Would she?

BANG, BANG, BANG. A knock sounded on the door.

Vincenzio rose with a shudder, eyes narrowing as he tried to figure out who would have the guts to knock on his personal chamber doors.

A voice sounded on the outside. "Sir, it's Zander. I have news."

"Come in," Vincenzio said calmly. "Lock the door behind you," he instructed the steward.

After doing so, Zander turned to his Commander. "I caught sight of several fires in the distance. It has to be the reinforcements you sent for, since a caravan of merchants wouldn't put up that much smoke. By my estimate, they'll be here within the next couple of days, depending on how many supply wagons they bring with them."

Vincenzio gave a terse nod. "Thank you, old friend."

The steward inclined his head. "Is there anything else I can do for you, sir?"

Vincenzio took a moment to look the gangly man over. "Actually, yes. Look at this letter. What do you think when you read it?"

Zander took the two pieces of Mirabella's letter in his hands and his eyes darted across the paper, reading the words previously reserved for only the Commander's eyes.

"Mirabella is missing." The steward's eyes widened in alarm as he looked up to meet Vincenzio's dark gaze. "It says here she's walking the riverbank…" Zander trailed off as he caught the look in his friend's eyes. "But you don't think she'd make the journey herself alone so close to the woods, do you? That seems unlike your wife," he stated matter-of-factly, disbelief at the words unsaid between them plain on his face.

"No, I don't think she's walking along the riverbank. I think that was a ruse to make sure I didn't look for her." Vincenzio stated with a closed expression. "But what motivations would she have for leaving?" Vincenzio pushed.

Zander looked at the words once more, rereading carefully before pinching his eyebrows together. "You don't think she's trying to find Duncan, do you? I thought those ties were cut years ago."

"Aye, but that was before our relationship was as strained as it is now."

"So you think she's going to Duncan to get back at you?" Zander asked.

"No, I think she's going to Duncan because she wants attention. She's not getting any more from me or Myra, so she's going to her brother to fill the void left by us." Vincenzio grunted.

"Would she have the balls to do that?" Zander probed.

Vincenzio gave him a hard look. "Based on Mirabella's disposition over the past few years, I would say no, but at one point, she was willing to turn her own brother in for a chance with me."

"I didn't know that."

"Mirabella led a very poor and uneventful life before Myra took her under her wing. I would bet my position this is all about getting the attention she seeks. See, being a mother is exactly what Mirabella needed. That little girl spent every waking moment needing her mother. It was a dream come true for someone as attention-seeking as her.

"But now that she's gone, my lovely wife needs to fill that void. Mark my words, she went to Duncan to mend the relationship and finally get the love and adoration she never got from him as a kid."

"So what are we going to do about it?" Zander asked carefully.

"Nothing, absolutely nothing." Vincenzio said with a smirk. "I'd bet you anything Duncan doesn't believe her or want anything to do with her. We just need to focus on finding Gemma before any of that can happen. Once that's done, Mirabella will have no choice but to come crawling back to us." His smirk turned predatory. "And if she learns a little something about the Magicae, who am I to stop her?" He gave a low chuckle, amused by his brilliance.

Zander chuckled as well. If he had any doubts, he hid them seamlessly, knowing all too well what befell those who disagreed with the commander.

"Anything else?" Vincenzo asked the steward.

"No, sir," Zander shook his head. "I assume you want me back on lookout duty?"

"Aye, tell me when they're about a day's ride out. Once our reinforcements come, we will exterminate these rats once and for all."

Zander gave a nod and left as quickly as he had come.

Vincenzio hobbled to the door, locking it behind the steward so he could get some peace before the reinforcements came. A good night's rest would go a long way in helping him get ready for the war to come. The Magicae infestation of the North would end one way or another. Vincenzio smiled to himself as he went back to his desk, writing a letter of thanks to Myra for sending him the troops he'd need to finally civilize the North.

Chapter Twenty-Eight

Nan watched the caravan go through set up with a slight crease on her forehead. Thoughts chased themselves around in her mind as the plan she came up with was brought to life.

An ache in her chest made her pause, the memory of falling off the wagon and hitting her head flashing abruptly.

She put her hand on the tree she stood under and pulled her long fur coat tighter, trying to steady herself. She could see a whisper of her breath as she took deep gulps of air. The world spun a little before righting itself. She gripped the tree with one arm and put her other to her temple, sending a silent prayer to the Huntress for strength.

It couldn't be her time to go yet. Not when her people still needed her.

When Nan had her episode outside of Heimat, it drummed up memories of her own Abuela. Specifically, her Abuela's arms, beckoning her to come and find rest. But she had pulled away, shaking her head and trying to find the words to explain that no matter how much she wanted to run into those arms, she still had a duty to her people.

And for the ones she loved, the fire of hope was not yet ablaze, but barely a spark. If she left now, there was no telling if her people would survive this drought of hopelessness.

The tightness in her chest eased, and she could breathe again. The sounds of her people found their way back to her ears and the smell of the woods overcame her nose.

"Abuelita? Why are you so far away from everyone? What's going on?" Javie asked.

Nan turned to her grandson and couldn't help but smile. "I'm just taking it all in, Nieto. Come, rest a minute. I need to talk to you."

"About what, Abuela?" Javie asked quizzically.

"Promise me you'll look after your Hermana. She needs you more than you know."

"Always. I know we fight sometimes, but Luc means the world to me. She's the only one that understands me." Javie spread his hands in front of him, still stunned when the plants on the ground responded to the slight movement. He looked back at the old woman next to him. "We don't talk about it much, but I know she didn't have the childhood I did because she was always so worried about me."

Nan smiled sadly, knowing the boy spoke the truth. She tried to give Luc a normal childhood, but raising a child in her fifties was a lot different from raising one in her thirties. Nan knew she hadn't always been the most attentive and Luc had been the one to keep a second eye on the mischievous young boy.

Nan had already been a mother, and all she wanted was to be a grandmother. She did her best, but her relationship with those kids was not the same as the one they had with their parents.

But that was okay.

She pulled her grandson close and rested her head on his shoulder, letting him lead her back to the caravan.

Luc played with the pendant around her neck as she danced on the balls of her feet and stretched her muscles out before their performance. Luc couldn't help but be impressed with her Abuela's quick thinking as she looked at the makeshift trapeze to her right.

They constructed it with J's help and the other elephants that afternoon, rigging together a rudimentary trapeze set made of two long poles set in the ground within sight of most of the platforms in the trees. Some Forgers and Herbalists had created a basic ring-like structure surrounding it, made of fell trees and some scrap metal. The whole thing was a hot mess compared to what they usually created along the road.

But it would get the job done.

Luc's eyes traveled upwards as she swung her arms back and forth, her gaze catching on the tight rope connecting both poles at the very top. She chewed on the inside of her cheek as she ran through the routine in her head. After the tightrope, the two acrobats would move to the swing for some partner work, Duncan joining them to put on a spectacle with the wind.

Luc looked up to the platforms above, noting the Elven were already milling about, watching their performance area intently. Chiara had spread the word among the Healers in the infirmary and anyone else she encountered when she went up to check in on the Shifters. She stayed in the trees, stirring up a crowd to watch the Circus set up their makeshift performance ring. Luc could feel the energy up above among the Elven and her lips turned upwards into a smirk.

Looks like we're not so different after all. The acrobat closed her eyes and lifted her chin to the sky, letting the energy of the gathered spectators wash over her, as she had done many times before.

Luc was still a little in awe that this was even possible. Finding the Elven she'd heard so many stories about as a kid was a dream come true.

If only it was under better circumstances.

She let out a sigh as she opened her eyes, still not sure they were fully prepared for this show. And regardless of whether the performance went well, she was still on the fence about whether this plan would even work.

Her Abuela laid out the skeleton, but Duncan and Chiara were the ones to flesh out the details. They insisted a single performance would win the Elven people to their side.

But what good will a show do? Luc clenched her teeth as she tried to drive the pessimism from her mind, unable to shake the feeling they needed to do more to get the Queen and her daughter on their side.

The acrobat danced on the balls of her feet again as she observed her fellow performers readying their acts. A nervous thrill crept up her spine at the thought of performing once again.

The energy among the performers was high as they considered and worked on what they would do for the show that night. Everyone was excited to use their Gifts in their performances and take a break from the fear of the unknown. Performing for an audience was as natural as breathing to the entire company, despite the holes left by those that left the caravan after Heimat.

Everyone was given a choice, and most had braved the Forest, but not all.

J and Eva were working on building a performance with the other two elephants and Wren. The young Crafter refused to be left out, persevering until Eva caved to the younger girl's demands. Now the two stood with heads bent toward one another as they discussed a new idea animatedly. J shook his head softly with a slight grin as the two devolved into giggles.

Zalia and the young fire Crafters were going to do a fire demonstration with the company's water Crafter on hand should anything go wrong. Zalia was demonstrating different moves, while the other two worked on following her lead. Her face was as harsh as ever, but Luc caught the hint of a smile on her lips as she continued her instruction.

Simeon and the other horsemen worked outside the ring on horseback. They were going to show their skills on horseback before doing a Teach and Learn on different aspects of horsemanship. Simeon had stepped up in Tyee's absence as head horseman, running the others through their routine. He was the closest to the missing performer, but he didn't let it show, keeping his face stoic as he gave directions to the other three.

At the end of their performance, they were going to invite anybody who wanted to come for a ride the following day. Simeon had thought of it as an easy way to entice some of the younger Elven to the ground for more interaction with the members of the Circus.

The acts were going to give the Elven a show unlike any they had seen before. Luc was determined to do her part, even if she didn't quite believe in the plan Duncan and Chiara concocted. It would buy them time to find Tyee and avoid taking the forgetting rune.

Luc chewed on the inside of her cheek and pictured their routine again.

Luc and Damien would open the show on the trapeze, with Duncan providing a little spice to their act. The three of them had practiced several times, but Luc was still nervous about adding an element that could go wrong. Not to mention performing without Rae and Zeke there to calm her nerves and offer their opinions. She continued to bounce on her heels as her thoughts spiraled into worry about the other two acrobats.

"Mi amor! Don't tell me the infallible Luc is nervous." Damien rubbed her shoulders as he came up behind her and tried to get her attention. "Talk to me." Luc stopped bouncing and shook him off. She turned to face him but kept her distance and started toying with the pendant on her neck, refusing to meet his eyes.

Damien furrowed his brows as he watched the young woman struggle with whatever was on her mind. Trying again, he cupped her cheek and brought her gaze to his.

They sat in silence, staring into each other's eyes for a few seconds before she offered. "Rae and Zeke would love this. It doesn't feel right without having them here."

"Aye, love. I would be worried if we didn't feel something about not having them here, but our fearless leader is going to make us look like badasses tonight."

Luc chuckled, but the humor didn't reach her eyes. "You can say that again. I still can't believe I agreed to this."

"Oh relax, mi amor. Mark my words, Duncan is a genius and we're gonna be great." Fire filled the young man's eyes as he stared into her eyes. "I got you, Luc, trust me."

Luc finally let go of the pendant around her neck. It was the necklace her Papa gave her on her fourth birthday, about a month before the Uprising. It was the only thing she had left connecting her to her father and one of her most prized possessions. She wore it around her neck to remind herself to be as compassionate and caring as he was.

She looked into Damien's dark eyes filled with honesty and placed her hand in his. Luc had apprehension about the show they were going to perform, but she also knew there was no going back. The Circus was on a path that only the Huntress could see the end of. She needed to trust in Damien, Duncan, and their people if they were going to get out of this mess.

Luc gave her partner a determined nod and pulled him to one side, getting out of the way of J and the other elephants. Her eyes scanned the outside of the ring until they landed on Duncan. The familiar feeling of disbelief he shouldered so much settled on her shoulders.

If she was apprehensive, Duncan had to be terrified.

The Circus was in a tough spot, disoriented in the forest and dependent on the Elven letting them go. Luc squeezed Damien's hand before pulling away.

"I need to speak with Duncan. It's time to channel our inner Rae if we wanna get out of this mess."

Damien chuckled and pulled her into a one-armed embrace. He kissed her temple and whispered, "Honestly, Luc? We don't need Rae right now. We need you."

Luc pulled back but didn't interrupt as Damien continued. "Rae is a force, as we all know, but this situation needs tact, not raw power. Follow your intuition, amor, your prowess in reading people is unmatched. Trust yourself and you might be surprised at the results you drum up." He chucked her chin and left with a nod, heading towards where his mother descended from the trees.

Luc gave a soft smile as she watched the man she loved walk away. Sometimes Damien's positive outlook got on her nerves, but other times, it lifted her spirits. Lately, it seemed like they bickered constantly, and Luc didn't know how to fix it. But then they'd have moments like this where everything was right between them. She blamed it on missing their friends and having too much time on their hands. Regardless, knowing she had his support made it easier for what she needed to do next.

"What was that old saying? A rock for each thought?" Duncan asked.

Luc gave a chuckle, thinking of the saying she and Rae coined. "Close. An agate for your thoughts is what you're looking for."

"Ah, of course. Unfortunately, I don't have an agate." He leaned down and picked a flower from a nearby bush. "But I do have this flower." Luc threw the older man a smile as she accepted the delicate bloom.

Duncan had always felt like family, being one of those people that made everyone feel welcome. He had a natural knack for remembering names and a genuine way of asking questions that made him popular amongst everyone in the Circus. But few people had the relationship with him she did. Of course, Rae's bond with the Ringmaster could never be matched, but Duncan would always be a mentor to her. His listening ear and gentle advice were invaluable when she was first elected as Head Mortal to the Governing Council.

The Ringmaster always made it a point to make her feel welcome and encouraged her to share her opinion. This time was no different as he waited for her to share her thoughts.

Damien's advice flashed in her head as she considered her words. *Maybe force isn't the best plan of action. But then what is?*

"I'm worried about the show tonight. Tyee's life and our own people's memories are at stake. Duncan, what if they take too much? What if we forget what happened in Heimat? What if we forget everything?" Luc spun the flower in her hands as the emotions bubbling inside came out.

She had kept her emotions reined in during the meeting of the Council but alone with the Ringmaster; they came tumbling out.

Duncan studied her carefully for a moment. "Luc, we take it one step at a time, just as we've always done. The horsemen are offering the Elven a chance to ride tomorrow after their performance, and I'm going to make the same offer for the other acts. The more Elven we entice down from the trees, the better. What do you think?" He lifted one eyebrow, waiting for her response.

Luc frowned. "But what does that accomplish? I guess I don't understand how winning over the Elven people gets Tyee back and lets everyone keep their memories."

Duncan sighed. "I forget how young so many of you were when the Uprising occurred. They always say that hindsight is twenty-twenty, but in this case, it's very much true. Looking back, there were so many opportunities to quell the fears of the Mortals, but we, meaning Andre and his advisors, didn't take those fears seriously. We didn't push for the integration that we have in the Circus; whole towns had dividing lines between the Mortal and Magicae sectors. Even Fernwen, with the highest concentration of Magicae, had divisions."

Duncan rubbed his palms together before meeting Luc's hooded gaze. "Mostly, there was little mingling other than those families that gave birth to children with Gifts. We didn't do enough of winning the public over when we were young and didn't realize the consequences that our actions would have." He put a hand on the acrobat's shoulder and his expression turned serious. "Never underestimate the power of the people, especially when they're discontent. We didn't listen or act swiftly enough, and that turned into a disaster. Have you been observing the Elven people? Really watching them?"

Luc toyed with the pendant around her neck before admitting. "As much as I can from the ground. I wouldn't say I've made any observations other than those I've made by sight."

Duncan's eyes softened and he gave a nod. "As I would expect, and the boat most of us are in. Luckily, Chiara and the other Healers could get a better idea of morale and the culture of the Elven. Luc, this is a lesson in politics. I know you're not the type that wants to play the game, but sometimes there isn't much of a choice. Chiara and the others reported a lot of dissension between the monarchy and the Elven people. The younger generations especially grow weary of a life limited to the trees. The Queen is beloved, but her favor wanes as it becomes clearer that her heir has a mean streak.

"Now's our chance to take advantage of the split between them."

Luc considered his words. The new information was a bit of a surprise, but Luc still had her doubts. "So you're assuming the Queen will listen to the masses to curry more favor for her daughter?" She waited for Duncan to nod before continuing. "But isn't that a gamble? What if the Queen is convinced the people will see it her way once she speaks?"

"That's just it. We need to force her hand into revealing what she's proposed."

Luc narrowed her eyes. "Dunc, I don't think that's the right course of action. The Queen and her daughter don't strike me as the types to fall into such a trap so easily."

Duncan patted her shoulder. "That's why we have to get their people to bring it up."

Luc's eyes widened. "You're going to tell them?"

"We need to get them to trust us first, and then we can ease them into it. Take heart, young one. They didn't slaughter us when they had the chance. Clearly, there is some sort of honor system. We just need to figure out what it is." Determination shone in the Ringmaster's eyes as he made his leave of her. "If you excuse me, my friend, I'm going to check in with the other acts, and then the show can begin." With a flourish, Duncan turned to go check in on the other performers.

Luc watched him go before making her way over to Damien and Chiara.

"Weight of the world on your shoulders. Some things never change, do they?" Chiara said, her eyes crinkling at the corners.

Luc let out a breath she didn't know she was holding. "I'm just worried," she answered. "So much could go wrong and there's so much we don't know. I hope this works."

Chiara put an arm around the young woman and pulled her close. "I get it, but there are good people here and it's not fair to judge a people based on their leaders. The Elven deserve a chance."

"And what if we regret giving them a chance?"

"Figure it out," Chiara murmured. "We figure it out just as we've always done."

"Light of my life, it's unlike you to be so negative. What else is weighing on your mind?" Damien asked, catching one of Luc's hands and bringing it to his mouth, placing a gentle kiss on her knuckles.

Luc caught his gaze and felt her emotions threatening to boil over again. She swallowed them down before answering, not wanting to look unhinged in front of the Head Herbalist. "I'm at a loss as to how a performance is going to help our situation and can't stop thinking about Tyee. Why are they keeping him from us? What do they want from him? I don't understand, and it puts me on edge." Luc confided in her partner and his mother.

An unconventional friendship had developed between the acrobat and the horseman while they traipsed through the forest, but Luc still didn't know his full story. Regardless, she recognized and respected his wit and the soft side beneath his gruff exterior.

Chiara glanced around the ring briefly before pulling the two young people to the side and out of earshot of the other performers. "As both of you know, I've been up in the trees checking in on our injured members. I've also been gathering information on the Elven themselves. I was talking with the head healer and he's sending people to look for our missing horseman. He told me this has happened before and the Elven are sick of it.

"They're sick of having leadership that isn't transparent with them. They respect and revere Queen Ulla, but Sylvia, heir to the throne and the acting general, is not liked by many. She doesn't have much support among the people because of her abrasive nature and quick temper. The way they see it, this is another example of why she's unfit to lead.

"Not only did she bring us here and risk the Elven's secrecy, but she's not willing to deal with the consequences and make hard decisions. That leaves her mother and the Elven people themselves to deal with her repercussions." Chiara kept her voice low. "The healers don't know what happened to Tyee. He's not in any of the healing facilities, not even the quarantine chambers where people are sometimes kept captive as a last resort. You both were with when we checked the caves, and there were no signs there either. There are only a few other places he could be hidden, if he's still alive."

Luc leaned into Damien before looking back at the Head Herbalist. "What can we do?"

"Perform as if it's your last show ever," Chiara said simply. "The Elven are excited about tonight, especially the younger ones, the ones that do not know of life beyond this forest. From what I've gathered, the Elven have much longer lifespans than us, so a lot of their elders remember a time before all the hiding. Their people have been doing this far longer than we have and they're curious. If we give them something to talk about, they'll be more likely to have a discussion with us."

Luc gave a nod, soaking in the older woman's words. "It feels wrong to perform when Tyee is missing and our people could lose their memories."

"Aye, but it's our best bet at getting out of this jam. The young ones are restless and ready for change. Those are the ones we must win to our side. The head healer is older, so he vaguely remembers the wars and finding refuge here, but his children do not. He told me his children's biggest critique was that they didn't choose this way of life. There are runes they have to allow them to blend in with the rest of Kamore. They argue they should be allowed to send a party into the towns and see for themselves whether hiding is still necessary." Chiara said with a grim expression.

Luc covered her gasp with a hand. "What did you tell him?" Her thoughts swirled with what the young Elven would encounter should they enter any of the towns dotting Kamore. *They will be met with hatred and the refusal to accept anyone with differences. They will only be met with disappointment.*

Chiara's response roused the acrobat from her thoughts. "I told him the truth. I said Mortals have come to, or at least most of them, live in fear of Myra and her soldiers. It's not that they're bad people. They're just easily swayed by their feelings of fear and wanting to feel secure in how they live by following someone like Myra. They don't have to think about the repercussions for those different than them and can convince themselves those who are different deserve what they get. The Mortals cling to Myra in hopes she will give them the stability they crave. They will defend her until the end unless what she says doesn't align with what they now believe. Myra has given them a voice to spread derision and the idea that one's own thoughts and beliefs should be more valued than those of anyone else.

"I told the head healer his children had a point, and they had a right to want more from this life, but that they should also be careful. The Kamore we know, wouldn't accept the Elven. One day? Maybe, but it's going to take a lot before that's possible. I told him that our company is considered an anomaly, being a collection of Mortals and Magicae that are not bonded by familial ties. I informed him of the harsh reality that more often than not, children are abandoned, neighbors are turned in and friends are hunted, all in the name of the greater good."

Luc's eyes widened.

"A little harsh, Ma." Damien said, his expression bewildered by his mother's candidness. "Not exactly the best way to get somebody to trust you."

"On the contrary, my son," Chiara reached out with one hand and touched her son's cheek. "That's exactly how you win someone's trust. You will not place much faith in someone who is dishonest. Respect grows when you share the truths, especially the hard ones. You can be tactful in how you word them, but you should never lie to those you're trying to win over." Chiara's lips turned upward into a slight smirk. "Unless it's to your loved ones. A white lie now and then doesn't hurt anybody. Like when I told you I liked your hair cut back in Galley."

Luc let out a chuckle, remembering when Damien tried to cut his hair into the shape of a hawk just to show Bane he could.

Damien shuddered at the memory. "Thanks for the reminder, Ma. Now I'll have nightmares for a week."

Chiara rolled her eyes at his dramatics and waved the two off, knowing they needed to take their places before the show started.

Chapter Twenty-Nine

Chiara sat on the sidelines as the Circus began its performance. The sun had started its descent moments ago, but it was already nearly dark beneath the trees. Her green eyes moved to the city of Verdencia, a satisfied smile lighting her lips.

By the light of the torches on the walkways, Chiara could make out hoards of Elven gathered for the promise of entertainment and some insight into a world outside the forest.

This has to work. The Head Herbalist thought as she strained her eyes to look closer at the people in the trees. She could only pray to the Huntress that this would win the Elven over.

Luc and Damien weren't the only ones skeptical of their plan. Chiara knew they could only place their faith in the powers that be to get their people out of this mess. Her eyes caught on the healer from the infirmary. He stood at the edge next to what had to be his grown children. She flashed him a smile, glad he supported his children instead of simply writing off their concerns.

She turned her attention back to the ring, where Luc and Damien were warming up for the show. Her eyes shone with pride as her son walked across the tightrope and Luc swung on the swing beneath. Damien balanced precariously, using just a wooden staff to help him balance, swaying with the movement of the rope and leaning into the crowd's energy.

Chiara's green eyes followed her son closely. Damien had an amiable smile on his face as he added his dramatic flair to the routine. He used the pole he was holding to shift his weight from one side to the other, pretending as if he was almost losing his balance. She smiled softly as her gaze shifted to Luc below him, hanging by her hands as she swung her legs to get momentum before twisting them into different poses.

Chiara held her breath as Luc finished her sequence. Her eyes became shadowed with doubt as she prepared for what was to happen next to her only child. She had always been fiercely protective of her son, sometimes to the point of suffocating him when he was younger. As much as she tried to hold him close when he was little, she eventually recognized his need to spread his wings. When he fell in with Luc, Rae, and Zeke, she was hesitant to release her tight grip on him. She compromised, inviting the three to join them for dinner and taking the time to get to know the friends her son had made. After a time, Chiara recognized the bond between them as something she should nurture, regardless of the questionable antics they frequently got into.

When Damien was younger, she had to close her eyes more often than not as he performed high in the air with nothing but a net and Zeke's skills and reflexes to catch him should something happen. A gasp from the crowd followed by a hush drew Chiara's attention back to the middle of the ring.

Duncan stepped out of the shadows, one arm aloft, wearing his signature top hat and purple overcoat with long coattails. The outfit brought out the lavender in his eyes as he held Damien aloft, suspended in the air and still clutching the long wooden pole.

Despite not watching it all happen, Chiara knew from rehearsal the idea was to make it look like Damien lost his balance and fell. The audience was left believing all that stood between Damien and catastrophe was the Ringmaster's quick thinking and impressive skills. The crowd's eyes were wide as they watched in stunned silence, fixated on Duncan's every move.

"My esteemed and honored hosts! I am so pleased that you are here with us tonight." As he spoke, he lifted his hand slightly, sending Damien into an upright position and hoisting him gently back up to the tightrope.

Chiara watched as he turned back to the crowd, a bright smile on his face, and mischief in his eyes. She chewed the inside of her cheek, hating this facade their Ringmaster put on. Every time he was in the ring, she knew it was necessary, but she saw how it weighed on her old friend. *He still owes me that conversation.* Chiara kept her thoughts to herself as her attention darted between Duncan and her son.

"It would be remiss of us not to perform for such a group as yourselves. You have been the best of hosts and deserve to sit back and let us entertain you with some things we've picked up along the way." Duncan paused and Chiara didn't miss the glance he shot toward the structure that housed the Queen. "I fear our welcome is waning, as expected, and we just want to express our gratitude in whatever way we can."

Chiara heard grumbling from the trees up above. It seemed as if the people gathered didn't approve of their Queen's absence or lack of welcome.

Interesting. Maybe this is a better plan than we thought. Chiara shifted her attention back to the center of the ring as Duncan continued.

"We will start with these fine young people on our makeshift trapeze. As you can see, we have no nets as we had to leave in quite a hurry. No big top either, so I welcome you to engage despite our humble equipment. Regardless, since there is no net, I will help ensure no accidents take place on the high line wire. I'm not sure how familiar all of you are with the Gifts inherent in us Magicae. I am what we call a Crafter, specifically a wind Crafter."

Chiara's lips turned into a small smile as Duncan lifted both hands and made flickering motions, calling the wind to ruffle the trees and the clothes of their patrons. She could tell Duncan's eyes were dancing with mirth as they watched the young Elven's eyes widen in surprise before laughing with glee.

Chiara's soft smile turned into a frown as she wrung her hands. Her heart gave a painful twinge as she watched the Ringmaster in the center of the performance area and thought about the young Elven they came to impress. So many of them had grown up sheltered and trapped in the forest, unable to take part in the world beyond their city. She knew this performance was about winning the Elven people to their side, but she couldn't help thinking part of Duncan's and Nan's ambitions were to also open the eyes of those young enough to yearn for something more. The Herbalist had a feeling they wanted to expose those young ones to what could happen should they decide to leave the forest. She thought of the healer and his children and could only hope they were doing the right thing.

Duncan cleared his throat and called the winds back. They made a tiny whirlwind around his person, fluttering the tails of his long coat as he turned to where he knew the Queen resided. Chiara's gaze followed his, trying to catch sight of the frosty queen she dreaded. She couldn't make out a figure but waited as Duncan spoke, regardless of her absence.

"My greatest thanks and praise must be sent to Queen Ulla herself. Without her grace and mercy, we would not be here today. The same goes for her daughter, General Sylvia, for finding us as we wandered around aimlessly. We owe them both a lot and dedicate this performance in their honor." Duncan cast a glance upward as the crowd grumbled once again at the mention of their monarchs. The Healers were right, the Queen and her daughter were losing the favor they once had. The Elven that gathered for the performance had no interest in what their monarchy thought.

They were here for a taste of something new.

Once Luc and Damien nodded their heads, Duncan cried, "let the games begin!"

Chiara could feel her heart pumping faster and louder, unable to contain the worry and trepidation she felt seeing her son perform without a net or the usual trapeze equipment.

The performance started with Luc hanging from the bar motionless, as if waiting for something. Damien let out a yip and dropped from the rope above, timing his jump to land feet first on her bar. Once both were on the bar, they started swinging in tandem, moving it back and forth at an impressive speed. Luc kept both hands on the bar, swinging her legs for momentum before pulling them up into a splits position as Damien kept the momentum going above.

After a couple of oscillations, Luc shifted her grip to make room for Damien to drop next to her, showing off his strength as he caught himself with one hand.

Chiara lost herself in the crowd as she cheered on her son and his partner, adding her screams and shouts to those of the Elven. Her heart pounded as the two continued their sequence, Luc climbing to replace Damien on top of the bar while Damien hooked his knees around it, suspending himself so his hands hung freely. Luc increased the swing's momentum before dropping suddenly, trusting in Damien to catch her by the wrists.

They did a couple more sequences with Damien spinning Luc around in the air, gripping her hands and ankles as she spun, imitating the routine Zeke and Rae did for the night performance.

Chiara's eyes moved to the side of the ring, looking for the Ringmaster. Relief filled her chest as she noted her friend's concentration, his gaze never straying from the acrobats above. Duncan's dedication to his role in keeping the two safe was a balm to her anxiety. The next part would be the genuine test of his skill in Crafting.

Damien held Luc by her wrists as they swung together, moving the bar faster and further than previously in the performance. As they reached the top of their arc, Damien propelled Luc upward. She tucked into a ball and spun rapidly up and over the tightrope. The Ringmaster used the wind to time her momentum with Damien as he swung back the opposite way.

Luc came out of her tuck, still high in the air, and plunged head first towards where Damien would end his oscillation. She reached her arms out, and he gripped her wrists with a confidence only developed from being performance partners for years.

Chiara felt the knot in her chest loosen slightly at the successful trick. They did a few more sequences similar to the first, with Luc launching into the air and either catching herself on the tightrope above or falling back down to be caught by Damien's unfailing hands.

Duncan did his part, making sure their timing was impeccable and helping prod Luc whenever necessary. It was a sight to behold, and the audience was easily transfixed by the athletic prowess of the acrobats.

They cheered as the two performers finished their set with a final yip, both of them releasing their grip on the bar and counting on Duncan to slow their fall to the ground. When they finally planted their feet on solid ground, Duncan made his way to the center of the ring and all three took a bow.

Duncan cupped a hand around his mouth and addressed the crowd. "Please give it up one more time for the Black Swan and White Raven!"

Chiara clapped along with the crowd, silently thanking the Huntress for keeping her son and his partner safe.

The sound of thundering hooves drowned out their applause. Chiara felt her anger rising as the horsemen appeared, incomplete, without their fifth member. Duncan stood his ground in the middle of the ring, letting the four horsemen file in around him. She watched as Simeon broke away from the others, only pulling up when his horse stood beside Duncan.

"Please give it up for our Midnight Riders!"

Chiara smiled at Duncan's words despite the heat in her chest, knowing this was a way to honor their missing Night Rider.

"These four impressive men need no introduction, so without further ado, I will let them take it away." Duncan gave a nod to Simeon, letting him know his voice was projected.

"We couldn't help but notice the lack of true horses here. We get it; the ponies are all you need. Horses are bulky and they take up a lot of room. Plus, I don't even know where to start to get them into the trees." He earned a chuckle from the gathered Elven as he planted the imagery of horses in the trees.

Chiara lost what the man said next when she became distracted by Luc and Damien making their way over to her. The performance continued in the ring as the two acrobats approached her. Damien gave her a sidearm hug and kissed her cheek.

"I told you I'd be fine," he said, referencing their conversation from earlier.

"As your mother, it's my job to worry and you can't expect me not to." Chiara replied, happy the performance was over and done with. A small part of her wouldn't be upset if finding a new place in the forest meant no more need for the acrobats to perform.

She took the time to study her son's partner. Luc was a very accomplished woman, kind, and gifted in the art of holding a conversation. Chiara could tell the two were very well matched and happy they found each other.

Everybody deserves that first love, no matter what happens in the end. She refused to think about Damien's father as she looked at the two and squeezed her son. She thought Luc seemed tense but carried on as if she hadn't noticed, keeping a close eye on the young woman.

"You two were breathtaking. I'm surprised you didn't mention anything about classes for tomorrow. I thought you were going to move the rope down lower and invite everyone to take a crack at it."

"Yeah, Duncan decided he would make an announcement at the end of the show," Luc responded without looking at the Herbalist. Chiara watched as the young woman cocked her head, puzzled by her uncharacteristic behavior. "Do you hear that?"

"Hear what, mi amor?" Damien asked, cocking his head as well with a slight frown.

"I don't know, maybe it's nothing, but I'm gonna go check on my Abuela just to be sure."

"Do you want me to come with you?"

"No, no, stay with your mom. I'll be back before you know it." Damien shrugged his shoulders as Luc scurried away.

"You should have gone with her." Chiara admonished, watching her son closely as his shoulders fell. "Something's going on with her."

Damien let out a sigh as he watched Luc walk away. "No, she just needs space. We fought before the trapeze. Nothing serious, just a little tiff, but she said she needs some space. I think spending all this time rehearsing with just me reminds her of our friends, bringing about her anxiety of the unknown and her concern for them. She needs to prove to herself she can handle this on her own. She'll be fine, and it's good for us to have a little space."

Chiara gave her son a soft nudge. "How did you become so wise?"

Damien took a half bow in ringmaster fashion. "It's because of all the years I've been alive, spending so much time with others. You'll understand one day, young one," he said with a wink.

Chiara chuckled and threw an arm around his waist, sending a prayer of gratitude to the Huntress for the son she knew she'd always fight for. She leaned her head on his shoulder as they turned their attention back to the horsemen in the ring.

Chapter Thirty

Luc's skin felt prickly all over as she listened for the sound she heard when she was with Damien and Chiara. She thought she'd heard the cry of a horse, but couldn't be sure until she investigated further.

A hair fell from Luc's top knot as she walked away from her partner and his mother. Swearing under her breath, she brushed it away. Luc wasn't the type to let her emotions get the best of her, but her transgression with Damien right before the show started weighed heavily on her mind.

"Luc, what's going on with you? You've been on my case for the past hour. Talk to me." Damien tried pulling her into a one-armed hug, but she pulled away before he could. She caught the hurt look in his eyes, but it didn't soften her response.

"Step off, Damien. If you were trying harder, I wouldn't have to get on your case." She toyed with her pendant as she continued. *"Lest you forget, we don't have a net."*

Damien shot her a look, frustration filling his eyes as the hurt dissipated. "I'm not that thick, Luc. I know the risks. We haven't stopped talking about them ever since they built this death trap." His eyes narrowed. "But that's not what this is about, is it?"

Luc hesitated before answering. "I don't want to hurt you."

"You hurt me more by not telling me what's going on."

She gripped the pendant around her neck and flashed him a glance, refusing to hold his gaze for long. "Dame..."

"Tell me, Luc. Please?"

She caught his gaze again before staring into the distance. "I think I need some space."

A tense silence formed between the two as Damien waited for her to continue, knowing she needed some time to put her thoughts into words.

"It's just been too much. Everything that's happened on top of having to perform today without Rae and Zeke. It's too much." Luc said in a rush.

"And what does that have to do with us?" Damien asked, drawing out his syllables.

Luc grabbed his forearms and looked into his eyes. "I love you so much, Dame. But between rehearsal and trying to deal with everything, we've been spending a lot of time together, just the two of us."

"And that's a bad thing?"

Her eyes pleaded with his. "No. It's not a bad thing, Dame." She cupped his cheek with one hand. "But I'm keyed up and worried about everyone, which doesn't make me the best partner. I need you to understand this isn't about you. It's about me knowing my limits."

Damien searched her eyes before giving a nod. He pulled her close and kissed her on the forehead. "Whatever you need, amor. As long as you come back when you're ready."

Damien was too good for her. She'd always known it, but this was another example of why it was true. She was frustrated with herself for needing space and frustrated with Damien for acquiescing so easily. Her mind was spiraling as it did when she got stressed, which is why she had to remove herself. Part of her felt bad, knowing she'd been looking for an excuse to leave the pair behind.

She would have to explain to Chiara at a later time. The Herbalist deserved that much after she left in a hurry.

But right now, she needed to figure out if what she had heard was real.

Another scream sounded in the distance. This time, Luc knew that it was coming from the horse yard and she rushed towards where the horses were held. As she approached, she saw Koko pawing the ground with one hoof before pacing and letting out another awful scream.

Something was wrong.

She went to the fence and called to the ebony stallion. "Koko! It's okay. What's going on, bud?" Luc had been helping Simeon take care of the horse as often as she could. Koko had taken to the raven-haired acrobat, letting her lead him around and bribe him with treats. Something was agitating the stallion and Luc wasn't sure if she'd be able to calm him. Luc narrowed her eyes as her mind raced.

There was only one reason Koko would act this way.

If he could somehow sense Tyee was in danger, he might act this way. *What else could it be?* Maybe if he'd done it the first day without Tyee, it could be explained away as anxiety, but knowing the horse had been without Tyee for several days, something felt different.

Luc trusted her gut and went to the gate.

Koko let out a scream and barreled towards her, barely giving her time to unlock and pull it open before the horse thundered past.

Her stomach dropped as she realized he might head for the ring. If he interrupted the performance, everything could be lost. Her heart pounded as she raced after the gigantic horse, doing her best to keep him in sight. He veered left instead of right, heading away from where the horsemen still performed in the ring. Luc didn't have time to breathe a sigh of relief, so she sent up a prayer of gratitude instead.

She pumped her arms faster, knowing she needed to keep up with the horse if she wanted to have a chance at finding Tyee. She kept running despite her heart feeling like it was going to come out of her chest and the burning sensation inside her lungs as her body struggled to keep up the pace.

Just as she was about ready to give up, she noticed Koko slowing down ahead of her. The horse resumed his anxious pawing and pacing before choosing a large oak tree and dancing circles around it. Every so often, he would look up and nicker softly, as if trying to call to the rider he still had a bond with.

Luc looked up into the tree as she approached and realized it was on the outskirts of the Elven city. There was only one bridge connecting it to the larger trails in the sky.

Reaching the oak, Luc put her hands on her knees and leaned over, gasping for breath.

It's been a long time since I've done wind sprints. Time to put those back on the docket. She thought to herself, knowing full well that if she wanted to be ready for the upcoming fight, she'd need as much endurance as she could get.

After catching her breath, she moved to the anxious horse and put a gentle hand on his front shoulder. "Shh, pretty boy, I'll go look. You stay here and be quiet." She looked him in the eyes, pointing to one side of the tree and the shadows beyond it. "I'll go check it out, but you need to settle down." She repeated her instructions, only turning her gaze to the tree in front of her once the horse did as he was bid. Luc shook her head in amazement, not quite believing how well the horse listened.

She didn't know what Tyee did to train him, but whatever he'd done, no one could deny Koko was one of the best-trained horses in the entire country.

Turning her attention back to the old oak, she ran her fingers over the rough bark, looking for the hidden handholds that would take her up to the house in the tree. Finding them, she shot a glance around before setting a swift pace upwards. Once she reached the top, she held her breath and peered over the edge, readying herself for guards, or anything else.

Her face scrunched into a puzzled frown when she realized no one was there. A loud bang had her ducking for cover as she heard angry footsteps march away. After a couple of beats, she peered back over the edge and watched Sylvia's figure disappear down the bridge. Wasting no time, she heaved herself up and over the edge, not thinking as she hurried inside the structure.

She took care in closing the door behind her as her eyes adjusted to the darkness within. With the sun fully set, only a flickering candle lit the cavernous room. Luc made her way to the table that held the candle, whirling around when she heard rustling to her right.

Her heart jumped into her throat as she realized a body lay on a table writhing in what she could only assume was pain. She grabbed the candle and brought it over to the person, not sure whether she hoped it was Tyee, or someone else. Luc didn't know if she could face the consequences of either scenario, but with a slight tremble, she lifted the flame to illuminate the person's face, anyway.

She had to stop herself from dropping the candle when she recognized the dark hair and lanky figure belonging to the horseman they were looking for.

"Tyee, what have they done to you?" She whispered before assessing the situation, knowing Sylvia would send guards at any moment. She could only pray they stayed outside, watching their post instead of checking in on the prisoner himself. Without thinking, she reached for the hunting knife that had been at her hip since entering the forest and cut the gag from Tyee's mouth.

"Water," he croaked. Glancing around the room, Luc searched for something to quench the man's thirst. Her eyes settled on the table next to him and she grabbed a waterskin from the worn wood. She sniffed it before taking a swig, making sure it was only water. Her Abuela taught her and Javie how to taste the difference between water and water that was mixed with something. They'd spent hours practicing until they could distinguish water from water with one grain of salt in it. She hated it as a kid but was grateful for it now.

There wasn't much water left, but she drizzled it into the horseman's mouth, concern flashing in her eyes as he guzzled the liquid. He cleared his throat before meeting Luc's gaze.

"We don't have time for that. Get me out of here as quickly as possible." Luc knew he referred to the concern in her eyes, so she pushed it away and went to undo the bonds that held his hands.

"Wait, don't do that yet. I could be wrong, but I think that might alert them to my escape."

Luc's eyes widened in alarm. "What about the gag?"

"No, I didn't see any runes on it when Sylvie took it out the last time. That's how we determine whether they'll send her an alert. Look at the straps on the bonds. Are there symbols on them?"

Luc brought the candle close so she could get a better look at the leather straps holding him. "Aye. They're small, but I can make them out."

"Hmm." Tyee closed his eyes for a moment, giving Luc time to study the constrained horseman. Dirt and bruises dotted the skin not covered by his clothes. Her eyes moved to his face, noting the bags under his eyes. She jumped when his dark eyes flew open and met hers. "I have an idea, but I need a little more juice. Did Rae or Zeke ever draw energy from you?"

"Yeah, they did when we were younger, but not recently." Luc couldn't understand why Tyee asked that question. As far as she knew, only the Magicae could call on the energy that ran through every individual's veins.

Unless the Elven can too.

The thought popped into her mind as she studied the rogue.

Luc didn't quite understand the mechanics of it all, but only those with Gifts in their veins could see and call upon that life-providing force. Besides, the Elven used runes to control the power in their blood. Surely they wouldn't need life energy to sustain them.

The question must have shown in her eyes as Tyee said, "I need you to trust me, please. It makes little sense and I'll explain later. If you're comfortable, touch my forearm and lend me some of your life energy."

Luc hesitated before doing what he asked. She didn't know of another way to release his bonds without signaling his captors and the last thing they needed was Sylvia or her guards to find them. She gripped his forearm and met his gaze.

"I trust you," she said with a nod. "I might understand more than you realize, but let's get you out of here before anything else."

He grunted before closing his eyes. Luc didn't know what it felt like to pull energy from someone, but she knew what it felt like when someone pulled energy from her. She braced herself for the slight tug but kept her grip firm on Tyee's arm. The questions swirling in her mind quieted as a familiar sensation of energy leaving her bloodstream made her heart pound.

Luc shifted her attention from Tyee's face to the leather bonds around his wrist. The symbols etched into the leather started emitting a soft glow, causing Luc to give a slight gasp. "Keep going Tyee. Whatever you're doing, keep going. I think it's working."

Luc braced herself again as she felt a slightly harder tug pulling at the blood in her veins. The slight feeling of dizziness started coming in full force as Tyee's emotions collided with hers. Flashes of memories and feelings whirled past her. She saw images of a woman singing in a strange language, followed by visions of a younger Silvia. Then there were a couple of flashes of horses and a stable before she saw Rae enveloped in a golden light.

A smirk formed on her face as Luc recognized the way Tyee remembered Rae. She had a feeling that whatever had happened between the pair ran deeper than a few stolen kisses and a roll in the sheets.

Before she could have another thought, the world went dark.

Chiara still stood next to her son as they watched Duncan make his way into the ring at the end of J's performance with the elephants and his young charges. J spent most of the performance in his half-Shifted form, highlighting the mechanics of what it took to transform himself into the friendly pachyderm. Eva and Wren had taken turns educating the crowd on elephant behavior, allowing the baby elephant to show off its skills and training.

The relationship between the three had taken hold of the audience's focus, especially that of the children. They watched in delight, taking in the sight of such marvelous creatures and secretly wishing they could switch places with either of the girls. Chiara knew they were hoping one of them would make the same announcement as Simeon had at the end of the horsemen's performance and they would be invited to interact with the friendly creatures.

She turned to her son, as Duncan bade J and his entourage goodbye before welcoming Jess and two other Forgers to do a demo on how they could manipulate their Material.

"Do you think we should be worried about Luc?" She asked in a whisper.

Damien gave her a sideways glance. "Ma, I told you before, she'll be fine. I told her I'd give her space and I need to be a man of my word. You wouldn't want me to go back on my word, would you?" He dared to raise an eyebrow at her.

She gently punched his shoulder, "Don't give your mother sass. I'm only worried about the girl since she's been gone a while when she said it'd be quick."

"I know, Ma, but—"

Chiara followed her son's gaze as a woman came flying into the arena, interrupting the performance. Her gaze quickly switched to Duncan, catching his lavender eyes filled with worry. Chiara was taken aback by the reaction as she inspected the woman in the center of the arena.

The woman collapsed in the middle of the ring, wearing ripped and dirty clothing. She squeezed her son's shoulder before making her way into the ring, knowing her services might be needed. Jess hastened her Forgers out of the way and cast a glance at their audience. This wasn't part of the plan.

Chiara disregarded all the eyes on her as she made it to the woman first, with Duncan following close behind. He addressed the crowd in the trees. "I beg your pardon, my friends, but it seems we need to take a brief intermission. Please, excuse us."

He leaned down and caught Chiara's green gaze while the crowd broke into whispers above. "Let's get her to my cabin."

"I think she needs to go to the infirmary," Chiara countered, not understanding why Duncan would insist a stranger be brought to his cabin. The woman wasn't Elven, but it remained to be seen whether she was Magicae or Mortal and how she'd gotten past the defenses and charms of the Elven. Their secret city was heavily guarded not only by individuals but by runes designed to convince would-be trespassers they were going in circles.

Duncan's eyes pleaded with hers as she helped lift the woman. Duncan pulled one of the unconscious woman's arms over his shoulder, and Chiara did the same with the other. They walked with the woman stumbling between them, mumbling quietly to herself once she roused a bit.

Chiara hissed when they were out of earshot of everyone. "What's going on,

Duncan? Who is this woman? Why do you want her in your cabin?"

Duncan licked his lips before answering. "Chiara, this is my sister."

The Herbalist furrowed her brows. "Your sister is in the Capital. I thought she married a general or something." She paused before whispering. "Isn't she the one that betrayed you? Betrayed Andre and all the Magicae?"

"Yes, yes, yes. This is the very same sister, but look at her." He gestured to the woman between them. "She's been through hell. I don't want anyone to see her or figure out who she is before I've talked to her."

The woman let out a cry of pain, causing Chiara to direct them to a tree. "Let's set her down here and try to assess all of this. Do you have any water on you?"

"Yeah, here, I always keep a waterskin on me if I'm performing. Take whatever's left."

Chiara gave a nod as she leaned down and offered the waterskin to the woman. "Hey, I need you to drink some water. You're in shock. Take some deep breaths and when you're ready, we have a few questions we need to ask you."

The woman guzzled the water down, followed by several deep breaths as she exhaled, about to speak, when hooves sounded on the path to their left.

Duncan and Chiara whipped their heads around in time to see Koko plodding through the forest with Tyee and an unconscious Luc on his back.

Chiara shared a glance with Duncan before asking, "To your cabin?"

Duncan rolled his eyes at her before nodding his head.

Chapter Thirty-One

Bane kept his breathing in time with the pumping of his legs as he chased after the man that attacked him and Gemma.

The thug was fast as he weaved through the narrow alley.

"I know these streets like the back of my hand. This is your last chance to split the reward." The man called over his shoulder.

Bane stayed silent but slowed his pace, trying to gauge whether the man would stop or keep going. They were reaching the end of the alleyway and the Shifter knew the man spoke the truth. Bane couldn't let the thug give him the slip, no matter the cost. The man realized Bane slowed his pace and did the same, hazarding a glance behind him.

"That's a good lad," he said with a smirk.

Bane came to a full stop and assessed his surroundings quickly. There was a pile of crates strewn across the left side of the alley and what appeared to be a couple of garbage cans to his right. He knew he'd have to be precise in his next moves to make sure no noise escaped the shadowy alley. The greedy man approached Bane slowly, the smirk still plastered on his face.

I'll never understand how someone can be so stupid. Bane thought to himself, blown away that the man thought he'd turn in the girl he'd defended mere moments before. It was clear this man was desperate or simply so deep in the dark underbelly he'd forgotten what a decent man looked like.

Idiot.

Once the man was close enough, Bane launched himself using muscles honed from physical training and the lingering power of his bear form. He barreled into the man, knocking him onto his back and the breath from his chest.

"Let this be a lesson. There are still people in this world that will not betray their own." Bane whispered into the man's ear.

Both men sucked in air, trying to recover from the chase and the tackle. The man on the ground tried in vain to headbutt Bane but only resulted in knocking the Shifter's hood back. He stared into the brown eyes of a bear in shock.

"You—you're—Demon," the man stuttered before hissing the last word.

Something snapped inside Bane at the slur that had haunted him all of his life. The weight of everything came crashing down as he started speaking with his fists instead of the words that would never communicate the pain and failure he felt.

Bane strangled the man and then punched him again and again. The man's screams quieted as he slipped into unconsciousness. Lost in his rage, Bane continued despite the state of the man, with the word demon still ringing in his ears.

The pounding of footsteps finally shook Bane out of his trance-like state. He went to wipe the blood and spit off his face and was surprised when he felt the wake of tears. Stunned, he was frozen until a hand gently shook his shoulder and guided him to a standing position.

Once standing, wiry arms embraced him and he let himself lean into the small comfort in a rare display of vulnerability. Getting ahold of his emotions, Bane straightened and rubbed at his face again. His eyes met Zeke's gray ones filled with concern, and he gave the Crafter a nod of thanks.

"What happened?" Zeke murmured.

Shame set his cheeks on fire as Bane looked at the bruised and bloodied man. "I lost control." Bane set his lips in a grim line and refused to meet the other man's eyes.

A hand on his cheek made him meet a falsely gray gaze. Zeke repeated his question. "What happened? You can tell me, Bane, I won't judge you."

Bane sighed but obliged. "He slowed down because I tricked him. I tackled him, but then he saw my eyes." The Shifter closed his eyes before recounting the next part. "He called me a *demon.*"

Zeke's eyes filled with sadness as he put a hand on Bane's shoulder, not sure if the man craved comfort or space. "I'm so sorry. You didn't deserve that."

Everyone knew the visceral reaction all Shifters had to the name demon. Ever since the Uprising, Shifters had been disproportionately targeted by the fearful and hateful Mortals following Myra. Countless babies were taken to the Capital and slaughtered as soon as their eyes changed.

"No, but I shouldn't have let myself lose it like that. We need to be better than those that hate us. What would my Da say if he could see this?" Bane hung his head.

Zeke felt dismay at the man hurting in front of him, but his eyes hardened, as did his resolve. "Then let's be better." Casting a glance around, he searched the alley for anything that could help.

Bane shook the guilt away and furrowed his brows. "Where are the other two?"

"They were giving the first guy a sleeping draught. I don't have any more of it though, so we'll have to improvise. Do you have any rope?" Zeke patted his pockets before looking at the Shifter.

"Here. It's not very thick but it should do the trick."

"Perfect." Zeke took it from him and wrapped the unconscious man's hands and feet together. "Now we need to get him under some of these crates." The Crafter made to grab and move the unconscious bloody man to the side of the alley.

Bane put a hand on the man's arm. "Wait." He shrugged off his coat and ripped several pieces of cloth from the bottom of his shirt. Working swiftly, he used the pieces to create a gag and tightened it around the man's mouth. "Okay, now help me move him."

They got him to the side of the alley, but Bane hesitated as Zeke started creating a wall around the thug. "Do you think he's going to make it?"

Zeke felt for a pulse. "It's slow, but I feel his heartbeat." He sent a glare at the man on the ground. "He'll live."

"Part of me wants to make sure nobody finds him. Part of me hopes he dies." Bane clenched his fists.

"Aye, but we both know you'll regret it later. Maybe we only partially cover him with crates?"

Bane nodded and did as the Crafter suggested. As they finished, Rae and Gemma came bounding up to them.

Rae kept Gemma close and pulled her towards the mouth of the alleyway after realizing what they were doing. "I'll take Red with me while you two finish. The other guy is taken care of." She frowned as she studied the bloodied man. She raised one eyebrow at her two friends. "I guess what they say is true. You really should see the other guy."

The two men chuckled as the women moved out of earshot.

Bane looked to Zeke and put a hand on his arm when he made to follow Rae. "Thank you."

Zeke's eyes widened in surprise. "For what?"

"For trying. I'm not the easiest person to get along with." Bane knew his eyes belied the emotions swirling within. It'd been a while since he felt such a pull towards another man. He struggled to find the words to communicate what he wanted to say.

Zeke sent him a knowing smile and squeezed his shoulder, letting his fingers linger. Bane felt the flush on his neck return as he searched once more for something to say.

"Come on, guys, the coast is clear, but we need to hurry." Rae's voice sounded from down the alley.

The two men shared one last look before jogging towards the Crafter and her charge.

"What's the plan, Rae?" Zeke asked in a hushed tone.

"The lady at the inn said they stayed for the night, but then left earlier today. That means something or someone spooked them into leaving. My bet is they took the time to find provisions and then headed to the forest. That was the plan we discussed before the *Vengeance* left." Rae said, taking charge as usual.

"Aye, but we don't know which direction they headed." Zeke furrowed his brows.

"No, but I think if we follow this main road, we should find the market we passed by before. That would be the place to get the supplies for the next part of our journey. Once we get to the market, I say we head straight into the forest and see what we find." Rae tapped her chin as she thought out loud.

Bane took time to digest Rae's words. "That seems like the best bet to retrace their steps, but let's stick to the alleys. I think if we crossed this main road and took a left, we could follow the alleys to that market."

Rae and Zeke nodded their agreement while Bane leaned down and tied Gemma's hood a little tighter around her chin.

"All right, Red. We're going to need to move quickly and quietly. You were so brave when those men came after us, but I'm going to put you on my back to make sure we go as fast as possible. I need you to keep a tight grip around my neck and don't let go, no matter what." He chucked her under her chin before she nodded furiously. "If your hood slips back, knee me in the back three times. That way, I'll know we have to stop. Is that clear?"

"Crystal," the little girl's gray eyes were like steel as she answered.

"You're a trip, Red." Bane said with a chuckle before crouching down so the little girl could climb onto his back. Once the little girl was situated, the three crossed the deserted main road under the cover of the night sky.

George dropped his head in his hands as Reg and Tamara kept arguing. He drowned out their bickering as he considered the options in front of them.

They'd waited almost two full days for Rae, Zeke, Bane, and Gemma to catch up with them and George was running out of hope they would find their group in time. He felt horrible even thinking about deserting the four Magicae, but he had to think about the children in his care first. The inn they'd gone to on Mouse's recommendation had been perfect, at least until the hawk delivered that one-word message.

RUN. That's all the ominous letter said, and the three had squabbled over its legitimacy for hours. That is, until the soldiers came.

Once Reg saw them ask for a room, the three leaders determined it would be best to move along. They had already gone to the stables and purchased several horses the day before to help carry supplies and children if needed. When the soldiers appeared, it set everyone on edge and put them in greater danger than before. They decided it would be best to purchase their provisions and head into the forest.

They could only hope the message hadn't been a trap to get them into the trees.

But now that they were here, the question remained, why wait?

Reg argued they should wait at least one more day while Tamara insisted they carry on and hope the other four made it without them. She claimed their provisions would only last so long and they did not know where they were going or how long it would take to get there. She thought it would be best to leave as soon as possible to make their provisions go as far as they could.

George was on the fence about what to do. He couldn't get past the idea of leaving without giving the other four some sign of where they'd gone. He lifted his head from his hands and looked at the trees, the different choices running circles in his mind.

There has to be something we haven't thought of.

With Reg and Tam deep in conversation, George was the only one who noticed the shadowy figure approach them from one side. As the figure got closer, it revealed itself to be one adult who had been in Reg's group when they fled from Heimat.

George stood, catching the attention of the other two. Reg and Tamara stopped their debate and turned to the man.

"Excuse me, I have a bit of information that you should take into consideration." The man said, knowing the dilemma their leaders faced. All the adults in the company knew there was a choice to make regarding what to do next and had voiced their opinions.

Nobody wanted to leave Rae and the others behind, but they were also worried about the safety of the children in their group. Rae and the others were accomplished Magicae who could fend for themselves. The children, on the other hand, needed as big of a head start as they could get.

George knew the group of adults could hear the three of them arguing. Maybe not the exact words, but they could hear raised voices. He knew this must be important for one of them to approach during the middle of such arguing. Reg and Tam automatically looked to him as the man waited to speak. George mentally rolled his eyes, already sick of the deference both Reg and Tamara gave him.

Makes me miss the Captain. George thought to himself. *Or even Freeman at this point.*

His thoughts about the poised and rakish Captain brought up unwanted emotions. Her devilish grin flashed in his mind as a shiver ran down his spine.

Best not to think about that right now. George forced his mind back to the matter at hand. He looked at the man and gestured for him to continue.

"One of the older kids just told us they overheard that one of the young Herbalists made a flower bloom in front of several people in town. Nobody said anything when it happened, so the kid didn't think she needed to tell anyone. But the older kids knew they needed to tell us as soon as they heard." His face remained impassive as he delivered his news.

"Did you talk to the kid that did it?" George asked, forcing himself to keep his tone even.

"We did, and she broke into tears. She knew she'd done something wrong, but one of the others dared her to do it. She wanted to be like Gemma, in her own words, so she did it."

Reg slapped his hand to his forehead while Tamara's lips formed a grim line. Her eyes were hooded as she stared right at George.

"You know what this means, George. We have to leave now."

George's mind raced, knowing Tam was right, but also not willing to give up on the other four. "Maybe there's a compromise we can come up with."

"What compromise, George?" Tamara snapped, fed up with his persistence in waiting for the others. "There's nothing we can do that wouldn't alert our pursuers to where we've gone."

"Unless we set up a bunch of fake ones…" George said slowly, a plan taking form as Tamara narrowed her eyes.

"Go on."

"We need to talk to the kids first to be sure, but we know people saw a Herbalist, right?" George paced as he thought out loud.

"Aye," Tamara replied for the group, her eyes following the lanky man as he moved back and forth in front of them.

"What if we make a big display of greenery with a path into the woods as if a Herbalist created it? They'll assume we left a path behind us because the child isn't in control of her powers." George paused and tapped his chin. "The question is, how do we let the others know that's a fake path without being too obvious about it?"

The man who brought them the news spoke up. "What about wolfsbane?"

"Brilliant." George's eyes twinkled with appreciation. "Easy enough to identify, yet the message is obvious."

"Wait, what message, Georgie?" Reg scratched the top of his head. "Wouldn't that just signal to 'em they're on the right path? I mean, com' on, wolfs*bane*? It's practically screaming the Shifter's name."

George frowned. "I see your point, Reg." He took a moment to think before holding up one finger. "What if we put wolfsbane on one side and have it trail off towards where the true path is?"

"I think that could work. Wolfsbane is known for being a poison, along with having roots in Shifter lore. But it also can symbolize mistrust of Mortals." The adult Magicae offered.

"So we just need to hope they remember their studies of different plants then." George said with a grin.

"Okay, great idea, but how do we let them know where we've actually gone?" Tamara asked.

"My beautiful, beautiful friend. We're going to use your glass." George thought of the supplies they carried that would allow Tam to use her Gift.

"How do you mean?"

"We are going to leave a path of glass shards, like breadcrumbs." A glint came into George's eyes as the plan took shape in his mind. They would use the flowers to show which way their companions should look, and some glass would show them they were on the right track.

"And what if someone stumbles upon the glass?" Reg asked.

George thought for a moment before snapping his fingers. "Bane can use his sense of smell. We'll leave a trail of glass, and then use the Shifter babe..." He trailed off as he tried to remember the child's name.

"Cade," Tamara offered.

"That's it. We'll use Cade's scent on some trees to get them to the next set of glass shards. We could rub his blanket on the trees." George looked at the other three to get their thoughts.

"It's a good plan, George." Tamara said begrudgingly, still exasperated by the lengths he would go to accommodate those still missing. "We should get it done as quickly as possible, though."

She led the charge back to their group, beelining for the horses carrying her supplies.

George sent up a prayer to the Goddess, giving thanks for Tamara's resourcefulness and ever-lasting need to have the supplies needed for her Gift close at hand. She'd insisted they get a large bag of sand in the marketplace, 'just in case' the need should arise for it. Not to mention the shards of glass from broken bottles on the street she was constantly tucking away.

That woman is always two steps ahead. George thought as he followed Tamara and the others back to the group from Heimat. Now they needed to prep their people and make sure nobody else used their Gifts within eyesight of outsiders.

Time to get to work.

Chapter Thirty-Two

Duncan felt his emotions rising as he struggled to decide which problem would be best to tackle first. He stood in the doorway of his cabin, glancing between Mirabella on the left and Tyee on the right. A noise outside had him reeling out the door to make sure Luc was still okay on Koko's back. He sighed in relief seeing her condition and position on the big horse's back remained unchanged.

His gaze traveled toward the direction Chiara had disappeared. Once they'd gotten Mirabella and Tyee back to his cabin, he sent the Herbalist to find Damien and Javie to help them get Luc into Nan's wagon.

Duncan had made sure Tyee was settled before taking up his position in the doorway, trying to keep a handle on all three people in his care. He pushed down the panic and questions of what to do next as he looked to the stars above.

Huntress, what do I do? He sent his question into the void, knowing it would go unanswered.

With a sigh, he decided the best thing would be to focus on Luc. He quietly closed the door of his temporary residence and walked to the horse's side. Duncan reached a hand out to touch the unconscious woman's hand and squeezed it. The horseman reassured them Luc was unconscious from giving him her life energy, but nothing could take the worry from his mind.

Chiara herself felt the acrobat's pulse and reported it was slow, but steady. Duncan held onto that as he dropped Luc's still limbs.

Sounds from the performance ring could be heard all the way to his cabin as

Jess continued the show in Duncan's absence. He had sent a runner to tell her to finish up the Forger display and move forward with the rest of the performances. There were only a few acts left and his second-in-command could handle it for the time being.

Guilt clawed its way up into his throat as he thought about disappointing his people.

Duncan pushed it down as hard as he could, trying to stay focused on what was in front of him. He could shoulder those feelings of shame and disappointment later, after he sorted through the tasks at hand.

He glanced at the performance ring once more. *I need to time this just right to close out the show. What's taking them so long?*

He tapped one foot as he peered into the darkness.

Footsteps thundered down the path toward him, and relief washed over the Ringmaster. Javie and Damien raced toward their unconscious loved one before coming to a stop.

"What's happened? Why won't she wake up?" Damien asked, his voice cracking as he reached up to stroke Luc's hair.

"She just needs rest," Duncan reassured him. "She's given too much life energy, but Abuela will have a tonic that will set her to rights. We need to get her in the wagon."

Pain flashed in Damien's eyes, but he nodded and pulled her off the enormous horse.

"Life energy? Who did she give her life energy to?" Javie demanded.

"Who cares, Javie? Help me get her in the wagon." Damien looked up from the woman he cradled gently in his arms.

Luc's younger brother opened his mouth to protest, but upon seeing his sister's still form, he met Damien's eyes and rushed to open the back door of the wagon. Javie hopped inside and helped Damien maneuver her onto a cot.

Duncan kept a hand on the stallion as he waited outside the wagon, keeping watch for any unwanted visitors. He turned back towards the performance ring as soft footsteps approached.

Chiara had her arm looped with Nan's as they made their way to the wagon, concern written on both of their faces.

Duncan looked at Nan and offered. "A lot is going on right now that I will explain later. Luc will be fine; she just needs a tonic to restore her life energy."

Nan nodded and said gently, "That's what Chiara told me." Her eyes were strained as she went to the wagon where her granddaughter lay unconscious. Before entering, she paused at the back doorway. "Chiara led me to understand there are a lot of moving parts you need to take care of." Her bright eyes held a questioning look.

"Yes."

Nan's eyes turned steely. "Let me finish the performance, then." Seeing the Ringmaster's hesitation, Nan said more firmly, "Go take care of that mess inside your cabin. I will let everyone know there's nothing to worry about. I'll say that the woman was a straggler from our group we thought we lost, but she's—"

"Tell them she's my sister," Chiara spoke up, causing Nan and Duncan to shoot her a look. "They'll be less likely to doubt your story if she's connected to one of us, but we don't want our people to know who she is just yet. At least not until we've had the time to question her."

Gratitude shone in Duncan's eyes as he looked at his old friend. She was one of the smartest people he'd ever met and once again proved that to be true. His feelings for his younger sister were complicated, but he at least owed her a conversation before the whole Circus realized who she was.

"I will do that as soon as I've seen to Luc," Nan said before entering her wagon and tending to her granddaughter, effectively ending the conversation.

Before she could, Duncan gripped her arm. "Thank you."

Nan patted his hand with a smile but said nothing as she waved him away.

That left Duncan and Chiara to take Koko back to where the horses were kept. The pair walked in silence on either side of the horse as they made their way to the paddocks. Duncan patted the horse on his haunches before closing the gate behind him. He turned to Chiara and offered her his arm, which she gladly took.

"Duncan, I have a bad feeling about all this," Chiara said as they walked back towards Duncan's cabin and the mess that awaited them. Duncan refused to meet her eyes as they kept walking.

"I do too. I can think of only one thing that would make Mirabella leave, and it's not good." He used his free hand to rub the back of his neck. "But finding Tyee is an enormous relief."

Chiara frowned and pulled her arm from his. "I think it raises more questions and more problems. I mean, how do we keep this from the Elven? Should we let them know we found him? Force them into a confrontation?"

It was Duncan's turn to frown as his hands found his coat pockets. "No, no, no. We keep this our secret for as long as possible. They're denying that they ever had him, so they won't come after him. And if they do, they'll be discreet about it. We need to let them think he escaped and left on his own."

The Herbalist's lips settled into a grim line. "We need to have a Council meeting about this," she said in a clipped tone, clearly not agreeing with Duncan's train of thought.

"We will, but let's leave it for the morning." Duncan shrugged his shoulders and placed one hand on the door in front of him. "Since Nan volunteered to do the end of the show, I can devote the rest of tonight to Tyee and Mirabella." He turned to the door in front of him and propped it open.

The sight inside was as they'd left it. Mirabella was still unconscious while Tyee dozed on the cot opposite her. As they hesitated in the doorway, Tyee stirred. Chiara immediately went to his bedside and offered him a glass of water.

"Here, take this, Tyee." The Head Herbalist put a hand behind his shoulders to help him sit up before putting the glass to his lips. "Then we have a few questions if you're up to it." Tyee drank greedily, taking the glass from her hands. Chiara grabbed the pitcher from the nightstand and refilled it.

Tyee nodded his thanks, but asked, "Will Luc be okay?" His dark eyes searched the Herbalist's green ones for any sign the acrobat was in trouble.

"Yes, she'll be fine as long as she gets some rest," Chiara reassured him.

Duncan noted the way Tyee's shoulders sagged with relief at her reassurances about Luc. *The loner sets down another set of roots, it seems.* The Ringmaster cleared his throat, knowing it was his time to speak up.

"We've been searching for you, Tyee. I want to clarify we didn't abandon you. We looked everywhere we could think of but found nothing. Chiara even asked some healers for advice on other places to look. Everyone we talked to agreed that Sylvia, the general, would be capable of something like this and had done so in the past. I'm sorry we couldn't find you sooner." Duncan's tone was nothing but sincere as he held the other man's gaze.

Tyee's eyes held an unknown emotion as he nodded. "I appreciate the sentiment, Duncan. Honestly, it's a wonder Luc even found me. I don't blame you for what happened or how long it took for rescue."

"Why did they keep you, Tyee?" Chiara asked. "Did you ever find out their reasons?"

Tyee met both Chiara and Duncan's gazes before dropping his eyes to where his hands toyed with the edge of his blanket.

Eventually, he let out a sigh. "Yes, and no. I found out the motivation why, but still have questions of my own."

Duncan pulled up two chairs next to the horseman's bedside and his lavender eyes prodded him to continue, so he launched into his story. Starting with the history between himself and Sylvia, Tyee let the words come tumbling out. Soon enough, Duncan and Chiara knew everything about the horseman from before he arrived at the Circus.

Neither of the Council members interrupted him as he weaved his tale. During the story, Chiara took his hand in hers as a way of providing gentle comfort.

Duncan listened intently to what Tyee had gone through. *No wonder he could never join the Circus completely. I doubt even Rae knows all this.* The Ringmaster was lost in thought when Tyee motioned for another glass of water before he got into the story of his capture. Duncan snapped his eyes back to Tyee when he saw the movement in the corner of his eye.

"I felt her voice in my head in the clearing and that's when I passed out," Tyee said after drinking another glass of water. "When I woke up, I was tied to a table. The first time I came to, it was only Sylvie and me, but the second time, her mother was there too. It took me a while to recognize Sylvie, but I immediately became suspicious when I realized she was the aristocrat from my past.

"She made a point of playing it off as if she was trying to get more information about the Circus, but she was just playing games. Same old Sylvie but…"

"But the Queen was there one time," Chiara repeated for clarity's sake.

"Aye, she was there one time, and she was the one that alerted me to the fact that this could be about my lineage."

"Your lineage?" Duncan asked with a frown.

Tyee nodded. "She asked something about whether I was the one that Sylvie went looking for in the first place all those years ago. It struck me as odd, so I waited for my opportunity to find out more. Earlier today, I saw my chance and asked her if I was half Elven. She didn't deny it."

Chiara struggled to follow the man's train of thought. "Okay, but why would you assume you were half Elven? Because you never knew your father?"

"No, no, no." Tyee shook his head. "I had this dream… I think it was a memory of my mother. And she was singing a song in a language I didn't recognize, but it stirred something inside. I thought back to all those other times I'd given my life energy to a Crafter or other Magicae. Rae said something to me, or she thought something… I—"

"Dreams are hard." Duncan gave the man an encouraging nod.

"Yeah, I couldn't tell if they were dreams or visions or what, but I had this feeling something was off. So I tried calling to the runes around my bonds and they would glow, but not enough to release me." He rubbed one of his wrists. "So when Luc appeared out of nowhere, I asked her if I could pull energy from her and it worked. I knew I pulled too much when she passed out, but my bonds released. I was in shock until I heard Koko's nicker below and I got to work getting us out of there. I don't know what this means, but they took me because of the blood in my veins."

Duncan frowned as he considered Tyee's words. The Elven leaders' shiftiness when it came to the horseman made more sense considering Tyee's heritage. What they needed to figure out now was how to keep Tyee's freedom under the radar from the Queen and her general.

"I won't lie to you, Tyee. I know nothing of the Elven people. At least nothing besides what we know from the stories and what we've observed from the ground. You need to get some rest before thinking about what you want to do next. You've been through some trauma and sleep would do you good." The Ringmaster patted his arm and made to stand up.

"Duncan, I don't want to stay here. Not after what happened." Tyee sat up, trying to get out of bed.

"Tyee, you need to rest." Chiara pushed his shoulders back to lie on the pillows. "Get a good night's rest and see how you feel in the morning. If you want to explore the Elven magic in your blood, I'm sure the healers would assist you. There are good people here, so sleep on it and we can discuss it more in the morning."

She handed the horseman a sleeping draught. "Drink it," she said when he hesitated.

His eyes darkened, but he took the glass offered to him and knocked it back in one gulp. Chiara dimmed the lantern by his bedside and gave a soft smile as the man dissolved into light snoring. She got up and moved her chair to the woman that was still unconscious.

"I think we need to wake her up, Duncan." She searched his face, trying to decipher what he was thinking.

"Shouldn't we wait until the shock wears off?" Duncan asked as he looked at his younger sister. Chiara bit the inside of her cheek and gently shook the slight woman.

"Mirabella. Mirabella, hon, I need you to wake up. Come on, darling. We need to talk to you." The Herbalist prodded the woman several times before turning to the Ringmaster. "I can give her an awakening tonic, but there are risks. The body puts itself in an unconscious state as a way of protecting itself, and if we wake her up, it could damage the healing process that's taking place."

Duncan sighed as his fears were confirmed. He knew they needed answers, though. "I don't think we have a choice, Chiara. If we wait for her to wake up, we're going to have to face more questions."

"I have a bad feeling about what she's gonna say," Chiara admitted.

"We owe it to our people to sort this out." Duncan insisted, punctuated by Tyee's snores.

Chiara didn't reply but nodded as she pulled another tonic from her bag. "Help me lift her," she stated, reminding Duncan of why her people voted her Head Herbalist.

He went to Mirabella's other side and put a hand behind her shoulders, gently lifting her into an upright position. Chiara tipped the tonic back slowly, pouring the mixture down the woman's throat.

Nothing happened at first, but eventually, the young woman let out a cough. Chiara lifted a glass of water to her lips despite her eyes being wild and filled with panic as she took in her surroundings.

Duncan watched as Chiara took her opportunity and moved the glass in front of the confused woman's sightline. "Please, Mirabella. Drink, you need water." Surprised by the use of her name, Mirabella did as she was told.

Slowly, understanding filled her eyes as the events of the last day replayed in her mind. Finishing the water, Mirabella pulled away and struggled to speak. "Duncan... I need Duncan."

"He's right here, hon." She motioned to the Ringmaster on the other side of the cot.

Mirabella's eyes misted over as she stared at the brother she hadn't seen in over a decade. Soft sobs racked her body as she struggled for words.

Duncan pulled his chair close. "Bella, talk to me." He placed a comforting hand on her shoulder.

"I'm sorry, Dunc. I'm so sorry. I didn't mean to... I thought, I thought it was for the best. They convinced me it was for the best."

Duncan's eyes clouded over as he remembered Mirabella's part in the Uprising. "We'll talk about that later. Why are you here? How did you find us?"

Mirabella couldn't face her brother anymore and dropped her head in her hands, giving in to the sobs that ran through her body. "I'm so sorry. I didn't know."

"Bella. I need you to focus, please. Why are you here?" He tried to guess why the woman had shown up unannounced. "Gemma's not here."

There was a pause as Mirabella processed that fact. Slowly, she calmed down enough to lift her head from her hands. "I knew there was a chance she wouldn't be here." She sighed in defeat. "I just thought that finding you would be the best shot at finding her."

Duncan gave a nod. "And what of your husband?"

Fear filled Mirabella's eyes as she gripped Duncan's forearm. "Duncan, they're coming for you. Myra knows you're alive, and she put out a kill order on you."

Duncan's stomach dropped as his worst fears came to pass.

Chapter Thirty-Three

Nan woke with a start in the darkness of her wagon. She fumbled for the lantern by her bedside as quietly as she could.

When she found what she was looking for, she paused and listened to the sounds within the wagon. She heard Javie's soft snores and a curious sound she couldn't quite place. It was as if water was falling drop by drop onto the floor.

She lit the wick of her lantern, shielding the flame from the others in the wagon. Dimming the light, she moved it towards where Luc still lay unconscious on the cot.

My reckless, reckless nieta. What am I going to do with you? She thought to herself. Shaking her head, she lifted the warmly glowing light to check on her grandson.

Javie was in the wagon's front, asleep on the makeshift cot he'd set up. Satisfied he was sleeping soundly, she turned back to her granddaughter. Nan did her best to keep quiet, moving closer to Luc. A soft smile formed on her lips as she noticed Damien asleep in the chair next to her.

Poor lad is gonna hurt his neck with much more sleeping like that. She tsked inside her head despite knowing this was the kind of love she wanted for her granddaughter.

Her thoughts strayed to a young Huntsman who roamed the woods years and years ago. She became lost in a memory for a moment before the *drip-drop* of water reminded her she was looking for something.

Sure enough, Damien must have knocked over the glass of water she'd placed on the bedside table. Luckily, the glass hadn't fallen, but what little water remained in the overturned glass was dripping onto the floor.

This must be what woke me. She thought to herself, grabbing a towel and studying the small puddle on the ground. She carefully eased herself down to the floor to mop up the water.

Still finding yourself cleaning up the messes of others. Some things never change. Nan thought as an amused smile lifted the corner of her lips. As she worked, her thoughts strayed back to the end of the performance for the Elven.

She knew there'd be a Council meeting in the morning to discuss the events of the night before, but Nan felt in her bones that trouble was brewing. Her eyes found her unconscious granddaughter once more and her heart clenched with fear.

She was still puzzled why her granddaughter offered her life energy to a part Elven like Tyee. Neither of the two young people realized the consequences of doing so could have been much worse. Nan slowly straightened, taking the drenched towel with her.

The fortune teller's lips were pursed as she grabbed the now empty glass from Luc's bedside. She could only hope the meeting in the morning would shed some light on why the pair took such a risk and give them clarity on what they needed to do next. Worry caused her shoulders to tense as she put the glass in the cupboard and the towel with other linens needing to be washed.

Slightly out of breath, the old woman sat on her cot for a minute and thought about everything that would need to be discussed with the others. She knew she would need to report on how the rest of the performance had gone.

Mirabella interrupted Jess and the other Forgers' performance, but after a brief intermission, Jess salvaged the rest of it and helped organize the rest of the performers. According to Jess, Gar went next, doing a raptor demonstration, delighting adults and children alike as they flew through the trees and ruffled their patrons' hair with their proximity.

Nan arrived as Gar was finishing, just before Conrad and Nymeria took the stage. They performed another Shifting demonstration using the big cats to illustrate their bond and ability to communicate with the impressive animals. Finally, Nan took the stage with Freya and a reluctant Javie to show what the Herbalists could do.

After their performance, Nan thanked the Elven people and asked all of them to come down the following afternoon to meet the performers and animals that performed with them. She promised them adventure, camaraderie, and an education unlike anything they'd ever experienced. She even hinted at the possibility of more Crafting demonstrations should there be enough interest.

Catching the air of suspicion hanging over the crowd, Nan also explained the woman who made an unexpected appearance was the relative of the Head Herbalist and was being monitored for health reasons.

Her heartbeat had finally slowed when she felt some of the tension release from the crowd.

All they could do now was pray to the Huntress it had been enough to win the Elven people to their side.

When the old woman could breathe easily once more, she stood up from her cot and went to her granddaughter. Keeping the dimmed lantern in hand, Nan tenderly brushed loose strands of hair from Luc's face and tucked them behind the young woman's ear.

Please wake up, mi amor, we need you. Nan felt the sinking feeling in the pit of her stomach that came when she saw Luc's collapsed form returning in full force.

She knew she needed some fresh air, and the stars to clear her head and calm her anxiety. With a determined look, she slipped out of the wagon and into the night.

Gar shuffled past the cottages that his people occupied under the cover of the stars. One lone falcon rode on his arm, still hooded from when he had put her to bed. He patted his pocket once more to make sure the ink and piece of cloth were still there.

Relief flooded his chest upon realizing the instruments were secure. His eyes caught on the path that would lead him to the performance area. His thoughts returned to the ring and his performance with the raptors. It went well, with the birds doing what they were trained to do despite Bane's absence. Gar was confident in the birds' training and his capabilities to execute it well, but the question always remained whether they responded to him or his son in falcon form.

The older man hadn't let the falcon on his shoulder join in the festivities and was punished for it later, having to take the bird for a late-night flight. He'd skipped out on the last bit of the performance to do just that.

I couldn't risk it. I couldn't risk losing the only tether to my boy. Gar willed his thoughts away from the bitterness he felt at not knowing where Bane was. He knew leaving the performance was petty and disrespectful to his comrades, but he resented having to put on a show for the captors who wouldn't let them leave.

Despite being on the Council, Gar felt like his voice and opinion were being silenced more and more. He understood that no decision would make everybody happy, but as of late, it felt like not every voice on the Council held the same amount of weight. Every fiber of his being railed at the idea of being held captive, but one man fighting back would amount to little. He needed to make them listen.

On his way back from the walk with the falcon, he had run into Chiara, leaving Duncan's cabin. She told him about the Council meeting in the morning and to be prepared for big changes. He pressed her for more until she told him about Mirabella's admission that Vincenzio was sending troops with a kill order on Duncan's head.

Returning to his bed with the weight of that information on his mind, he tossed and turned for hours before finally giving up. He would not wait until morning to take action, no matter what the repercussions were. Gar had shown his son's letter to Duncan and the others, agreeing to wait to send a response once the Council conferred upon it.

But Gar wouldn't wait any longer.

This was why he took another walk late in the night with the falcon on his shoulder. It was risky taking the raptor out again so soon, which was why he kept her hood on. The longer the bird stayed calm, the more energy she could conserve for the long flight ahead.

As he kept walking further and further through the line of cottages, he came upon Nan's wagon. His eyes widened as he saw the old woman slipping from the back door.

He hurried his pace but kept his footsteps as quiet as only a huntsman could. Once he was close enough where he didn't have to yell, he hailed her.

"Be careful there, lass, otherwise someone might catch you making off to see your lover in the middle of the night." His eyes danced with mirth as he teased the old woman.

Nan whirled around upon hearing the voice, but her eyes crinkled with happiness as she threw a smile at her old friend.

"I could say the same thing about you, dearie." She replied, before linking her arm through his. They continued on in silence, neither wanting to break the stillness of the night, as they took in its beauty. Soon enough, they reached the part of the forest where the trees were thinner and there was a magnificent view of the stars. The clear skies and new moon made them twinkle even brighter.

"And where are you taking me on this fine evening?" Nan teased.

Gar chuckled before replying. "Only where the most serious of lovers go. Into the forest, lassie." The two laughed before Nan rose one eyebrow at him, a silent question on her face.

She pulled him to a stop and nodded towards the falcon, demanding an answer.

Gar's eyes clouded with pain. "Myra put a hit out on Duncan," he whispered. Nan's arm tightened around his as her eyes widened. "That's what Mirabella reported to him and Chiara. She also said Vincenzio's troops aren't far behind her."

Nan remained quiet as she processed this turn of events.

"I'm writing a letter to Bane." Gar's tone left no room for argument as he stared the old woman down.

"I would never try to stop you." Nan's eyes drifted back towards the wagon. "Doing something for the ones you love is the noblest of pursuits." She struggled to hold back the tears as she continued, "We must do all we can to protect them for as long as we're able." She met the falconer's gaze. "Let me help you. I think there's a rock up ahead that we can use to write on."

Gar nodded his thanks as he led them the way Nan indicated. Upon reaching the rock, the two got to work crafting a letter to Bane and the others.

Gar wrote in code as quickly as he could, brandishing his knife quickly and confidently. With the soldiers on their doorstep, he double-encoded it just in case the worst were to happen. Gar's eyes got misty as he finished the last line of the letter.

Ride the winds, but don't forget the way home.

That was what he always told Bane when his son went flying. He shook his head and rolled up the cloth before tying it to the falcon's leg. Gar removed the falcon's hood and stared straight into her eyes.

"Fly straight and true. Don't stop until you find him." He whispered before throwing the falcon in the air and watching her disappear into the night.

Nan wiped a tear from his cheek before patting it. "Come on, old friend. Let's go back and try to get some sleep."

With one last look back, Gar led them out of the forest and back to their beds.

Tyee was lost in a dream again, but this time, all he saw was gold.

Rae faced him, her eyes dancing as she taunted him. Her lips pulled upwards into a wicked grin as she sidestepped his halfhearted thrust.

"What's next, Drifter? Another sad excuse for an attack?"

The Crafter's words fell on deaf ears. Tyee's eyes drank her in, despite knowing she was toying with him as they sparred. Using the wind to knock him off his feet, Tyee felt a knot in his chest as he noticed once again the absence of her fire.

The feeling of steel reverberating in his hands called him from his thoughts as he met the woman's twin daggers once more.

Her fire might be gone, but not her spirit. He thought to himself, before standing and going on the attack again. She danced nimbly out of the way, sending a smirk his way.

Tyee lifted the sword in his hand as the vision of Rae drifted into the distance. Acting before he could think, Tyee broke into a sprint, chasing after the woman. He heard her calling his name, urging him faster, but he couldn't reach her. The voice sounded louder and louder, but Tyee became engulfed in darkness.

One moment he was watching Rae's outline disappear and the next he was slowly opening his eyelids, realizing it was Duncan calling his name and shaking him awake.

"Sorry, son. I need your help. I mean to get the Queen and bring her to the Council meeting this morning. She deserves to know what's happening."

Tyee stared in shocked silence as he rubbed the sleep from his eyes. His thoughts spiraled as he felt his heart leap into his throat.

"Duncan, I gotta stay low. I can't face her after what she did." His dark eyes leveled a steady stare at the Ringmaster. "She can rot for all I care. Let's just get the hell out of here."

Duncan shook his head gently, breaking eye contact with the horseman. "And what would we do with the elderly?" He held his hands up in surrender. "Son, I know you're angry. I know you want revenge for what happened, but there are innocent people, innocent kids, who don't deserve to die. Will you sentence them to death?"

Tyee gave the Ringmaster a long look. He knew the older man was playing on his heartstrings. "No, of course not, but I can't risk getting taken again."

Duncan sat in the chair next to him. "I need you, Tyee. You're one of our best fighters and we need our best to get out of this mess. I have a plan. All I need is for you to trust me." Tyee studied the Ringmaster but was only met with sincerity.

With a grumble, he asked, "What does this plan consist of?"

Duncan drummed his fingers on his leg, "Trust me, it's better if you don't know."

Tyee's eyes narrowed. "That's not giving me much to go on, Duncan." Lowering his voice to a whisper, he asked, "How many know?"

Duncan furrowed his brows. "Know what?"

"About me."

"Only the Council members know." Duncan clenched one fist and seemed to struggle with his next words. A feeling of dread came over Tyee as he waited. "I intend to take you with me to go see the Queen and her General. We need to convince them we have a solution to the problem we face and we will announce it at the Council meeting. Bringing you will prove they can trust us to be open and forthright."

"Using me as a sign of good faith? Duncan, that makes no sense." Frustration rose in Tyee's chest, making it feel tight and overwhelming the fear deep inside. "Have you thought about what they could do to me? They could take me with a snap of their fingers; you saw what they did to us in the clearing."

"Not in front of their people, Tyee. The healers will be right behind us. Chiara has spent enough time with the head healer to witness the respect given to him and the rest of the healers. She's also reported there's dissension among the people regarding the Queen and her Heir. They can't risk losing what little favor they have." Duncan's tone was nothing but patient as he countered.

Frustrated by the Ringmaster's persistence, Tyee tried a different angle. "Duncan, Sylvie, and I have history. She will not let me go that easy, no matter what her people think. Maybe she won't do it today, but she'll come in the night, out of sight." He clenched and unclenched his fists. *Tell him.* His mind urged him, despite the fear in his heart. "She knows about Rae, Sir, and Sylvie's not the type to share."

Tyee met the Ringmaster's searching gaze and watched emotions flit across the older man's face.

"Tyee, what can I do? The troops are coming and Myra knows I live. Mirabella confirmed as such. The soldiers are less than a day out. Bringing you is political. As much as I'd like to avoid it, I don't have a choice anymore. Having you by my side at the table shows we will be bold and put bygones aside, considering the new conflict. The risk will give weight to the news we bring. It's the only way to make them believe my words are true, and not just a tactic to get out of their ultimatum." Duncan's eyes pleaded for Tyee to understand. "We can't get out of this mess without the Elven."

Tyee closed his eyes. Rae's face came unbidden, a smirk on her face and an eyebrow raised in challenge. *What's it going to be, Drifter? Coward or champion?* The horseman shook his head and sighed. "When's the meeting?"

"As soon as you're dressed."

Duncan handed the man a change of clothes and left the room, giving him a little privacy. Tyee scanned the room and noticed Mirabella, fast asleep in the bed next to him. Rising too quickly, Tyee's world spun. He reached a hand to the wall to brace himself until he felt steady on his feet again.

Focusing on the smooth wood beneath his fingers, the world righted itself. Shedding his clothes, he donned the ones Duncan left for him as guilt panged in his gut. *I never asked about Luc.* Tyee strode to the door with purpose, promising himself he would rectify that as soon as possible. Grabbing his coat from the rack, he pulled its hood over his head and left the safety of the cabin.

Duncan straightened from where he leaned on the wall of what had been his home for several days. Moving without a word, he started towards the city in the trees.

"Duncan, wait. I never asked about Luc. Has she woken up yet?" Tyee asked in a loud whisper.

Duncan whirled around with a finger to his lips. The somber expression on the Ringmaster's face was all the answer Tyee needed, despite Duncan shaking his head, anyway. "We'll talk later. We're late as it is. Come." Duncan said quietly before resuming his march towards the Queen's quarters.

Tyee pulled his hood closer as they came upon the tree they needed. Duncan wasted no time and quickly clambered up, using the handholds carved into the tree itself.

Tyee took a deep breath before climbing up after him, the trepidation and fear threatening to overtake his control. He swallowed it all down and settled a mask of indifference on his face. When he reached the last of the handholds, he swung himself up to the bridge above.

He kept his hood on as he watched Duncan conversing with a guard outside the door to where they aimed. Eventually, the guard turned and knocked loudly. After a couple of moments, the door opened a crack, allowing the guard to relay the message in hushed tones to whoever was behind it.

Slowly the door opened to reveal Sylvie and her mother, both frowning at the interruption. Tyee winced in response but quickly schooled himself, relaxing the fists that clenched on instinct. He took deep breaths to calm his racing heart as he looked at the two women who held him captive.

Ulla took one long look at the two men before gesturing them inside. She offered them drinks, saying, "I take it you've decided on when the forgetting runes will be given to your people." The Queen's tone was frosty as she met Duncan's eyes, disregarding Tyee's hooded figure altogether.

Duncan licked his lips before replying, "On the contrary, you and I have a problem." His gaze shifted between the two women, but he stood his ground. "We have word from Heimat, the city we fled, that a legion of soldiers is in pursuit. They should reach Verdencia within the next day or two, according to the woman who interrupted our set last night. She followed us to warn us before it was too late."

The Queen's stare was like daggers as she hissed, "You mean to tell me you were being pursued and conveniently left that out? How do I know you're not lying to me?" She whirled on her daughter. "Can you confirm what he says? Or is your intelligence incapable of that as well?"

"Mother..."

"I am your Queen and you will address me as much." Ulla spat before turning back to Duncan. "Don't think I misunderstood what you were trying to do last night. Your people will take the forgetting rune and go before your so-called pursuers can find this place." Sending a look to her General, she said with a growl, "Prepare your soldiers and rally our guests; it's time they stop taking advantage of our hospitality."

"Your Grace," Duncan held his hands up and gestured for Tyee to come forward. "Give me one minute to explain before you proceed." Without waiting for a reply, he motioned for Tyee to pull his hood back.

Tyee thought of Rae before taking a deep breath and doing what Duncan asked.

Silence permeated the small structure as the two women processed who was before them. Sylvie recovered first and lunged toward him. Duncan used the wind to hold her back.

"Before you do something rash, know that Chiara is bringing the head healer here as we speak. He knows we found Tyee, and he's prepared to tell your people what you've done to an individual with Elven blood in his veins." Duncan kept the wind at his fingertips as the two women blanched at his words. Tyee felt the tightness in his chest loosen slightly, but not disappear completely as the wind Crafter continued. "I need both of you to come to our Council meeting so we can discuss the next steps and what it will take for our people to work together against a common enemy."

The Queen's eyes narrowed. "That sounds awfully close to a command, Duncan." Her voice was still icy, but Tyee noted the slight bit of weariness that had crept into her voice. Giving Duncan a hard look, she asked, "Where will the meeting take place?"

"Mother, you can't be entertaining this farce."

"Sylvia," Ulla snapped. "Stand down, General. We would be fools not to use the resources at our disposal. If you interrupt again, you will be dismissed from your position." The Queen's tone was iron as she stared down her daughter. Sylvie dropped her gaze to the ground and stayed quiet despite the angry red dots that formed under her nails as she clenched her fists.

Ulla turned to Duncan and repeated her question, refusing to acknowledge the horseman in front of her. "When and where's the council meeting?"

"In the amphitheater in an hour," Duncan said.

The Queen nodded before turning away, dismissing them. "We'll be there."

Duncan gave a nod before turning back to the door they entered from. Tyee followed, giving both women one last look. Sylvie's eyes flashed with anger but she didn't utter a word as he followed Duncan out the door and down the tree.

The horseman only let relief wash over him when his feet touched the ground, and the pair walked back towards Duncan's cabin.

Pursing his lips, Tyee tried again, "How's Luc doing?"

Duncan started before answering, "She's resting. I will let you know if I hear anything." Tyee nodded his thanks as the leader of the Circus became lost in his thoughts again. The horseman clenched his jaw as he prepared mentally for what was to come next.

Coward or champion? The choice is yours.

Tyee knew which one he had to choose if he wanted to look Rae in the eye again.

Chapter Thirty-Four

Rich locked the doors of the bakery with a heavy heart. Taking a moment, he rested his palms against the rough wooden door one last time and gazed up at the old building. The decision to leave was a hard one, but when Rob said he was taking the girls to Tommy's mom's farmhouse, there wasn't much left to discuss. Anna left no room for argument in joining their son-in-law and granddaughters at the farmhouse. Rich felt guilty for shuttering his doors but knew this was what he needed in order to heal.

With one last pat, he whispered, "This isn't goodbye. It's I'll see you later."

Grabbing his small bag of possessions, he turned away from the place that had been his home since he was a child. Thoughts weighed on his mind as he started the long trek to the outskirts of town.

Rumors were Myra's reinforcements would be in sight soon. They had yet to see the smoke from their fires, but Rich knew it was only a matter of time. Vincenzio was only giving them three days to prepare because he was banking on his reinforcements needing that much time to arrive. After being humiliated, the self-declared mayor was in no position to be merciful. Everyone knew once the troops arrived, Vincenzio's revenge would be swift and fierce.

They may have won a battle, but the war was far from over.

And what a toll did that battle take.

Those who lived in the Fringe or knew Johanna had taken it the hardest.

Rich would never forget her good humor, kind heart, or the way she persevered, no matter the cost. She'd always stood up for the Magicae of Heimat and her quiet leadership would be sorely missed. Thoughts of the younger woman danced in his head, causing the baker to take a detour.

He took the long way so he could stop by the tannery one last time.

Simone had organized a memorial service for her dear friend the night before. Eddy had convinced some of the young sailors to help him in retrieving her body from where Vincenzio hung it like a trophy. The memorial service was inspirational without a dry eye in the crowd, especially once Eddy returned with Johanna's body. The chance to send the heroic Forger's body to a final resting place was a relief and devastating at the same time.

Both of them were hurting more than they cared to admit, and Rich knew neither of them had been willing to go through their deceased friend's things. Neither of them wanted to risk finding more reminders of the woman they lost. Rich could do this small act for the two who knew her best.

Rich passed down the street, taking in the signs of rebuilding that had taken place since Vincenzio ordered the fires to burn while searching for his daughter.

It was like the forest after being decimated by a fire. The charred remains were still visible, but dots of new life and structures could be seen if you looked hard enough.

The baker had a sinking feeling it was all in vain and would be destroyed when the mayor's reinforcements arrived. He'd been talking with Tommy and knew they needed to evacuate those Magicae that remained within the city limits. There were enough smaller towns in the area or along the coast that they could send people to as long as they were discreet about it.

Lost in his thoughts, Rich came upon the tannery sooner than he expected.

Flowers lined the street outside her door, and candles littered her front stoop. A beautiful drawing of the young woman was plastered to the door.

A single tear fell from Rich's eye as he traced the woman's likeness with one finger. It was a perfect depiction of the Forger, complete with laughing eyes and a knowing smirk. The tanner's wit preceded her despite the low profile she kept within their community. Rich took his finger off the door and touched it to his lips before sending it upward to where the Goddess resided.

"Keep her safe. Take her home," he whispered to the higher power he'd refused to acknowledge since losing his daughter. He sank to his knees before the wooden door as the tears came faster.

The old man broke into sobs that racked his whole body as he wept for Johanna and the daughter he still missed every minute of every day. He let himself weep until he was emotionally drained and his tears ran dry once more.

He rubbed a hand roughly across his face as he composed himself.

The grief continued to come in waves, and it was impossible to predict when it would strike again. But Rich was doing his best to move on; gone was the man who stumbled blindly in the streets.

He found purpose again in being the leader his community needed, helping Tommy and the others strike back and find vengeance. Despite Rich's good-natured personality, losing his daughter broke something inside of him and he didn't know if he'd ever get it back. He had a duty to those around him, and he would not go down without a fight.

With one last look at the memorial outside Johanna's door, he dragged himself up, grabbed the duffel bag next to him, and entered the lifeless tannery.

He took one step inside and immediately regretted it.

This place felt like a tomb, with Johanna's tools left out and projects still half-done on various racks. The smell of rotting animal skins assaulted his senses as he paused at the entrance. His heart panged when he realized the Forger had been planning on coming back to finish what she started.

Rich grabbed the lantern by the door and wandered into the bleak space.

His eyes wandered around the room until they snagged on a box at the only desk in the space. There was an envelope attached to it. Rich furrowed his brows and moved closer to the humble desk, grabbing and opening the letter attached to the box. Johanna's handwriting was horrid, and he could just barely make out the words scratched on the paper.

The color drained from Rich's face as he realized what it was.

Quickly assessing the size of the box, he recognized it would not fit in the bag he had with him. Searching desperately around the room, he found a small cart he could use to transport the box. With trepidation, he slipped the envelope into his pack and picked up the box.

He couldn't bring himself to open it alone, deciding it would be best to take it to Tommy's. He placed it into the small cart along with his duffel and draped a couple of blankets over both of them. With a grunt, he lifted the cart and took it to the back exit used for deliveries. With determination, Rich pushed what would become Johanna's legacy towards the farmhouse.

Chapter Thirty-Five

The group of four Magicae made their way along the outskirts of town until they were directly across from the display of greenery. Bane knelt so Gemma could climb onto his back again.

"One more time, Red, you've been doing so well." The Shifter encouraged her. Gemma gave a determined nod as she linked her arms around his burly neck.

The two men waited for Rae to give the signal she was ready. Her hazel eyes contained specks of gold as the tonic hiding her true eye color wore off. She met Zeke's gaze and gave him a nod. He settled into a crouch and used his hands to redirect the winds coming their way.

Through gritted teeth, he said, "You're good, Sparks, give us some cover."

Rae took a deep breath and pulled some of the water from the air, coaxing the water droplets closer together until a slight haze settled over the field in front of them. She added some of the fog she created from the power within until a dense fog lined the way to the trees.

Without breaking her concentration, she said, "Go quickly and quietly. Walk straight and keep your eyes on your feet until we reach the trees."

The three of them took off with Gemma holding tight to Bane's back. Rae gritted her teeth as the water threatened to expand again. She had to hold on for as long as possible to make it more believable. They reached the other side without issue and Rae slowly let the fog disperse. Her head was pounding at the power she needed to keep the water atoms from dispelling back into the air. Her sheer willpower was all that kept the fog in place for as long as it did.

As it lifted, Rae fought to stay conscious, keeping her eyes on the greenery in front of them. She bent over, putting her hands on her knees as she gasped for breath.

"Does anybody have water?" She asked between gasps. Zeke rushed forward with a waterskin.

"I don't have much, but take it."

Rae accepted gratefully and took deep gulps of the lukewarm water.

As Rae caught her breath, Bane studied the greenery in front of him. While he was lost in thought, Gemma gripped a branch and coaxed it to set her down on the ground.

Bane looked to the young Herbalist, unfazed by her resourcefulness. "Red, what are these flowers?" He pointed to one of the delicate blue blooms.

The little girl cocked her head and touched one flower. The puzzled look on her face evaporated once she touched the delicate petals.

"It's wolfsbane," she said with delight. "I've never seen wolfsbane before."

Bane shot a glance at Zeke, who was watching the girl intently. Catching the Shifter's look, the wind Crafter shrugged his shoulders.

Bane put a hand on Gemma's shoulder and asked her, "Does that happen a lot? Where names come to you?"

Gemma cocked her head again, "Um," biting her lip, she glanced around. Shaking her head, she answered, "No, I've seen pictures of them in my books."

"In your books?"

"Yeah, Momma said not to, but it was the only way to feel connected to them. Momma never let me go outside without her, so I could never feel the plants."

"Wolfsbane," Rae panted as she straightened. "Wolfsbane means something."

"Well, clearly it's a message for us," Zeke said. He walked toward the greenery, feeling it with his hands. He kept his eyes on the blue flowers as he crossed to the other tree that completed the archway. The acrobat frowned. "There's no wolfsbane over here, just another blue flower."

Rae's golden eyes met Zeke's silver ones. "Do you think George was worried about someone else seeing this?"

"Maybe?" Zeke's reply was more of a question than anything else.

"Do we go left then? The side that the wolfsbane is on?" She asked, stepping back to take in the full archway. *We need to hurry.* The Crafter thought to herself, absentmindedly biting her lip.

"I'll scout ahead and see what I can find." Bane said, deciding for the group. "Stay here, Gemma, and catch your breath. Stay out of sight." He nudged the girl towards the other two before striding to the left, not looking back at the Crafters or the little girl.

Zeke walked back to Rae and took her hand in his. Rae jerked her hand away when she felt Zeke's life energy touch her own.

"Z, I can't."

"Just take a little, Rae. You and I both know you need it. We can't have you passing out if it means we have to carry you. Even if Bane carried you, we'd lose too much time." Zeke argued, holding out his hand once more.

Rae gulped, but gave him her hand and accepted his offer. As she took some of Zeke's ice-cold energy, a memory came to the surface.

She was enveloped by the warm maroon of Tyee's life energy. She felt his admiration of her spirit and the spark of attraction that always pulled her back to him. Their kiss at the lake, fingers leaving trails of fire over bare flesh, the night in the forest when they fought; all of it marched through her mind as Tyee's voice sounded all around.

"I'm not scared of getting burned, Birdie."

The second time she pulled energy from the horseman came to mind. She was still lost in the warm maroon, but this time, it emitted a soft glow. Bewildered by the detail she'd forgotten, the memory slipped away despite the Crafter trying to hold on tight.

As quickly as it came, it was gone again.

Rae blinked her eyes, trying to bring herself back to the present as Zeke released her hand. She caught a look of concern on his face as he asked, "What's on your mind, Sparks?"

Rae bit her lip, uncertain she wanted to go down this road. "Do you think he hates me?" She finally asked, knowing Zeke was the only person who would understand why Tyee was upset with her.

Her trapeze partner's eyes softened. "No, I don't think he hates you. I think he's frustrated with you, but I—"

Footsteps from their left interrupted Zeke's train of thought. Both Crafters instinctively took up positions in front of Gemma, only relaxing when they realized it was Bane returning with information.

"What did you find, Bane?" Zeke asked.

"We need to go this way." Bane gestured back to the way he came from. "Shifters have a distinct smell. I followed it until I found a trail marked with shards of glass." He paused. His eyes found Zeke's as he said, "Wolfs*bane*. It was pointing to a trail only I could find. But the scent is stale. We won't catch them if we keep going on like this."

Rae watched as the two men spoke volumes to each other with just a look. *If I wasn't so happy for them, I'd be telling them to get a room.* She was about to distract Gemma and let the pair have a moment when Bane spoke again.

"I'm going to try something." Something was off in the usually confident man's tone.

Zeke threw him a quizzical look, catching the change in Bane's tone. "What do you mean?"

Bane answered Zeke's question, but his eyes focused on hers. "I need to see if what Rae and I talked about is true. I need to see if I can Shift into more animals."

Rae didn't break eye contact as she put a hand on his arm. "I understand. But is now the right time to try?"

"I don't think we have a choice." Bane's eyes blazed with determination as took off his shirt and dropped to all fours in anticipation of the Shift.

Rae and Zeke exchanged a look while Bane closed his eyes.

Excruciating minutes passed before Bane spoke again.

"It worked." Rae's eyes met Bane's and found pure awe. It was a feeling she knew well. "Give me a moment."

Before any of them could say another word, Bane's muscles and bones re-configured themselves until a large stallion stood in his place. He pawed the ground once in impatience as Rae and Zeke recovered from their shock. Gemma watched from Rae's side, eyes wide as she took in the Shifter's abilities once more.

Rae recovered first and used the horse's mane to swing one leg over his broad back. Zeke picked Gemma up from under her arms and held her up for Rae to grab. The little girl giggled at being lifted so high in the air as Rae settled her in front of her.

Once she was satisfied the girl was stable, she leaned down to help the wind Crafter. Zeke shot her a smirk before using the wind to catapult himself behind her.

Rae rolled her eyes and shook her head, muttering, "Show off," under her breath. Before he could respond, Bane was off, following the trail left for them to follow.

The Great Northern Forest was an eerie place to walk in the dark.

Sounds of insects and strange rustling in the bushes filled the night air with a haunting melody. The occasional cry of an animal offered the only dissonance to the music of the forest's underbrush.

George ran a hand through the locks that had grown out since leaving home. *Goddess, I need a haircut.* He thought to himself, effectively distracting himself from the decision he was supposed to be making. Taking another look behind him at the people in his care, he gave a sigh.

"You're right, Reg. We need to stop."

"I've been telling you that for the past hour. Nice of you to finally listen, Georgie." Reg responded with a clipped tone.

George held up his hands. "I know, I know, I'm sorry. Old friend, please forgive me."

Reg gave him one more look before letting out a sigh of his own. "You know I can never stay mad at you, Georgie. I'll spread the word."

George gave a crisp nod. *I shouldn't be so hard on him.* He turned to Tamara, a scowl on her face.

"Please don't, Tam. Our people are tired and need a break. We've been going hard for almost half the night. They deserve to rest until tomorrow."

Her only response was to pinch her lips tighter before turning around to spread the word.

So Tam's pissed at me... again. It's so fun being the leader, isn't it? George thought back to his days as a young kid, hiding from anyone and everyone. He wished he could be that invisible yet again. He knew his people were depending on him, but he couldn't help longing for simpler days. His shoulders drooped as he turned back to help his people bed down for the night.

All too soon, it was George's turn to take watch. He clasped his forearm with Reg and took up his position on the outskirts of the camp. As the night wore on, he felt his eyes getting heavy. Slapping his face gently, he willed himself to wake up. Reaching for the waterskin at his hip, he decided a drink might be the wake-up call he needed.

Despite all his efforts, George still felt himself dozing.

As he gazed into the dark line of trees, his ears perked up at the sound of what could only be hoofbeats. Drawing a short sword from his side, adrenaline in his veins, he took up a defensive position. Straining his ears to listen once more, he picked up the distinctive sound of a single set of hoofbeats.

His eyes traveled to the instrument hanging from one branch of the tree next to him. He wasn't convinced he needed to ring the bell just yet.

Hope caught in his throat at the thought that this could be the ones they left behind.

George met the intruder in hopes they weren't an enemy. Moving quickly but quietly, he stepped towards where the sound was coming from. As he moved closer, the hoofbeats became more and more pronounced.

Tensing his muscles and keeping his sword at the ready, George was prepared when a big bay stallion burst through the trees.

George stepped in the animal's path, calling, "Halt! Who passes through this forest?" He used the most menacing voice he could muster as he studied the three figures on the beast's back. His heart throbbed in his chest as the adrenaline pulsed through him.

"George, it's us! Lower your weapon."

One figure slid down the horse's back, with the other quickly following suit. Both individuals approached slowly with their arms raised.

As George focused on the two coming towards him, he recognized Rae and Zeke. They were a little worse for wear than when he'd left them, but still unmistakably the two Crafters. His mind raced as he looked back at the big horse and the little girl still astride him.

"Where's the Shifter?"

Rae cocked her head before giving a slight chuckle. "You're looking right at him," she said.

George made a face. "I'm not stupid. Bane's never been a horse. A raptor or an alligator, sure, but not a horse."

Rae and Zeke shared a look before Zeke took a step towards him. "No, George. Bane can be anything."

George frowned. "So he's like you?" He directed the question at Rae. "Like all-powerful or something?"

Rae gave a nod.

George considered them for a minute. "Did anyone follow you?"

Both Crafters shook their heads. "No, Bane got us here quickly. And Zeke did his best to direct our scent in a different direction. When I was up for it,

I doused the trail with water to wash away the footsteps as best I could." Rae explained.

George gave a terse nod. "I'm glad the plan worked. And that you found us."

Without any more ceremony, George turned around and led them to the camp. He showed them a quiet place where they could lay out bed rolls before returning to his post.

He hadn't let the relief he felt at seeing the four Crafters show, but inside, it washed over him like rain. He hadn't realized how on edge he'd been without the power and leadership of the three adult Magicae behind him. The security they provided had been sorely missed.

He sent a prayer to the Goddess thanking her for her mercy. After that ordeal, George had no problem staying alert while he kept watch into the wee hours of dawn.

Bane walked through the trees a little way outside of camp. He was seeking refuge among the sights and sounds of the woods. It was a relief to be out of Lockewater, away from the stony rigidness, and back among the flowing greenery.

He felt like he could finally breathe again.

Being amongst Mortals outside of the Circus or Heimat was always exhausting. He constantly felt like there was a target on his back and one wrong step would mean his end. It was no wonder that so many Shifters opted for life in the wild, as opposed to dealing with the prejudices and dangers of life in the city.

Closing his eyes, he let his senses wander, taking in the auras of the things moving in the trees before wandering back to the camp. The Shifter babe stuck out like a beacon in his mind's eye. The others had done a great job of creating a path for them to follow without being too obvious to Mortals that meant them harm. Taking a last deep breath of fresh air, he turned back to where the others gathered.

The sound of raised voices made its way to his ears. As he walked, his heightened sense of hearing picked out both Rae and George's voices.

"You went into the woods without a single thought about where you were going?" Rae asked incredulously. "There are children here, there's a baby. You can't do anything half-assed like that. It's too dangerous."

"Rae, again, we didn't have a choice." George's tone relayed the frustration that his face did not. "We had to leave Lockewater as soon as we discovered there had been a sighting of one of the Herbalists. There was no time to debate other options if we wanted to keep everyone safe."

"But this doesn't keep anybody safe. We can't just wander and waste time and energy that we don't have." Bane watched Rae pace in the small clearing where the leaders gathered to discuss their next steps. The Crafter was like a coiled spring, all tension, with frustration and anxiety rolling off her in waves. He stayed just outside the clearing as she continued. "And we can't stay here. The ship we intercepted could be after us as we speak and there's a trail pointing straight at us. We are one huntsman or tracker away from losing everything."

"What else were we supposed to do, Rae? Leave you without a way to find us?" George threw his hands in the air. "Damned if we do and damned if we don't."

Bane finally entered the clearing and made his way to where Zeke and Reg stood to one side.

"What's going on?" He asked the two.

"Oh, you know, the two lovers are go'ng at it again." Reg said, a wicked grin on his face.

Zeke raised his brows. "Lovers?"

"Oh, c'mon. They fight like an old married couple," Reg insisted.

Bane sent a puzzled look to Zeke. "I thought she and Tyee were an item."

Zeke gave a shrug. "Who knows anymore? I'm just sick of the arguing."

"Well, tell the lass to step down," Reg said.

"Why?" Bane asked. "She makes good points."

Reg held up his hands. "I'm not here to argue. George took charge once we got to Lockewater. He's been doing his best since he volunteered to be a liaison between Heimat and the Circus years ago. We wouldn't have made it as far as we have without him. That's all I'm saying."

The three men turned back towards the pair as they continued to argue. While they observed, Tamara strode from the cluster of tents to their right, holding the Shifter babe.

"Will you two knock it off?" She hissed, keeping her voice level while she sent daggers to Rae and George. "This doesn't help. You both have an incessant need to be right, and it's unbecoming."

She walked towards the three men and offered the babe to Bane. The Shifter's eyes went wide as he instinctively held his arms out to catch the baby should Tamara drop him. Tamara ignored the hesitant way he took the baby and made her way to Rae and George, determination in her steps.

Bane held the baby at arm's length, unsure of the best way to hold him. Picking up on Bane's discomfort, the young Shifter started crying. Panic welled in Bane's chest as he bounced the child up and down.

Reg made a tsking sound before taking the upset child from the Shifter. "Give him to me. Hey there, someone's a little cranky. Why don't you let Uncle Reg take care of ya?" He babbled to the baby as he rocked him. Catching the puzzled looks on Bane and Zeke's faces, Reg shrugged. "What? I have nieces and a nephew. It takes more than a few tears to scare me." He continued rocking the baby and started walking, murmuring words of soft encouragement to the little one in his arms.

"Not a baby person?" Zeke asked with a smirk.

"Can't say I have a lot of experience there. When you're a bird most of the time, there's little opportunity to hold a baby." Bane answered.

"Right," Zeke winced. "Sorry."

"Don't be sorry, Crafter. I've known the burden I would bear ever since I joined the troupe. The sacrifice is worth it." Bane said with a far-off look in his eyes.

"Is it though?" Zeke ventured while his gaze moved back to the fire Crafter. She argued with both George and Tamara. "Rae and I talk about it a lot. Some days, I wish I'd never been blessed by the Huntress. I wish I could give this Gift back."

"You don't mean that," Bane said as he studied the acrobat closely. "I've seen the way you look when you call forth the wind. Losing your Gift would be like losing a limb."

"Exactly. Devastating, but not impossible." Zeke countered. "It would make our lives so much easier."

Bane shook his head, "But it wouldn't be. If we didn't have our Gifts, we would be Mortal and Mortals always oppress those who are different. If there were no Magicae, they would just find some other way to discriminate against certain groups. Depending on where we fell in line, we might be the ones doing the discriminating. That doesn't sound easy. It sounds exhausting."

Before Zeke could answer, Bane held up a hand. Listening instinctively, he turned towards the sound of beating wings. He took two steps outside of the clearing and held up his arm.

Sure enough, a falcon exploded from the trees to land on his outstretched limb. Bane looked at Zeke with wide eyes. It took Zeke a moment to register the bird's significance, but when he realized it was the same falcon Bane sent to the Circus, he spurred into action.

"Sparks! I think we have the answer you need." He bellowed.

Rae, George, and Tamara looked up from their argument. Zeke pointed with emphasis at the falcon on Bane's arm. George and Tamara looked confused, but understanding blazed in Rae's golden eyes.

"Is that from your father?" She asked, leading the other two towards them. Bane gave her a grunt as he untied a missive strapped to the falcon's foot.

The others held their breaths as his eyes darted across the page, looking for the three dots that would indicate where to start. When he realized the letter was double-encrypted, he looked up.

"This is going to take me a bit. He used the double code, which isn't as easy to read. I have a bad feeling about this." Bane felt his stomach drop as he tried to decipher why his father would go to such lengths to keep his words from prying eyes. He turned to the others. "I need a piece of paper and something to write with."

"I'm on it." Tamara rushed back to the tents she came from.

"Can someone explain what's going on?" George asked with a frown.

Quietly, Zeke obliged, explaining the birds Bane sent before the storm hit. "This bird should lead us back to where our people are." The acrobat finished.

Understanding lit George's eyes as Tamara ran back to them carrying an inkwell and a piece of birch bark. "This is the best I could find on short notice." She offered both of them to the Shifter.

"It's perfect, thank you." Bane took the supplies and brought them to a nearby rock. He shut out the roiling emotions of the others as he focused solely on the message in front of him.

He turned the piece of cloth so the three dots were in the left-hand corner and looked diagonally for the next clue on how he should decode it. Once he figured out which code it was written in, translating would be easy.

Bane worked as quickly as he could, but it still took close to an hour. He could feel the tensions rising in those around him as they forced themselves to give him space to work.

When he was done, he looked up into Rae's golden orbs.

"We have a problem," he said.

Chapter Thirty-Six

Duncan paced back and forth on the stage of the amphitheater as he waited for the other Council Members to take their seats. He was trying to decide on the best way to present everything quickly and concisely. He licked his lips as he paced once more across the stage, deciding it was time.

He went to the front of the stage and sat down, beckoning everyone to come closer.

The Queen and her daughter were nowhere in sight, but Duncan didn't want to waste any more time. He could only hope they would join soon.

Meeting the gaze of everyone gathered, he began.

"For those of you who don't know, Luc found Tyee last night. To be brief, during the escape, she was injured and is resting in Nan's wagon for the time being." His lavender gaze caught Nan's kind eyes. "Since Luc can't be here to relay the events of the night, I have asked Tyee to do so in her stead. He will give an update and then help us strategize."

"Strategize for what?" Conrad grumbled.

"To prepare for what is coming, given the information I gleaned from my sister." Duncan waited to let his revelation sink in.

"Isn't your sister married to Vincenzio?" J asked gently.

"And responsible for the past decade of living on the run?" Conrad accused.

"Please, just wait." Duncan held his hands up. "You're all going to have questions, but there are bigger things at stake that we need to get through first. Tyee needs to share what happened with the Elven." The Ringmaster motioned the horseman forward.

Tyee shot him a hooded look.

Duncan felt sweat gather on his brow as he met Tyee's dark gaze. *Come on, Tyee. I know you can do this.* Whatever Tyee saw in Duncan's gaze did the trick.

"The General and I have history. Ultimately, because of this connection, she thought I would be the one she could use to get answers." He flashed a wicked grin at the members of the Council. "She was disappointed when I never did." He sobered quickly after earning appreciative glances from the gathered leaders. "But I wouldn't be standing here today if it wasn't for Luc." He held Nan's gaze and gave a nod, recognizing her granddaughter's heroic actions.

Tyee paused to look at the older members of the Circus and swallowed before his next words. Duncan watched with furrowed brows, not sure where this was going.

"I know I haven't always been the most willing community member. But finding myself tied to a table and enduring a brutal interrogation, all I could think about was how stupid I'd been.

"I don't blame anyone for not finding me sooner or my being taken. I know Duncan, Chiara, and others were looking as hard as they could. But on that table, I felt so alone. I vowed to make a change if I made it out of that hellhole. This community is stronger when we work together, and I am committed to getting us through this. When Duncan takes the floor again, know that I am here to help in whatever way I can."

The Council sat in stunned silence, never expecting to hear those words from the horseman. Nan beamed at the young man before clapping her hands. Slowly, the other members of the Council joined in. Duncan let them applaud the horseman before calling for order.

"Thank you, Tyee. Our community will always be here for you. Now, onto the next matter at hand. There's one more thing we need to discuss." The Ringmaster's gaze flicked back to where he expected the Queen and her General to make their appearance. "I was hoping to include the Queen and her general, but this news is too urgent to wait."

"Who said anything about waiting?" the frosty tone of Queen Ulla sounded behind the Ringmaster. Duncan whirled around before inclining his head.

Gesturing for the pair to sit, he said, "My apologies, your Grace. Please, join us. We were just getting to the part we need you for."

Sylvia let out a hiss as her eyes locked on Tyee. She whispered under her breath, but Duncan couldn't make out the words. He studied Tyee carefully, noting the color leave his face, but when the young man met his gaze, only determination shone in his eyes. Duncan paused as he took in the man's clenched jaw and white knuckles, but the horseman's eyes pleaded for him to continue.

Turning to the members of the Council, Duncan continued, "As many of you probably recognized, the woman who interrupted our show last night was my sister. And yes, the very sister that led to our downfall. She's spent the past half a dozen years married to Darren Vincenzio, the man that led to all of this." He sighed, running a hand through hair that was too long. "She was young when the Uprising happened, and Vincenzio and Myra manipulated her into doing what she did. It excuses nothing, but she is trying to make amends now."

Duncan noticed the way everyone on the Council's eyes hardened at the mention of Mirabella. The Queen and Silvia looked bored while Nan and Chiara were the only friendly faces in the room.

Locking on Chiara's green eyes, he drew a shaky breath. "Mirabella sent her and Vincenzio's only daughter with Rich—"

"What does this have to do with us?" Sylvia drawled.

"Let him finish. He's getting to it." Chiara snapped, her patience wearing thin.

Duncan shot her an appreciative glance but hurried through his next words all the same. "We can only assume the girl is with Rae and the others. She's the reason Heimat was sacked, and Vincenzio is not letting her go without a fight. He's sent soldiers into the forest after us. Mirabella said they were less than a day behind her. They march with a kill order on my head from Myra herself." The gathered Council members watched in shock as Duncan turned towards the Queen. "Queen Ulla and her general are here to help us develop a strategy against this new threat. The wards around Verdencia are strong, but not impenetrable. We need to set our differences and grievances aside to form a united war council."

"Duncan, you can't expect us to trust them after what they've demanded from us," Conrad said with a growl. Standing up, he pointed to Tyee. "And what about what they did to one of our own? We can't let this go unpunished, Duncan. Leave them to rot. I would rather risk the soldiers than get into bed with our enemy." He spat on the ground next to him.

Chiara spoke up. "We were all upset when Duncan brought news of the Queen's ultimatum, but our elderly and our children are depending on us to put our grievances aside. You don't have to like it, Conrad, but this is the best chance for both of our peoples. The Elven don't know what they're up against and their warriors are few. If we forge an alliance, we can protect our own and send a message to Myra herself."

Sylvia started to speak but was cut off by her mother. "I'm not an easy woman to get along with," she acknowledged slowly. "But that doesn't mean I can't see what's in front of my face. It was naïve of us to think we could continue living our lives as we have. We've lived in isolation for too long. Our young people do not remember the wars between the Elven and the Mortals. They do not understand why we hide and I would be a fool to think I could keep them here much longer." She pursed her lips and gave her seething daughter a stony look, giving her warning not to interrupt.

"You're young, old, and sick are welcome to shelter in the trees. But now we need to come up with a plan to save both of our peoples." She directed her last words at Conrad, the most vocal of dissenters. Midge and J were also quiet, mulling over their options.

"It's a lot to ask, I know," Duncan said. "But it's the best way to keep everyone safe." The sound of a body crashing through the undergrowth reached Duncan's ears. Puzzled, he looked at the sound.

The Queen and her daughter were on their feet in an instant and moved quickly towards the noise. Duncan followed, leaving his people at the amphitheater, as an Elven guard broke through the treeline. Reaching the Queen, he dropped to his knees and gasped for air. "Intruders—a battalion of soldiers are at our doorstep."

The Queen wasted no time, turning to her General, saying, "The time has come. Ready your troops." Silvia dashed off and Ulla shot a look towards the Ringmaster. "Gather your young and old and send them with the healers. Bring all of your fighters back here as quickly as possible."

With those last words, she sped after her daughter, calling commands to those above.

Duncan felt as if he was in a dream. Time seemed to slow down and all he could hear was the blood roaring in his ears.

Turning back towards the Council, everyone now at their feet, he stumbled towards them. Familiar arms caught his, and he stared into comforting green eyes. "What is it, Dunc?" Chiara asked, fear and trepidation in her eyes.

Duncan swallowed, taking a moment to clear his thoughts. "They're here. Chiara, Midge, and Nan gather all the young, old, and anyone who needs shelter. Meet them by the ladder beneath the infirmary. The healers will help you get everyone up into the trees." He turned to the others. "Everyone else, I need you to gather anyone and everyone willing to fight. Bring them here and we'll meet up with the Elven."

The members of the Circus's Governing Council wasted no breath as they rushed towards the cottages to assemble their people.

Duncan called after Tyee. "Horseman, stay with me. We need to discuss strategy before the battle begins."

Tyee met his lavender gaze. "I have an idea."

The pair put their heads together as Elven and Magicae rushed around them.

The sounds of yelling hit Luc's ears first. Followed closely by the feeling of being jostled.

Still unable to open her eyes, Luc's eyelids fluttered as her other senses took in what her eyes couldn't. Restraints running across her legs, arms, and torso kept her in position on what could only be a cloth stretcher. She felt her body being hoisted up to who knew where.

Strange smells assaulted her nose as the sound of heavy footfalls accompanied more screaming. Suddenly, she felt the tension on the stretcher release, causing her to free fall. The line holding the stretcher finally caught, jerking her to a stop. That was all Luc needed to convince her eyes to open, revealing the trees before her. Her throat felt like it was on fire as she struggled to force the words from her throat. She tried to turn her head but realized it was held tightly in place by a strap across her forehead. Panic formed a tight knot in her belly as she realized she was immobile and unable to speak out.

While Luc struggled, she felt the rope above her resume pulling her closer and closer to the leafy canopy. Tears sprung to her eyes when she saw her Abuela's face above hers. Her grandmother's gentle eyes widened in surprise when she realized Luc was awake.

"Oh, child, you were supposed to still be asleep. Here, take my hand. They're gonna carry you to the infirmary and then we can get you out of this, okay?" Concern filled the old woman's eyes as she waited for her granddaughter to nod. Luc did what she could and inclined her head in a slight nod. Abuela's wrinkled fingers squeezed her own.

The acrobat tried to clear her throat but Nan replied, "Child, just wait until we can get you on a bed and I can get you some water." Her hand slipped from the familiar wrinkled hands as leaves raced above her and she was transported to what she presumed was the infirmary.

Luc finally inferred she was in the trees amongst the Elven. The only question was, why?

Her mind was a mess as she struggled to remember anything from before she woke up. Memories of Koko and climbing a different tree flashed in her mind. She remembered finding Tyee in a similar position as the one she found herself in, although for much more sinister reasons.

She remembered him asking for her life energy and she remembered agreeing. But beyond that, her world was dark. She hoped the horseman was okay, but still couldn't understand why she was in the trees.

Her chest tightened as the panic returned in full force. *The forgetting runes. Maybe it's my turn to get one.* Luc's stretcher was jostled as a scream pierced the air closer to her person. Luc reeled in panic, trying to look for the wrinkled face that had always been there for her. She knew her Abuela would follow behind them, but she'd give anything to have the comfort of those crinkled, wise eyes and a reprimand for her worry.

The furious pace of those that carried her continued, although Luc could feel one person carrying her now ran with a limp that hadn't been there before. Her carriers came to a stop and maneuvered her through the door of what could only be the infirmary.

Her chest relaxed ever so slightly as the bonds holding her loosened. Luc tried to sit up but was maneuvered onto a bed before she could make any movements herself.

"You're awake." A familiar voice sounded to her left. On instinct, she turned her head towards the voice, but moved too hastily, sending spots across her vision.

"None of that now. Drink some of this water. You're coming off quite the sleep."

Luc felt someone hold a glass to her lips and gently tip it upwards as cool water ran down her throat. She drank too fast and dissolved into a fit of coughs. The glass left her lips to be replaced by a hand on her back. After she recovered, the acrobat looked up at the person who tended to her, meeting Chiara's green eyes.

"Take a breath, Luc. Your body put itself into a coma after Tyee took too much life energy. It needed rest in order to heal. Give it some time to wake up."

Once Luc regained the ability to talk, she asked, "What's happening?" Her speech was stilted, but her point came across in the few words she spoke.

Chiara's eyes turned dark as she answered. "Vincenzo sent soldiers. We're working with the Elven to stop them from destroying this place and both our peoples. I need to check on the others as they bring them up. Your Abuela will be here soon with a tonic. Your body still needs rest." Chiara's tone was like steel as she made to move to the next bunk.

Luc's eyes widened as she realized the Herbalist's intentions. "Wait, Damien." She gritted the words out, forcing her vocal cords to work despite being unused for so long. This time, green eyes filled with sorrow.

"He's joined the others to fight. Once they're organized, they march."

Luc felt her heart shatter as she replayed the last conversation she had with the man she loved more than anyone. Sharing a last look with the Herbalist, Chiara left her bedside without another word.

Still exhausted from the entire ordeal, Luc closed her eyes.

Huntress, keep them safe. I'm begging you. I'll do anything, just keep them safe. She thought before her mind drifted to unconsciousness once more.

Chapter Thirty-Seven

R ae swallowed as she hazarded one last glance behind them.

Upon hearing the letter Bane received from his father, the group decided it would be best to split up. There was no point in bringing the children and those with no fighting capabilities into the mess that awaited them.

Guilt left a bitter taste on Rae's tongue as she thought about leaving the little redhead with the other group.

"Red, you have to stay here. It's not safe." The Crafter was crouched at eye level with the young Herbalist. She tucked a stray curl behind the little girl's ear, admiring the fiery hair and the spirit that matched it. Tears streamed down the little girl's face as she launched for Rae once more.

"No, please. I'll be good. I promise I'll be good."

Rae gently pried the little girl off of her and held her firmly at arm's length. "Gemma, you need to stay here. We don't know what we're walking into. If you're there with us—"

"I can help." The little girl insisted. "I helped with the ship."

Rae's heart broke, knowing she was going to crush the little girl's dreams. "I know, I know, and you did so well. But we're not prepared, Red, this isn't like the ship. It puts us all in danger if we have to worry about protecting the people with us and fight the ones that mean us harm. Reg will take good care of you, and as soon as the battle is over, we'll come to fetch you." Rae pulled the little girl into a tight embrace. "We'll be reunited before you know it."

Rae swallowed again, trying to chase the regret and memory from her mind.

"She couldn't come with us," Zeke said as he walked beside her, guessing at the reason behind her tormented expression.

"I know," Rae sighed. "I just can't get over that look of betrayal in her eyes."

"The kid will get over it, but none of us would if something happened to that little spitfire. It's for the best." He repeated, nudging her shoulder.

Reg had stayed behind begrudgingly with the others, on strict orders to continue northward to the coast. Once there, the group was to set up camp and stay put within the confines of the trees. As soon as it was safe, Bane would send a bird to guide them back to their people and final settlement.

Rae and Zeke traveled with Bane, George, and Tamara, along with some of the other adult Magicae from their group. Most of the Herbalists had stayed with the children and the elderly, but one was with them in case they ran into trouble on the way. He was a fine marksman as well, an asset in any fight.

Rae's stomach had been in knots ever since Bane translated that letter. The faces of those she loved ran through her mind's eye as crippling anxiety threatened to take over. They alternated between jogging and walking, Bane leading the way, following the falcon towards the Elven city in the trees.

They didn't stop to rest, keeping a relentless pace towards the ones they loved.

"Huntress, I think we're gonna jog again," Zeke complained.

"I guess Luc was right. We need more cardio," Rae replied, sadness filling her eyes.

Zeke squeezed her hand. "We'll get to them. It'll be okay. We only have to make it through this insufferable run first." Zeke said in exasperation, earning an appreciative glance from the other Crafter.

Rae picked up her pace as Bane urged them into a jog. *I will do whatever it takes to protect the ones I love.* Rae vowed inside her head, determination fueling her forward.

After hours of traveling through the darkness before dawn, the sun finally started peeking through the trees. Rae was exhausted trying to keep up with Bane's pace, but every time she wavered, she pictured a different face in her head. Her loved ones urged her legs forward despite them feeling like they would collapse at any moment. Her ears caught the cry of the falcon and her eyes snapped to the Shifter ahead.

He signaled for their party to come to a stop.

Rae listened carefully and heard the sounds of a skirmish up ahead. The falcon cocked its head and stared intently at Bane before taking off in the battle's direction.

Bane closed his eyes as he focused on his connection with the bird he sent on ahead. Rae knew he was using the falcon as his eye in the sky.

"The battle is in full force, or so it looks to be—," Fear contorted Bane's face as he hesitated. "There are so many. The main battle is happening about a league away. The falcon had to skirt around some trees. I can only guess that's the city my father mentioned. They have a small force and they're fighting, but I don't know how long they're going to last." Opening his eyes, Rae watched him chew on the inside of his cheek, lost in thought.

"We don't have the manpower or the numbers." She said simply, looking at those gathered. "We have a decision to make. There is no doubt we have the spirit and drive, but it comes with a risk."

"There's always a risk." Tamara insisted. "We all knew this could happen. We're prepared."

The two women shared a look.

Without warning, Bane whipped his head to the right. Furrowing his brows and licking his lips, he glanced back at the Crafter.

"Do you trust me?" He asked her, echoing her words from their mad dash in Heimat.

"Absolutely," Rae said without hesitation.

"They're focusing all their energy towards the north. If you guys snuck around and hit them from the southwest, you have the best chance of catching them unaware. I'll be back as soon as I can."

Rae's eyes widened in surprise, but she gave the Shifter a nod as he took off without a backward glance.

This is it. We march to save our people.
I'm coming for you, Drifter.

Tyee's arms shook as his sword met the blow of another soldier's blade. With gritted teeth, he pushed the man back, putting all his weight behind the Elven sword in his hand. He parried twice before wrenching the weapon from the man's hand and sending it flying.

He aimed for the spot between the soldier's leather pads and struck true. He removed the thin blade with a squelching sound as it came out blood red.

Panting, the horseman didn't have time to wipe the blood from the blade before the next was upon him.

Tyee was flanked by Jess and Simeon. The three of them led the charge against the main part of Vincenzio's battalion. They were joined by many of the others, while the Elven fought along the Northwest line. Archers from both sides hid in the trees, pelting and littering the battlefield with arrows.

Tyee met his next opponent with determination, blood roaring in his ears. He'd spent hours sparring with the other stable hands during their downtime and made it through the occasional bar brawl, but nothing could've prepared him for this. Sheer grit kept him on his feet as he engaged soldier after soldier. He became numb as he sliced down more and more of the enemy.

With one last slice to the gut, the woman Tyee faced crumpled to the ground, and he risked a glance to the left.

His eyes widened in horror and he yelled as loud as he could, "SIMEON! WATCH OUT!"

Tyee lunged toward the man who was like a brother to him. He met the blade that was intended for Simeon's neck with his own. The two fought in tandem, finishing the soldier in quick secession. Simeon grunted his appreciation before throwing himself back into the fray.

Jess had closed the gap Tyee left open in his swift departure to save Simeon. She moved back towards Duncan as Tyee returned to his post. Nymeria and Conrad were twin tempests, all fangs and claws as they kept close ranks around the wind Crafter.

Tyee's whole body ached as the sounds of battle warred around him. The Magicae and the Elven were putting up an extraordinary front, but they were growing weary as the battle raged. The sheer mass of soldiers streaming through the trees hinted at hundreds, if not thousands, of men and women waiting for their chance to engage with the ones they hated most.

Tyee struggled to catch his breath between soldiers but was snatched from his reverie as one brute barreled toward him. Pure instinct raised his blade just in time to catch the powerful swing of a broadsword. Tyee's teeth rattled with the force of the blow, but he stayed on the defensive, parrying blow after blow.

Too late, he realized his last block would miss. He braced himself for the blow that never came.

An enormous wind almost pushed him over, but its true strength hit the soldier, toppling him to the ground.

Tyee swallowed the bile down and refused to dwell on what could have been, flashing an appreciative glance at the Ringmaster. He didn't dare risk being caught unaware again and faced the wall of soldiers once more.

We can't keep this up. He thought as his sword danced with his next opponent. He refused to send a glance towards the Elven, but he knew their numbers were small and their powers finite. Sylvia had apprehended them with one snap but couldn't reproduce those results sustainably. She could never send all those soldiers into unconsciousness without using every drop of power in her veins. The General would never leave her people in such a vulnerable state. The Elven had to use the magic of their runes sparingly and strategically as they protected Verdencia and their secrets.

With a grunt, he slid his sword into the next soldier. Arms trembling, he clenched his jaw and searched for his next opponent.

A dash of light caused him to look up.

The few fire Crafters they had were to Duncan's right, putting on a formidable display as they kept the soldiers at bay. Tyee's blood ran cold when he realized this light came from behind the soldiers to the southeast. Alarm caught in his throat as thoughts of Vincenzio enslaving Crafters came to mind.

There's no way. We're screwed if he did. He thought to himself, panting, as more and more soldiers came through the trees. Curiously, Tyee couldn't figure out if they were marching towards the fight or fleeing from the flashes of light.

The world seemed to be in slow motion as the light inched closer and closer. Tyee's stomach dropped as it made its way into his sightline.

Tyee stilled in shock when he could finally make out the fighter holding two swords set ablaze.

Rae was a spinning balderdash, her golden braid whipping behind her. Her movements exuded the grace of the acrobat she was as she sliced down anyone in her way. Hope flared in Tyee's chest when he realized she wasn't alone.

Zeke fought next to her with George and Tamara flanking them. Behind the four were half a dozen of the adult Magicae from Heimat.

They did it. They made it. With renewed vigor, Tyee kept fighting slowly but surely, making his way to meet Rae and the others. The reinforcements fought to where the members of the Circus were concentrated. Having to fight on two fronts, the soldiers' forces wavered.

Tyee, Simeon, and Jess led the charge, doing what they could to meet their friends. Finally, Rae burst through the ranks of soldiers, leaving chaos in her wake.

She spun to a stop in front of Tyee and flashed a wicked grin. "I didn't know you were the damsel in distress kind of type, Drifter." She gulped for air as sweat beaded on her brow.

"Neither did I, Birdie," came Tyee's response as he drank in the woman who had never left his thoughts. A smirk graced his lips, but before he could say what he wanted, the clank of steel on steel brought him back to reality.

Tyee shot her one last look, his eyes promising what his voice couldn't. They would talk once the fight was over.

The two turned shoulder to shoulder and faced the oncoming hoard as one.

Chapter Thirty-Eight

The moon rose high over Heimat on the cool, clear autumn night. Tommy and Melody's widower, Rob, walked the riverbank once more as a slight wind loosed the leaves from their branches. They moved soundlessly with the hoods of their cloaks pulled tight to hide their faces.

Tommy led the charge, only stopping once they reached the stretch of river hidden by a high hill. Crouching down, he removed his hood and studied the sky above.

"They should be here soon," he murmured to his companion. Rob followed suit, crouching down and removing his hood.

It had been several days since Rich brought the box back to the farmhouse, and the town leaders discussed their options. There was no doubt in anyone's mind that Vincenzio's revenge would be swift and ruthless.

And Myra's soldiers had been spotted on the horizon earlier that day.

Tonight was the only night they had to evacuate as many people as they could. Their only saving grace was that the children had left with the Circus or on the *Vengeance,* leaving only adult Magicae in town. It would be easier and swifter to move adults.

The four heads decided evacuation was the only way to save the rest of their people. Rob insisted he take Rich's place in leading their people to safety. There were long arguments, but Rob's logic won out. His girls would stay with Rich and Anna at Tommy's Mom's farmhouse until Rob delivered his group to their safe house.

He and Tommy would divide their group and head to two different surrounding towns. Simone and Eddy were doing the same thing on the other side of town.

Both men slid packs off their backs from under their cloaks. Inside was Johanna's legacy.

The box Rich found contained another one of her cloaks that mimicked its surroundings, along with the instructions to make more. In the letter that accompanied it, she dubbed it her farewell gift should her plan go terribly wrong. Her ingenuity was the best thing she could have given to her people in her absence.

Rich and the others wasted no time in getting the example and its instructions to the other Forgers who worked with animal skins. Once they grasped the basic concepts of molding the atoms that comprised the skins into becoming changeable, it was fairly straightforward. Each group took a dozen cloaks to help hide themselves on the long road ahead.

Tommy's heart squeezed when he thought of Sara and their kids. They were also staying with his mother at the farmhouse. They had stripped the property of anything Magicae-related, just in case. It was doubtful the soldiers would bother with the farmhouse since it was so far from town, but it was better to be prepared.

Sara, his mother, Rich, and Anna were ready to protect themselves and the children, should it come to that. Tommy knew it was the best they could do on such short notice, but it still rattled him to think he didn't know when he would see his wife and family again.

He thought back to the picnic they'd hosted when George left and gave a soft smile. Little did he know that would be his own farewell picnic as well.

Rob caught the small smile and asked, "What is it?"

Tommy gave a bitter chuckle. "I always thought George was mad for agreeing to leave should it come to this. But here I am doing the same damn thing."

Rob's eyes softened. "You and me both."

Tommy gripped his friend's shoulder before pulling him into a brief embrace. "You and me, we'll get through this as we've always done. This one's for Melody."

"For Melody," Rob echoed in a somber tone before pulling away.

The two men went over the plan one last time, staying as quiet as they could. Soon enough, the sound of light footsteps caused both men to look up.

They shared one last glance before handing out cloaks and relaying the instructions to those that gathered. In one hour's time, they would disappear into the night without a trace.

Chapter Thirty-Nine

Rae's skin buzzed with energy as she fought side by side with the other members of the Circus. Her core hummed with delight as Rae wielded her Crafts against their enemies. It took every ounce of control she had to use her energy wisely and effectively. She didn't want to admit it, but fighting with her Crafts gave her a release unlike anything else. She felt more and more like herself as she fought soldier after soldier.

Risking a sideways glance, she watched Tyee take down another soldier with the sword in his hand. He moved with a newfound swiftness and power that emanated from his very person as he dodged and parried every sword that came near him. Something was different about the loner that Rae couldn't quite put her finger on.

But, damn, is it working for him. She thought while she watched the man move with a grace he'd never shown before. Tyee caught her stare and sent her a smirk before launching into an impressive succession of sword strikes that effectively took out his next opponent.

Jerking back to the reality of battle, she focused on the soldier coming towards her and kicked the legs out from underneath her. Once on the ground, Rae used wind and soil to blind her, and with a sickening crunch, she felt her dagger pierce through blood and bone.

I will never get used to that sound, she thought grimly. But as long as it was us against them, Rae would do what she needed to defend her people.

While Tyee fought on her left, Zeke flanked her right with Jess, Duncan, and the Shifters further right. He used the wind to direct throwing stars and take out as many soldiers as he could. He reverted between using his stars and the thin rapier he held in one hand, trying to save as much energy as he could. Zeke used all of his acrobatic grace as the enemies kept coming in droves.

It was clear Vincenzio had intended the worst for the members of the Circus.

Despite the Gifts at their fingertips, Rae knew it was only a matter of time before the number of soldiers outlasted them. Every time she met another opponent, her strength wavered. The battle kept on for what seemed like hours, although Rae knew mere minutes were passing by.

Panting, she rubbed the sweat from her brow.

A blood-curdling scream to their right had her shaking to her core. *Duncan.* Her heart jumped into her throat.

Risking a glance in that direction, Rae saw red.

A soldier stood over Jess as he thrust his sword past her armor once more. Icy dread sank in Rae's stomach as she saw the Forger crumple to the ground. Not wasting any time, she launched herself towards the assailant.

In a fit of rage, she forgot herself, setting the man ablaze, leather armor and all. Tears streamed down her face as she swung desperately, memories of the kind, protective woman filling her head. She stood over Jess, as a mother bear stood to protect her young ones. Rae let herself be consumed by the rage and grief inside, letting out a roar.

Her twin daggers struck like lightning as she wept. Working through the emotions inside, Rae was soon panting from the effort. She stepped back before unleashing the wind upon the enemy lines, affording herself a slight break.

As she caught her breath, she looked back to the position she'd left, fear coating her insides. The battle seemed to take place in slow motion as one soldier slipped past Zeke's guard and sliced his side.

Acting on instinct, Rae punched wind and rock forward, knocking the man off his feet. Zeke yelled in pain, gripping his side and struggling to hold his sword aloft.

Rae bit her lip, wanting nothing more than to go to her friend, but she couldn't leave such an enormous gap in the line. Duncan, Conrad, and Nymeria would be exposed on their left flank.

"Duncan!" she cried, projecting her voice as the Ringmaster had done on numerous occasions. Duncan's head whipped toward his adoptive daughter, concern and grief etched on his face.

"I need to help Zeke." She pleaded.

Duncan inched towards the Crafter, positioning himself and the feline Shifters closer to Rae so she could go to Zeke.

She fought her way to him and briefly gripped his shoulder.

"Hold on, Z, you're not dying today." Rae's daggers were a blur as she parried another woman's short sword.

Tyee and Simeon shifted closer to her, not breaking stride as they engaged with soldiers along the way.

Rae set her feet and gritted her teeth, keeping her focus on the woman in front of her. With a final flourish, she sent the soldier's sword flying. She saw fear in the other woman's eyes but didn't hesitate as she spun and slit the woman's throat.

Rae thought she was going to be sick with how easy killing was becoming. She didn't have time as another soldier took the now-dead woman's place. Rae gritted her teeth and engaged, the clash of steel roaring in her ears.

We won't make it, she thought. *Where the fuck did Bane go?* She questioned as she swallowed and held her daggers aloft once more, keeping herself between Zeke and their enemies.

The pounding in her head warned her not to use more of her Crafts, lest she wanted to risk losing consciousness. Looking to the far right, she noticed Zalia's flames dying as the other fire Crafter used the last of her life energy. The same story told itself again and again as the Magicae of the Circus flagged from hours of battle.

Rae knew it was only a matter of time before she lost more of the ones she loved dearly.

Every fiber of her being urged her forward, but in her mind, she knew retreat was the only way to save the rest of the Circus.

Preparing to yell for a retreat, her eyes caught on where the Elven held their ground. Their tanned and weathered skin from a life outdoors was slick with sweat as their long, dark hair hung in braids behind them. They fought with swiftness and grace, but Rae noticed the holes in their lines. All she knew of the Elven was what had been contained in Gar's letter. Magic flowed in their blood, but she didn't know how long their reserves would last. *Not much longer if looks aren't deceiving.*

Keeping up with the soldier in front of her, Rae projected her voice to the horseman on her left.

"Tyee, we can't—we can't keep going like this." she panted. "We need to retreat," she said between sword thrusts.

Keeping their enemies at bay, Tyee kept fighting as if he hadn't heard her.

Frustrated, she threw herself into the fray once more. Sweat came off her in droves; from exertion or fear, she didn't know. With a grimace, she had to put her emotions aside despite the fear in her heart for friends who were more like family.

"Birdie, I don't know if that's still an option for us." Tyee finally replied, yelling to be heard over the sounds of battle. "At this point, it's keep fighting or surrender." His tone and expression were grim as his sword slid between another soldier's ribs.

Rae kept going. *He's right,* was all she could think as she desperately sliced with her daggers.

Resigning herself to do what she could for her people, she threw one last look at Tyee.

"Drifter, I'm sorry. I'm sorry for everything." She caught the look of confusion on his face but refused to elaborate as she called on what was left of the power within.

Her entire being went up in flames as she threw herself towards the line of soldiers.

Fire and blood were the last things that swam in her vision before everything went dark.

Bane flew as fast as he could.

He willed his wings to beat faster as the distant sounds of battle sounded. Behind him trailed an army of Shifters in various forms.

The Shifters of the Forest were coming to join the battle.

He could only hope they weren't too late. The falcon that led them to their people in the first place still waited near where the battle raged. Bane called on her once more to circle the field and help him decide where to hit first.

Ice filled his veins when he realized his people were losing.

Through the falcon's eyes, he watched as Zeke was cut down and Zalia's flames faltered. The rest pushed on, but he could tell they were weary. Urging the falcon to patrol the other side, he realized the Elven looked just as bad. They moved with greater swiftness, taking down two or three soldiers at a time, but holes dotted their lines.

As much as Bane wanted to go to his friends, he had a duty to save as many as he could. From his father's words, he knew there was more at stake than simply those fighting for their lives.

Silently thanking the falcon for her service, he released his tie to her. Shifting course ever so slightly, he directed the army between the Elven forces and those of the Circus from the south. That was where the highest concentration of soldiers was and where the Shifters would make the most impact.

He maneuvered them to attack at the soldiers' backs, opposite their allies. Bane let out a piercing cry as he reached the first lines of soldiers. He heard roars and growls behind him as the Shifters of the Forest attacked as well. Several of them, also with forms as birds of prey, followed Bane's lead.

He directed them into formation to create an aerial attack. As they dive-bombed their first set of soldiers, he caught the sight of an inferno in the corner of his eye.

Rae, no, was all he thought before beelining for the impressive Crafter. The other avian Shifters followed suit and attacked the soldiers, threatening the now unconscious woman. Bane had seen her fall as the flames around her died and heard Tyee screaming in anguish. He used his avian brothers and sisters to flank the horseman as he stood over Rae's body.

Slowly but surely, the Shifters made ground as they compressed their enemies against the combined forces of the Elven and the Circus. Bane's strategy worked and, given enough time, the soldiers' forces dwindled.

As the last two dozen soldiers comprehended their fate, they bolted from the field, running as fast as they could from their failure. Bane saw the feline Shifter he convinced to follow him dispatch several of the hound Shifters after the stragglers.

They won't last long, Bane thought to himself as he circled in the sky. He let out a cry before landing on Duncan's shoulder.

He chattered in the Ringmaster's ear before spreading his wings and coasting down to Zeke's still form. Duncan knelt next to the Shifter, forcing Bane to really look at their decades-long leader.

The Ringmaster's hair was longer than Bane remembered and peppered with more gray than before. He could tell that every muscle was screaming at the older man to rest as worry lines appeared on his forehead. Duncan felt for Zeke's pulse and let out a sigh of relief.

"He'll be okay, Bane. Stay with him until the Healers come. I need to check on Rae."

Bane let out a cry in answer, inclining his head towards where he'd last seen the acrobat. Duncan nodded his thanks before heaving himself up and towards Rae's collapsed form.

Looking down at the young man Bane had spent so long traveling with, he willed the Crafter to wake up.

Come on, Z, don't die on me now. We have unfinished business to settle. He kept watch over the acrobat as the Elven, Shifters, and Magicae collected themselves and the wounded after a battle many didn't think they'd survive.

Chiara studied each face as more and more Elven and Magicae were brought to the infirmary.

She was searching for the ones she loved.

Chiara was no stranger to treating the wounded, but never had she seen such bloodshed. She grew up in a small village that engaged in skirmishes with neighboring towns, but nothing could have prepared her for this.

The worst part was having to lay a sheet over the newly departed. She dreaded it every time she neared a bed that was too still.

It was a blessing from the Huntress Herself that they survived a battle with Vincenzio's own trained soldiers, but the cost was too high. Their numbers didn't allow for runners to bring the wounded back quickly enough. Too many people were lost before they even came in.

If only they'd been brought in sooner. Chiara thought more often than not.

Her stomach was in knots every time a new body was deposited at the door. She feared more than anything finding her son's face among the deceased. Taking a deep breath, she centered herself. Panicking wouldn't change the fate of her son, but it would change the fates of those she could help.

She continued her rounds, handing out tonics as she saw fit. Her expression was grim as she handed out more and more pain tonics for those whose bodies would have to do the work on their own. Even Herbalists blessed with Gifts from the Goddess could only do so much. For many, it would be up to their spirits to keep them alive through this dark night.

"Chiara," a voice called from the door.

Her head turned to where Freya stood, just outside, triaging patients as to which section of the infirmary they should be brought to.

"It's your son."

Ice entered her veins as she marched towards the door, scared to death of what she would see on the other side.

Chiara let out a sob when she saw Damien standing there with only a few minor scrapes and cuts on his face and a limp in his step. She pulled him into her arms and squeezed as tight as she could.

"Easy, Ma. Watch the leg. I got hit by an arrow, but Freya put me on the mend."

Chiara couldn't form words past the lump in her throat. Pure joy chased away every other emotion as she held on to her son.

Remembering who she was and her duties, she gave him one last squeeze before pulling away. "Let me see," she said, looking at the leg he wasn't putting weight on. Sure enough, there was a wrap around his upper thigh.

"It wasn't too deep, but I left it in just as you said and waited until a Healer could take it out." Damien winced as his mother's light fingers danced across the bandages.

"Good boy." She beamed, satisfied with her examination of his wound. She patted his cheek, taking care not to touch any cuts or scrapes.

"I knew you'd want to see me, so I got here as soon as I could."

Chiara glanced around before pulling him to one side. "What happened out there?" She asked, taking her first break since the battle started.

Damien's expression turned grim. "It was awful. The screams, the chaos... Half the time I didn't know who I was aiming at."

Damien's eyes had a hollow look that had never been there before. Chiara's joy quickly faded as she realized her son was unrecognizable after such trauma. She gripped his shoulder as he continued.

"We were losing terribly. I think Rae and Zeke showed up hours ago. Time meant nothing as those soldiers kept coming. They helped for a while, but there were so many." He put a hand to his forehead, hesitating.

"Go on," she insisted.

"Our ranks were thinning. Even among the archers, many had fallen. When suddenly, an army of Shifters came through the woods."

"The same ones from the clearing?" she asked.

"Aye, at least as far as I could tell. They're the only reason we survived." He hesitated again.

"Ask it." Chiara said, knowing what her son wanted and that she wouldn't have the answers he sought.

"Have you seen them? Rae? Zeke?" He asked, staring into her green eyes.

Her eyes filled with sorrow. "I haven't seen them. They haven't been brought up yet."

Damien swallowed and clenched his fists, determination blazing within his own green eyes. "What about Luc?" The fear was palpable in this tone.

"She's awake. Nan moved her next door to the outpatient building. Do you want to see her?" When Damien nodded furiously, she said, "I'll take you to her."

Chiara linked arms with her grown son and guided him to the smaller building off the main Infirmary. In the wake of the battle, the healers and Herbalists decided it would be best to put those recovering and not in danger of death in the outpatient building. It was extremely crowded, but Chiara knew it was the right move.

They weaved between beds and chairs until they reached the far right corner. As soon as Damien saw the woman he loved, he took off, crushing the acrobat in his embrace.

Chiara met Luc's gaze and watched her mouth 'thank you.' Chiara gave her a nod before heading back to the infirmary, giving the two the space they needed.

Besides, her work was far from over and she'd taken as long of a break as she dared.

Tyee was in shock.

He'd watched Rae go up in flames and hurl herself at the enemy line with the ferociousness of a wild animal. He could only watch as she used the rest of her life energy to take out as many enemies as she could. As soon as her body dropped, spent from the use of such power, he raced to protect her.

He'd stood over her body, ready to kill anybody who tried to get to her or die trying.

Once the Shifters turned the tide and the soldiers disbanded, Tyee was left feeling hollow, a ringing in his ears. He sank to his knees beside the woman he admired while his world shrunk to include just the two of them.

His heart was pounding as he searched for a pulse. Fear drenched his insides when he couldn't find one.

"Fuck this," he growled, grabbing at his hip for the small knife he kept there.

Taking a deep breath, he reached inward. Tyee didn't know what he was doing, but he needed to act quickly if Rae was going to have a chance.

A sudden memory flashed of Zalia cutting her arm to give more life energy to Rae that night in Windemere.

I can do better than that.

He focused on trying to remember the runes the Elven placed on their weapons, walls, and even the bindings during his capture. The runes seemed to be where the Elven drew power from. He just needed the right one.

Knowing he was running out of time, Tyee reached for the one that came to mind the clearest. Keeping the shape in his mind, the horseman took one of Rae's hands in his own. He used the knife to carve the three lines that formed the rune into her palm. Bright red blood beaded, slowly trickling from its confines beneath the Crafter's skin.

Wincing, Tyee did the same to his own palm before clasping Rae's hand so their blood intermixed.

Tyee let out a gasp as he was thrown into Rae's consciousness, shocked by how still it was. Rae was fire, full of dancing warmth that could burn if you were careless, not this hollow emptiness.

Despite the fear, Tyee knew all he could do was offer his life energy and hope it was enough. Rae would have to do the rest on her own. He willed his life energy to flow fast and strong through the blood bond formed between their palms.

His head spun from the outflowing of energy, but he gritted his teeth. He was half Elven and that had to count for something. He watched his energy flow from his core into hers, and sure enough, it was glowing once more.

The last thing Tyee saw before he passed out was the unmistakable spark of flame at Rae's core.

Huntress, let it be enough.

Chapter Forty

Luc leaned on Damien as they walked back to the infirmary to keep watch on their friends. Luc had finally recovered from giving too much life energy to Tyee. It was a wonder that she even survived; Tyee must have depleted her reserves to dangerous lows for her to have taken so long to recover.

She was given the okay to leave the outpatient building days ago, with orders to take it easy. In true Luc fashion, she'd insisted on pushing it instead of following Chiara's orders.

She had convinced Damien to take her to the Council meeting with Queen Ulla, Sylvia, and two head Shifters from the Forest.

The meeting went as well as could be expected. Queen Ulla dropped the idea of the forgetting rune as a peace offering to the Circus in exchange for all they did during and after the battle. The Elven were grateful for the help during battle and in healing their wounded but insisted the Circus move on from Verdencia all the same. Luc was relieved about the forgetting rune being dropped but rankled at having to leave so soon.

Beggars can't be choosers, I guess.

The Shifters of the Forest, the ones that apprehended the Circus members in the clearing, were even more arrogant after saving both the Elven and Magicae from ruin. They claimed they had done it for Bane, but Luc secretly thought they were just territorial and didn't want any soldiers on land they deemed as theirs.

The battle may have ended, but their journey was far from over.

The pair reached the doors of the infirmary, but Damien paused before entering. He gazed into her deep brown eyes. "Promise me."

Luc crinkled her eyebrows. "Promise you what?"

He cupped her cheek gently. "Promise me that no matter what happens, you and I are endgame."

Luc lifted one brow. "Damien Rutter, is that your idea of a proposal?"

He pulled her into a kiss. "I'll take that as a yes."

"You're going to have to do better than that." She rolled her eyes despite the butterflies in her belly at the thought of her heartmate asking for her hand.

Rae is going to flip when she hears this.

Luc's stomach dropped at the thought of her friend.

Rae had yet to wake from the coma her body put her into. Her pulse was strong, but nothing indicated when or if she would wake.

Steeling herself for more disappointment, Luc led Damien into the infirmary, but quickly stopped in her tracks.

Damien ran right into her back. "Whoa, sorry amor, I didn't think you'd stop so suddenly."

Luc didn't respond as she ran straight for the woman who was like a sister to her.

Rae had finally woken up.

Reaching the Crafter's bedside, Luc couldn't help but launch herself at her friend, silent tears leaving tracks down her cheeks. Luc took a moment to hold her friend close, murmuring in her ear.

"Don't you ever do that to me again, Hermana. I was so worried about you. I don't care how many children need you, I come first."

Luc felt Rae's chest rumble with silent laughter as her words had the desired effect. The Crafter's arms weakly wrapped around Luc's middle as laughter turned to tears and tears turned to relief.

As long as we're together, we'll be okay. We can get through this as long as the four of us stay strong.

Finally, Luc gave Rae one last squeeze before gently pulling away. She moved to a sitting position at the foot of the small cot.

"What the hell? How come I didn't get that kind of greeting?" Zeke's familiar voice asked in indignation as Damien helped him into a chair next to Rae's bed. The Crafter sat gingerly, wincing as he lowered himself into the seat. He had a wrap around his middle for the slash to his side. Tonics helped the healing process go faster, but he was still in recovery.

"Settle down, Zeke. You told me not to hug you because of your side." Luc shot him a look.

Zeke gave her a fake pout. "Still. You could've done something."

Luc rolled her eyes at Damien and Rae.

Silence fell over the four friends as they took in the new bruises, scrapes, and hidden wounds each sported.

"We have a lot to talk about," Luc said softly. "Who wants to start?"

"Go for it, amor." Damien beamed, reaching for her hand.

With a smile, Luc began, filling Rae and Zeke in about everything that had happened since that fateful day in Heimat. The four acrobats stayed up late into the night, sharing adventures, scars, and their hopes for the future.

Despite her fear for what came next, Luc leaned into the feeling of contentment that came with being surrounded by the friends she loved dearly.

It had been about a week since the battle, and the Circus was finally ready to leave. They'd spent the week deciding on where to go, gathering provisions, and healing.

They lay Jess and the others who gave their lives to rest in the forest.

Tyee had never been close with the Forger, but even he felt the absence of her steady and confident leadership. He watched from the trees as the wagons were packed and the horses were loaded.

"It looks like your time's up, Drifter." Tyee turned to the right, where Rae walked stiffly from the infirmary. Luc raised a hand to the horseman as she guided Damien and Zeke towards the ladder that would take them down to the caravan.

The four had been inseparable ever since reuniting, much to his chagrin. Tyee knew they'd been through a lot.

He just wished he could've had more alone time with Rae.

The horseman had regained consciousness a couple of days prior only to find himself in a bed next to Rae's. Seeing his confusion, she claimed Freya owed her a favor.

Despite their proximity, they seemed to never share a moment alone.

The other three were constantly around, sometimes including Tyee and other times letting him sleep. It was a gracious gesture, but Tyee knew he'd never truly be one of them. The four acrobats had a bond that nobody could reproduce.

He finally talked with Rae the night before, after Zeke was discharged. They'd stayed up all night, sharing everything they'd been through.

"So you're half Elven?" The Crafter asked.

Tyee looked at his outstretched hands. "I guess." He hung his head. "Not that it amounts to shit."

Rae gave him a look. "What does that mean?"

"You didn't just ask me that." Tyee spat. Seeing Rae's hurt expression, he softened his tone. "Sorry. I just mean there won't be any Elven where we're going, so how can I expect to learn anything? No one to teach and nothing to learn means nothing changes."

Rae swung her legs from her cot and grabbed for his hand. Tyee moved over to give her some room, inviting her to share what little space he had. Sitting down, she kept his hand in both of hers. Catching his gaze, she murmured, "You could stay here." Tyee snorted, but Rae continued before he could interrupt her. "Hear me out. It wouldn't have to be forever, just until you learn what you need to." She shifted her position so her body angled towards his. Leaning down, she put one hand on his chest. "You deserve an opportunity to learn about where you come from and who you are."

Tyee's heart was thumping so loud he was sure she could feel it beneath his thin shirt. With a gulp, his eyes made it back to her face. Rae's expression was uncharacteristically open and as honest as he'd ever seen. Her sincerity made his heart pound faster.

Narrowing his eyes, he retorted. "If you didn't want me around, all you had to do was say so, Birdie." He flashed her a smirk to make sure she didn't take it personally.

Rae rolled those damning golden eyes and made to take her hand away, but Tyee had anticipated the move. Swiftly, he grabbed her arm while keeping a firm grip on the hand that still held his. Gently, he pulled her, so she lay on top of his side, one arm around his middle and the other trapped by his arm.

Rae let out a quiet chuckle, no doubt thinking about the others in the infirmary who could be watching. She snuggled closer, tilting her head back to look him in the eyes. Keeping one hand tucked around her, Tyee used his other to stroke her hair and cheek. He lost himself looking into those golden eyes, still in disbelief she was in his arms once more.

As he leaned in for a kiss, she whispered, "Think about it, Tyee. Promise me you'll consider staying and learning about the power in your blood."

Tyee searched Rae's face. Finding no trace of humor, he nodded once. "I'll consider it. No promises I'll do it, though."

She cupped his cheek. "I heard your ex is quite the piece of work."

"And that's putting it lightly." He leaned closer to her so their lips brushed each other as he kept talking. "But I don't want to talk about her."

"What do you want to talk about?" Tyee felt Rae's smile against his lips.

He kept his hand on her cheek as he kissed her slowly instead of answering, letting his actions do the talking. After a few more kisses, they drifted off to sleep in one another's arms.

"Tyee? You there?"

Tyee's eyes widened as he turned to the voice, willing himself to return to the present. Realizing Rae stood next to him, he sighed. "Sorry, what were you saying?"

"Lost in thought? Hopefully, it was about me." Rae shot him a smirk. He shook his head and motioned for her to continue. "I was asking whether you had made your decision yet. Mantaga Lake with the Circus? Or staying here with the Elven to learn your fate?"

He slung an arm over her shoulders and guided her to the ladder that her friends had taken down to where the caravan gathered.

"You'll have to wait and see Birdie."

Chapter Forty-One

Darren Vincenzio sat in the former town hall writing a letter of gratitude with a smirk on his face. Myra's reinforcements had been everything he could've hoped for. They arrived the day before and reported for duty early this morning.

On his orders, they were sacking the city as he wrote. He couldn't keep the smile from his face as he thought about all the Magicae they would root out from within his city.

And this was only the start.

Once Heimat was cleansed, Vincenzio intended to do the same to all the neighboring towns and cities in the North. His name would go down as a legend when their history was recorded.

He could almost taste sweet, sweet victory on his lips.

A knock on the door put a pause on writing his correspondence. The sharp *rap* could only belong to one man.

"You may enter, Zander!" Vincenzio called, returning his eyes to his letter. He heard the steward enter and called, "Those soldiers of Myra's are everything a battalion of soldiers should be. Strong, obedient—"

"Sir, I beg your pardon, but there's someone here you need to see." Zander interrupted.

Vincenzio's eyes snapped to his friend's face, knowing it was unlike the steward to interrupt his commander. When Zander stood at attention but didn't elaborate, Vincenzio's eyes narrowed.

"Bring them in." The burly man's voice bellowed his command.

Zander nodded before motioning someone forward from the other side of the doorway. Vincenzio pursed his lips as he stared in shock at one soldier he'd sent into the forest after the Circus.

"Well? Speak." Vincenzio's haughty tone communicated his impatience.

And then the soldier launched into a story that challenged everything Vincenzio had known to be true. His battalion of soldiers was useless against the Magicae and their new allies. For the first time in a long time, Vincenzio felt dread in the pit of his stomach.

Dismissing the man and Zander, Vincenzio threw his fists down on the already cracked podium. With a roar, he threw it across the room, where it splintered into hundreds of pieces.

Seething, he let himself rage, destroying furniture and punching walls. Tomorrow he would come up with a strategy to destroy the Circus once and for all.

Naomi braced herself as heavy footsteps sounded on the cobblestones leading up to her cell.

Here we go again. Let's see what new torture you have today, Miserable Myra.

The former First Lady winced at the venom in her thoughts. Anger and petty insults wouldn't get her anywhere. She needed to keep her cards close to her chest now that Myra knew Duncan was alive. Goddess, she hoped he'd gotten Rae to safety.

Her tongue tingled with bitterness as she thought of her golden-haired beauty. Myra had taken everything from her, but losing her children's younger years would always be the most devastating.

Naomi was jarred back to the present as her iron door rattled on its hinges. Her eyes widened in shock as a young man, almost in his twenties, shut the door behind him. He wore his golden hair cropped short with hazel eyes framed by thick eyebrows. He was dressed in the formal dress of the palace guard with an air about him that hinted at leadership.

This was Mallick, Myra's adopted son.

And Naomi's true son.

He was still in her womb when the Uprising happened and Myra took him from the former First Lady as soon as he was born, without hesitation.

It had been the worst torture Myra could have concocted.

Naomi had gone over her options time and time again, but couldn't decide what was the right thing to do. At this point, it was doubtful Mallick would even believe her when she finally spoke the truth. She always thought she needed to wait until he was older and had a chance of escaping Myra's grip.

She just hoped she hadn't waited too long.

It cut Naomi to the bone every time she looked into eyes that didn't recognize her for who she was. Even now, all she saw was contempt as she met those hazel eyes.

"You're in trouble, Freeman." He drawled, pacing in front of her, ready to pounce. "Mother sent me in here since I seem to always get you to sing."

Naomi's body tensed, waiting for the blows that were to come. Mallick had become a brute growing up in Myra's court. Naomi accepted every blow from her son, knowing it was what she deserved for not getting him to safety.

This was the penance she had to pay.

"I need you to tell me everything you know about this Duncan character."

Sadness filled her eyes as she turned her vision to the floor. Letting her mind float, she disassociated herself from the body that was so bruised and broken; it was unrecognizable. She had to make it look believable when she fed her son lies that had been put in place decades ago.

She couldn't do much, but she could do this one thing to protect the ones she loved.

I forgive you, my son. She thought those familiar words as he prepared to strike.

The day to act would come soon enough. She just needed to hold out a little longer.

C hapter 1

Gemma was cold. It was always too cold by the sea, but by the sea gave her a better view of the landscape around them. The cold was worth possibly seeing the bird Bane had promised he would send.

The redhead pulled her coat closer as the wind howled around her. She looked to the trees, taking comfort in the greenery that grew there.

At least I'll always have the plants. She thought to herself. *They grow for me and reveal their secrets when I ask nicely.* She furrowed her bushy eyebrows. *And they never tell me I have to stay back.*

Being left behind by Rae, Bane, and Zeke stung more than the little girl cared to admit.

She had been such a good girl, but it wasn't good enough. It was never good enough. Not for her mother and not for her new friends. Gemma felt tears prickling at the corners of her eyes at the thought of her mother. All she wanted was to make her mother proud and it seemed like she would never be able to make that happen.

Gemma looked to the ocean and watch the waves roll in. She rubbed at her eyes, trying to keep the tears at bay. The Herbalist spent as much time as she could away from the others in the group. The adults were nice enough to her but the kids called her names when the adults weren't around.

"Aren't you the general's daughter?" One of the little boys asked.

"Yeah, she is!" Shouted a little girl.

"So you're the reason why mommy sent us away." Sounded another little boy, clutching a toy rabbit close.

Gemma had closed her eyes tighter, hoping they would think she was still asleep. When they didn't go away, the redhead grabbed her coat and left for the solitude of the sea.

Before she could escape, one of the older girls said, "there she goes again. Running away instead of facing the sins of her father. Just wait until she realizes her parents didn't want her because she's one of us."

Gemma could feel her anger and frustration surfacing again.

Those kids assumed they know everything about her when they had no idea what her life looked like. Gemma knew her parents were wealthy but being wealthy wasn't the same as being free. Her life had been dictated by a set of rules that was ever-changing as she grew older. She didn't understand why so many people talked about her father and whispered as if they were afraid of him overhearing their conversation. Gemma couldn't comprehend why fear clung to the people that seem to always surround her father.

All she saw were strong arms that picked her up and spun her whatever she wanted, a smile that lit up the room, and eyes that danced with joy. Her father yelled sometimes but so did everyone else in their household. Even her mother raised her voice when she got frustrated. Gemma refused to believe her mother sent her away because her parents didn't want her anymore. She couldn't bear the thought of being abandoned by the two people she loved most in this world. It had to be a big misunderstanding.

The Herbalist found her gaze wandering to the trees once more. Acquiescing the pole in her blood, Gemma moved closer to the forest. She held her hands out and watched the vines creep forward until they draped themselves upon her hands and arms. She giggled as their leaves tickled her skin and wash with wide eyes as flowers began to bloom up and down the vines.

The loud cry of a falcon caused Gemma to look up to the sky with hope in her heart.

The little girl scrambled to disentangle herself from the plans before turning back to the sea. With her heart thumping frantically and the blood roaring in her ears, she sped towards the sound of the cry.

Soon enough she saw Bane's unmistakable falcon form beelining for her.

At least she hoped it was Bane.

"Bane!" Gemma flailed her arms trying to make sure she got his attention. As he approached, she heard a chattering sound. Confused by Bane's behavior, the little girl cocked her head and stared intently up at the raptor. Gemma racked her brain, trying to think of what Bane was trying to communicate to her.

A memory flashed in her mind and Gemma instinctively held up one arm. The falcon let out a cry before swooping down to land lightly on the arm she offered. Bane walks up her arm until he perched on her shoulder and nuzzled her cheek. He chattered once more and held out one leg. A piece of cloth was tied to his proffered leg and Gemma could just make out the letters R-E-G.

"You need help finding Reg, don't you? Hold on, I'll take you to him." Gemma's steps became filled with purpose as she strode into the forest, ignoring the way the plants reached for her and the connection she could provide.

Sign up for my newsletter to stay up to date on what happens next in the Chronicles of Kamore: https://authorcalewis.com/landing-page/

Newsletter
Sign-Up

Cast of Characters

On Board the *Vengeance*

Bane- Shifter, Raptor forms, son of Gar, Star of the Raptor Show

Cleo Starski- Mortal, Captain of the *Vengeance*

Gemma- Herbalist, Grower, Daughter to Mirabella and Darren Vincenzio

George- Mortal, Liason to the Circus, Brother to Tommy, Best Friend to Reg

Luna- Mortal, Mother to a Shifter Baby

Miriam- Mortal, Sailor

Mouse- Mortal, Sailor

Rae Freeman- Crafter, Fire, Acrobat, Daughter to Naomi and Andre, Lighting Crew, Golden Eagle

Reg- Mortal, Resides in the Barracks, Best Friend to George

Sebastian Adams- Mortal, First Mate to Captain Cleo

Tamara- Forger, Glass Material, Resides in Artist's Row

Zeke- Crafter, Wind, Silver Falcon

The Circus and the Forest

Betsy- Mortal, Head Cook

Carlos- Herbalist, Head of Medical Tent

Chiara- Herbalist, Healer, serves on the Governing Council as Head Herbalist, mother to Damien

Conrad- Shifter, Tiger form, serves on the Governing Council as an Elder, Big Cat Performer

Damien- Mortal, Acrobat, Son to Chiara, White Raven

Duke- Mortal, Strongman

Duncan- Crafter, Wind, serves on the Governing Council as Head Crafter, Ringmaster

Eva- Forger, Wood, Elephant Performer

Freya- Herbalist, Healer

Gar- Mortal, serves on the Governing Council as an Elder, Head of the

Raptor Show

Izzy- Crafter, Unknown, Young girl that loves Nan's storytelling, Daughter to Marv

Javie- Herbalist, Grower, Brother to Luc, Grandson to Nan

Jess- Forger, Iron Material, Strongwoman

Juno- Shifter, Elephant form, serves on the Governing Council as Head Shifter, Elephant   Performer

Kaiser- Mortal, Son to Nymeria, Big Cat Performer

Kim- Mortal, Young girl

Luc- Mortal, Acrobat, serves on the Governing Council as Head Mortal, Black Swan

Mac- Mortal, Head Cook

Marv- Mortal, Ticket taker

Midge- Forger, Cloth Material, serves on the Governing Council as an Elder

Nan - Herbalist, Healer, "Abuela," serves on the Governing Council as an Elder, Fortune Teller

Nymeria- Shifter, Lioness Form, Mother to Kaiser, Big Cat Performer

Solomon Thorne- Herbalist, Grower, Tutor to Javie

Sylvia- Elven, Elven General and Heir, Daughter to Ulla

Tyee- Mortal, Horseman

Ulla- Elven, Queen of the Elven, Mother to Sylvia

Wren- Crafter, Unknown, New Recruit from Windemere

Zalia- Crafter, Fire, Lighting Crew

<u>City of Heimat</u>

Anna- Mortal, Baker, Wife to Rich, Mother of Melody

Darren Vincenzio- Mortal, Myra's right-hand man, Husband to Mirabella, Father to Gemma

Eddy- Mortal, Wharfman

Johanna- Forger, Animal Hide Material, Resides in the Fringe

Mirabella- Mortal, Wife to Vincenzio, Mother to Gemma

Rich- Mortal, Liason to the Circus, Baker, Father to Melody

Rob- Mortal, Husband to Melody

Sara- Mortal, Wife to Tommy

Simone- Mortal, Resides in the Lower Districts

Tommy- Mortal, Resides in the Norther River District, Brother to George, Husband to Sara

<u>In the Capital</u>

Mallick- Mortal, Son to Myra

Myra- Mortal, Tyrant of Kamore

Naomi Freeman- Mortal, Former First Lady of Kamore, Mother to Rae, Best Friend to Helene

<u>Deceased</u>

Andre Freeman- Mortal, Former President of Kamore, Father to Rae

Helene- Herbalist, Healer, Best Friend to Naomi

Jason- Herbalist, Healer

Jose- Forger, Metal Material

Melody- Mortal, Baker, Daughter to Rich and Anna, Wife to Rob

Mikel- Mortal, Resides in the Upper Districts

Naveen- Mortal, Sous Chef

Rocky- Mortal, Carnival Tent Worker

Acknowledgments

Writing my second book was a whirlwind. Just like raising a child, crafting a book takes a village. I am blessed to have such a powerful one behind me every step of the way.

First and foremost, a huge thank you to Joseph for always supporting my dreams. I'm still working on that promise to make it up to you one day. Every step gets us closer.

To Val for taking the time to edit the thousands of words I've put on paper. Your unwavering support and keen eye have helped make this story look its best.

To the best Beta readers around, Amy and Kate, you challenge me to write clearer and give more depth to my characters and storyline. Thanks for catching those pesky plot holes.

To Rachel for creating another extraordinary cover and blowing me away with her creative genius. You work magic when you bring my characters and setting to life. Can't wait to see what you do with Book 3!

To all the friends and family that have encouraged me along the way. Your excitement, enthusiastic purchasing, and constant wondering about when book two was coming out always made my day. Special shout outs to Mom, Dad, Adam, Sophia, Cody, Emma, Grandpa, Deb, Greg, Neal, Peggy, the Cabin Crew, my aunts, the Kickball Team, Laura, Abby, Tyler, and Sydney for never failing to ask about how everything was going.

To everyone that took a chance on me and this story. It fills my heart to know others connect with these characters as much as I do. Thank you for making my wildest dreams come true.

And finally, to my Grandma and all the other loved ones that have passed on from this world. You made me who I am today and taught me to never take anything for granted. You will live on in my heart and the memories I will cherish forever.

About the Author

C A Lewis grew up reading stories filled with dragons, swords, and adventure. Her books transport readers to other worlds where magic and fantasy reign. Her debut series, The Chronicles of Kamore, highlight themes of found friendship, defying the odds, and perseverance despite what life throws at you. She is based in the Twin Cities of Minnesota with her husband, Labrador Retriever, and two cats.

https://authorcalewis.com/

Sign up for my newsletter at: https://authorcalewis.com/landing-page/